D0240155

SOUTH ATLANTIC REQUIEM

ALSO BY EDWARD WILSON

A River in May
The Envoy
The Darkling Spy
The Midnight Swimmer
The Whitehall Mandarin
A Very British Ending

SOUTH ATLANTIC REQUIEM

Edward Wilson

A

Arcadia Books Ltd
139 Highlever Road
London W10 6PH

www.arcadiabooks.co.uk

First published in the United Kingdom 2018

A catalogue record for this book is available from the British Library.

ISBN 978-1-911350-31-6

Typeset in Minion by MacGuru Ltd
Printed and bound by TJ International, Padstow PL28 8RW

Arcadia Books distributors are as follows:

IN THE UK AND ELSEWHERE IN EUROPE:
BookSource
50 Cambuslang Road
Cambuslang
Glasgow G32 8NB

IN AUSTRALIA/NEW ZEALAND:
NewSouth Books
University of New South Wales
Sydney NSW 2052

To the memory of Wendy Blair, 1947–2017

'The wriggling writhing worms will now eat you at the ships, far from your parents, when the dogs have glutted themselves upon you. You will lie naked, although in your house you have fine and goodly raiment made by the hands of women. This will I now burn; it is of no use to you, for you can never again wear it, and thus you will have respect shown you by the Trojans both men and women.'

In such wise did she cry aloud amid her tears, and the women joined in her lament.

Andromache mourning for Hector from *The Iliad*
(translated by Samuel Butler)

Holy Trinity Church, Blythburgh, Suffolk: 18 August 1982

It was a funeral without a body. Instead of a coffin containing even a token bone or two, there was a regimental sergeant major bearing a gold-tasselled scarlet cushion with the colonel's medals and honours. There were over four hundred mourners in the church. William Catesby recognised only a few of them, even though Blythburgh was very near where he had been born and brought up. The person that Catesby knew best was the one who wasn't there. In fact, he hadn't known the colonel that well at all, but he felt obliged to pay his respects for what they had shared. From time to time Catesby and the colonel had been seconded to JIC, the Joint Intelligence Committee, and they soon discovered a shared sense of humour – something that often bonds people more than ideology or upbringing. It was inevitable that their mutual appreciation of things bizarre would lead them to a lake in central London. It was a dark secret pleasure that gave them both delight: the pigeon-eating pelican of St James's Park. Their fascination with the psychopath pelican was, however, only one of the secrets they shared.

The summer had begun with a blazing early June, but August had turned stormy and unsettled. Catesby suppressed an unfunereal smile. It was Black Shuck weather. As children, he and his Suffolk pals were spellbound by tales of the hellhound with blazing eyes. It was, in fact, during an August thunderstorm in 1577 that Black Shuck had run amok through the congregation of Blythburgh Church tearing open throats with his teeth and disembowelling guts with his razor-sharp claws. Catesby glanced at the door on the north side of the chancel. You could still see the claw marks of the devil dog scored into the ancient oak – looking like what someone could have done with a red-hot poker. Catesby suspected that the colonel would have loved a funeral service in the shadow of Black Shuck – a canine cousin of the pelican of St James's Park.

Catesby wondered why the family hadn't chosen Iken rather than Blythburgh for the funeral. The colonel had once confided that Iken churchyard, loud with curlew cries and overlooking the tidal flats of the Alde, was his favourite place, but maybe that was another secret he hadn't shared. The views, however, from Blythburgh Church, were even more stunning: the marshes, the winding river, the Blyth estuary, the distant sea. As a boy Catesby had often cycled to Blythburgh to swim in the river – and still did as an adult. There was a shady footpath that led from the church to a patch of rabbit-cropped grass where you waded into the river at high tide. The water was muddy, but so much warmer than the North Sea.

The service had begun with the organist playing Bach's 'Fantasia and Fugue in G minor'. The music was so moving and beautiful that Catesby imagined that the Black Dog had stopped in his tracks and now lay mourning among the tombstones with his muzzle between his paws. The colonel hadn't been a great man, just a good man – which is, perhaps, better.

Catesby furtively studied the faces of the congregation. It was something that spies were trained to do: *Don't turn your head; swivel your eyes.* There were four major-generals and thirty or so other officers in uniform. The government was represented by two junior ministers. The MP for Waveney, also a junior minister, but very out of favour, was present as well. Catesby recognised a number of local landowners, who were probably friends and family of the widow. She was a somewhat imperious woman who came from a prominent Suffolk family. The colonel often joked that he had 'married above himself'. Something else they shared in common. 'Let's face it,' Catesby had once joked, 'we're just a pair of gigolos.' The colonel had replied with a broad smile.

Catesby looked down as the vicar quoted the lines from Job: *We brought nothing into this world, and it is certain we shall carry nothing out. The Lord gave, and the Lord hath taken away; blessed be the name of the Lord.* There was the sound of someone nervously clearing his throat in the pew behind him. Catesby was sympathetic. Job wasn't exactly a bundle of laughs.

Catesby turned his eyes to the ceiling. The angels always cheered him up – as they must have cheered other church visitors for centuries. There were twelve wooden angels on the nave roof arranged in pairs. The androgynous angels had flowing hair and faint smiles. Presumably, they had survived destruction at the hands of the Puritan iconoclasts because they were too high up to remove – nearly ninety feet above the floor. Unable to reach them, the Puritan soldiers had used the angels for target practice instead. You could see the holes from the musket balls – but the angels were still smiling.

The inaccessible Blythburgh angels survived, but a wealth of artwork had been destroyed: more than two hundred paintings, two crosses, twenty cherubim and the stained-glass windows. Wanton destruction by humans depressed Catesby, but it didn't surprise him. The need to destroy beauty and peace out of self-righteous conceit was a human trait that had never disappeared.

The funeral ended with the National Anthem:

Send her victorious,

Happy and glorious...

followed by 'Nimrod' as the regimental sergeant major carried the cushion bearing the colonel's decorations down the aisle and out of the church. Catesby fought back tears. Elgar's 'Nimrod', always played at British military funerals, was beautiful and heartbreaking – but the moving music would not bring back the dead or erase human stupidity.

The service was now finished and the organist played Bach's 'Prelude and Fugue in E flat' as the mourners left the church. There were seven people in the family reception line: parents, a brother, a sister, two sons and the widow. Catesby had never met any of them, so he didn't make conversation beyond polite condolences. But when he got to the widow, she grasped his hand firmly and fixed him with eyes that glistened more with anger than tears.

'You are, I believe, William Catesby.'

'Yes, I am.'

'John was very fond of you – and told me a few things about you.' The widow lowered her voice. 'I'm not sure that there is anyone else at this funeral that I could say this to.'

Catesby leaned forward. 'Yes.'

The widow's eyes flashed like lightning. 'I hope that fucking bitch rots in hell.'

King's College Cambridge: May 1979

Catesby met Basil, his old tutor, in Basil's rooms overlooking Front Court.

'Do you remember coming here for your tutorials on medieval French literature?'

'Yes. My biggest concern was hiding my lack of preparation. I wasn't enamoured of *La Chanson de Roland*.'

'Why?'

Catesby smiled. The tutorial seemed to have recommenced after nearly four decades. 'The *Chanson* was far too long-winded – and, at the time, the Fall of France in 1940 seemed more relevant than the Battle of Roncevaux in the ninth century.'

'The battle actually took place in 778.'

'Lack of preparation again.'

'And, I suppose, you were eager to get in uniform and do your part.'

Catesby looked out the window at the late Gothic splendour of King's College Chapel. 'I had delusions of glory – and I also felt guilty basking in warm safe privilege while others were dying. In that way, I was probably an embarrassingly boring young man.'

Basil folded his long fine fingers. 'It would be unkind of me to reply.'

'Thank you.' Boring or not, Catesby was certain that Basil had recommended him for the Secret Intelligence Service – but that was after the war when he returned to complete his degree. And perhaps the Catesby who had been parachuted into occupied France in 1943 was no longer as callow and boring as the earlier version.

'Would you like a snifter of port?' said Basil. 'It helps my arthritis.'

'Did you get it on the NHS?'

'You're still a socialist, aren't you, Catesby?'

'I would rather describe myself as a loyal servant of Her Majesty's Secret Intelligence Service.'

'Quite. By the way, I voted Labour last week – that woman is simply ghastly.'

Catesby smiled.

'So you will have some port?'

Catesby nodded.

Basil filled a thimble-sized crystal glass and nodded to a small pile of folders on his desk. 'Those are the most promising candidates. It hasn't been a vintage year. Why don't you have a look while I mark a batch of Tripos papers?'

Half an hour later Basil was snoring and Catesby was finishing his notes on the recommended final-year students. The tutor was right: it wasn't a vintage year for likely SIS recruits. But there was one who stood out. Catesby stared at the old prof and coughed lightly.

'Oh dear,' said Basil, 'I must have nodded off. What do you think?'

'I don't suppose you've seen *Evita*?'

'Evita who?'

'*Evita* is a West End musical.'

'Good lord. No, I haven't.' Basil gave Catesby a condescending look. 'Is it any good?'

'I'm not a music critic, but it alerted me to some important issues.'

'If you don't mind my asking, why did you go to see a … a musical?'

'My wife, Frances, ended up with two tickets. A rich admirer wanted to take her to see it. When she turned him down, he insisted she keep the tickets.'

'And how is the charming Frances?'

Catesby remembered that Basil had met his then wife-to-be when he had returned to Cambridge in 1946. Basil, not normally someone with an eye for women, had been impressed with Frances's upper-class manners tinged with a strong hint of Bloomsbury unconventionality. A wartime fling had left her with twins whom she paraded unashamedly as 'little bastards out of wedlock'.

'She's fine,' said Catesby not wanting to go into details about an estranged wife who worked for MI5.

'Are you reconciled?'

'A bit – or, I assume, Frances wouldn't have turned the rich bloke down.'

'Was he broken-hearted?'

'I hope so – but she thought it would be fun to see the musical after all. It actually wasn't that bad.' Catesby lifted up one of the folders. 'And your student reminded me of it.'

Basil looked at Catesby over his half-frame reading glasses. 'I suppose you're referring to Fiona Stewart. She spent her year abroad in Argentina researching Borges. In fact, she's gone back. She has, I've heard, formed an *attachment*. In any case, she's not someone I thought would have interested you.'

'On the contrary, I would like to interview her.'

'And what about the others?'

Catesby shook his head. 'I believe that the Secret Intelligence Service has already surpassed its quota of white public schoolboys.'

Basil smiled. 'I think you will find Fiona Stewart posher than any of them. She is, in fact, quite a madam: the Conservation Association tried desperately to recruit her.'

'And she turned them down?'

'Actually, I think she found them a bit common.'

'Perhaps she was playing a game, a role.'

'All undergraduates do – even you did, Catesby.'

Catesby smiled bleakly and returned to Fiona Stewart's folder.

Buenos Aires: May 1979

Fiona Stewart thought the Argentine naval aviator was the most beautiful man she had ever seen. His hair glistened like wet coal. He was so intent, but she wasn't relaxed enough. She gently cupped his head in her hands knowing that he couldn't see her indulgent smile or read her thoughts. She knew that he needed her so much – and trying so hard to please her was part of that need. 'Let me do you,' she said.

He rested his cheek against the inside of her thigh. 'But I want to give you pleasure.'

She stroked his head. 'You give me pleasure by being so beautiful.'

'But I want to make you come. I want you to quiver all over – like you do to me.'

Fiona pulled his head up so she could look at him closely. 'Why are you so intense? You seem so nervous.'

'I want to give you back the pleasure that you have given me before it is too late.'

'What do you mean too late?'

'Ever since Inés died I have had premonitions of my own death.'

The Argentine aviator was referring to his wife who had died the previous year after a long illness. The Englishwoman came level with him and held him closely.

'Do you miss her?'

'I don't miss her because she has never gone away.' He looked at the ceiling. 'But I wish that I had loved her more.'

'And not been unfaithful?'

'That is a cruel thing to say.' The Argentine smiled. 'But I wish that she hadn't found out about my affairs. Why are you laughing?'

'Because you are so honest – even when it shows you in such a bad light.'

The Argentine was no longer smiling. 'But you must remember that I did love Inés, sometimes more than life itself.'

'Who else do you love more than life itself?'

'My son, of course – and, I know you think this silly, but I love my country more than life itself.'

Fiona propped herself on her elbow and stared at the Argentine. When he was wearing his naval officer's uniform, he was even more handsome than in his polo kit – and he wore that uniform with such pride. Part of her regarded his military preening as a child's game, but she understood how much it meant to him. Although the aviator was seventeen years older than her, Fiona felt that he was a younger brother who needed to be protected and taught about the real world.

Her lover smiled. 'I can see what you are thinking behind your hooded ironic English eyes. You are laughing at me.'

'Laughter can be a sign of love – women often love men who make them laugh.' She felt his penis, no longer hard and thrusting, lying limp against her thigh. She reached down and stroked it. 'I want to put you in my mouth.' He immediately stiffened.

'You're playing games with me.'

'But you love games – I saw that the first time I met you.' She wanted to add *and fell in love with you*. But at the time, it wasn't so much falling in love as falling in lust.

London: September 1979

Recruiting more women wasn't just a matter of equal opportunities; it was also a professional necessity. A long-running problem was that SIS officers looked pretty much alike – and the same applied to MI5 officers, although, as Catesby and his colleagues pointed out, their knuckles dragged a bit lower. For years MI5 surveillance teams had been a joke. Two bored white men in trilbies and overcoats sitting for hours in a government motor pool Humber fooled no one. Sometimes they tried to improve their cover by changing the number plates – even though they were using the same car. On one occasion, the 'diplomat' under surveillance gave a friendly rap on the car's window to inform the driver that his rear number plate was not the same as the front one. The Sovs always recognised the 'watchers' and loved to play games with them. The favourites were high-speed chases through the centre of London – no fear of speeding tickets with diplomatic immunity – as the Russian driver tried to 'lose his tail'. When the *rezidentura*, the spy office at the Sov Embassy, wanted to replace an ageing car at the British government's expense, they instructed a driver who was being closely pursued to slam on the brakes.

According to SIS recruitment criteria, the important thing about Fiona Stewart wasn't her gender but that she was a brilliant linguist in Spanish and Portuguese – both languages in which SIS was understaffed. Ironically, the intelligence service had many fluent speakers in the world's most difficult tongues – including Hungarian and Mandarin – but few Spanish speakers. It was as if the Spanish Armada and the War of Jenkins' Ear had never happened. The saga was one of Catesby's favourite lessons from British history. The smuggler Jenkins had his left ear sabred off by the leader of a Spanish boarding party. The severed ear was later displayed in Parliament to stoke up war fever. In the end, Jenkins's ear was the first of 20,000 British casualties in a war that also cost Britain 407 ships lost. Catesby feared that it could happen again – but no one listened to him.

Catesby's interest in Latin America began when he had been on temporary duty in Havana during the Cuban Missile Crisis. He realised there were issues of culture and history that few in London understood – issues that could prove lethal, as they nearly had in October 1962. His interest was rekindled sixteen years later when he was temporarily promoted to be Dir/Americas while the normal holder of the post was recovering from a ski injury. Catesby grasped that being Dir/Americas was a job that meant dealing with Washington and little else – Canada and Latin America could go hang. When the real Dir/Americas shed his plaster and finally hobbled back to his desk at SIS HQ, Catesby pointed out his section practically ignored Latin America.

'If you want that lot,' said Dir/Americas, hanging up his walking stick, 'you can have it.'

The DG approved the transfer of responsibility and Catesby's job title expanded to Head/SovBlocTSection/Dir/LatinAmerica – but he was still on the same pay scale.

Catesby stared at the Fiona Stewart folder that lay open on his desk and wondered what to do next. She was almost too English and too posh – a younger version of his own wife. Pity she wasn't black, Asian or working class. On the other hand, she lived in Argentina and Fiona's style and looks were what

Anglophile Argentines expected in an Englishwoman. Catesby knew that many of the Argentine elite liked to swan about in tweeds and Jermyn Street shirts. They also played rugby and cricket and sent their children to expensive private schools to learn British English rather than the American variety. Catesby leaned back and frowned. Was he falling into the English habit of labelling South Americans? That's why he needed an agent in place who could see beyond the stereotypes – who could recognise nuances, strengths, frailties and the contradictions of the human factor. It was called HUMINT – Human Intelligence – and was no longer very popular. HUMINT required more personnel and was a lot more expensive than SIGINT – Signals Intelligence – which was the current rage. Would he get the funding even if she accepted a post?

Normally, interviewing a family member of a potential SIS recruit was frowned upon at best and totally forbidden at worst. But as Fiona's father was a former army officer who had won the Victoria Cross and was a sometime member of the Royal Household at Sandringham, Catesby was certain that Major Stewart could be treated differently. In fact, Major Stewart enjoyed the rare distinction of being one of those who had been awarded the VC *posthumously* – but who then turned up alive, but not well, to pick up the medal in person. The major had been reported dead when, in fact, his badly wounded body had been taken prisoner by the Italians. Following the surrender of the Italians in Africa, Stewart had been repatriated and received the Victoria Cross at Buckingham Palace.

Stewart met Catesby in an office that had been constructed in the rambling garden of his North Norfolk farmhouse. The outbuilding was traditional East Anglian design, black shiplap planking and pantile roof. There was also a Black Shuck weathervane – the infamous hellhound got everywhere. The garden office was furnished with shabby and broken antiques that the major's wife had expelled from the house. There was also a pair of binoculars and a collection of bird books – and a drinks cabinet. There were piles of leather-bound legal books that needed navigating around and which Stewart used as side tables. The major had studied law after leaving the army and rose to the level of Recorder, a part-time circuit judge, before he chucked in legal work.

'Whisky,' said the major, 'G&T – we can even do a cup of tea, but the milk's gone off.'

It was ten o'clock in the morning. 'I'll have tea, please – and don't worry about the milk.'

The major, whose right eye had been shot away in Africa, wore a black eye patch. He gave Catesby a one-eye wink of reluctant agreement. 'Well, I'll join you.' He switched on the kettle, which seemed to do nothing. 'Fucking thing.' He gave the kettle a firm shake and it began to gurgle. 'Good. Did you come far?'

'Only from Suffolk – I've got a place there.'

'Thought I detected a hint of an accent – and, if you don't mind my saying so, your name is fascinating.'

Catesby gave a tired smile. Being reminded yet again that he shared a surname with the leader of the Gunpowder Plot was tedious beyond belief.

'My own ancestors,' said the major in a low conspiratorial tone, 'were Recusant Catholics hiding Jesuits in every nook and cranny. So I am honoured to meet a Catesby.'

Catesby smiled. In this case at least, his name was useful.

'But despite the Jay connection I didn't go to Stonyhurst, I went to Ampleforth.' Major Stewart paused. 'But you haven't come here to talk about me; you've come to talk about my daughter.'

'But I know, Major Stewart, that your own life is very interesting.'

'I'm not sure what my own life is. I can't focus.' The major stared out the window. 'Look at that bugger.'

'Where?'

'That old apple tree. There's a great spotted woodpecker.'

'Lovely birds,' said Catesby, 'but they pecked the lime mortar out of my chimney and I had to have it rebuilt.'

'It's the price we pay for living in period homes. Where was I?'

Catesby smiled. 'You said you couldn't focus.'

'How apt.' The major paused. 'But it's nothing recent. I haven't been able to focus since I got back from the war. That's why I went to university and read law. I needed something hard and definite to concentrate the mind – and for a while I was quite successful.' He nodded at a hat rack adorned with a long white judge's wig. 'As soon as I got promoted to the bench I lost interest. That's when I bought this farm and started breeding rare sheep – and orchids too. Am I boring you?'

'Not much.'

'Ah, but one more thing. I still have a part-time interest in the legal business. I serve on the board of the Mental Health Review Tribunal – and as such I meet a lot of psychiatrists.' The major smiled. 'Useful for free consultations. In any case, I confided in one of the shrinks about my lack of focus and he asked me about the war. Apparently, there's this new thing called PTSD – Post-traumatic Stress Disorder. At first, I thought it was a lot of nonsense – and part of me still does – but maybe there's something in it. What did you do in the war?'

'SOE.'

'Ah, maybe you'd better have a word with this shrink too – and then let me know what you think.'

Catesby blinked nervously. He didn't need a psychiatrist to tell him he was fucked up.

'Good lord,' said the major, 'there I am going on about myself again when you're here to talk about Fiona. God, isn't this tea awful?'

'It's drinkable.'

'Should have had it black; milk's gone sour. Fiona is the youngest – the brightest and the wildest.' The major smiled. 'I think she gets it from her mother.'

'How many children are there?'

'Five – all girls. Don't say it, I know. Tried with the wife on top and every other position, but still ended up with a girl every time.'

If, Catesby thought, SIS ever gave him permission to publish his memoirs, Major Stewart was going to get a mention.

'Now, Fiona was difficult from day one – and didn't get any better until we sent her to boarding school as a teenager. At first I thought it was a cruel decision, but I gave in to She-Who-Must-Be-Obeyed and her whim of iron – and the sisters, who had had enough of her too, also thought it the right decision.'

'And it worked?'

'Indeed. She settled down and eventually became Head Girl.' The major paused and looked out the window. 'I don't know why. Maybe the hormones settled down. Can't say it was being in an all-girl environment – she was in that here, even the cat is a girl. The school certainly encouraged her sporting prowess: tennis, running – her PE teacher thought she had a chance of qualifying for the Olympics in the Women's Pentathlon. I think, for the first time, Fiona began to feel good about who she was.'

'What an amazing person.'

'We certainly think so. But Fiona's biggest change was discovering her extraordinary brain – and God knows where she got that from, not either of us. The first stage, I believe, was Fiona developing a crush on her Modern Languages teacher – a most extraordinary and charismatic woman. In any case, Fiona blossomed intellectually and got into Cambridge – where she took up sculling.' The major smiled. 'But she dropped it because she thought it was making her arms and shoulders too bulky. For the first time, she became aware that she was a stunning beauty – and didn't want to waste it. Her new hobby became breaking hearts...' A dark look crossed the major's face. 'And I hope she continues to do so.'

'By the way,' said Catesby, 'how would you feel, as a father, if Fiona decided to join the Secret Intelligence Service?'

Major Stewart stared out the window. 'There's that woodpecker again. I don't know. At the risk of sounding like a drunk at the local Tory club, I love my country – even though we have done some bloody awful things. I also love my daughter – and loving her is not always easy either. When I was in the army we were fighting a bloody fucking monster. It was easy to be a patriot. On reflection, I think Fiona would only thrive in the intelligence service if you provided her with challenges and excitement. She is easily bored. Fiona is a spirited girl who loves taking risks – maybe too many…'

'I must be honest, Major Stewart; personal relationships do play a part in determining a person's suitability for SIS.'

'So you would weed out someone whose lover was a KGB agent?'

Catesby laughed. 'On the contrary, we would recruit them with alacrity – and make sure their briefcase was always stuffed with false information for the lover to copy and pass on to Moscow Central.'

'I see. It's complicated.'

'I fully appreciate, Major Stewart…'

'Stop calling me that, my name is Ken.'

'I fully appreciate, Ken, that you might want to keep your daughter's private life private.'

'Well she never has. She broadcasts the details of her love life without an ounce of shame. But maybe not so much now; it could have been an adolescent need to shock.'

Catesby nodded agreement.

'I think things started to go wrong – well, wrong in my opinion as a parent – when she went to Argentina for her year abroad. It's part of the Modern Languages degree course at Cambridge.'

Catesby put on an old fogey face. He wanted to bond with the major. 'I was on the same course in the forties – they parachuted me into France instead.'

'Quite. Not long after arriving in Buenos Aires, Fiona became friends with a fabulously rich American girl named McCullough. Apparently McCullough isn't her surname but her Christian name.' The major frowned and shook his head. 'I've never heard of a St McCullough, have you?'

Catesby shook his head.

'In any case, I began to think that McCullough might be a good thing. Rich Americans are much more generous and friendly than rich Brits. Now, I always thought that Fiona had – how should I put this – a Sapphic side?'

Catesby nodded.

'Which is fine by me. In fact, I would much rather have girlfriends around the house than boyfriends. But, as usual, I was wrong about Fiona – and the relationship with a fabulously rich American woman never blossomed.' The major looked at Catesby. 'I don't suppose you're a polo fan?'

Catesby shook his head.

'Neither am I – my regiment was far too unfashionable for that sort of carry on. But in Argentina, polo is a very popular sport – almost like rugger or footer here. And polo, it seems, was the reason that McCullough ended up in Argentina. Not that she plays it herself – I'm not sure that women do – but her filthy-rich father does and owns several strings of polo ponies. Not a sport for paupers. In any case, the billionaire daddy keeps a few luxury flats in Buenos Aires – which, I suppose, attracted McCullough there for a university course or two. I have the impression that McCullough is one of those young people who quickly gets bored with a degree course and then drops out and starts another. I shouldn't be critical – maybe it turns them into Renaissance men and women. Where was I?'

'I assume then,' said Catesby, 'that Fiona met McCullough at the university?'

'Exactly – and introduced Fiona to the world of Argentine polo, which she now adores. Going to a polo match is a lot different from going to see Norwich at Carrow Road – champagne and designer everything. But I think Fiona is attracted more to the speed and athleticism of both the men and the horses – and, of course, the danger.' The major paused and frowned. 'And it was at her first polo match that Fiona met him.'

'Met whom?'

'Ariel Solar.'

'Wonderful name.'

'And a wonderful polo player too – one of the highest-ranked amateurs in Argentina.'

'And, if I may be frank,' said Catesby, 'what don't you like about him?'

'And, by the way, don't think for one moment that I don't like him because he's a foreigner or a hot-blooded Latin. I'm much more broadminded than that. I am, however, worried about the fact that he is a lot older than Fiona – and started the affair with her when his wife was still living.'

'The wife died?'

'Yes, after quite a long illness. I suppose we shouldn't judge Ariel going astray. But what most bothers me about him…'

'Yes, go on.'

'I don't think Ariel is anywhere near as intelligent as Fiona. His English, for example, is very poor whereas Fiona's Spanish is native speaker fluent.'

'Does he have a job when he's not playing polo?'

'Yes, I can't fault him on that. He's a naval aviator with the equivalent rank of an RAF Squadron Leader.'

A voice in the back of Catesby's head was going *yes, yes, yes.*

Fiona's father let out a loud laugh. 'Or the equivalent rank of a British Army major – just like daddy.'

'Is this Ariel Solar well connected with the Argentine elite?'

'I am sure he is now – but I suspect he is of humble birth. You have to admire him. He has clawed his way up on the basis of prowess on the sports field and in the cockpit. And I am sure he is also brave and courageous. Otherwise, Fiona wouldn't have given him a second look.'

Catesby bit his tongue. He wasn't going to say *just like daddy*, even though it was blatantly obvious.

The William Brown Polo Club, Greater Buenos Aires: October 1979

The year that Fiona had spent apart from Ariel was the unhappiest of her life. She began to write to him every day when she returned to complete her final year at Cambridge. When, however, she realised that his wife was dying she thought it best to let him have time to concentrate on his wife and family. Ariel wrote to her the day that Inés died – a quick note full of sorrow and shock. Their correspondence began again in earnest a month later – and became more and more passionate. Fiona wondered if it was right to be exchanging such letters with a husband still in mourning. But, as Ariel said: *Life goes on*. She realised that it wasn't the most profound thought in the circumstances, but Ariel wasn't always a profound or complex person – and Fiona admired him for it. He was a breath of raw life and fresh air after the self-analysing intellectuals of Cambridge. But it was now two o'clock in the morning and Ariel wasn't there.

Fiona's reason for returning to Argentina was to research a PhD on Jorge Louis Borges – at least that was the story she told her father. But her real intention was to be with Ariel Solar. It was, however, impossible to be with him every night – or even most nights. His duties as a navy pilot often took him away. He was now at the Río Grande air base in the south of the country – closer to Antarctica than he was to her. And when he wasn't occupied with military duties, he often spent time at the family home with his teenage son, Gonzalo, who was being looked after by Ines's mother, who also lived there. Fiona appreciated it was a delicate situation – still a little too soon to introduce her to 'Gonzalito', who was missing his mother, and far too soon to present her to Inés's mother as his future wife. They had discussed marriage – even though Fiona wasn't sure that lust had changed into lifelong love. But she did miss him and so wished that he was beside her in bed. She put her hand between her legs – but she decided not to pleasure herself. Or to use the vibrator that McCullough had given her – that she still hadn't tried. McCullough was a treasure, and although she didn't always get things right, Fiona loved her American directness even when it was a bit gauche.

McCullough's generosity to Fiona also included use of her father's luxury flat in Recoleta, Buenos Aires's most exclusive neighbourhood, when her father wasn't there. It occupied the top storey of a French-style building in Uruguay Street. Fiona found the 'French' style of Buenos Aires more French than anything she had ever seen in France. The flat was where Fiona and Ariel often made love. But, as it was now the height of the polo season, the flat wasn't available. Even though the Recoleta flat was a bit over the top, Fiona preferred being in the centre of town to her room at the William Brown Polo Club. The club accommodation came with the job. In addition to her job, Fiona was also enrolled as a student at the university's *Facultad de Filosofia y Letras*. She continued to do some perfunctory research to justify her paltry grant, but she soon realised that her heart wasn't in writing a thesis on Borges.

It was Ariel who told her about the polo club job. *You'd be perfect*, he said – and he was right. Many of the club's members and visitors were English-speaking – and Fiona, being an athlete who was fluent in both languages, impressed the directors as the ideal candidate for Assistant Manager. She also did her homework on the man the club was named after. William Brown, unlike many of the club's patrons, was certainly not an Anglophile – he had been press-ganged from an American ship to fight against Napoleon. Brown was a County Mayo-born Irish adventurer who rose to command the Argentine Navy in the wars against Spain, Brazil and Uruguay. The polo club had several oil paintings of *Almirante* Brown and Fiona felt that his eyes were following her with distrust.

Fiona got the job and grew to like it. The work wasn't hard and it was a fabulous place for someone who loved sport. It wasn't just about polo – even though there were four polo fields and stables for two hundred and fifty horses. The club had a golf course and twenty-one tennis courts – in addition to the eleven hard courts, there were four clay and six grass. There were also pitches for cricket – including several practice nets – and rugby, swimming pools and squash courts. And when you had showered and slipped into your tweeds or flannels, there were bars, restaurants and hotel rooms. The place was, thought Fiona, not only sporty, but a little bit decadent.

Fiona rolled on her side and touched herself gently – *god how she missed Ariel.* She liked to remember how it began – and none of it would have happened if it hadn't been for McCullough. Fiona stroked herself and smiled. What would Ariel say if she ever suggested a threesome?

Fiona loved McCullough from the moment the American described herself as a 'spoilt rich bitch'. Fiona adored her for both her honesty and perceptiveness. McCullough certainly was a spoilt rich bitch and she wore that piece of self-knowledge like a suit of armour. Nor did she tolerate those who disagreed with that self-assessment. Fiona's own background in England had been privileged, but the codes were different. It took Fiona a while to realise that McCullough wasn't a surname, but a first name – and that 'only assholes wear black polo boots'. Likewise, Fiona soon found out that McCullough's universe was a crumbling dystopia wrecked by hordes of assholes who multiplied faster than she could eradicate them with her supercilious smile of loathing. The most 'unspeakable' of McCullough's assholes were rich American males – and her own father headed the list.

Monster approaching alarm bells began to sound the first time that Fiona met McCullough's father. Talbot – not a surname either – was handsome in the way that only rich men are: perfectly groomed, combed and gym-fit. What Fiona found most chilling about Talbot were his eyes. She had never seen eyes that were as cold and uncaring. His eyes, of course, undressed her – those of many men did that. But Talbot's obscene stare wasn't so much lechery, as evaluating the worth of a piece of merchandise. His brief introductory smile seemed to say: *I could, of course, fuck you if I had the time and could be bothered. But I probably won't.*

Talbot turned away and resumed talking to another American, obviously filthy rich too, but not an Alpha Plus Apex Predator like Talbot. *My handicap is still four. Of course, that's pretty damned good for an amateur – but I want to improve. And that's why I stay here three months a year. For all their faults, the Argentines still play the world's best polo – largely because of the horses. Where do I stay? I've got an apartment in Recoleta – the neighbourhood looks a bit Parisian if you like that sort of thing. The only problem is that it's too close to the Presidential Palace. Every time there's a goddamn military coup the tank fire cracks the ceiling cornices. No, no, the blond one's my daughter – the brunette is an English friend. My daughter's name? McCullough. Nice piece of ass, isn't she?*

McCullough rolled her eyes and took Fiona by the elbow to guide her away. 'Didn't I tell you that Talbot was an asshole?'

At the time, Fiona had given a thin smile and stayed silent. Back then, she still thought it best not to comment on McCullough's family. But frankness eventually replaced reserve. Fiona hugged her pillow and pretended it was McCullough. She needed a friend with whom she could share things – everything. She closed her eyes and remembered the first time she had met the American.

UBA, the University of Buenos Aires, had no central edifice but had sites scattered all over the city. The Facultad de Filosofia y Letras was located in a stately nineteenth-century building on the Calle 25 de Mayo. The road was BA's equivalent of London's Whitehall. Fiona had quickly discovered that many of the students had Leftist leanings. One had sidled up to her, nodded towards a young male with short hair and whispered, 'Watch him, I don't know who he is – maybe pretending to be a student. The problem with this place is that we're so near the Ministerio del Interior and the Secretaría de Inteligencia too – only a five-minute walk. The goons from SIDE, the Secretariat of State Intelligence, don't have far to go to keep an eye on us. They've never forgotten that Che Guevara studied medicine here.'

'Thank you for the warning,' said Fiona. They both were distracted by a tall blond woman looming near them.

'Shhh,' said the Leftist.

At the time McCullough had been doing an intensive Spanish course in the same faculty. She had tried to eavesdrop on the whispered conversation to see how much she understood. McCullough thought Fiona had a friendly face and began to speak Spanish to her. She was pretending to ask for directions to the library, but really wanted to practise her Spanish. After they struggled through a few sentences McCullough admitted that she was a '*gringa*' and Fiona shifted to English.

'God,' said McCullough, 'you sound awfully British. Did you study there?'

'No, I am British.'

'Oh *god*, I'm *so* sorry!'

'Nothing to be sorry about. I don't suppose I look like a typical English rose.'

'You're much prettier.'

'Thank you.' Fiona wasn't used to having her looks complimented by another woman who wasn't family.

'And I love your voice – you sound so upper-crust.'

'I'm sometimes embarrassed by it.'

'Why?'

'It's difficult to explain.'

'Bad *gringa* manners again. I shouldn't be so intrusive.'

'You're not intrusive – I apologise if I sounded brusque.'

'Have you time for a coffee?'

'That would be lovely.'

They hit it off – even though it was mostly McCullough doing the talking. *I didn't* flunk *the History of Art major at Vassar – even though that's what Daddy tells everyone – I just didn't finish it. Things sort of went wrong when I took a year off to study the Renaissance in Florence. If you don't mind, it's not something I like to talk about. But since then I've become* passionate *about Latin American art, particularly Pre-Colombian. You could say I've gone straight from Michelangelo to the Mayans.*

A few weeks later McCullough invited Fiona to the annual Gringo-Gaucho Match at the William Brown Polo Club. McCullough's father was captain of the Gringo team. Fiona's first impression of the club was that it was a parody of an England that only existed in the minds of Hollywood film directors. Or a parody of a parody. Like one of those film versions of an Indian hill station where the British Raj went to escape the summer heat – and to play polo. The voices were mostly the Italian-accented Spanish of Argentina, but sometimes those voices lapsed into a dated English that sounded like that of actors playing posh roles in a 1930s film. She heard several 'spiffings' as well as a haughty 'balderdash'. There were modern British voices too coming from a cricket net, but most of the non-Spanish voices around the polo field were American – except for that of one Irishman playing for the Gringos.

Although *la cancha*, the playing field, was over three hundred yards long, Fiona's first impression was of a densely crowded space full of horses and riders. In addition to the eight *jugadores*, there were two mounted umpires in black-and-white striped jerseys. It was a hot November day and the place smelled of horse, human sweat and cooking meat from the hospitality tents on either side of the field. The Gauchos were wearing sky-blue jerseys with white trim; the Gringos white jerseys with red and blue trim. Fiona was sure that two of the Gaucho *jugadores* were speaking Welsh to each other – making everything more surreal. Nothing seemed to connect: there was the twentieth-century ostentation of Rolex watches, popping champagne corks and designer sunglasses, while a few yards away there was a world of mounted danger that looked and smelled like a medieval tournament. The helmeted player-knights held their mallets upright like lances and the horses twitched for action.

Fiona began to feel intoxicated even before the cool touch of a champagne flute caressed her bare arm.

'Get some of this down you,' said McCullough. 'My father's paying for it.'

'Thank you.'

'You should be thanking the American taxpayer. Ultimately, they're the ones who paid for it – as well as Daddy's string of polo ponies.'

'Cheers,' said Fiona clinking glasses.

'Finish that so I can give you a refill.'

Fiona smiled and brushed her hair back. 'Sure.' She finished off the remaining champagne and held out her glass. She noticed the bottle in McCullough's unsteady hand was nearly empty.

'You don't ask many questions, do you?' said the American.

'Well actually, I was just about to.'

'What three questions would you like to ask me most?'

'Have you had a lot to drink?'

'Yes.'

'Is it because of your father?'

McCullough nodded. 'Both no-brainers. You've just wasted two questions.'

'So I've only got one left?'

'I'm not interesting enough for more – I'm just a boring, spoilt rich bitch who is typically fucked up.'

'I would never say that.'

McCullough stood back and looked at Fiona. 'God, you are absolutely stunning.'

'If I look less frumpy than usual, it's because of your dress.'

'I wish that we had taken it up more. You have beautiful legs and should show more of them.'

Fiona stirred a little uneasily. But it was a beautiful dress. It was tailored from marble-grey hand-painted chinoiserie silk.

'It looks so much better on you,' said McCullough. 'I'm too tall and gawky. By the way, it doesn't have any cum stains on it now and I don't want to find any when you give it back. It cost my trust fund nearly two thousand bucks.'

Fiona didn't react to the American's staged crudeness. She knew it wasn't genuine. It was part of a persona that McCullough cultivated. 'So,' said Fiona touching the fabric, 'the American taxpayer didn't pay for this lovely dress.'

'I suppose they paid indirectly.'

Fiona swallowed more champagne. The combination of the heat and the cold bubbly made her feel lightheaded. 'I've got one more question – and one we would never ask in England. Where does your family's money come from?'

McCullough smiled. 'You English certainly wouldn't ask it, but you would sure as hell find out in other ways.'

'That may be true.'

'My family made their money from chemicals. They first got rich in the nineteenth century from producing textile dyes and soap – but then they went into petrochemicals and explosives and got super-rich.' McCullough gave a dark smile, leaned forward and sniffed the fabric of the chinoiserie silk. 'Can't you tell? My dress smells of napalm.'

'I hadn't noticed – but I can see how you feel. Poor you.'

'Well, I'm hardly poor because of it. My family made a lot of money out of Vietnam.'

Fiona looked into McCullough's grey eyes – and saw they were wet. She reached out with her fingers and touched the American's freckled forearm.

'Don't you dare feel sorry for me. Let's talk about something else – the polo. It's a wonderful game. Women play it too – I'm taking lessons. Would you like to?'

'I have ridden. My father insisted; he was a cavalry officer…' Fiona stopped and looked again at the American. Another layer of mystery disappeared. McCullough was an athlete. Her body was lean and supple – the classic gamine. Fiona could see that the American felt more at home in jeans and a T-shirt than wearing a silk dress.

McCullough turned and looked at the polo field. 'The ponies are lining up. I think they're about to begin.'

Fiona watched one of the mounted umpires lift a solid white ball. There was a temporary hush. The only sound was the ponies nervously pawing the ground. The umpire rolled the ball between the two lines of players and the ponies rushed forward. It was difficult to see what was happening. Suddenly a *jugadore* wearing the livery of the Gauchos broke free of the pack. His grey pony was at full gallop, but he drove the ball goalwards with easy graceful swings of his mallet. A Gringo on a bay pony was in pursuit and gaining, but unable to deflect either ball or rider before both passed through the goal. The *banderillero*, the goal mouth official, verified the goal by waving a large red flag in both hands.

'That was Ariel Solar,' said McCullough. 'He is magnificent – he has a handicap of four, good enough to be a professional, and he is their best player. And a lot of women think he's gorgeous.'

'Do you?'

McCullough shrugged and sipped her champagne.

'Which one is your father?' said Fiona. 'It's difficult to see their faces in those helmets.'

'He's number two. For some reason he's being less of an asshole than normal – he usually hogs the number one position which should go to your best goal scorer.'

On cue, the Gringo number one shouted, 'Take the man!' and McCullough's father guided his pony into Ariel Solar, preventing him from getting near the ball. The Gringo number one came up fast on a gallop, hitting the ball towards the goal with a smooth forehand. Ariel managed to disengage himself and galloped towards Gringo One who was rising into the half-seat position to take a shot at the goal. Just as he extended his arm backwards to take his stroke, Ariel hooked the Gringo's mallet. There were calls for a penalty from the Gringos, but the umpire ignored them. The rest of the chukka passed without further goals and the *jugadores* dismounted to change ponies.

'What do you think?' said McCullough.

'I can't believe they are amateurs.'

'Two of them aren't. Gringo One is a professional with a handicap of six – hot stuff.'

'He didn't sound American.'

'He isn't. He's an Irishman called Hugh something.'

'And I suppose Ariel Solar is the other pro?'

'Oddly not. He is their best player, but spends most of his time flying fighter planes for the Junta. The other professional is Ramón Evans, the son of a cattle rancher from Patagonia.'

'I think I heard him speaking Welsh.'

'Probably to his brother, who is the Gaucho number three when he isn't looking after the *estancia*.'

The southern sun and the champagne made Fiona's head spin, but everything felt gorgeous and sensual. The riders had remounted; an umpire with a straggling black moustache tossed the ball underhand between them with a gesture of almost careless contempt. Fiona squinted into the chaos and wanted to embrace all of it with outstretched arms. She wanted to run her hands up and down the tight-fitting white jodhpurs of at least one of the players. Reality had been turned upside down. November was late spring – and a Welsh-speaking gaucho was cracking lances with an Irish knight.

The game went back and forth for the next two chukkas. The Irish Gringo scored two goals in quick succession – before Ariel, who had been roughly fouled by McCullough's father, hammered home a penalty from forty yards to equalise. Talbot quickly replied by slamming home a deflected ball in front of the uprights – and then a thirty-yard penalty. Finally, with seconds left in the final chukka of the first half, Ramón Evans stole the ball from his Irish counterpart and passed it forward to Ariel who gracefully slid a nearside backhand, an almost impossible shot, through the legs of a Gringo pony and into the goal. As the hooter sounded, the Gringos were winning 4–3.

At halftime, the spectators went on to the playing field to stomp in the divots. It was, explained McCullough, a custom started by the British – and meant that the women wore 'sensible shoes, instead of sling backs and stilettos'. The divot-stomping also gave the spectators a chance to mingle with each other as well as the dismounted players. Fiona found a spectator, a conservatively dressed man of around fifty with a sharply trimmed moustache, staring at her – and her blood chilled. She couldn't see his eyes because he was wearing dark glasses, but she could feel his stare.

'That's Mussolini,' said McCullough.

'Is that his real name?'

'No, but they also call him El Loco.'

'The Crazy One.'

'Loco is a generalissimo who used to be military governor of a province. He did such a good job that he's been promoted to command a whole military region.'

'Why's he looking at me?' said Fiona. 'Does he think I'm a guerrilla?'

'He looks at everyone if he doesn't know them – he'll later write you up in his notebook. Loco is very thorough.'

Fiona stared blankly at the sun-drenched field. She had grown up with respect for the military, but not adulation. Even her father admitted that senior officers were not always 'the shiniest pebbles on the beach'. But she knew that her father had pushed himself and his men to the limits of what is humanly possible – even though he himself was dismissive about his 'gong'. He kept the medal hidden away in a sock drawer and never referred to it or put 'VC' after his name.

McCullough was busy stomping a torn-up turf the size of a big coffee mug back into its hole. 'There are,' she said, 'some real lizards who belong to this club. It's pretty scary when they turn up in uniform – but they look as though they are in uniform even in civilian clothes.'

Fiona was aware of *La Guerra Sucia*, The Dirty War, and the disappearance of thousands of people. But she had somehow separated it in her mind from the great talent and cultivation of Jorge Louis Borges. If he could exist with it, so could she. Life was full of discordant notes – and modern music reflected it. While Argentine detainees were drugged and thrown naked into the sea from aircraft, their country's greatest author gave lectures on 'The Role of Myth in World Literature'. And often Borges's audiences were full of high-ranking military officers in uniform. It was as if intellectual refinement was a way of having a soapy bath that removed the stains of blood and shit. But if one became obsessed with injustice and pain, one forgot to enjoy the moment – Fiona sipped her champagne.

The general called El Loco was talking to Ariel Solar. He had taken off his sunglasses and gestured with them towards Fiona and McCullough. One of the Gringos joined Ariel and Loco.

'There's my dad,' said McCullough. 'He wants us to join them.'

'Okay.'

'I bet what you really want is to meet Ariel. Personally, I think his beauty is too obvious.'

Fiona didn't reply.

The Argentines were speaking English for the benefit of Talbot, McCullough's father. The general's English was very good, but Ariel's was almost non-existent and it was obvious that he was embarrassed and finding it difficult to follow the conversation. Instead, he made eye contact with Fiona – a look that was almost desperate.

'I am worried,' said General Loco giving Talbot a concerned stare. The general then slowed his words in the hope that Ariel would understand, 'Worried that *Capitán de Corbeta* Solar plays so much polo. He is one of our most valuable and talented naval aviators – and we would hate to have him injured.'

'Surely,' said Talbot, 'the game improves his eye-hand coordination.' The American looked at Ariel and translated, '*su coordinación ojo-mano* – an essential skill for a fighter pilot.'

Ariel looked vaguely uncomfortable at being patronised, but

his eyes were fixed on Fiona – and hers on his. He mouthed, '*Encantado*.' She nodded back. It was the moment their affair had begun and there was no turning back.

The second half of the match was more frantic than the first and the pounding hooves even louder. There was something, Fiona realised, about the sound of a galloping horse that made the blood quicken. It was a sound that was primal, dangerous – and thrilling. A sound that was beyond morality and cool reason. In the end, the Gauchos came from behind to beat the Gringos 11–10. Ariel scored four of their second-half goals. Each time he drove the ball through the uprights he looked for Fiona among the spectators – and when he found her, he lifted his mallet like a knight of Aquitaine saluting his lady.

They became lovers a week later. McCullough had invited Fiona back to the polo club to see a game of *pato*: *It's an incredible sport – you can't believe how they stay on the horses.* Fiona, of course, accepted the invite – not so much to see a game of *pato*, but to see Ariel Solar. She had researched the game – and it was incredible. *Pato* had originally been played with a *pato vivo*, a live duck in a basket. The game involved dozens of horsemen galloping over miles of pampas. The first team to reach its own *estancia* with the duck – usually no longer living after hours of being snatched and tossed about – was the winner. *Pato* often turned violent with knife fights and gauchos being trampled. The Church threatened *pato* hooligans with excommunication and refused burial rights to any player killed in a match.

In modern *pato*, the duck is replaced with an inflated leather ball with handles. Goals are scored by tossing the ball into a rimmed net – like a large basketball hoop – mounted on a tall post. The player in possession of the *pato* has to hold the ball with an outstretched arm so other players can snatch at it. The fights for possession of the *pato* are the most exciting part of the game. And, as McCullough had said, it was utterly unbelievable how far the players could lean over the sides of their horses to pick up a dropped *pato* from the ground without falling off.

Ariel's team won 12–7 with him scoring five of the goals. No one was knifed or trampled – and the mood seemed more friendly and relaxed than the previous week's polo match. There were fewer spectators and only Spanish was spoken. The winning team was presented with a magnum of champagne in front of a marquee emblazoned *Asociacion Nacional de Jugadores de Pato*. Cameras clicked and the champagne spurted. A moment later, Ariel was at Fiona's side.

'Would you like to meet the horses?' he whispered.

'Yes, that would be nice.'

'I'll see you at the stables in twenty minutes.' Ariel slipped away.

McCullough had been eavesdropping from arm's length. 'I heard pretty boy say something about *caballos*.'

'Ariel wants to show me the horses.'

'What a smoothy. That's the first line they teach you in Getting Laid 101. Would you like me to come along as a chaperone?'

'Only if you want to.'

'I think not.'

Fiona sensed that McCullough was trying to put on a brave face.

'I hope we meet up later,' said Fiona.

'Don't worry about it.' The American walked away.

The stable block was a large neat building that accommodated nearly two hundred horses. Ariel was sauntering on the drive that led up to it from the clubhouse. He was wearing light grey trousers, a dark grey linen jacket and an open-necked white shirt. Fiona had to admit that he looked a bit of a spiv. Ariel had his hands in his pockets and was shifting nervously. His black hair shone still wet from the shower. Like many military men, he looked ill at ease in civilian clothes – unless they were for sport.

'Hello,' he said, 'I hope you are interested in horses – I must realise that not everyone shares my passion.'

'I love horses, but I don't know enough about them.'

'They are the real heroes. They are much more noble and brave than we are.'

She realised that Ariel needed to do the talking. It was his way of coping with his nervous shyness. Despite the age difference and Ariel's status, Fiona knew that she was stronger and more confident than him in every respect. She had already begun to play with him.

'Did you know,' said Ariel, 'that most polo ponies are mares – probably 90 per cent of them?'

'Why is that?'

'They are far more aggressive than geldings – but easier to manage than stallions. Having said that, a well-bred docile stallion can be an excellent polo pony.'

'So I've heard.'

'Where did you hear it?' Ariel's voice had a note of suspicion. 'Are you laughing at me?'

'No,' she lied, 'not at you. At the idea of well-bred stallions being docile. It's the sort of thing we would have wished for at BSG.'

'What is BSG?'

'Berkhamsted School for Girls. I went there. And I'm not sure that any of the girls ever said that about stallions, but many would have agreed.'

'Is it a famous school, like Eton?'

'Not particularly, but Clementine Churchill went there.'

'What is she famous for?'

'Mostly, I suppose, for being the Prime Minister's wife.' Fiona frowned. 'I'm sorry.'

'For what?'

'It's difficult to explain.' Fiona had been brought up to be superior, cool and disdainful of men; even if they were docile well-bred stallions. It was something she needed to lose before it destroyed her and made her incapable of warmth.

Ariel led her into the stables, which smelled of hay and urine and horse. 'Talbot,' he said, 'has the best polo ponies – many are former thoroughbred racehorses. They must have cost a fortune.'

'Where are your horses?'

'I don't own any horses. I borrow them from rich friends. In any case, the ones I rode in the *pato* match are now being walked and rubbed down.'

They came to a stall and stopped. It was dark. Fiona could barely make out the figure of the bay mare.

Ariel reached out and gently touched the polo pony's muzzle and the pony raised her head in greeting. 'This is Monsoon.' Ariel's other hand was resting on the gate of the stall. He then rubbed it along the top slat. 'This is bad.'

'What is?'

'She's been chewing wood. It means she hasn't been getting enough exercise and stimulation. Horses need to move about. They need to canter, gallop and roll on the grass. They need to play with other horses. When you keep them in a stall, they should have a view of outside. Horses like seeing the world go by – people and cars; the wind in the trees. They are curious creatures and want to be part of it all. They love movement.'

'I'll tell McCullough about the wood-chewing.'

'It may be best if I deal with it – sorry, if I sound too bossy.'

There was a moment of silence. Ariel touched his lips to Fiona's forehead. She raised her face and they kissed with open hungry mouths.

They made love in Ariel's room near the stables. It was part of a block of spartan rooms reserved for players and officials. The bed was narrow metal frame – like the ones in barracks or boarding schools. Ariel still had his shirt on when they began and Fiona shifted under him to remove it – she wanted all of him uncovered. Then she stopped and pushed him away. It had all happened so quickly – and he wasn't wearing a condom. But he had wanted her so much. There were other ways.

That first time had troubled Fiona – for there was nothing of Ariel in the room other than his own body. Not a book, not an ornament, not a photo of his family. She knew that he was married and had a son, that his wife was very ill. Fiona always wondered why he had shown no guilt – but he did show grief, a heartfelt mourning that informed his every look and gesture.

As soon as Fiona woke up, the memory of that first encounter disappeared as if it was a half-remembered dream. But a photograph of Ariel on her bedside table suggested otherwise.

She picked up the portrait – *¡Buen día!* – and gave his image a perfunctory kiss. She still missed him, but things were less passionate in the early morning light. She looked at the calendar as she slid into her sports clothes. It had been nearly two years since they became lovers in the room down the corridor. But now tennis was on her mind. Twice a week she played tennis with the club pro. He was a tired-looking man in his late forties who drank too much, but still won most of their sets. On this occasion, she managed to win two of the five – her best effort yet.

'See you Thursday,' said Fiona as they parted.

'Just a second…' The pro finished lighting a cigarette.

'Yes.'

'Someone was looking for you yesterday evening.'

'Who was it?'

'No one I've seen before. I think he was an Englishman.'

'Do you know what he wanted?'

'No, but I suggested he try again today. I said late morning might be a good time – before the lunchtime rush.'

'Thanks.'

The man from the embassy met Fiona in an empty lounge. He was wearing a light grey suit with that slightly tussled look that British diplomats abroad practise to perfection. He greeted Fiona with a wry smile and an envelope in his hand.

'This is a delicate matter, so I would like to confirm a few things.'

'Please confirm away.'

'What is your full name and date of birth?'

Fiona told him.

'What pets do your parents have?'

'Only a cat.'

'And what is his name?'

'It's a her and her name is Wandapuss.'

'I think that will do.' He handed over the envelope. 'We hope you will consider our offer of a free trip home – perhaps to coincide with Christmas.'

Fiona kept a straight face as she stared at the diplomat. There was no need to tell him that he was being a complete prat. His half-hidden ironic smile admitted it. For a second she almost fancied him. They both shared a certain public school insouciance – something she could never have with Ariel.

The diplomat gave a barely detectable cough.

'I look forward to reading your letter.'

'And when you have, would you please destroy it – regardless of what you decide to do.'

Fiona watched as her fellow countryman left the polo club lounge. He didn't turn around. She stared at the unopened letter – and suddenly felt that she needed a drink. For a second, she wondered if she shared a gene with one of her aunts who was a total lush. She shrugged and said, 'Who gives a fuck?' and walked over to the bar for a stiff brandy. She poured it into an espresso cup to disguise what she was drinking in case someone walked in. Fiona smiled. She was already acting like a spy.

She went back to her seat and opened the letter. It was standard civil service, with CONFIDENTIAL stamped at the top and bottom of each page. But it was terse and gave little away. There was nothing in the letter to indicate it was an invitation to apply for a post as an SIS intelligence officer, but she would still destroy it as instructed.

Fiona stared out the window at the extravagant greenery of a November spring. Everything in Argentina was upside down. And the country had turned her inside out. The chap from the embassy – and he wasn't a guy or a bloke, but a chap – was a reminder of who she was and what she was renouncing. No, there was no turning back. The first time she had lived abroad she had found British people annoying – and tried to steer clear of them. But, from time to time, there were relapses into sentimental homesickness – particularly for her father. God how she loved that silly gentle man – and how he could always make her laugh. Fiona picked up the letter. 'I bet,' she said, 'this has something to do with you, Daddy.'

She finished her shift later than usual and was glad to be alone when she went back to her quarters. She had kept the letter from London on her person the entire day, its edges like a prodding knife. Fiona placed the letter on top of her dresser. She had brought matches from the bar so she could burn the letter and flush its ashes down the toilet – but first she wanted to copy out the contact details in case she changed her mind. A free trip to England for Christmas was tempting – and money was tight. She could hear Argentine voices in the corridor; muffled by a wall, their accent sounded even more Italian. Going native meant never going back. It was a matter of pride. The ultimate test for an expat was listening to the Shipping Forecast on the BBC World Service. In Argentina, it was broadcast just before 4 a.m. – a vulnerable time of night. If you could listen to *Sailing By* and make it past Viking, the Utsires, Trafalgar and Fair Isle without a lump in your throat, you were no longer a Brit. Fiona had never managed it.

Fiona picked up a pen and pulled out the top dresser drawer to find her personal diary. It was leather-bound and packed with cards, letters and memorabilia. As she opened her diary, a photo fell out. Her father had a larger copy – and she had *begged* him not to display it where others could see it. Fortunately, he saw the point and kept it under cover. Daphne, the second youngest, was sixteen and big sister Margery had just turned twenty-one. The five Stewart sisters are naked – and the most beautiful and sensuous, as always, is Noël. Her willowy small-breasted body is in profile to the camera. The photo had been posed and snapped by an art student who had been besotted with Noël. It had been taken on Holkham Beach in early summer at low tide when the golden sands are endless. The water is still lapping around their ankles. Noël, her hair wet and untidy in ringlets, has obviously braved a swim. They are posed around an ancient tree stump exposed by the falling tide. Fiona reminded herself that she must never show the photograph to Ariel – for, surely, he would fall in love with Noël. Everyone did. Noël would soon qualify as a junior doctor. Fiona felt another pang of jealousy as she imagined her sister – hair pinned back, white-coated, stethoscope-bearing – gathering admiring glances as she made the ward rounds. And what, thought Fiona, had she become? A failed PhD student skivvying in an Argentine polo club because she had fallen hopelessly in love with a beautiful Argentine pilot whose every touch and glance set her on fire. Fiona's eyes turned flinty as she stared at the letter from the Secret Intelligence Service.

London: December 1979

There were three on the interview panel: Catesby and two from Dir/PA. One of the admin types was from DD/Finance, the other from Positive Vetting. They all agreed that Fiona Stewart would be an ideal recruit for SIS. She had already passed the assessment tests with flying colours and only the vetting process remained. 'But,' said DD/Finance, 'I'm not sure that she wants to be part of us. She could certainly make a lot more money elsewhere.'

'The City always prices us out of the market,' said Positive Vetting.

'She doesn't want a job in the City,' said Catesby. 'She wants to do a PhD on Latin American literature.'

DD/Finance was nibbling the end of his reading glasses. 'It often happens that way,' said Finance. 'It did with my own kids. They leave university all full of ideas and a thirst for knowledge – then they discover money.'

Catesby smiled. 'But we didn't.'

'Perhaps,' said Positive Vetting, 'no one else would have us.'

'Except,' replied Catesby, 'the Russians.'

Positive Vetting gave Catesby a weary look.

'Shall we call her back in?' said Finance.

The interview recommenced with the usual formalities: she 'would receive a standard government letter' within a week; if the letter made a 'provisional offer of a post', she would be told whom to contact for the next stage.

'Have you,' said Catesby, 'any questions for us?'

'If you make an offer, do I need to give an answer immediately?'

Catesby looked at Finance.

'Within ten working days,' said DD/Finance, 'is the usual call.'

'But in your case,' said Vetting, 'we could be flexible.'

'We never,' said Catesby, 'put candidates under pressure to make a quick choice. Joining us is a serious decision – and there is no turning back.' He gave Fiona a close look. 'Have you any other questions?'

'Yes. What is the worst part of this job?'

'I think' – Positive Vetting addressed Catesby by his cover name – 'that you had better answer that.'

Catesby stared at the desk. 'The worst thing, for some of us, is when an agent you are running is arrested, tortured and executed. The agents we run are, of course, not innocent civilians caught in the crossfire.' Catesby paused and looked up. 'But their families may well be – and they often suffer as well. The human consequences of what you do will haunt you for the rest of your life.'

'I suppose,' said DD/Finance, 'that you are wondering why anyone would do this job.'

Fiona smiled nervously. 'What then is the best thing about a career in the Secret Intelligence Service?'

'I'm glad you asked that,' said Catesby. 'It's a great job for someone with a curious mind – you uncover secrets and find out how the world works.' Catesby smiled. 'But the best thing, the very best thing, is telling truth to power.' He stopped and looked at Fiona. 'I think you have another question?'

'Does power always listen?'

'That,' said Catesby, 'is top secret. But if you join us, I am sure you will one day find the answer.'

Fiona kept a straight face. The assessment tests had appealed to her sporting instincts – and her sense of sibling rivalry. She always needed to win and was proud she had taken straight sets from the SIS assessors at Fort Monckton. The evaluation procedure, which lasted two days, was a hard grind that tested the candidates physically, mentally and emotionally. The most difficult personality test was called Emotional Detachment and Instinct. The problem was that you didn't know whether they were looking for cuddly types or psychopaths. Fiona decided to be completely honest in her answers – and that's exactly what they wanted. She now wondered whether she should continue to be honest and tell them that she had decided not to accept the post. On the other hand, she didn't want them to think she had conned them to get a free trip back home for the Christmas hols. She decided to wait.

In the end, it wasn't a matter of Fiona Stewart saying yes or no – or a bad mark from Positive Vetting. It was a question of budget cuts. The new Tory government was taking an axe to public spending – and the intelligence services and the military were no more exempt than social services. Catesby sent Fiona a standard civil service letter with a contact number asking her to make an appointment – which she did promptly. The only other person in Catesby's office for the interview was a woman from TS, Training Section, called Gwen who had a military background and wore sensible brogues.

'What am I supposed to do?' said Gwen.

'Make her feel more comfortable.'

'No one's ever accused me of doing that before.'

'In any case,' said Catesby, 'there's a directive floating around.'

'What sort of directive?'

'That interviews shouldn't take place between members of the opposite sex when there isn't a third person present.'

'But there's only the two of us here now,' said Gwen.

'Should I get someone else to come in?'

'That won't be necessary, Catesby. If you pounced on me I would break your neck in two places.'

'*Have some Madeira, m'dear, I've got a small cask of it here.*'

'Actually, I wouldn't mind a drink.'

'I'll buy you one in the canteen.'

'I thought you inherited Henry Bone's Chippendale drinks cabinet.'

Catesby smiled. Henry Bone still haunted SIS. He had been Catesby's mentor when he first joined the service. Bone, despite having been a close friend of Anthony Blunt, had risen to director level in SIS. The jury was still out on whether Bone had exposed the Cambridge Spy Ring or helped them escape – or both.

'He took it with him,' said Catesby with an enigmatic half-smile

'Do you ever see Henry?'

'You sound like you're from Positive Vetting.'

'Only asking.'

'From time to time. He's living in happy, but nervous retirement.' Catesby didn't know Gwen well enough to say more. The change of government meant more than budget cuts. It meant the likelihood of a witch-hunt, even though the witches were dead, buried or gaga. There was a knock on the door. Fiona Stewart had arrived.

Catesby began the interview by explaining to Fiona that, although she was the ideal candidate, new financial restraints meant it was impossible 'at present' to offer a full-time post. He couldn't go into detail about his conversation with the Foreign Office mandarin who controlled the SIS budget: 'I'm sorry, Catesby, but new staffing is cut back to bare essentials – and it's hardly likely that we'll be going to war anytime soon with a Spanish- or Portuguese-speaking nation.'

Fiona sat composed with her hands folded. 'I'm not,' she said, 'certain that I would have taken up the post in any case. I had wanted to go back to Argentina to continue my studies – and for personal reasons too.'

Catesby nodded. He had been expecting that answer – and that was the reason why he had invited her to the interview. Fiona had been open about her relationship with an Argentine naval aviator. It wouldn't, Catesby had thought at the time, be a disadvantage to her recruitment. In fact, a file in his brain had ticked 'very useful'. Perhaps more useful than a salaried intelligence officer. Catesby had cleared it in advance with DD/Finance. The cuts didn't affect SIS's 'unaccountable funds' budget – a pot of cash that notoriously lured East Bloc agents with prostitutes and champagne among other things.

'I'm going to come straight to the point,' said Catesby. 'Would you consider working for us in another capacity?'

Fiona tilted her head and looked at him hard. 'In what capacity?'

'You would be what's called a NOC: it means "non-official cover". It's the terms we offer most of our agents – not an actual contract, you'd be freelance.' Catesby didn't add that 'non-official cover' also meant no diplomatic immunity. NOCs could be arrested as spies by the host country – and even executed – and there was nothing that London could do about it, other than a spy exchange if the NOC was important enough. Business persons operating in the Soviet Bloc were the usual victims. 'But we would,' said Catesby, 'train you and pay you.'

'So,' said Fiona, 'I wouldn't be an intelligence officer, I would be a spy.'

'That's right – and, by the way, you would be on a retainer of two thousand pounds per annum. A useful top-up,' smiled Catesby, 'to your student grant.'

Fiona didn't smile back. In fact, there were financial difficulties. Her family weren't as grand as they seemed. 'What would I have to do?'

'Nothing that you felt uncomfortable with – you could spend most of the time researching your thesis.'

This time Fiona did smile. 'I think there's a catch.'

'It would be useful if you got to know people close to the centre of power – but also the general mood. We're not interested so much in open-source intelligence, that's what we call newspapers and stuff – I hope our embassy in Buenos Aires takes care of that. We want intelligence about human beings. In the trade, we call it HUMINT. Gathering it requires close observation and intuition too.'

Fiona wondered if Catesby was making a not-very-veiled reference to her lover. If so, she was tempted to lean forward and say, *Fuck off!*

'Would anyone like a cup of tea?' said Gwen.

'Once the wood-burner is roaring this place gets stripping-down-to-shorts-and-T-shirt warm.'

But it was just after breakfast and her father's office in the garden was still cold. Fiona held her hands over the delicious warmth of the glowing fire.

'I suppose being in Argentina has made you forget the invigorating chill of a British winter.'

'I do miss England – but there are compensations.'

'I am pleased that you've accepted the job – but I think it's best we don't say anything to your mother or sisters. They love intrigue.'

'I certainly wouldn't have accepted a full-time post – and I am having second thoughts about accepting this one.'

'That's normal.'

'I feel that I am deceiving Ariel.'

'That's understandable. You obviously can't tell him.'

'Were there secrets that you kept from Mum?'

Her father smiled bleakly. 'There still are – and this is one of them. Relationships are complicated and sometimes withholding the truth is better than causing hurt. It doesn't mean you don't love the other person.'

'Have you ever lied to me?'

'No. You should never lie to children.'

Fiona remembered the double bluffs her father used to play on the tennis court against her – the unpredictable combinations of drop shots and lobs. 'I'm not sure that's true.'

The major laughed. 'By the way, how does Ariel feel about you being away for so long? He must miss you.'

'He does. He wasn't surprised that I came home for Christmas, but is disappointed I'm staying so long.'

'Because of the training course?'

'Which won't be until a week after New Year.'

'SIS and booze. It takes them a long time to stir after a holiday.'

'But it is a short course – only ten days – the one they give to us bargain-basement part-timers. Apparently, it's mostly about covert communications.'

'I am proud of you, Fiona – but, of course, I will be worried about you too. Just like when you went on skiing holidays.'

Fiona smiled. 'I might take it up again. There are some excellent ski resorts in the Andes – it's a great country for sport.'

Fiona paused. 'But now, because of this training course, I've got to think of a cover story for getting back to Argentina so much later.'

'I'm sure we can invent a family crisis or two.'

Brompton Oratory, London: May 1980

The sign in front of the confessional, *Nederlands Sprekende Priester*, wasn't so much to attract Dutch-speaking penitents as to keep everyone else away – everyone, that is, who didn't have a rendezvous with Catesby operating under *priester* cover. The Provost, the priest in charge of the Oratory – who always referred to the place by its proper name, the Church of the Immaculate Heart of Mary – gladly accepted a small donation in return for Catesby's clandestine use of a confessional. The Provost never asked questions, but must have known that the Oratory was a notorious spy venue. While the posh Catholics of Kensington and Chelsea went to mass and communion, Sov agents from the *rezidentura* crossed themselves and muttered Hail Marys as they emptied and filled dead letter boxes hidden under pews.

There wouldn't be a problem if an actual *Nederlands* speaker came in to confess their sins. Catesby's Antwerp-born mother had brought up both him and his sister as speakers of French and Flemish *Nederlands*. It was the only thing they inherited – and was largely the reason Catesby progressed from state school to Cambridge and on to SIS. In any case, only one *Nederlands* speaker had ever come into the confessional. It was an elderly woman who was visiting her London-based daughter. Her sins weren't very interesting – if they were sins at all. Confession was for the woman a fortnightly habit. The only other person not on spy business who ever came into the dark booth was a whacked-out young man who wanted to know the best places to score drugs in Amsterdam.

The recent Soviet invasion of Afghanistan meant that Catesby had to concentrate on the Head/SovBlocTSection part of his job rather than the recently tagged on Dir/LatinAmerica. That's budget cuts for you. Catesby felt guilty about not paying as much attention to Fiona as she deserved. He still hadn't had a chance to read her latest decoded cables, but had brought them with him. They were difficult to read beneath the low-wattage bulb in the confessional. Catesby squinted as he made notes on Fiona's latest messages. She was obviously torn between her love for the naval aviator and her detestation for the Junta – who were right bastards. Catesby knew what she was feeling because he had experienced similar personal conflicts in his own career – and hoped that Positive Vetting never probed them. He finished Fiona's cables and slipped them back into a trouser pocket underneath his candlewax-stained cassock. Catesby looked at his watch. SLIME was late. The codename broke a fundamental rule. Aliases should never describe the agent – and SLIME was slime.

Catesby didn't like dressing up as a priest. He was a fallen-away Catholic who had embraced atheism with a convert's passion. Nonetheless, the Oratory did appeal to his sense of humour. He found it a surreal Disneyland version of a Roman basilica – a pile of expensive ecclesiastical tat that took the breath away. But being a spy meant you had to play roles. Catesby always thought that drama school would provide better training for new intelligence officers than marksmanship courses. On this occasion, Catesby had been summoned to play priest-confessor because of a call made from a payphone that uttered the password for an Oratory *Treff* – short for *Treffung*, meeting. Everyone still used the German abbreviation, which had become spy slang in 1950s Berlin, even if they were operating in Burma.

SIS had been cultivating SLIME, a major in the KGB, for some time – ever since the American station in Ankara had rejected him. As luck would have it – and luck was one of the intelligence officer's most important tools – SLIME was assigned to the London *rezidentura* where he spent more time buying luxury goods for high-ranking apparatchik wives than he did spying.

The biggest reason the Americans didn't want SLIME as a defector was because he was a dyed-in-the-wool communist who hated capitalism. He had great nostalgia for Stalin – even though SLIME was too young to remember much of his rule

– and thought the Soviet Union had been going downhill ever since his death. When he told his American contact in Istanbul that, if they didn't accept him as a defector, he was going to apply for political asylum, the American laughed out loud. SLIME swore at him in Russian.

The CIA station chief in London had shared the report on SLIME with SIS – largely because he thought SLIME was a great joke. The American report concluded that SLIME was 'mentally ill' and 'dangerously unstable'. It stated that any intelligence gleaned from him would be 'totally unreliable' as the result of 'attention-seeking sensationalizing'. Catesby thought the Americans had been too busy looking at SLIME's ideological contradictions and not enough at the reasons for his personal turmoil – and how that turmoil could be exploited. Catesby wrote an addendum to the CIA report with attached suggestions and sent it 'eyes-only' to the DG. Catesby was soon given permission to take on the case.

Catesby finally heard the door open and the creak of wood as the Russian knelt on the narrow kneeler. 'Are you there?' said the Russian in English.

'God is everywhere,' said Catesby.

'You make joke or are you priest?'

'Sorry, it was a joke.'

'What you think of offer I make last time?'

'We are interested in the offer, but we don't understand why you want to leave the Soviet Union – forever.'

'One word, corruption. The Soviet ideal has been lost forever.'

'Can you explain?'

'I go now, you are stupid. I don't want talk to you.'

Catesby realised that SLIME was drunk – and the best way to get on with a drunk is to agree with him. He was wired up and everything was being recorded. Catesby knew that if the tape fell into the wrong hands, his words might be edited, misconstrued and used against him – so the tape, like much else in the Secret State, was going straight into the burn bag even though it would be useful for blackmailing SLIME. 'I hope,' said Catesby, 'you don't leave. Many of us share your noble ideas. The shining beacon that was once the Soviet Union has now been extinguished.'

SLIME seemed unfazed that a British intelligence officer had just praised the old Soviet Union. 'Maybe,' said the Russian, 'only way we can light torch again is from exile.'

'Do you want to bring your family with you?'

'Yes – she hates my wife.'

Catesby was confused. SLIME was drunk and rambling on about something that he thought he had already mentioned, but hadn't. Catesby shifted into Russian. 'Кто это … Who is this person who hates your wife – and why does she hate her?'

SLIME, seemingly unaware that he had been addressed in Russian, answered in English, 'Because she wants me in her collection – on shelf next to her jewels from Georgia.'

Catesby finally twigged. SLIME was a handsome man who had once trained as a ballet dancer. He was pretty certain of the woman's identity, but wanted to make sure. 'Does she look like her father?'

SLIME laughed. 'She look just like him – same cheekbones, same black swept-back hair. Going to bed with her would be like going to bed with General Secretary of Communist Party.'

It all fitted into place. SLIME was being pursued by Galina Brezhneva. The files on the daughter of the Soviet leader were ripe reading – and had been passed around the Sov sections at SIS with great amusement. Catesby had studied them with care, but had not been so much amused as saddened. No daughter of a Soviet leader had ever grown up normal and happy. Galina was an alcoholic who collected men and expensive jewellery – and notoriously flashed her knickers dancing on tables at wild parties.

'And,' said SLIME, 'she almost as fat as her father.'

Catesby suppressed a laugh. Despite his good looks, SLIME was far from gallant. In any case, Galina's father had more serious health problems than being overweight. The CIA delighted in passing around a list of Leonid Ilyich Brezhnev's ailments and weaknesses: alcoholism, insomnia (and consequent addiction to barbiturates), heavy smoking, gout, arteriosclerosis and emphysema. It was clear that Brezhnev, after eighteen years as leader, might not be long for this world – and who knows what would come next. SLIME was right: the Soviet Union had stagnated and deteriorated under Brezhnev's rule. And as he grew older, Brezhnev's ego needs increased the more his health failed. On each of his birthdays Brezhnev was showered with new medals and orders. There was something childlike about his love of medals – an addiction to shiny things his daughter seemed to have inherited.

Catesby could just make out SLIME's silhouette through the wire mesh of the confessional window. He felt he was giving Last Rites, rather than absolution, to an empire in its death throes.

'Will you help me?' said the Russian.

'What was your last job before you came to London?'

'I still have same job. Only come to London on temporary duty.'

The news confirmed Catesby's suspicion that SLIME's primary function in the UK was to go on shopping trips for the *nomenklatura*. The diplomatic bag was a better way of getting the goods to Moscow than dragging stuff back after a holiday.

'And what,' said Catesby, 'is that job?'

'I am still in First Directorate, but transfer from Turkey to Latin American section – and taking Spanish language course. I ask for change after argument with Turkey boss.'

Catesby reflected. The Ankara KGB *rezident* had probably picked up a whiff of SLIME's disloyalty. 'Where,' said Catesby, 'do you think will be your next overseas posting?'

'Mexico or Argentina – Argentina is very important target for First Directorate.'

Catesby stared into the darkness. Was this just luck? Or had the *rezidentura* twigged that Catesby's additional title was Dir/Latin America? Was SLIME a plant? This was why no one liked dealing with defectors and doubles.

'Listen,' said Catesby, 'if you don't tell me the truth – and everything you know – we are going to leave you to the sweet embraces of Galya.' Catesby thought about throwing in a blackmail threat, but decided to save that for later. 'But if you do give us everything we want, we will receive you and your family with open arms – and pay you a retainer.'

'What is retainer?'

'Money. Question one, is the First Directorate supporting the Montonero guerrillas fight against the Junta?'

SLIME laughed. 'You must be crazy, *mucho loco* as they say in Argentina.'

'I'm pleased that your language lessons are going so well. But why would I be crazy for thinking you would support a Marxist revolution?'

'Because Soviet Union need beef and grain today more than it need revolution in Argentina tomorrow.'

'Really?' said Catesby pretending surprise. He already knew that Russia accounted for 30 per cent of Argentina's exports – and what, as any fool could guess, Argentina would want in return? And yet no alarm bells were ringing in Whitehall. Could no one see why the Argentines were stocking up weapons?

'Argentine thing started after Afghanistan,' said SLIME.

Catesby nodded. Foreign affairs boffins like to call such things 'unintended consequences', but you didn't need a degree in international relations to work out what would happen. The United States declared a trade embargo against the Soviet Union as the result of Moscow's invasion of Afghanistan. Meanwhile, the Junta in Buenos Aires were suffering from Washington's ban on arms sales as the result of human rights abuses. Hey presto, Russia and Argentina swap guns for food. 'Tell me more about your job,' said Catesby.

'I am responsible for liaison with the Argentine Communist Party.'

At first, Catesby had a vision of SLIME's agents making clandestine contacts in jungle hideouts – but then he remembered. It was one of those odd facts that stick in an intelligence officer's brain with a question mark attached to it. Even though everyone and everything that took a Marxist line had been driven underground by the Junta, the small and elderly Argentine Communist Party were still allowed to function and even to publish a newspaper called *Que Pasa*.

'Why,' said Catesby, 'has the Junta not banned the Argentine Communist Party?'

'Because they are useful idiots.'

Catesby laughed ... It was a term that usually referred to 'fellow travellers' being duped by communists, but in this case it was communists being used by a right-wing Junta. The secret world was a looking-glass gallery of deception and unexpected turns.

'In fact,' said SLIME, 'the Junta prefers weak Communist Party to Peronists.'

The Russian might have been drunk, but he had put his finger right on the button. The biggest challenge to the Junta was Peronism, a movement founded by a general and his wife who rejected both capitalism and communism. *Los Descamisados* – the shirtless ones – had adored the Peróns for they had given them low-cost housing, free medical care, paid maternity leave and subsidised holidays. Catesby remembered a conversation with an ex-Tory minister comparing Eva Perón and Thatcher. The former minister had confided, laughing: 'The difference is that the "shirtless ones" who voted for Thatcher will remain shirtless.'

'But,' said Catesby probing for more, 'the Argentine Communist Party support revolution?'

SLIME smiled. 'Sure in El Salvador and Nicaragua, but not in South America. They know what Junta will tolerate.'

'You say your job is to liaise with the Argentine Communist Party?'

SLIME nodded.

'What do you liaise about?'

'Arms sales.'

Catesby sat up as he heard a bell in his brain go 'ping'.

SLIME continued. 'We use the Argentine communists as middlemen, as brokers, between the Kremlin and the Junta. The Junta cannot approach us directly to discuss these things – the Americans would find out and go crazy.'

'I suppose,' said Catesby, 'the Junta want weapons to carry on their war against the Montonero guerrillas.'

SLIME laughed. 'I don't think they need ship-to-ship missiles and submarines to fight guerrillas in jungle. They also want Sukhoi-22 attack planes – and I think you know why.'

Catesby did know why. The SU-22 was a big worry for NATO because of its ability to jam radar systems – which rendered NATO surface-to-air missiles useless against attacking planes. Catesby found the expensive game of military one-upmanship depressing. The superpowers were going to spend each other into the ground.

'Why I tell you this – you give me nothing in return.'

'If you want political asylum for you and your family, I can arrange it.'

'How can you promise that? You not Prime Minister. You not Queen of England.'

Catesby wasn't going to say 'trust me' – everyone in the trade knew that 'trust me' was spy talk that translated as 'fuck you'. Instead he said, 'There are conditions. We are going to provide a haven, a safe house, new identities and a job. In return, you will provide a complete list of all the weapons systems that Argentina has expressed an interest in – and the names of everyone involved in the negotiations. We would also like up-to-date technical information about the SU-22. And finally, the First Directorate's assessment of the Argentine leadership – everything from drinking habits to sex life to position in the power structure.'

'You are asking for a lot. I think I provide most of it, but information on SU-22 is highly classified and I might not be able to get.'

'I understand, but try.'

'How much you need for deal?'

'All the Argentine stuff.'

'I can do that.'

'Can you get your family to England?'

'Not sure. That could be difficult.'

'Turkey or Switzerland?'

'Turkey would be easier.'

Catesby paused. There were also a number of rat-lines for

extricating defectors from East Bloc countries with weak border controls, but Catesby didn't know whether he could trust SLIME enough to mention them.

'Would you,' said Catesby, 'consider leaving on your own?'

'I might.'

'Basically, I don't give a toss whether you come out alone or with your loved ones. I've told you what I want. Contact me when you've got it – and we'll safe-house you with champagne and whatever else you want.'

SLIME slid out of the confessional. He didn't say goodbye.

Buenos Aires: July 1980

Fiona had more or less given up on her PhD thesis. She had begun to suspect that the works of Jorge Luis Borges were the emperor's new clothes. The broad diversity of his learning may have been owing to a youthful addiction to encyclopaedias. His use of symbolism was often strained. What annoyed Fiona most was the writer's sly and smooth ability to conjure up the profound out of the banal. But Borges was certainly a wizard – and Ariel adored him. Fiona had to be careful not to criticise Borges in front of Ariel. The writer was a national treasure and attacking him was an insult to Argentina.

In any case, Fiona had begun to prefer her new job as a duty manager at the William Brown Polo Club to the dry loneliness of academic research. She no longer felt like a skivvy. Her job description emphasised the importance of 'interacting with club members and their guests'. She not only loved the social life, but it also provided information to encode and send to London. The other aspects of the job – maintaining stock levels, budgeting, monitoring – appealed to her sense of efficiency. Fiona came to realise that she was more cut out to be a businesswoman than an academic. Nonetheless, she kept her contacts at the university because they were excellent for intelligence gathering.

As it was the middle of winter, too late for the autumn polo in April and May and too soon for the spring matches in September and October, Fiona had free use of Talbot's flat in Recoleta. It was also a good place to stash the radio transmitter because of the secret safe. She felt uncomfortable keeping the radio transmitter in her quarters at the polo club. There was a safe there too, but she suspected *el gerente general*, the head manager, also had access to it even though she had changed the combination. Spying was exciting, but it also made you paranoid.

The Recoleta flat, unlike her ground-floor accommodation

at the club, also had the advantage of height. Her radio came equipped with a high-gain directional antenna which Catesby had instructed her to point to different compass points depending on the date and time. One of the receiving stations was code-named Three Ships. Even though the station's location was top secret, Fiona laid a compass on an atlas and reckoned it had to be Ascension Island. She did the same for Spirit Voice and discovered it must be in New Zealand. She then found a Maori dictionary in the university linguistics department library – and found that Spirit Voice translated as *Irirangi.* She also discovered there was a New Zealand naval base named *Irirangi* near the small town of Waiouru. None of this was information she needed, but it wasn't idle curiosity either. Basically, Fiona had discovered that SIS security was often crap. And that discovery made her wonder about her own safety as a secret agent without diplomatic immunity.

There was one more receiving station, but that one was on the move – and Fiona had to wait for him to contact her. She loved the fact that there was a real human on the other end. She played back and decoded the message from HMS *Endurance*, the elderly Antarctic ice breaker that patrolled the southern ocean like a tired but loyal Labrador: AVAILABLE TO RECEIVE YOUR TRAFFIC BETWEEN 2300 AND 0200 ZONE TIME STOP PLEASE ACKNOWLEDGE

Fiona knew that the person receiving her message on *Endurance* wouldn't understand a word of her encoded transmission. It wouldn't be decoded until after it was bounced back to London, probably via GCHQ – and she hoped that no one other than Catesby would see it. He had advised her to be free and open in her reports – and not to worry about including personal impressions and unsubstantiated rumour. It seemed to Fiona an unprofessional way of doing things, but Catesby explained that intelligence wasn't just a science, it was an art. 'It's like being a poet: you throw away 95 per cent of your images and ideas, until eventually you discover the lines that echo and ring true. But the difficult part of being an intelligence officer is realising that you may never find those true lines – that you would have been better off learning a useful trade or, alternatively, getting a job in a bank.'

Fiona took out her rice paper notebook – if someone walked in the door she could swallow her report – and began writing. *A woman of about fifty came to the Recoleta flat seven days ago, 02/07/1980. She seemed surprised to see me. She hesitated at first, and then asked if Talbot was there. It seemed unlikely that she didn't know that Talbot is never in Argentina between the polo seasons. Perhaps she was looking for McCullough – or maybe she wanted to see who was in the flat. The woman was tall and had blond hair. She spoke careful fluent English – she sounded like a European royal who had learned upper-class British English at a boarding school. I doubt if she was one of Talbot's girlfriends – she wasn't young enough. I saw her again yesterday. As requested, I have been monitoring the Mothers of the Plaza de Mayo demonstrations...*

Fiona stopped writing. She thought she had heard a noise in the outside corridor. She put the notebook under a sofa cushion and went to the door. She opened the door and looked down the marble entrance hall – there was no one there. Fiona knew that she was becoming more paranoid and jumpy. She wished that Catesby hadn't asked her to check out the Plaza de Mayo demos – every time she went there she felt a thousand eyes boring into her back. The demos took place every Thursday afternoon at three thirty. The weekly protest march was an attempt to bring the world's attention to those who had disappeared since the military coup in 1976. The Mothers of the Plaza de Mayo were those who had lost sons and daughters.

...and was surprised to see the same woman. I am totally certain that it was her. She gave me a brief look of recognition, before looking away again – she didn't look pleased to see me. She was carrying the picture of a young man with dark hair and beard. I didn't ask any questions and pretended that I was just passing by and had no interest in the demo. I have since found out the identity of both mother and son...

After she had encoded and sent the message, Fiona took her written report to the sink where she usually burned the pages before washing the ashes down the drain. But the demons of paranoia were leaping and jeering – she imagined an Argentine intelligence officer deep in the bowels of the building armed with plumbing wrenches to look for the guilty evidence of burned paper. Instead, she ate the rice paper and washed it down with red wine.

Near Geneva: August 1980

The minister's cover story was a painting holiday in Switzerland. He had set up his easel facing Madame de Staël's former château at Coppet. Meanwhile, Catesby was walking a Bernese Mountain Dog which was the size and shape of a two-seater sofa. He found it difficult to control the dog without dropping the smart leather bag slung over his left shoulder. The bag contained doggie treats, a water bottle – and documents. But the dog provided perfect cover: spies never went to rendezvous with pets or children – which is why Catesby recommended that his agents do so whenever possible. Prams with babies were perfect dead letter drops – and had been part of his own Moscow Rules. The Sovs were none the wiser until a double agent under torture had revealed the Gorky Park pram ruse.

Catesby struggled to steer the dog towards the minister and his easel. When he got near, he called out, '*Ça va*?'

'I hope,' said the minister, 'we can speak English. I find all this hush-hush business a bit tedious.'

'I must say,' said Catesby, 'that I am inclined to agree. I hope you don't mind my asking, minister, but who do you think we are hiding from?'

'Our own backbenchers and the press.'

'Just,' said Catesby, 'like Cavándoli wants to hide your rendezvous from hard-line members of the Junta – probably for similar reasons.' Comodoro Carlos Cavándoli was the minister's counterpart in the Argentine government – and part of Catesby's reason for being in Switzerland was to bug the *comodoro*'s hotel room.

The minister reached out to stroke the Bernese Mountain Dog. 'Where did you get this wonderful animal?'

'It belongs to the owner of the guesthouse where I'm staying. I told him I loved dogs.'

'Could you move him so he's in line of sight with the château. Don't worry, I'm not going to paint you – just the dog.'

Catesby led the dog about twenty yards in front of the easel.

'That's good. Can you make him lie down?'

Catesby leaned on the dog's shoulders, but only got him to lie down when he sat on the grass next to him. As he sat cross-legged by the enormous Bernese Mountain Dog, Catesby reflected on all the other bizarre duties he had carried out during his thirty-three years as an intelligence officer.

'I like the glossiness of his black coat,' said the minister, 'and the way the reddish-brown of his legs is brought out by the white of his neck and chest. Thank you, it will only take a few minutes.'

Catesby stared at the faded grandeur of the château. The topography and the tall grass hid the ornamental lake, but the unseen water added to the colour. The pinkish-beige of the château walls seemed to shimmer. He could almost hear a string quartet as he imagined Madame de Staël leading her lovers into her literary salon. Catesby knew that he would have been an awkward guest. Madame de Staël's most famous quote – '*Tout comprendre rend très indulgent*'; 'Understanding everything makes one very indulgent' – had always infuriated him. Madame de Staël had never witnessed an SS atrocity.

'I've done enough of the dog,' said the minister. 'I can tidy him up later.'

Catesby walked back to the easel and looked over the minister's shoulder at his watercolour.

'What do you think?'

'You evoke a sense of world-weary decay.'

The minister sighed. 'I suppose I'm too obvious.'

'No,' said Catesby shaking his head, 'I like it – both as a painting and a cover story.'

'But you don't like us.'

Catesby shrugged. The minister had obviously read his file. Catesby had a reputation as being a member of the awkward squad – and that he had stood unsuccessfully as a Labour candidate in the 1945 election was never a fact that eluded the notice of Conservative ministers.

'My personal politics,' said Catesby, 'have never interfered with my loyal service to whichever government is in power.'

'Well, actually, your having a different point of view could be very useful. But we'll come back to that later. How did it go?'

'I've got a complete recording – and already have a transcript of the relevant bits.'

'Your translation?'

'I didn't need to translate – they were practising their English.'

The minister frowned. 'Perhaps they knew we had bugged their room and they were ridiculing us.'

'It didn't sound that way – and, by the way, Vice Comodoro Bloomer-Reeve speaks absolutely fluent English with a slight Scottish accent.'

'Isn't he Cavándoli's private secretary?'

'And confidante. They both come across as utterly charming and are looking forward to meeting you.'

'Bloomer-Reeve,' said the minister. 'I find the number of such British-sounding names in Argentina disconcerting.'

'There are,' said Catesby, 'a hundred thousand Anglo-Argentines and seventeen thousand British passport holders.'

'Would it be fair to say that there is no country in Latin America with which we have as many cultural and ancestral ties? And is it not ironic that British Argentines outnumber Falkland Islanders by more than fifty to one?'

It was clear to Catesby that the minister wanted to get rid of the islands and was looking for excuses to do so. He suspected that the Anglo-Argentines were more interested in polo ponies than cultural ties.

'Did we learn anything interesting from our eavesdropping?'

Catesby took an envelope out of the leather bag and handed it to the minister. 'Verbatim from Cavándoli: "If the British offer a ninety-nine-year leaseback we must take it." They then go on to discuss whether the Junta would accept it – and they both have their doubts – which is why the negotiations must be top secret.'

'It's all to do with image,' said the minister. 'The Junta need press photos of the Argentine flag flying side by side with the

Union Jack over Government House – even if it won't mean a thing for the next ninety-nine years.'

Catesby remained silent. An inner instinct told him that things were going to go badly. He knew that Cavándoli and the minster would charm the pants off each other – and both would leave Switzerland with a completely wrong impression of the other's country.

'Do you know something?' said the minister as he tinted a sliver of sky. 'Heath once asked me if I would like to be Arts Minister. I tried not to laugh. But I managed to tell him that having a ministry for the arts was an absurd waste of taxpayers' money. Why not have a Minister for Having a Good Time with Junior Ministers for Wine Drinking and Love Making? In any case, I ended up on the backbenches.'

It was obvious that the minister was a Tory 'dry', one of those who wanted to cut government expenditure through the bone and into the marrow. 'There are,' said Catesby, 'those who think that properly financing the Secret Intelligence Service is also a waste of taxpayers' money.'

'We expect results.'

'Well, don't expect many results from Latin America. We have one SIS officer to cover the entire continent of South America as well as Central America and the Caribbean.'

'That's not true; you've got two.'

'Not strictly true. The second agent is a part-timer, a NOC on two thousand quid a year.'

'Like the vacuum cleaner salesman in *Our Man in Havana*?'

'She's much better – and probably more useful than our man in Buenos Aires who has his hands tied.'

The minister looked puzzled. 'Why are his hands tied?'

'Because he's openly declared as an intelligence officer. In fact, he works closely with the Argentines to counter Soviet influence – and remember, this poor guy doesn't just cover Argentina, but *all* of Latin America.' Catesby paused. 'Because of budget cuts we have to ration our resources to concentrate on the Soviet Union and the East Bloc.'

'Which means,' said the minister, 'that you haven't the luxury to spy on every junta and every drug runner from Tierra del Fuego to the Texas border at taxpayers' expense.'

Catesby could see that the minister was an obstinate man – who could also be abrasive. He knew that one-to-one arguing was pointless. If you wanted to win an argument, you needed to do so at a committee meeting where you could humiliate your opponent. You made enemies, but you changed bad policies. Catesby looked at the minister, nodded and smiled.

'It's simple really,' said the minister. 'We have to cut the Gordonian Knot. When I took over this job I was handed a fat file marked The Falklands. It has been a headache for all of my predecessors – but it won't be for me. What would be your solution?'

'I don't like or trust the Junta. I would keep a submarine and a frigate on station.' Catesby noticed the minister's cadaverous face twist into a superior smile. 'And yes, minister, I realise that would require two frigates to have a permanent presence as well as two Royal Fleet Auxiliary tankers as no South American country would provide refuelling facilities.'

'I'm pleased that you realise the cost. Sabre-rattling is ridiculously expensive and doesn't solve the problem.'

Catesby shrugged. 'I see your point.'

The minister returned to his easel. 'The only permanent solution would be a mutually face-saving transfer of sovereignty. Ideally, it should take place after Argentina returns to civilian rule – but that could be a very long wait. We should also fund any Islanders who want to resettle in the UK or Commonwealth.'

The huge dog seemed to have developed an affection for the minister. He pulled away from Catesby and lay at the minister's feet with his head resting on his ankle.

'He must like being painted,' said Catesby.

The minister leaned down and stroked the dog. 'Nice lad.' He turned to Catesby. 'Now, if the Falklands produced wine instead of sheep, I might have a different view. In fact, I believe that we have a long-standing claim to Bordeaux that needs looking into.'

Catesby smiled, 'Would you like us to prepare an intelligence assessment?'

'Not yet. I haven't actually asked the Prime Minister about annexing Bordeaux, but she is a bit prickly about the Falklands.'

Catesby had wondered if the minister's meeting with his Argentine counterpart had been arranged with the PM's knowledge and approval, but thought it best not to ask. But he did know that there were conflicts between her and her senior ministers.

'There is,' said the minister, 'from our South America desk, a very confidential paper laying out four options for the Falklands. No one wants it to circulate outside the FCO – but I think you should see a copy and then pretend you haven't seen it.'

Catesby frowned and bit his lower lip.

'You don't look happy.'

'It's infuriating.'

'What is?' said the minister.

'The number of times that the Foreign Office hasn't shared things with SIS?'

The Bernese Mountain Dog began to bark.

Catesby smiled. 'See. He agrees.'

'Keep the dog out of this. Why do you think this is a problem?'

'Because the FCO is packed with languid dilettantes flourishing Oxbridge double firsts who think that anyone outside the hallowed precincts of the Foreign Office is a total idiot who can't be trusted.'

'I believe, Mr Catesby, that you have a double first from Cambridge.'

'Perhaps, minister, I'm just a state school ragamuffin with a chip on my shoulder.'

'You would get on well with the Prime Minister. She doesn't like inherited privilege either.'

Catesby gave a bleak smile. 'In any case, I hope you have seen my report on SLIME?'

'I glanced at it – very busy, you know – and then passed it on to Defence and Intelligence for evaluation and comment. And I am well aware you and your colleagues find the process annoying.'

Catesby nodded. It was a running sore in the Secret

Intelligence Service that other Whitehall departments, notably FCO and MoD, had their own in-house intelligence sections.

'Duplication of effort and second-guessing?'

'I have, minister, heard those thoughts expressed.'

'I am sorry to say, but they thoroughly rubbished your SLIME report. "Total nonsense," they said. "Moscow would never sell arms to the Junta." The consensus is that SLIME is a planted double who is spreading disinformation.'

'I think I may be a better judge of that.'

'Has SLIME contacted you again?'

'No – and I don't think he will,' said Catesby. 'The Galina Brezhneva saga has taken another twist. She seems to have given up on SLIME and set her cap at another KGB officer. I also think that SLIME has finally realised that the Brezhnev era is coming to a close.'

'Is Brezhnev ill?'

'Very. But, minister, my report isn't rubbish and I would like to explain why.'

'Go on.'

'Intelligence is rated according to source and information. A1 means that the source is totally reliable and the information confirmed. I rated my report as C1 – meaning that although SLIME may have been a doubtful source, the information he conveyed was completely true. Argentina's military shopping list – air-to-ship missiles; ship-to-ship missiles; radar-blocking gear; submarines – isn't just one they've passed on to Moscow. They've gone shopping all over the world for this stuff.'

'Have you proof?'

'A report will be on your desk when you get back to London. And may I add, minister, that air-to-ship missiles are not the kit you use to fight guerrillas in the jungle.'

The minister smiled. 'I know what they'll say.'

'What?'

'They'll say the Junta needs that stuff to beef up their navy and air force to confront Chile over the Beagle Channel.'

'I bet they already have.'

The minister nodded.

Buenos Aires: September 1980

The visit to Palermo Viejo was an important step in McCullough's radicalisation. The neighbourhood was the oldest district of Buenos Aires. The street was worn-down cobblestones and lined by mature trees unfurling early spring buds. Che Guevara had lived in the neighbourhood when he was a medical student – and Borges had lived there too and written a poem about it. It was clearly the type of place where intellectuals and artists lived. McCullough could see it was a more interesting and tasteful area than Recoleta, where her father had chosen to buy his flat among the ostentatious and wealthy. In fact, her father's place embarrassed McCullough – and letting Fiona stay there gave her an excuse for not using it. But there was another reason too.

Maria was a woman in her sixties who McCullough had come to admire and adore. The understated culture and dignity of Maria's home seemed to reflect her personality. The paintings, the books and the furniture handed down the generations were not there to impress, but for daily living. There were, however, no family photos – the security forces had taken them all. And, likewise, there were gaps on the bookshelves where anything considered subversive – such as the plays of Federico García Lorca and Bertolt Brecht – had been confiscated.

'I came to your father's flat,' said the older woman, speaking an English that to McCullough's ears sounded very 'upper-crust' British, 'to warn you not to have anything to do with that person you told me about – even though you were so determined. It was urgent – I was so worried about you.'

McCullough smiled. 'I wasn't going to go any further until I had asked your advice.'

'I understand your idealism. You remind me of my son and the people he tried to defend, but what you want to do is very dangerous. The Junta has won – the ERP hasn't existed for over two years.' The woman was referring to the *Ejército Revolucionario del Pueblo*, the People's Revolutionary Army.

'He was,' said McCullough, 'very convincing – and seemed a passionate believer in the cause.'

'I have since found out that he is almost certainly an agent provocateur.' The woman gave a sad smile. 'The Junta have run out of guerrillas to kill so they want to create more. You are not the only young idealistic person they have tried to recruit. They need to justify their brutal emergency powers.'

'He came to find me again – at the university – only two days ago. He said his name is Mateo, but I doubt if that is his real name. Many other students, radical ones, seemed to know him. Could he be genuine?'

'Even if he is, it is not worth the risk. What did he say this time?'

McCullough stared at the empty spaces on the bookcase and tried to remember the conversation. 'What surprised me was that Mateo, who you think is an agent provocateur, knew a lot about Fiona.'

The woman looked concerned.

'He knows that she is having an affair with an Argentine Navy pilot – who also is a polo star – and he knew the pilot's name and when he visits her in the apartment.'

'Did he say anything else?'

'He said it was a useful coincidence that *Capitán de Corbeta* Solar had a mistress in my father's apartment.'

'Did his voice sound menacing?'

'More sad than menacing – which is why I don't think he is an agent provocateur. One of them would have pretended to be delighted with the prospect of killing one of the Junta's best pilots.'

'Perhaps he was a good actor.' The older woman looked closely at McCullough. 'If you became part of an underground guerrilla movement, and your commander ordered you to kill this naval aviator, what would you do?'

'I hope that I would obey my orders – as I am sure that Che would have.'

The woman gave a weary smile. 'I often think Yeats could have been writing about Argentina instead of Ireland:

Too long a sacrifice
Can make a stone of the heart.
O when may it suffice?'

McCullough vaguely remembered the lines of the poem from English 101.

'But,' said Maria, 'I often think that if Yeats were an Argentine of today, he would be a supporter of the Junta.'

'Like Borges.'

The older woman smiled ironically. 'Our national treasure. Borges is a complex man who hated Perón – and now he hates democracy and supports Videla and the Junta. Borges says that most people are too stupid to understand poetry or mathematics, so why should we trust them to make decisions about how we are governed – which is even more complex than differential calculus. Am I boring you?'

'I'm not bored. But I am not an intellectual – they spend all their time talking and not doing.'

The older woman smiled. 'Did Mateo tell you that?'

McCullough laughed. 'Yes, he did.'

'But if you don't think before you act you might do something that hurts your cause – and waste a lot of beautiful lives.'

McCullough brushed a lock of hair out of her eyes.

'Violence, at this point, cannot defeat the Junta. Our only weapon now is peaceful protest which will turn world opinion against the Junta – and maybe stop the murders and arrests.'

'But they have killed members of your movement – your peaceful protest movement.'

The older woman looked at a painting of another woman on the wall – a woman with firm lips and an angular face. 'On the first day, there were thirteen of us in the Plaza de Mayo. The beginning was the most dangerous – within nine months three of our original thirteen had disappeared. But now we are hundreds – and there have been no more kidnappings or murders.' Pride showed on the woman's face. 'Jorge Rafael Videla is afraid of us – you can see his lip quiver beneath his moustache.'

McCullough stared at the woman. She wished that one day she would be that beautiful – and that noble and brave. 'You make me feel inadequate.' McCullough frowned. 'I wish I hadn't said that. My feelings shouldn't matter.'

'Your feelings do matter.'

'But my anger is meaningless – I'm just a poor little rich bitch. I haven't lost a child – the Junta has never hurt me or anyone that I love.'

'Who do you love?'

McCullough looked away. 'That's a tough question. I loved my first horse – and cried my eyes out when she was put down. I never loved my parents.' She wanted to add, *Not like I love you*. But she knew that would be too forward. There was another person she loved – with an uneasy jealous passion – but she didn't want to mention that either.

'Tell me more about the woman who is living in your father's flat?'

McCullough blushed – and then smiled to disguise her blushing. 'She has never been one of my father's mistresses.'

'I wouldn't judge her if she had been.'

'Her name is Fiona Stewart. She's a Cambridge University graduate – a very smart woman – who was doing a PhD on Borges, but she doesn't spend a lot of time at the university. She's now got a job at the William Brown Polo Club – not washing dishes, but some kind of manager. She's difficult to get to know, she has a sort of English upper-class reserve. But there's something about Fiona that doesn't add up.'

'She sounds interesting. I'd like to get to know her better. Is that all right with you?'

'Sure – and you know where to find her.'

Recoleta, Buenos Aires: November 1980

At first, Fiona had felt guilty about receiving two thousand pounds a year stipend from the Secret Intelligence Service. But no longer. Finally, she had a real piece of intelligence to report and couldn't wait to transmit it.

It had been a long weekend. Fiona had worked two shifts at the polo club. It had been busy because of a match between Ariel's team and a team from the Carrasco Polo Club in Montevideo. Ariel's team had a handicap advantage of four, which meant they had to score at least five more goals than the Uruguayan team to win. They just managed it, 13–8. Ariel scored four goals, but felt very beat up by the match. He had fallen off and badly bruised his shoulder and hip. Afterwards, Fiona took him to her flat in the club which had a long steel bath. While he luxuriated in the soothing water, Fiona mixed him a Cinzano and lemon. She handed him the drink and then reached under the water and gently squeezed his *cojones*.

Ariel smiled. 'We're just like an old married couple.'

Fiona kissed his forehead. 'I think, maybe, that old married couples in Argentina are different from those in England.'

'Or in Las Malvinas,' said Ariel playfully. 'We need to treat them to what the French call *une mission civilatrice*. We need to teach *los Kelpers* to drink wine and fondle their wives instead of their sheep.'

'And will you convert them to become good Catholics?'

Ariel frowned. 'Being a *good* Catholic is an ideal, an unattainable ideal, rather than a reality.' Ariel reached out of the bath and slipped a hand inside Fiona's blouse and inside her bra. 'Your nipple is hard and erect.'

'You excite me.'

'It won't be like that after you've had five or six children.'

'Is that what being a good Catholic is all about?'

'Of course. Condoms are the work of the devil.'

'Then why do you wear one?'

'Because you want me to.'

Fiona reached under the water again and closed her hand around his penis which quickly hardened. 'Then I am a work of the devil?'

Ariel looked at her closely. 'Perhaps you are. I never know what you are thinking. Your eyes don't give anything away.'

'I was thinking of getting in the bath with you. Couldn't you see that?'

'Hoping and seeing are not the same thing.'

Fiona began to unbutton her blouse. 'Do you want me to join you?'

'I'm not sure you can. This is a British bathtub.' He brushed the suds away from a metal disc under the taps. 'Made in Stoke-on-Trent, Staffordshire, England. Warning: No sex or naked bathing allowed.'

Fiona continued to undress. 'The ones we export to Latin America have an exemption. I'll show you.'

'I bet you will.' Ariel turned and looked at the naked Fiona.

'Don't stare.'

'I can't help it. You're so beautiful.'

Fiona slipped into the bath and Ariel spread his legs to make room. His face contorted in pain.

'What's wrong?'

'My thigh. I bruised it when I came off – and my shoulder too.'

'I'll be careful.'

Afterwards, Ariel fell asleep while they were still in the bath. The water was turning lukewarm and Fiona thought about running the hot tap, but didn't want to wake him. He looked so young, beautiful and peaceful amid the soap suds. She wanted to paint him as much as to hold him. His eyes gradually opened. 'You must,' he said, 'have saved me from drowning.'

'Shall we get dressed?'

'I could stay here forever.'

'But the water is getting cold.'

'And I am getting hungry.'

'Shall we eat here or in the restaurant?'

'Let's stay here. It's more intimate – and there are too many air force in the club. I want to get away from them.'

Fiona knew there was friction between the Argentine Navy and the air force. It was something that she had reported to London – and Catesby had asked her to find out more. But she also had a need to know these things for herself. She wanted to learn more about Ariel's life, even if the facts were state secrets, because it made her feel closer to him and part of him.

'Is it,' she said, 'because they are jealous of your uniforms – you all look so much more handsome?'

'I thought I was the only handsome one.'

'Such modesty.'

'It is not,' said Ariel, 'a question of uniforms, but of political power.'

Fiona wasn't going to press further. Asking too many questions revealed your hand. Her training had taught her to be indirect. The best information comes from a source who is talking freely – particularly when they want to show how much they know. She knew that Ariel wasn't a complete show-off or name-dropper, but he sometimes wanted to show that his insider knowledge was more than that of a *capitán de corbeta*, a lieutenant-commander. She found his male pride endearing – and liked to humour it.

She ordered *matambre arrollado* from the kitchen. They were thin slices of beef rolled around a stuffing of hard-boiled eggs, olives, onions and bell peppers and then barbecued. Fiona opened a bottle of Malbec.

'How are your bruises?' she said.

'I have had worse: two broken wrists, a fractured arm, two concussions, torn ligaments and numerous sprains. But many polo players have suffered far more serious injuries.' Ariel smiled. 'Especially the ones who died.'

'Is polo more dangerous than being a fighter pilot?'

'Hmm, good question. It depends on what you mean by dangerous. You are far more likely to be injured playing polo; but far more likely to die flying a jet fighter. But I've never flown in a war – that changes the odds enormously.'

'You never bombed the Montonero guerrillas?'

Ariel gave a sad smile. 'That's not flying in a real war.'

Fiona poured him another glass of Malbec. 'Do you think there will be real war?'

Ariel shrugged and drank the wine. Then he looked at Fiona. 'I hope it won't end up in war.'

'With Chile?' Fiona was referring to Argentina's dispute with her neighbour about three islands in the Beagle Channel.

Ariel shook his head and smiled. 'No, the Pope has intervened – and as good Catholics, both of our countries have accepted the Vatican's mediation. But England is not a Catholic country – and we don't speak the same language.'

'Have you ever been to the Falklands?' said Fiona.

'Never heard of them,' said Ariel laughing. 'Where are they?'

'I mean Las Malvinas.'

'That's better. No, I haven't.' Ariel gave a mischievous smile. 'But one of Thatcher's ministers has just been – and the Kelpers humiliated him.'

'Was it on the news?'

Ariel put a finger to his lips. 'Shhh. No, but I'm sure it will be.' Ariel lowered his voice. 'I have a friend who is an admiral – he was here today for the polo – who told us about it in the bar afterwards.'

Fiona remembered the admiral as a sinister character who gave her strange looks.

'We have an agent on Las Malvinas who sends us secret messages by radio. I don't know who he is. I think he may be an Argentine married to a Kelper woman – or maybe a Kelper who realises they would be better off as part of Argentina. Who knows?'

'So what did the Kelpers do to this poor minister?'

'They shouted insults at him and sang "Rule Britannia".'

'Why?'

Ariel smiled. 'I can't tell you. It's a state secret!'

'Just a hint. I promise I won't tell anyone.'

'I am so tired, Fiona. I want to lose myself in your beautiful body.'

It was four o'clock in the morning. Fiona had slept soundly until she had been awakened by Ariel's restive turning. 'Are you all right?' she said. 'Is it your shoulder?'

'Partly. I must lie on the side that isn't bruised.' He reached out and stroked her face. 'But I can't sleep anyway. I often worry and lay awake at this time of the morning.'

'Is it your son?'

'It is him and everything.' He paused. 'I think there is going to be war – I heard them talking about it in the bar. The humiliation of the British minister by the Kelpers means that a peaceful settlement is no longer likely. We were willing to give them everything. They could have preserved their British way of life – with warm beer and hot water bottles – for ninety-nine years. They could have used our hospitals and schools and sold fish in our markets. It was something called leaseback.'

'What was that?' Fiona knew what it was – she was sent regular briefings – but asked anyway.

'It meant that we would have owned Las Malvinas, but in name only. It meant that the Kelpers could live there rent-free for the next century. The hardliners in the Junta hated the lease-back deal – they thought that the Foreign Ministry was giving too much away.' Ariel smiled. 'Some blame it on their wives. The wives are almost English.'

It was something that Fiona found surreal. President Videla's Anglo-Argentine wife, Alicia Raquel Hartridge, was a parody of a well-born Englishwoman in the way she dressed, behaved and spoke. Her sister, Maria Isabel, was married to the Foreign Minister and shared the same British affectations. But then things started getting mixed up. The Foreign Minister's name was Carlos Washington Pastor – the middle name an homage to the USA. And the family name, Pastor, oddly apt, for the full title of his department was The Ministry of Foreign Affairs and Worship. Conducting relations with other countries wasn't just a cynical jockeying for power, but a matter of religious faith. Fiona wondered if these were cultural differences that London could ever grasp. But when she sent her next clandestine message from the flat in Recoleta she would try to explain.

London: December 1980

Back in the old days, when SIS headquarters were located in Broadway Buildings, going to the Foreign Office involved a gentle six- or seven-minute stroll that cut a corner through St James's Park to the Churchill War Rooms and then down King Charles Street to the main entrance of the imposing FCO. Catesby usually took a detour by the lake in St James's Park. He liked to have a look at the pelicans – particularly the one that was known to attack and eat pigeons. He had only seen the pelican gobble one pigeon, but the very sight of the ominous omnivore reminded Catesby that he lived in a world of 'nature red in tooth and claw' and prepared him for whatever meeting he was going to. Sadly, the downmarket relocation of SIS, from St James's to Century House in Lambeth, deprived Catesby of the opportunity to commune with the pigeon-killing pelican. But the longer walk did involve a bracing crossing of the Thames via Westminster Bridge. The iconic views of the seats of power were stirring. Although Catesby tried to restrain the patriotic mood, not everyone did. On one occasion he had been walking close behind a broad-beamed Conservative Member of Parliament who, unaware that anyone was close enough to hear, was singing 'Rule Britannia' in a low voice.

The mood music at the meeting in the Foreign Office was less stirring; it was more Fauré's 'Requiem'. The minister, who had been mocked in the Falklands, had suffered an even more savage mauling in the House of Commons. The meeting was chaired by the Deputy Secretary of the Cabinet, who – despite an Oxford double first – Catesby did not regard as the sharpest knife in the bistro kitchen. The venue was SAD, the South America Department, a cubbyhole in the Old Admiralty Building. The minister was not attending, but the civil service secretary who accompanied him to the Falklands was. The secretary was so young that

Catesby wondered if a sixth former from Westminster School had somehow wandered into the room as a lark. The DCDI, Deputy Chief of Defence Intelligence, had sent his apologies, but the MoD was represented by the colonel who headed up DHO, Defence Humint Organisation.

The FCO mandarins were the biggest fish at the meeting – and the head of the South American desk certainly knew about big fish. He had been stationed in Vientiane towards the end of America's war in Southeast Asia when a rare and enormous Mekong catfish had been caught. Lao tradition required the fisherman to offer the fish to the King of Laos. The king immediately announced a state banquet and invited the diplomatic community to share the catfish, which was eight feet long and weighed a quarter of a ton. The ambassador, a keen amateur chef, realised that the catfish might be the largest freshwater fish ever caught and asked the king if he could send the head and skeleton to the Natural History Museum in London. The king agreed and it fell to a senior dip, who was now head of SAD, to arrange transport of the fish remains to London before they rotted and putrefied in the tropical heat. He successfully did so with skill and aplomb. Catesby wondered if he would handle the Falklands crisis with the same dexterity and competence.

Within a few minutes, Catesby realised that the meeting was a waste of time. It had always been obvious that the Foreign Office wanted to get rid of the Falklands – which Catesby agreed was a rational policy. But in this case, rationality met opposition from Parliament, the Prime Minister and the Falkland Islanders themselves. Once again, it was obvious that the festering problem in the South Atlantic was being kicked into the long grass. Catesby watched the FCO mandarins reduced to ironic nods of agreement. The chairman, the Deputy Secretary of the Cabinet – who had been mauled by the PM – knew that boat-rocking was futile. The story of what had happened to him in Downing Street was no secret. In fact, the Deputy Secretary relished telling the story. Thatcher had only been Prime Minister for a few weeks when she summoned him to discuss a report. She opened the discussion by saying: 'I think only someone as stupid as you could have written this paper.' Stories of her appalling rudeness, often whisky-fuelled, were common currency in the rumour mills of Whitehall. In any case, the Deputy Secretary had ignored her verbal abuse and argued his brief. But in the end she didn't change her mind one bit. According to the Deputy Secretary, 'She listens, but only so that she can later claim she listened.'

Within less than a year, the new Prime Minister had become a Whitehall nightmare known for obsessing with the trivial and ignoring the important. The worst meetings were those scheduled around lunchtime. If the department hosting the meeting had not arranged lunch, they were hopelessly incompetent and inconsiderate: *Did it not occur to you that some of us might be hungry?* On the other hand, if food was laid on, the PM's reaction would be: *Oh, I'm far too busy to eat lunch!* In response, the mandarins developed a contingency plan known as The Designated Omelette Eater, which dealt with both scenarios. The lunch had to be simple and frugal – and omelettes were safe choices that spared the taxpayer. If the Prime Minister abstained, the Designated Omelette Eater stepped in and wolfed down the PM's serving to assure there was no waste – and later subtracted the estimated cost from his expenses.

The thing that worried Catesby most about Thatcher was the way she combined conviction with irrationality. The first agenda item was the minutes of the last OD meeting – that the SAD committee was to 'discuss', which really meant rubber stamp. The OD was an acronym for the Defence and Overseas Policy Committee whose permanent members included the PM and her four key cabinet ministers: Home, Foreign Affairs, Defence and Exchequer. But the tone of the minutes echoed Thatcher's personal views. A paragraph that began, 'In discussion it was generally agreed…' implied that the PM had got her own way. As the Deputy Secretary read out the key passage that had concluded the OD discussion on the Falklands, Catesby could hear Thatcher's own voice: 'No agreement could be contemplated which did not have the positive support of a majority of the Islanders.'

Catesby picked up his copy of the OD minutes and flipped to

the next page. 'Look,' he said, 'the rest of the meeting was about cuts in defence spending.'

The FCO's head of Defence and Intelligence cut in. 'I don't understand the point you are trying to make. Defence spending is a completely separate issue – there is no connection.'

The colonel who headed MoD Humint, and was regarded as a very bright and rising spark, looked vaguely amused and winked at Catesby.

Catesby had circulated a report that he had written on the dynamics within the Junta, partly based upon Fiona Stewart's observations, but he doubted that anyone had read it. 'There is a definite connection,' said Catesby, 'between UK defence cuts and the perceptions of the Argentine Junta regarding our determination to defend the Falklands.'

The Head of SAD stifled a yawn and the director of FCO Defence Intelligence rolled his eyes.

'The Argentine military,' continued Catesby, 'are now...'

'Can you please be brief?' said the chairman.

'I wouldn't have to speak at all if any of you had read my report.'

The colonel raised his hand. 'I have. It's excellent and I totally agree with your conclusions.'

'Thank you, but bear with me while I outline the argument for our colleagues. In purely military terms, the Argentine Junta are doing very well. They have crushed the Montonero guerrilla insurgency. It was a brutal victory, but a decisive one. The danger of a war with Chile over the Beagle Channel has now been resolved by none other than his Holiness Pope John Paul the Second.'

'Not a form of mediation,' added a wag from the FCO, 'that would go down very well in Northern Ireland.'

'Good point,' said Catesby, 'and your comment underscores the cultural differences between the UK and South America. There are many in Whitehall who dismiss the Argentines as temperamental Latinos. They are wrong. The Junta's decisions may seem emotional ones, but the decisions are based on logic and calculated risk.'

The Head of SAD nodded agreement. 'And emotions in South America – and in Britain too – are real political capital.'

'Indeed,' said Catesby, 'and, just as the 1966 World Cup helped Harold Wilson win an election, Argentina winning the cup in 1978 was an enormous boost for the Junta.'

'We seem,' said FCO Defence and Intelligence, 'to be going off piste.'

'I thought,' said Catesby, 'we were talking about my report – which does mention the 1978 World Cup and its effect on the Argentine national mood.'

'Please let him continue,' said SAD, 'or we'll never get out of here.'

'Thank you,' said Catesby. 'Although the Junta have been successful in terms of internal and external security, they have made a total mess of the economy. Inflation has risen to 600 per cent and real wages are down by 20 per cent. Put yourself in the shoes of the Junta.'

'Or their jackboots,' said the wag from FCO.

Catesby grimaced and continued. 'Argentine inflation is out of control. Unemployment is rising. The trade unions are planning a general strike. There is public unrest and you are in serious danger of losing power. So, if you're the Junta, what do you do? You invade the Falklands and you've bought your regime a lease of life.'

FCO Defence and Intelligence shook his head, but without much conviction. 'Relations between the UK and Argentina are amicable and stable – or seem to be. The problem with scaremongering is that it could seriously damage those relations. If we upgrade our military presence in the South Atlantic, as you seem to be suggesting, it would send a clear message to Buenos Aires that we are not sincere in our negotiations about a transfer of Falkland Islands sovereignty to Argentina.'

Catesby laughed. 'But we are not sincere about those negotiations in any case!'

The Head of SAD gave a weary sigh. FCO Defence and Intelligence looked out the window and yawned.

'Actually,' said SAD, 'those negotiations are going to resume early next year in New York.'

If, as Catesby often thought, you wanted to understand

British Foreign policy, ignore the works of Machiavelli or von Clausewitz and study Lewis Carroll instead. He found himself quoting beneath his breath: '*Why, sometimes I've believed as many as six impossible things before breakfast.*'

'Could you repeat that, Mr Catesby,' said the chairman, 'I didn't hear what you said?'

'I was talking to myself.'

'I heard what you said,' smiled the FCO wag. 'You think we are all mad. But let me try to prove that we are not. Argentina will never invade the islands as long as there is a possibility of an eventual transfer of sovereignty. Our job is to continue to assure them that the transfer is in the offing – just a question of a bit of arm-twisting in Downing Street and Parliament.'

'You sound,' said Catesby, 'as if someone has been leaning on you – and teaching you to sing a tune that you don't really believe.'

'Ah,' said FCO Defence and Intelligence, 'you've finally got it. Some of us thought you would never get there.'

The chairman looked at Catesby. 'Is there anything that you want to add? I'd like to get on with the meeting.'

'UK arms sales to Argentina.' Catesby picked up his report and began to read. 'Two Type-42 destroyers, two Lynx helicopters, 44 Seacat GWS-20 series surface-to-air missiles, 120 Blowpipe anti-aircraft missiles, 370 vehicle radios, 135 Tigercat SAMs, periscopes, ejector seats, gunnery trainers…' Catesby paused. 'The list goes on. And the current government has already approved export licenses to Argentina for a battle tank, ship-borne torpedoes, a Vulcan bomber, half-track Land Rovers – and much more.'

The chairman, who had been nodding approval as Catesby ticked off each item, responded. 'Pure genius. It not only helps our trade balance, but proves to the Argentines that we are confident that the Falklands dispute will be solved by peaceful negotiation.' The chairman gave a patronising smile. 'Otherwise, why would we be selling all those weapons to the Junta?'

Catesby felt he had just passed through the Looking Glass. Was he the only one who could see the Jabberwock? Had the

FCO mandarins turned into slithy toves who could only *gyre and gimble in the wabe*? Catesby cast his eyes around the committee table. Many of those present had personally experienced the horror of war. Could they not see where their complacency was leading? One of the mandarins seemed to read Catesby's mind and gave him a knowing smile. It wasn't complacency. It was the world-wearied self-possession of those born to rule. It was the simple reality of power: Downing Street was trampling over the rest of Whitehall and the mandarins could do nothing about it.

The rest of the meeting was devoted to the effect of defence spending cuts on Britain's NATO commitment. It occurred to Catesby that if a Labour government tried similar cuts to the armed forces they would be accused of surrender or treason. Any-other-business was mercifully brief and Catesby soon found himself in the crisp December air of St Charles Street standing beside the colonel from MoD.

'Are you in a hurry?' said the colonel.

'I'm from Suffolk. I'm never in a hurry.'

'I often go shooting there – my in-laws live near Saxmundham. But if you're not in a hurry, would you fancy a stroll through St James's Park? There's something that I would love to show you – if you like blood sports.'

'You've discovered the pigeon-eating pelican?'

The colonel nodded. 'There are now two of them. I think he's set up a training course.'

'Let's have a look then.'

As they walked past the bronze statue of Clive of India, who founded the British Raj and amassed an enormous personal fortune in so doing, Catesby thought of the tangled webs that empires weave.

They crossed Horse Guards Road and set out across the park. There was the clatter of horses' hooves and the shouting of orders behind them as the Household Cavalry practised their ceremonial duties.

'Do you not think it odd,' said the colonel, 'that we end up on the same side?'

Catesby frowned. He wondered if the army officer was referring to the dark days of the mid-seventies when elements of the military were getting fed up with strike-ridden Britain.

'We've always been on the same side,' said Catesby. 'We are both loyal servants of Her Majesty the Queen – and her democratically elected governments.'

'Many of us,' said the colonel, 'were appalled by what was being said by some of our colleagues – and they were firmly told to shut up.'

Catesby remained silent.

'I fear I haven't expressed myself very well.'

'Is that one of the killers?' Catesby nodded towards a pelican that was swimming in the lake.

'D'you know? They all rather look alike.'

'Let's sit here,' said Catesby. 'I'm fond of this bench. We once caught one of the Portland ring having a rendezvous here with a Sov agent.'

The colonel smiled. 'I've heard it's also a popular place for other things.'

'I hate it when they call it the "oldest profession".' Catesby smiled with pride. 'We're the oldest profession.'

'Look, he's come out of the water – and has that glazed look in his eye.'

'How do you know it's a male?'

'The plumage is the same, but males are slightly larger.'

Catesby was impressed. But the colonel was an intelligence officer and the trade was about learning to observe.

'Fingers crossed,' said the colonel, 'I think we're going to be lucky.'

On cue, the pelican began to stalk a plump waddling city pigeon that was stuffing its own face. In one quick and graceful move, the pelican dipped with his long beak and scooped up the bird. At first, it all looked in slow motion, but the pigeon was now flapping frantically. Despite its agonised convulsions, the pelican devoured the bird with stately languor. After a few seconds, most of the pigeon was in the pelican's throat pouch which extended under its lower beak. Only a single grey wing protruded out of the predator's closed beak – the wing seemed to be flapping.

'They're delicious,' said Catesby. 'I especially like wood pigeon breasts pan-fried with olive oil and butter.'

'What about pheasant?'

'They're fine too.'

'Next time we're shooting, I'll drop you off a brace.'

'Why are you being so kind?' said Catesby.

'Because we're under siege and need all the allies we can find.'

'Defence cuts?'

'Actually, I wasn't speaking personally. But I am the youngest of six and won't inherit a bean. I need at least five more years' service to look after me and my wife – but the way the axe is flying…'

'School fees?'

'Crushing. Needed to go begging to my father-in-law.'

Catesby stared across the lake at a council worker who was picking up rubbish.

The colonel cleared his throat. 'I must sound like something of a twit. It will be much worse for ordinary soldiers who get the boot – they haven't got anything to fall back on.'

Catesby was relieved he didn't have to make either of the points himself.

'But I don't really want to talk about redundancies. One still has a higher duty to the Crown – and this government is pursuing a disastrous policy in the South Atlantic.'

'Why didn't you submit a report for the SAD meeting?'

'We did. It wasn't circulated. Our man in Buenos Aires has been ringing alarm bells which have consistently been ignored. He speaks fluent Spanish, better than most of his Foreign Office colleagues, and knows a lot of Argentine military officers socially.'

Catesby agreed. The lot of the Defence Attaché wasn't a happy one. The to-the-manor-born dips didn't regard the military types as real diplomats, but as clumsy amateurs who didn't understand the rules or how to behave. Catesby had been the victim of similar disdain. SIS officers operating under dip cover were often treated as embarrassments in waiting – and sometimes rightly so. Many ambassadors lived in constant fear of the SIS station creating a diplomatic incident – from bugging to agent-recruiting to blackmail to kidnapping – that would result in a noisy PNGing, a declaration of persona non grata for the SIS thug involved, and a souring of relations with the host country. The FCO number-crunchers also resented paying the salaries and expenses of the military and SIS officers attached to embassies. It added insult to injury.

'Look,' said the colonel, 'you can see the pigeon sliding down his throat and into the gullet. I'm sure it's dead now.'

Catesby smiled. 'I see what you mean. The pelican is the Junta and the pigeons are the Falklands.'

'Actually, I hadn't thought of that. It's a…'

'Metaphor?'

'No,' said the colonel, 'I'd call it an analogy. And you shouldn't rely too much on analogies when making decisions. At least, that's what they used to tell us at staff college. But on the other hand.'

'You were talking about your DA in BA.'

'He has to step very carefully, otherwise he'll get sent home. It's not a matter of offending the Argentines – who like him – it's a matter of offending the Foreign Office. They seem to think that he should concentrate on being a sales rep for the British arms industry.'

Catesby frowned. Pursuing commercial interests was becoming a bigger and bigger part of the UK diplomatic service.

'I don't mind selling a few trinkets to the natives,' said the colonel, 'but the thought that those trinkets could one day be used to kill members of the British armed forces rather sticks in my gullet.'

'Your man in Buenos Aires,' said Catesby, 'I think I've met him. Artillery officer, keen wildlife photographer?'

'That's him.'

'Does he sup with the devil?'

'If you mean officers from the Junta and sympathetic defence attachés from the diplomatic community, quite a bit. They have a nice place in a smart suburb with a swimming pool – and do a lot of dinner parties.'

'Is he good at walking a tightrope?'

'He has to be.'

'Who,' said Catesby, 'does he send his reports to?'

'As you know, everything has to go through the Ambassador – not that he has the time to read them all – and then, read or unread, they get rubbished by the FCO. Embassy protocol means we can't bypass the communications system.' The colonel smiled. 'I believe it's different for your chaps.'

Catesby nodded. The real dips hated it, but only the SIS Chief of Station had the privilege of sending UK EYES ALPHA cables that absolutely no one else in the embassy had access to. Catesby could see that the colonel was angling at using the SIS man in Buenos Aires as a conduit to bypass the Ambassador and the FCO.

'Well?' said the colonel.

'It's difficult. Our man in BA is more of a dip than a spy. He's openly declared as an intelligence officer – and even has an Argentine liaison officer assigned to him who looks over his shoulder. Basically, the purpose of SIS in Argentina is to support the Americans in helping the host country fight communist subversion.' Catesby frowned. 'This arrangement, I must say, was made before I took over Latin America.'

The colonel smiled. 'I didn't realise you were Hernán Cortés.'

'Cortés never got south of Mexico. Oh, no – I operate on a much grander scale than Cortés. I, and my army of two, have responsibility for all of South America, Central America and the Caribbean.'

'I didn't know there were three of you.'

'I'm also running a part-time NOC in BA – who I worry about.'

'Should our chap get in contact with your NOC?'

'Not yet. I don't want to put her cover in jeopardy. Let's do it this way. Get your man to have a quiet word with our man – who I will tell to cooperate and pass on information outside the approved channels. But both of them will have to be extremely discreet.'

'It's ironic, isn't it? We spend more time keeping secrets from each other than we do the Russians.'

Catesby thought of the extreme secrecy that had surrounded the minister's visit to Switzerland to meet his Argentine counterpart. Both men had been hiding the sovereignty talks from their own governments. And now it had all gone tits up.

'I'd better get back to the office,' said the colonel.

'I'd better not go with you. It's best we're not seen together.' Catesby watched the colonel walk back towards Horse Guards. Whitehall was a dangerous jungle full of prying eyes, fragile egos, paranoid fears and vicious ambition.

Buenos Aires: January 1981

It was a hot summer's day and, unaccustomedly, McCullough was wearing a short skirt as she walked down Guatemala Street. There were no problems with the men of Argentina for they took great pride in respecting women. In fact, McCullough felt more comfortable revealing her body in Argentina then she would have in the USA – there were no stares or wolf-whistles on the streets of Buenos Aires. But there was a lot to whistle at, for the women of Argentina took great pride in their looks – and McCullough appreciated their efforts.

McCullough knew the sky-blue Ford Falcon was trouble even before it slowed down to walking pace and began to follow her. She had been car-stalked more than once in the USA. Drunk fraternity boys were the easiest to deal with: you just gave them the finger and said, 'Go fuck yourselves, assholes.' They usually shouted a childish insult or two and roared away. But the jerks wearing dark glasses in the Ford Falcon were playing a more dangerous game. Three of them in smart civilian clothes – one in Gucci shoes and designer sunglasses – got out of the car. McCullough smiled at the contrast between the cheap crap American car and the expensive Italian gear. Two were armed with submachine guns; the Gucci man with a pistol still in a holster. Another blue Falcon pulled up from the opposite direction and three bigger thugs got out dressed in jeans and T-shirts: they were all carrying submachine guns. They clearly weren't taking chances.

The Gucci man was in charge. He looked at McCullough and shouted, 'Put your hands behind your back.'

McCullough had been trying really hard. She held the tops of her thighs close together and was pulling in her lower abdomen to restrain her bladder – even though every bit of her was shaking. She wanted to keep what was left of her dignity.

She had succeeded until one of the T-shirt thugs touched her from behind. As soon as she felt the cold metal of the handcuffs close around her wrists, her bladder gave way. She felt the warm urine stream down her thighs, curve around her knees and then divide into several tributaries as it coursed down her calves on to her ankles. She felt some of the urine pool in her sandals, still warm, against the soles of her feet, but most spilled on the summer-hot tarmac. She couldn't bear to look, but could smell it. If the men had noticed what had happened, they didn't say so. They bundled her into the back of the first Falcon squeezed between two thugs who smelled of aftershave. She felt her skirt, now damp and cold, clingy beneath her.

The facade of the Escuela de Mecánica de la Armada, with its white Doric columns, made the place look like an old-fashioned American university hooked on Greek ideals. But the only subjects taught at ESMA were interrogation, torture and death. It was the most feared building in Argentina – the point of no return. There was no more adrenalin coursing through McCullough's body and she was no longer shaking: she was now terrified to the point of numbness. The rush of panic and bladder release had passed into cold fear and resignation. The speechless silence of her captors was more menacing than even the worst words.

As soon as they got her inside the building they put a hood over her head, which was tightened with a drawstring around her neck. There was one on each side guiding her. The echoes suggested a corridor. There were noises of orders being barked and muffled screams from what seemed the floor above. McCullough peed herself a second time. The person on her left spoke. It was the first voice she had heard since being abducted: '*¡Cuidado!Aquí estánlas escaleras.*' Her toes touched a step before the meaning registered: *Careful. Here are the stairs.* The warning words seemed the kindest and most human thing anyone had ever said to her. She wanted to embrace her captor – and then she realised that the stairs led to where she had heard the screams coming from.

McCullough's mind began to fill with thoughts of self-contempt. An inner voice was shouting at her: *You didn't have to do this – you're going to die and it's all your own fault! You could have lived out your days as a spoilt rich bitch lounging around in Florence, St Tropez and Aspen – and for adventure you could have gone off-piste at St Anton. Silly cow! You could have had children and naked showers with the au pair when the kids were napping. The world was all yours. But instead you had to go off on a fucking idealist ego trip. You hated your birth right; so you tried to become a revolutionary.* But that chic posing was far from the reality. She was headed for the torture chamber. And what would the torture be like? Apparently, they didn't rape; the Junta's thugs were supposed to be good Catholics fighting a war against communist barbarism. But they might attach electrodes to her labia. And, if that gave them hard-ons, would they confess their dirty thoughts to the priest next time they went to confession? And despite the electric shocks and the beatings and the fact that she would tell them everything that she knew, she would still have a one-way ticket on a *vuelo de la muerte* to the big adios. A few years ago bodies had been washed up on beaches a hundred miles to the south. They got the currents wrong – or didn't go far enough out to sea. There were no bullet wounds, so it looked like the victims had been pushed out of the airplanes or helicopters when they were still alive. What would it be like to be fully conscious during that final drop?

They took her up the stairs and to a room where she was pushed on to what felt like a bed. Someone reached behind her, unlocked the handcuffs and removed them. She heard footsteps going away, a door being closed and a heavy lock turned. McCullough was certain that she had been left alone. It felt good to have her hands and arms free. She reached up and found the drawstring that had tightened her hood. She managed to undo the knot. At first she was afraid to take off the hood – she feared that someone might be watching and would punish her. But curiosity won and she removed it. There was little to see. The room was darkened, but a few slivers of light crept in under the door and through the cracks of a boarded-up window. She could see that she was sitting on a bare mattress on a narrow-framed metal bed. She got up to walk around and her foot hit a bucket. There was a splash and a smell of urine. She sat down again and felt rigid with fear. She curled up on the bed in the foetal position and put her thumb against her mouth. At the age of three and four she had had a black nanny called Florence – whom she had loved more than her mother or anyone. She felt betrayed when Florence had been sent away – and even more betrayed when her mother made brief showy attempts at parenting.

She didn't know how much time had passed when a light switched on. It was a low-wattage bare bulb hanging from the ceiling. The switch must have been outside the room. She heard someone rattling a bunch of keys; McCullough decided it would be a good idea to put the hood back on and quickly did so.

Once again, there were no words – only large firm hands guiding her by the elbows. They went down the stairs again and along two corridors. One of her minders knocked on a door and an inner voice said, '*Pase, por favor.*' They entered and the same voice said, '*Quite la capucha.*' The hood was removed and McCullough found herself facing the chief kidnapper again, who had swapped his Gucci gear for a naval officer's uniform. Her leather shoulder bag – which she had forgotten all about – was on the desk in front of him. For the first time, she saw the irony – her shoulder bag was also Gucci. The naval officer nodded behind her at the two men who had taken her to his office. McCullough heard them shuffle and leave, closing the door behind them.

The naval officer stared at McCullough as if she were a rare specimen. He then spoke in formal English with only the slightest Argentine accent. 'I must offer you my most humble apologies. There has been a case of mistaken identity. We thought that you were a dangerous terrorist who closely matches your description. She is a tall attractive woman of Northern European background. I cannot tell you more.' The officer nodded at McCullough's bag. 'When we examined the contents of your bag – apologies again for the invasion of privacy – we found your identity documents and discovered our mistake. Would you like to look in your bag to see if anything is missing?'

McCullough picked up the bag and looked through it. If anything, it was tidier – even the spare tissues were neatly folded. She wondered if they had gone through her address book and checked her bank details. 'It looks okay,' she said.

The naval officer continued looking at her. 'You come from a very distinguished family.'

McCullough suspected that 'distinguished' was an Argentine euphemism for 'rich'. She frowned, but didn't say anything.

'Because of your special status, we feel that you could be in danger. The people we are fighting are desperate and will stop at nothing. They want to bomb and murder their way to power. Many of my closest colleagues have been assassinated by these extremists – and thousands of innocent civilians have been killed, wounded or abducted by these fanatics.'

The American remained stony-faced. She didn't want to reveal what she thought of the officer's propaganda lecture. She knew that the actions of the guerrillas were often bloody, but always targeted at the Junta and its bullies.

'Your father,' said the officer, 'is highly respected by the loyal and patriotic people of Argentina – and is a very talented and brave polo player. I know for a fact that subversive elements are planning to kidnap you and hold you for ransom. They rob banks and will do anything to fund their cause.'

McCullough looked at the naval officer. He was actually quite handsome and seemed quick and intelligent. She wondered if he believed what he was saying or was following a script. Everyone knew that the Junta had crushed the guerrillas and were now going after anyone who disagreed with the ruling dictatorship.

'I am sure that you would like to get back home. If you like, I will give you a lift.'

'That would be kind of nice.'

The car was another Ford Falcon. This one was dark blue and tidier than the abduction vehicles. The officer had taken his naval insignia off, but still looked the part. It was dark as the car headed south into central Buenos Aires. They were driving down the eight-laned Avenida del Libertador, the grandest boulevard in Buenos Aires. The street was lined with parks and grand embassies, but the most imposing structure was the Facultad de Derecho. The law school was a magnificent classical building that looked out over a Buenos Aires that was deaf to what it represented. The Spanish word, *derechos*, also meant rights – as in *derechos humanos*. McCullough felt a slight frisson of fear. The naval officer wasn't taking her back to her new apartment in Old Palermo. Where were they going? She decided not to say anything.

It had begun to rain: a semi-tropical summer downpour. The grand tree-lined boulevard had turned into a swirling impressionist painting. McCullough had no idea where they were heading and the Falcon's windshield wipers weren't able to cope. The naval officer finally turned off Avenida del Libertador. The first thing she recognised was the cemetery. Was he taking her there? A late visit to Eva Perón? They passed by the end of the cemetery wall and McCullough breathed a sigh of relief. They were in upmarket Recoleta. The naval officer was taking her to her father's apartment. Why? If he wanted Talbot to give his daughter a stern parental word, he was wasting his time. He never disciplined her; at most, he shook his head in despair. In any case, her father wasn't in Buenos Aires. Another thought occurred to McCullough. Maybe he didn't know where she lived now. The thought cheered her.

The naval officer stopped in front of the building. McCullough smiled. The Ford Falcon was probably the crappiest car that had ever parked there – even the taxis were classier. The officer turned off the engine and glared at McCullough, leaning towards her as if he were about to give her a kiss. She felt the fear again and pressed her knees tight together in case he was going to put his hand up her skirt.

The officer leaned closer and whispered. 'Once again,' he said, 'I must apologise for our mistake – and can understand how terrible it must have been for you.'

'Don't patronise me.'

The officer lifted his hands from the steering wheel in an ironic gesture of surrender.

McCullough was feeling stronger and wanted to punch his

face. It bore the smug self-confidence of a good-looking man who knows he is in control.

'We are,' said the officer, 'a country in turmoil. Sometimes love of one's country leads a person to make mistakes. But we are not monsters.'

McCullough decided not to reply.

'I hope we can part friends. My job in the future will be to protect you.' The officer took a notepad out of his pocket and began writing on it. 'I am going to give you two secret telephone numbers. When someone answers – and I hope it will be me – identify yourself as Dulche de Leche, that will be your codename.'

McCullough felt her stomach turn. *Dulche de leche* was Argentina's national dessert, a creamy pudding made from whole milk and caramelised sugar.

'Ring anytime there is something you want to discuss. Advice about restaurants, the weather – or something you find strange. Remember we are your friends and protectors.' The officer neatly tore the page from his notebook and handed it over.

McCullough put the note in her shoulder bag and tried not to laugh. The naval officer was obviously attempting to recruit her as an informant. 'Is that all?' she said.

The officer touched his brow as if saluting and started the engine.

McCullough went up to her father's flat. She had no idea whether Fiona was there, but was dying for a bath and a change of clothes. She knocked on the door – and no one answered. She put her ear next to the door; there was only silence. She let herself in.

In a way, McCullough was pleased to be alone. It would have been difficult to explain things if Fiona and her naval aviator lover had been there. What would she have said to Ariel? *One of your colleagues just kidnapped me and I was lucky to escape torture and execution. But now we're friends and he wants me to be an informer.* But the priorities now were the drinks cabinet and a hot bath.

Ten minutes later McCullough was soaking in a hot bath and wishing that Fiona was with her. But that was never going to happen. It was painfully obvious that the Englishwoman preferred boys. Why? Boys don't know about tenderness and stroking and patience and how to satisfy a woman. They just want to spurt. McCullough's few experiences with males had been awful – and sometimes brutal. She was surprised the Argentine naval officer hadn't tried to rape her. That's what men in a position of power always did. It was a simple mathematical formula: maleness + money + influence = brutality. She saw it in her father, but in a more cunning way. Perhaps Talbot found dominating women too easy and had decided it was more sporting to dominate other rich and powerful men: hence, polo and his obsession with sport – and business. He didn't do business for money – he already had more than enough of that – he did it as part of a power game. And he wasn't the only one. McCullough smiled and soaped between her legs. She was playing a game too: a much more dangerous and exciting game than her father was playing. She wanted to break up the system.

La Boca, Buenos Aires: February 1981

The sign, *prohibido escupir en el suelo* – no spitting on the floor – suggested that it wasn't a particularly upmarket café. McCullough's rendezvous with Mateo was in La Boca, one of the poorest and roughest districts of Buenos Aires. The café owner must have decided that covering the walls in advertisements was easier and cheaper than painting and decorating. There was a peeling Cinzano ad, which made sense since they sold the drink. But also adverts for soap, washing powder and truck tyres. McCullough and Mateo were drinking espressos.

'I don't think,' said Mateo, speaking English with an oddly Irish-sounding accent, 'that it was a case of mistaken identity. I think they wanted to frighten you, to warn you.'

So far, Mateo was the only person to whom McCullough had confided her ordeal. There was something in him that inspired trust, despite her older friend's warning. She decided to tell him about that too. 'I have been warned about you,' she said.

Mateo gave a weak smile. 'I don't know whether to be surprised or flattered – maybe a little of both.'

'I have a friend who is one of the founders of the Mothers Plaza de Mayo. She lives in Palmero Viejo – and I was on my way to see her when I was kidnapped.'

Mateo gave a knowing nod. 'Is her name Maria?'

'Yes.'

'I know of her. She is a very brave and noble woman.'

McCullough took a deep breath. 'She was the one who warned me about you. She thinks you may be an agent provocateur working undercover for the Junta.'

'I can understand why she warned you. Agents of the Junta have infiltrated the forces who oppose them. That is true – but it is also in the interest of the Junta to exaggerate the extent of their penetration because it sows distrust.' Mateo smiled. 'Perhaps you shouldn't trust me.'

McCullough didn't answer at first, but then broke into a smile. 'You can prove yourself. Let's go and kill a pig – and do it now.'

'And you can prove yourself too.' Mateo leaned close. 'I've got a gun – a Browning 9mm. Have you ever fired one?'

McCullough nodded. She had spent a lot of time on firing ranges in the States. America's gun culture cut both ways.

'Here's what we'll do. I give you the gun. You ride pillion on my motorbike – and we take out a traffic cop. That will prove that the Junta haven't recruited you as an agent.'

'Okay,' said McCullough without blinking, 'when can we do it?'

'I'll need to get false number plates for the Yamaha – and give you some practice with the pistol. Next week?'

'Sure.'

Mateo looked closely at McCullough. 'Did you know that I'm a priest?'

'No.'

'See you next week.'

The William Brown Polo Club: February 1981

It was a beautiful summer's evening and everything was green and fresh after a torrential rain. Fiona Stewart was sitting in a deck chair outside her quarters enjoying the view of the lake that bordered the golf course. The skyline of Buenos Aires was just visible over the trees. It wasn't, however, an aspect that pleased her. In fact, she had to admit that she didn't much like any of the scenery around the polo club. The combination of mock-Tudor architecture with blue striped awnings shading the windows just didn't go together. It was kitsch Englishness in the wrong climate. And a cricket match was going on. The perennial sound of an English spring, 'the thwack of willow on leather', was rendered surreal by Spanish voices calling for an lbw. Fiona sipped a Pimm's as she turned the pages of an Agatha Christie detective novel translated into Spanish. Part of Fiona enjoyed her role in the charade – but another side of her was fucking fed up.

Fiona put the novel down and did an inventory of key events from her past. Her first menstrual cycle and losing her virginity were no very big deals, but discovering that she enjoyed sex had been important. And being ditched by her first boyfriend, whom she loved desperately, was certainly her first experience of an emotional pain and, at the time, it seemed fatal. It temporarily destroyed her self-confidence. At first, she got it back by hurting others as he had hurt her – and later she realised that a few of those she hurt were much nicer and more attractive than her first love. It soon became too late to put that right – and she loathed herself for hurting one in particular. But these events, life-defining in some ways, were ones that only concerned her and her emotions. What changed Fiona most was discovering the excitement of learning. It began with a charismatic teacher in the upper-sixth, but fully flowered in her second year at university. Fiona's first passion was learning languages, not because of the grammar, but because when you begin to speak and think in a new language you become a new person and take on a new culture. But Fiona was now moving beyond that, beyond speaking Spanish with an almost Argentine accent. She was at the point where other issues intervened and could no longer be ignored. Injustice certainly existed in Britain, but there was little violence. In Argentina – rapidly becoming her second country – there was plenty of both.

Fiona becoming a friend of Maria was largely the work of McCullough. The American had gushed that Maria was *so British.* And, indeed, when Fiona finally went to tea at Maria's home in Palermo Viejo, she found the house more genuinely English than anything at the polo club. Although Maria had never lived in England, she spoke with an assured, clipped accent and her calm poise reminded Fiona of the wives of her father's regimental friends – particularly the ones who had lost their husbands or were coping with the alcoholic remains of those who had survived. Fiona had not just inherited her father's sense of adventure, but she shared the unspoken – the never spoken – horror of what had happened to him in the war. It was a horror that separated her father from her mother, but oddly drew Fiona closer to him. Being a secret agent in a land ruled by a murderous Junta enabled her to share the abyss.

There was a photo of Maria's disappeared son on the sideboard in the dining room. He had been a handsome young man with a beard who had disappeared when he was twenty-eight. The son had never been a guerrilla fighter, but a lawyer who defended political prisoners. Next to the framed photo was Maria's white headscarf, which she wore every Thursday afternoon to the Plaza de Mayo.

Maria saw Fiona looking at her son's photograph. 'He didn't want to be a lawyer; he was at heart an academic who wanted a career as a law professor. He vanished soon after the coup in 1976.' The older woman paused. 'I no longer mourn him as a grieving mother.' Her eyes flashed. 'But I fight for him as a cause – and I will never cease that fight. I apologise if I sound too emotional. May I pour you some tea?'

'Yes, please.' Fiona looked at the woman. She was more than beautiful; she was magnificent. Fiona knew that Maria wasn't looking for sympathy or comfort. She was seeking something far more important. 'How many,' said Fiona, 'have disappeared?'

'No one knows the exact number. Some say nine thousand; some say thirty thousand. But I would imagine that the figure is at least twenty thousand. What is so unbearable, so frustrating, is the secrecy. Secrecy is worse than lies. You can laugh at lies, but you can't laugh at the unknown. Secrets are poison.'

Fiona tried to hide her shame by staring again at the photo of Maria's son. She was also part of a secret world. 'How,' said Fiona, 'can I help your movement?'

'You are a well-educated Englishwoman – and I am sure you know influential people. One of our aims is to make the world aware of what has happened in Argentina. We want governments and international organisations to put pressure on the Junta to reveal what has happened to our children – and to stop the abductions.'

Fiona knew that Maria was playing a dangerous game and was lucky to be alive. Three of the thirteen women who founded the movement had already been disappeared. Fiona felt another pang of shame. Her life in England had been so privileged and protected.

'You know,' said Fiona, 'that my lover is a naval officer – and that I'm a manager at a polo club frequented by a number of the Junta.'

'All of us have to live with conflicts. I have close friends who are married to members of the Junta.'

Once again, Fiona felt that coming to Argentina was like passing through a time warp. The elite districts of Buenos Aires seemed like Renaissance palaces where silky courtiers stalked each other with hidden daggers.

La Boca, Buenos Aires: March 1981

McCullough's kidnapping may have left her traumatised, but it was also an initiation. She had finally talked about it with Fiona

– swearing her to secrecy – over a few bottles of wine. Fiona had seemed warmer than usual and said she admired her for having 'stared into the abyss' and come back to talk about it.

McCullough had also trusted Maria with the story of her ordeal, who advised that she report the incident to the US Embassy.

'I would never do that,' said McCullough.

'Why?'

'Because I don't trust them. Especially now that that nincompoop Reagan is President. He's a friend of the Junta.'

Maria nodded. The result of the American election had been disappointing. Carter had been an advocate of human rights.

McCullough admired Maria, but doubted that the Mothers of the Plaza de Mayo would ever do more than dent the Junta. The only way to get rid of the Junta was by a revolution. And for this reason she had grown closer to Mateo.

The café in La Boca was even grottier than before and so were the customers. Mateo leaned towards McCullough and whispered, 'Are you ready to kill that policeman.' He patted a leather bag on the chair beside him. 'I've brought my gun.'

McCullough wondered if Mateo was serious or if he was calling her bluff. Regardless, she was suffering severe period pain which had started in her lower abdomen and spread to her back and thighs. The pain put her in a bad mood, but not one that wanted to kill. On the contrary, it made her want to get pregnant. At least there would be nine months without period pain – and she had read that the pain usually alleviated after having children. She stared at Mateo. He was oddly asexual – perhaps it was a part of his being a priest. But that made her feel comfortable with him. She wondered if he would consider being a sperm donor – and what he would think about as he masturbated into the beaker.

Mateo sipped his espresso and gave a bland smile. 'You don't look very happy today.'

'It's a personal matter.'

'Perhaps popping off a traffic cop or two will cheer you up.'

'To be honest, I'm not in the mood.'

'Maybe next time.'

'Sure.'

'There are,' said Mateo, 'more important targets. You know, by the way, that we are soon going to have a new president. The Junta are fed up with Videla – he's made a mess of the economy.'

McCullough closed her eyes and tried to blank away the pain.

'I can see you are not well – so I will be brief. Videla's successor will be Roberto Viola, another army officer. This may signal a change of tactics. Next time you're at the William Brown Polo Club, keep your ears open.'

'Let's go kill a cop.'

Century House, Lambeth, London: May 1981

Catesby had been privileged to see an advance draft of The 1981 Defence White Paper (Officially titled 'The UK Defence Programme: The Way Forward'). The defence cuts proposed were substantial, but were not going to affect the UK's stance against the Soviet Union. To accomplish this, huge cuts had to be made in other areas. Thinking of his South American responsibilities, which his colleagues regarded as a joke assignment, Catesby quickly flicked through the White Paper to see what it had to say about the Falklands.

He didn't expect to see a chapter, but maybe a paragraph or two. In fact, there wasn't even a single paragraph about the Falklands – not even a complete sentence. The islands had to share one solitary sentence with three other areas of responsibility: Our forces will also continue as necessary to sustain specific British responsibilities overseas, for example in Gibraltar, Cyprus, Belize and the Falkland Islands. Catesby had begun to underline the sentence as a prelude to making a comment in the margin when the telephone rang. It was the colonel from Defence Humint.

'I'm sure,' said the colonel, 'that you've got your copy by now.'

'Just finished reading it.'

'She still wants to stand up to Ivan, but no one else.'

'So I gather.'

'I've just heard an interesting snippet from one of my navy friends, but it's not quite official yet.'

Catesby reached for a notepad. 'Go on.'

'They're going to scrap *Endurance*.'

Catesby scribbled HCABSFS. It was a coded message that had got him into trouble in the past because it wasn't that difficult to break – the HC decoded as HOW CAN and the final S as STUPID – but never had seemed more appropriate. Thatcher had dismissed the HMS *Endurance*, the ice patrol ship that prowled the South Atlantic, as something that could only go *pop, pop, pop*. But in reality *Endurance* not only carried lethal Wasp helicopters, but was an important symbol of the UK's presence in that far-flung region. Announcing the ship's withdrawal was essentially telling the Junta that London didn't give a fuck about the Falklands. HCABSFS with bells on.

Recoleta, Buenos Aires: June 1981

Winter was setting in and it was going to be Fiona's last transmission to HMS *Endurance* until the ship came back in the spring. She had grown fond of the covert receiver/transmitter that she had been trained to use during her extended 'Christmas break' in England. It was, in fact, a Russian radio: a Strizh – which translates as Swift. Her instructors at Fort Monckton, the SIS training centre overlooking the Solent, had explained that Non-Official Cover agents such as her were often given Soviet Bloc equipment. The idea was that if the police or security services of the host country found the stuff, they would think that the spy was working for Moscow and not London. The problem was that real Russian spies used equipment from the West for the same reason. 'I suppose,' admitted one of the instructors, 'we should do a double bluff and give our agents genuine British gear.'

Fiona admired the Strizh because of the way it combined ingenuity with simplicity – and its compact solidity. You wrote your message and then used an OTP, one time pad, to encode your message into numerals. Unless someone had a copy of the OTP, the coding was impossible to break. You then keyed the numbers in groups of five into the DSU, the Digital Storage Unit, which also contained the burst transmitter and burst receiver. When you were ready to send, the burst transmitter compressed your message and flung it out at high speed – a thousand words per second. This minimised the risk of interception and detection by reducing time on air.

Fiona enjoyed the drama of the process, but wondered if it was needlessly cloak and dagger. At the end of her training, she had a final briefing session with Catesby and said, 'Why can't I just pass a note on to the embassy – or have a chat with your man on a park bench?'

'Because,' said Catesby, 'we don't want to ruin our relations with the Argentines. Our man in Buenos Aires is an openly declared intelligence officer who is on good terms with the Junta. They regard him as an ally in their fight against communist subversion. If he – or anyone else in the embassy – were seen to be spying on the Argentines, the ambassador would pack them off on the next flight to the UK.' Catesby paused. 'By the way, Miss Stewart, may I remind you that you have signed the Official Secrets Act and are now a member of the Secret Intelligence Service?'

Fiona nodded.

'And what I am telling you is not idle chat, but a briefing which is highly sensitive and confidential. Our resources in Argentina are very limited. The staff at the embassy are unable to carry out the counter-surveillance procedures that are daily routine in Moscow. And, to make things worse, our SIS guy has been assigned a liaison officer from Argentine naval intelligence, who, I suspect, is often looking over his shoulder. So you can see why you shouldn't...' Catesby feared that he was beginning to sound patronising, so he shut up.

'Basically,' said Fiona, 'if the Argentine security services saw me meeting someone from the UK Embassy, they would become suspicious.'

'Exactly.' Catesby spread his hands. 'I haven't a clue to what extent our people are surveilled by the Argentines – or even if they are. But your meeting them or passing things on to them through dead drops is a risk we cannot take – and it could put you in danger.'

Fiona smiled. 'And I haven't got diplomatic cover.'

'It is a risky trade – and you're going to be our only spy in Argentina.'

'I understand that.'

'But, Miss Stewart, I am not sure you have been apprised of the worst-case scenario.' Catesby gave her a look of almost fatherly concern.

'I think, Mr Catesby, I can work that one out myself.'

'Go on.'

'If Argentina invade the Falklands, there may be a war. In which case, diplomatic relations would be broken off and many British people would be expelled from the country.' Fiona gave a composed smile. 'But I, because of my relationship with an Argentine naval officer, would probably be allowed to remain – one very lonely and isolated Brit.'

'Let's hope that doesn't happen.'

Fiona took a large sip of red wine before she began to compose her message. *ANTI-JUNTA ACTIVITIES: WANDA…* For a codename Fiona had christened McCullough with the name of the family cat. Despite the security of the OTP code, Fiona had been advised not to transmit actual names. *…continues to be an unwitting agent and continues to become more radical owing to her kidnapping/arrest. Cannot confirm WANDA was involved in drive-by shooting of policeman. Cannot confirm Soviet or Cuban involvement with any subversive group…* It was a subject on which London was particularly keen to have information. She hoped to involve McCullough in finding out. *Principal opposition group remains Mothers of the Plaza de Mayo. Still cannot comment on question of violent opposition to Junta owing to lack of information. Violence seems restricted to small number of individuals.* Fiona continued to the next section of the report. *JUNTA DEVELOPMENTS: Saloon-bar gossip suggests that Viola's economic policies will lead to recession and destabilise his position. Lot of whispers about sacked head of navy Massera. Travel to Romania? Connections with Masonic Propaganda Due and Mafia? Doubt if Viola's regime will survive. MILITARY: ICARUS* – Fiona would later regret her choice of codename for Ariel – *is now qualified for Super Étendard as well as Skyhawk and Mirage. Often away for training at Río Grande and on carrier 25 de Mayo. At dinner party teased fellow pilot for claiming he buzzed* HMS *Endurance: 'You must have scared the ship so much the British are withdrawing it.' END OF MESSAGE.*

Fiona poured herself another glass of wine. She felt that her messages were unprofessional and useless. They contained few facts; only gossip and information that could be easily picked up through OSI – Open Source Intelligence, such as newspapers and broadcasts. But did it matter? One of her trainers at Fort Monckton had confided that 99 per cent of intelligence received was what the trade called 'cabbages and kings' – useless chatter.

As soon as the transmission was complete, Fiona began to pack up the radio. She loved its practical compactness: you could fit the whole thing in a small rucksack – not that you needed one. The radio had its own sand-coloured canvas bag with back straps – which looked quite smart. Fiona was often tempted to openly heft it through the centre of Buenos Aires on one shoulder. She could imagine someone from the Russian Embassy, perhaps a military attaché, staring at her with open-mouthed astonishment. No, it wouldn't be a good idea. In fact, moving the radio around and hiding it was a problem. Her first act of spy craft on Argentine soil had been picking up the radio, which had been secreted in a sports bag, from beneath a park bench. She knew that the Strizh had been dispatched to Buenos Aires in a diplomatic pouch and then covertly left for her by someone from the embassy – but there were no fingerprints leading back to London. If a member of the Argentine security services had searched her bag, he would have known she was a spy – but finding out for whom would be a question of interrogation and torture. Followed, of course, by a non-return flight to the sea. The radio being discovered was a constant nightmare for Fiona. When she was in the Recoleta flat, she kept it hidden beneath floorboards in a little-used clothes cupboard – not loose floorboards, but ones that she tightly secured with a screwdriver. At the Polo Club, she kept it in a safe in her room. But at times she wanted to find a lonely bridge and drop it in the river. Even though it was a bit of a lark – she imagined that one day in the far future she might share her adventures with her sisters or BSG friends during a boozy evening – she wasn't sure the job was worth the money and risk. The other thing was Ariel. She wondered if she could tell him about her 'secret life'? Would he see it as a bit of a joke? Did Ariel love her enough not to betray her? Would he agree that betraying a person who loves you is worse than betraying your country?

London: August 1981

Catesby was now a member of a newly formed committee called LACIG, the Latin America Current Intelligence Group. Oddly, the one thing that they didn't want to discuss was the possibility of Argentina invading the Falklands. It was almost a taboo subject, like Stephen Ward, Profumo and the Cliveden country party capers in 1961 – and the high-ranking member of the establishment who served dinner guests naked wearing only a black mask and a chain. Afterwards, the masked VIP ate his own dinner out of a dog's bowl. Catesby had been informed that the man was 'definitely' not a member of the cabinet – and also told to mind his own business. Even though, as an intelligence officer busy tracking down Soviet spies, it was very much *his own business.*

Although it involved nothing as tantalising and tasty as the Profumo business, Catesby suspected that another cover-up was taking place – and what they were covering up was irrationality and incompetence at the highest level. The Prime Minister would not listen to anyone except the voice in her own head. Sadly, Whitehall and the cabinet were complicit by doing little to oppose decisions emanating from Downing Street that ignored reason and fact. Occasionally, Catesby was invited to club-land to have off-the-record chats with former or serving government ministers. No London club could rate itself as truly exclusive that didn't have a high-ranking SIS officer or two as part of its decor: spies were as much a part of the ambience as the dark leather armchairs and the mildly erotic eighteenth-century oil paintings. The invites did tickle Catesby's vanity – and the whispered conversations were often enlightening. Vanity, however, was no excuse for stupidity. Catesby always covered himself by reporting such meetings to C and writing a brief minute about what transpired – but did not include *everything* that was said. The feeling in club-land was that Thatcher was a disaster heading for oblivion after the next general election – if not before. *Don't get in her way. Give her enough rope.* This non-confrontational strategy was usually expressed by One Nation Tories – the ones the PM and her inner circle called 'wets'. The idea was that after her fall, the Conservative Party would return to 'normal'.

Buenos Aires: September 1981

SLIME had become reckless since being assigned to Buenos Aires. His careless behaviour was partly due to changes in his personal circumstances. Brezhnev's daughter had ditched him because SLIME was drinking too much and losing his spruce athleticism. SLIME's wife had also ditched him, taking the children with her, to set up house with another KGB officer. It was one of the reasons why the First Chief Directorate (Foreign Ops) decided to pack SLIME off to Argentina.

Buenos Aires hadn't quite become an end-of-career backwater for KGB officers and Sov diplomats, but the election of Reagan as US president meant that the Soviet Union was no longer dependent on Argentina for food imports. Reagan, grateful for the support of Midwest farmers, had ended the grain embargo that Jimmy Carter had put in place in response to the Soviet invasion of Afghanistan. But the US arms embargo against Argentina for human rights abuses was still in place and the country remained a big potential market for Soviet weapons.

SLIME's top-secret pre-deployment briefing wasn't something that the Soviet leadership would like to have broadcast to the world. Moscow's aim in Argentina and South America was no longer to foment revolution, but unashamed *Realpolitik*. The job of Soviet diplomats and spies in Buenos Aires was to promote trade and increase Moscow's influence in the region – even if it meant cosying up to juntas who regarded Marxist-Leninism as Satan's spawn. One of SLIME's tasks was to persuade the Argentine Communist Party and other left-wing groups to lay off revolution and to find 'areas of mutual interest' with the Junta. The most obvious common ground was Argentina's claim to Las Malvinas. It was an issue that united Right, Left and Peronist; followers of Che Guevara with followers of the Junta.

SLIME blotted his copybook less than a month after arriving

in Argentina. It wasn't a tiny ink-stain, but a great spreading scarlet spill that became an espionage legend among a small group of insiders. SLIME, who had once trained in ballet, had never lost his love for dancing and found a louche tango club as soon as he arrived in BA. His regular tango partner was a tall raven-haired beauty with long perfect legs. They put on a superb performance combining skill with the smouldering eroticism of the genre – and were cheered on by the other dancers. One thing led to another and after a whisky-fuelled dance evening they went back to the raven-haired beauty's flat. She performed an act on SLIME with consummate skill before she had even taken her clothes off. The video camera in the ceiling rose was whirring away and caught every one of SLIME's gasps of pleasure. The raven-haired beauty turned the lights out before she took her clothes off. SLIME was a little disappointed because he had been looking forward to a striptease that would reinvigorate him for the next session. Raven-hair, now naked, returned to the bed and placed herself in the *soixante-neuf* position – where SLIME was about to greet her with protruding tongue. Then a funny thing happened: the lights came on again, even though neither of them was near a light switch.

The Argentine intelligence service's video camera captured SLIME's expressions as they turned from pure bliss, to astonishment, to utter disgust. The huge penis next to his face and mouth was the last thing he expected to see – but, in retrospect, he realised there were telltale signs of transvestism that he should have picked up: the slim hips, the stiff artificiality of the breasts.

It was only seconds before two armed officers from SIDE were in the room. Presumably, they wanted to protect their star dancer in case SLIME turned violent – but he was a gentle man and nothing was further from his mind. The raven-haired beauty blew a kiss as she left the room. SLIME sat naked on the side of the bed and shook his head in self-contempt for his stupidity and lack of precaution – honey traps were the oldest trick in the book. The two officers from SIDE holstered their guns. They were polite, professional and even a little apologetic – like cops handing out a speeding ticket for going 35 in a 30-mile zone. The intelligence officers made no secret of the fact that the honey-trap op had been intended to compromise SLIME. They also seemed to want to downplay the seriousness of the situation. They gave SLIME contact numbers and passwords. *We only want a little cooperation, that's all. If you help us, no more will be heard of what happened tonight.*

SLIME did what every compromised intelligence officer should do – but few actually do – and immediately reported what had happened to the *Rezident*, the KGB Head of Station at the Soviet Embassy.

The *Rezident* looked at SLIME with a face that showed more sorrow than anger. 'I am not, Volodya, going to tell you that you were stupid because you already know that. I will, of course, have to inform Moscow. But don't worry – not *too* much – and come to see me tomorrow afternoon.' As soon as SLIME left the room, the *Rezident* shook his head and laughed. He suspected that the First Chief Directorate would be more amused than annoyed – and thought they might even ask him to press SIDE for a copy of the video so that they could pass it around the office.

The next day a hungover and worried SLIME reported to his boss as directed. The *Rezident* stared at his disgraced subordinate with a cable from Moscow in his hand. 'You're very lucky, Volodya, they are not asking for your immediate return.' The *Rezident* leaned forward and whispered, 'So I don't think you are going to be executed.'

SLIME twitched nervously. If Moscow knew about his meetings with Catesby at the Brompton Oratory, it would be a return ticket to the cellars of the Lubyanka and a bullet in the back of the head.

The *Rezident* glanced at the cable. 'I have argued, and the First Directorate agrees with me, that we can use what has happened to our advantage.'

'Thank you, comrade.'

'SIDE are not a particularly sophisticated intelligence service – if the KGB can't run rings around them, we should all be sent to the Lubyanka. We want you to go to the Argentines and pretend that you are in great fear of retribution by Moscow – and will tell them whatever they want to know and do whatever they want.'

'And then report back to you.'

'Exactly. It will, of course, be a great opportunity to pass on disinformation as well as finding out what the Argentines are up to.'

La Boca, Buenos Aires: November 1981

SLIME had dressed down for the rendezvous. It was a sleazy café and he wanted to look like a workman. It wasn't difficult to fit in: Argentina, owing to a large population of European immigrants, was an easy place for a Russian to pass unnoticed. SLIME looked at his watch. Mateo was five minutes late. He had been dead on time when they had met before. SLIME wondered if Mateo had worked out that he was being manipulated.

The Argentine intelligence service was happy to deep-six opponents of the Junta, but now they also wanted to use them. A Leftist urban guerrilla like Mateo could supply information about other Leftists who would then be hunted down and disposed of by the Junta. But experienced guerrillas like Mateo were too savvy and suspicious to provide names to anyone – even a tried and tested Leftist comrade. Informers were everywhere. SLIME's Argentine handlers had hoped that Mateo would trust the Russian because he was a fellow communist. SIDE would have liked more names for future reference, but Mateo would not have been able to give many even under torture. His organisation operated on the basis of three-person cells. The leader of the cell only knew the identities of the two other cell members and an additional person that he or she received instructions from and passed information to. No urban guerrilla could identify more than three fellow fighters. In fact, their numbers had so dwindled that even a full list of active guerrillas would hardly pack a prison cell. SLIME had known this even before he arrived in Argentina and everything he gleaned from Mateo suggested it was true. The Junta's vicious counter-insurgency war had been very successful, but they didn't seem to want to believe it – and were now striking out at those who were not dangerous militants. Paranoia runs deep.

There was, however, another strand to SIDE's thinking about how to use the remnants of the Montoneros and other guerrilla groups: false flag ops. One of the things that impressed the Argentine intelligence services most about the urban guerrillas was their skill as divers who carried out underwater demolitions. A few years before, the Montoneros had nearly sunk an Argentine destroyer with limpet mines. One idea doing the rounds at SIDE was tricking the guerrilla frogmen or frogwomen into attacking an American warship visiting an Argentine port. The anti-US attack would persuade Washington to give more support and military assistance to the Junta – and stop nagging about human rights issues and drop the arms embargo. It was, however, important that the guerrillas be unwitting and unaware that they were carrying out the Junta's wishes – and who better to assist them than a Soviet intelligence officer. As far as the Argentines were concerned, SLIME was their secret weapon

SLIME sipped his espresso and pondered over what he had to do. From Moscow's point of view, blowing a hole in a US Navy ship was a crap idea. The *Reszident* agreed: *Utterly shit and counter-productive. Our aim is to increase Soviet influence in Argentina, but that would play into the hands of the American Right. Don't go along with it.* It put SLIME in an awkward position. His job was to keep SIDE's trust, but also serve Moscow's interests. If he didn't do both, his own future could be tricky.

The café door opened and the wind stirred the dust on the unswept floor. Mateo had arrived. He nodded at SLIME and winked an order at the proprietor who started the espresso machine. It sounded like a cement mixer and shook the café's foundations. Mateo came over to SLIME's table.

'Greetings, comrade,' whispered Mateo in Russian as he shook hands.

'How are you?' said SLIME in poor Spanish. 'Should we speak English?'

Mateo nodded in relief as a waiter brought him his coffee.

'I am sorry,' said Mateo, 'that I am late. I think I was being followed.'

'Is it safe to talk here?'

'Safer than on the streets. There are no Junta spies in here – and no one who speaks enough English to know what we are talking about.'

SLIME needed to find out what the Argentine intelligence services were after so he asked the question directly. 'What is your view on targeting Americans?'

Mateo gave a smile of pure pleasure. 'I would love to. They are war criminals and oppressors – and I was pleased that for years rich and powerful Americans lived in fear. We taught them a lesson when we kidnapped that consul and shot him between the eyes.'

SLIME knew that the US Ambassador still travelled in a bulletproof car with bulletproof tyres and fully armed guards.

'In the old days,' continued Mateo, 'the logic of kidnapping Americans was mostly about getting ransoms or prisoners released.' Mateo frowned. 'But our strategy has changed. We are now more concerned with exposing and publicising the human rights abuses of the Junta – such as through the Mothers of the Plaza de Mayo.'

'And how successful is this new strategy?'

Mateo shrugged. 'How much is a matter of opinion. But at the moment terrorism against Americans has been called off. The problem is that if we popped off a few gringos, Reagan may lift the arms embargo against Argentina.'

SLIME was tempted to add *and you totally lost your guerrilla war.* But that would be rubbing it in.

Mateo sipped his espresso. 'Our struggle is in a hiatus.'

'But,' said SLIME, 'I understand you still have some very skilled fighters – particularly in area of underwater demolition.'

Mateo gave a proud smile.

'Are there any circumstances in which you would make peace with Junta – and perhaps help them?'

Mateo laughed and shook his head. 'But maybe...'

'Maybe what?'

'If the Junta had the courage to take back Las Malvinas, we would cheer them on – and maybe show them how to sink a ship or two.'

SLIME stared out the window and thought of his last meeting with Catesby. *How could the British be so stupid? Couldn't they see the obvious?*

William Brown Polo Club, Greater Buenos Aires: December 1981

Fiona was pleased to get away from the club because the atmosphere seemed tense and nervous – especially among the serving military officers who came there. It was a beautiful early summer's evening and she was happy when Ariel suggested they go for a walk. They began with a stroll through the formal gardens now in full bloom. The sounds were oddly like an English summer: the swishing hiss of oscillating hose sprinklers, the thunk of a croquet mallet followed by polite clapping.

Ariel took Fiona's hand. 'Shall we see the horses?'

'I'd rather just walk in the open. I want to be outside.'

'Good. I wouldn't want the horses to see us – they can read the expressions on human faces.'

Fiona smiled. 'I can't see anything wrong with your face – it's as handsome and loving as ever.'

'Ah, that shows that you're not a horse.'

'Is something wrong, Ariel?'

'You know that the President had a heart attack?'

For a second Fiona thought that Ariel was talking about Reagan, but then remembered that the Argentine President, General Roberto Viola, had been in hospital for 'hypertension'. 'So,' she said, 'it was more serious?'

'A lot more serious than a heart attack. There's been a coup.'

Fiona froze. She imagined tanks on the streets and bombs

dropping on the Casa Rosada. 'Has there been shooting? Violence? You must stay with me.'

Ariel shook his head and gave a gentle laugh. 'No, it's been a quiet coup. General Viola gave up office without a whimper.'

'Any idea who has taken over?'

'It looks certain to be Leopoldo Galtieri.'

'The one who looks like Paul Newman?'

'I must tell him you said that. I'm sure we'll get invited to dinner at the Casa Rosada.'

Fiona smiled. 'Will that improve your chances of promotion?'

'We'll have to wait and see. Galtieri is an army officer, but he did a deal with Admiral Anaya to get his support.'

'What sort of deal?'

'The sort of deal that you shouldn't know about.'

'I didn't realise that you kept secrets from me.'

'And you keep secrets from me. How did you lose your virginity?'

The conversation had taken a weird turn – from military coups to burst hymens – but Fiona held her ground. 'It was with a rugby player from Berkhamsted School for Boys – down by the canal. It was quick, painful and not very good. Any more questions?'

'I wish I hadn't asked – and I wish that you weren't English.'

'What an odd thing to say.'

Ariel stared at the ground.

'I'm sorry,' said Fiona, 'I suppose our attitudes towards sex are a bit different.'

'You're wrong, completely wrong. You have no idea why I said that I wish you weren't English.'

'You can't say it's religion – I was brought up as a Catholic.'

Ariel smiled. 'But not a Latino Catholic. I remember you once bragging that all the best English families were Catholic because you alone had the courage and power to stand up against the Protestant Reformation.'

'I must have been a bit drunk.'

'I think you were – but would your noble English family have guided Spanish Armada soldiers ashore with signal lights on a stormy midnight?'

'Fortunately, that is a dilemma that my ancestors never had to face.'

'But maybe,' said Ariel with a strange smile, 'it is not too late to find out.'

'You are in a strange mood – and you talk in riddles.'

'I sometimes wonder who you are.'

'I am someone who loves you with all my heart, mind and body.'

'I so want to believe that.'

Fiona looked at Ariel. He was close to tears. 'Let's go back,' she said. 'I want to take you to bed.'

Their lovemaking was quiet and intense. Afterwards, Ariel slept in her arms with an angelic smile. Fiona realised how much he needed to be loved and how much he needed her. He awoke on the stroke of midnight.

'Why,' said Fiona caressing him, 'did you say such strange things?'

'What strange things?'

'That you wished that I wasn't English.' She smiled. 'And what side would I be on if the Spanish Armada invaded.'

Ariel laughed gently. 'Because they were true.'

'I don't…'

'Listen, my darling, you don't know what happened today – with the coup.'

'How does it affect us?'

'More than you can imagine.' Ariel's face darkened. 'Admiral Anaya supported Galtieri on one condition.'

Fiona felt a chill of premonition.

'Anaya,' continued Ariel, 'offered his support on the condition that Galtieri invade Las Malvinas – the islands that English people call the Falklands. Now do you understand what I said and why I said it?'

Fiona smiled to hide her nervousness. 'You didn't need to translate the name of the islands.'

'I apologise if you think I patronised you. But I fear that our two countries could soon be at war.'

'I doubt it. I am sure there will be a diplomatic solution – or the UN will step in.'

'What I have told you, Fiona, is top secret. I could be executed for treason for sharing that information with an Englishwoman.'

One part of Fiona thought that Ariel was being melodramatic and exaggerating the risk of war. Another part of her wanted to send a radio message to London as soon as possible. She put her hand on his cheek. He needed to shave. 'Why did you tell me?'

'To show you how much I trust you; how much I love you.'

Fiona held him close.

'So what is your answer to my question? Would you, as a good Catholic, help the Spanish Armada?'

'I'm not a good Catholic – and I don't think the Armada needs my help.'

'Or put more simply: do you love me more than your country?'

She kissed him passionately. 'I do, I do, I do – you must believe me.'

'I believe you. And now a second question: will you marry me?'

'Yes, yes, yes!'

They made love again: slower and more deliberately. Later, as Fiona lay awake in the dark watches of the night she thought about what she had said – and she knew that every word and every promise was true. She wondered what she should do about the information that Ariel had passed on. She probably would pass it to London – and imagined that the chaps at SIS would laugh at her. She loved Ariel, but knew that he was a little insecure and liked to impress by sharing and embroidering insider gossip. Reporting the improbable Argentine plan to invade the Falklands was the easy bit; telling her parents that she was going to get married was the difficult one.

London: January 1982

Catesby had finally been told off for his memos headed HCABSFS: *Neither the language nor the tone is appropriate – and the encryption fools no one. Please cease using this acronym.* On reflection, many of those Catesby castigated weren't 'fucking stupid', just complacent or unaware of how they could alter the Prime Minister's collision course. On the other hand, there were those who were genuinely stupid and discounted the mounting evidence of an invasion. Unfortunately, these were the ones who had most access to Downing Street – one of whom dismissed the intelligence report Catesby had received from Fiona as *saloon-bar gossip passed on by a self-dramatising young woman with little experience in the world of intelligence.*

It was too cold to make their usual visit to St James's Park, so the colonel from DHO who was still deputising for the DCDI at JIC invited Catesby for a drink at his club. It was a dingy basement and most of the members were officers from unfashionable regiments and the Intelligence Corps.

'My wife won't come here,' said the colonel. 'She thinks the place is squalid. She says she could get me into the Cavalry and Guards – but I told her I don't want to be a waiter. And she didn't laugh, she never laughs at my jokes.'

'I know the feeling,' said Catesby sipping his beer. His own on-again off-again marriage was certainly not based on a shared sense of humour.

'Cheers. God, doesn't one need a drink after that debacle. JIC is getting even worse.'

'In any case, thank you for your contributions. Without them, our woman in BA might have seemed a bit of a drama queen.'

'I don't think it makes any difference. They think our Defence Attaché is a drama queen too – and now they think HMS *Endurance* is a ship full of drama queens.'

The colonel was referring to a series of reports from the DA in BA which consistently linked increasing Argentine frustration with the stalled Falklands talks to military preparations. And now these preparations had been eyeballed by the crew of HMS *Endurance* during the ship's annual visit to the southern Argentine port of Ushuaia. Normally, *Endurance* was greeted with a great deal of goodwill and fellow-sailor friendliness by her Argentine hosts, but on this occasion the Argentines had seemed furtive and stand-offish. Normally, Catesby would have been sceptical about Fiona's report – or any standalone report that wasn't supported by other intelligence sources. But on this occasion several alarm bells were ringing at the same time – and he was sure it wouldn't be long before GCHQ, who had easily broken all the Argentine codes, would also chime in.

'The attitude,' said the colonel, 'to scrapping *Endurance* is unbelievable. What did that Foreign Office guy say? I wrote it down: "The decision to withdraw HMS *Endurance* in no way implies a lessening of our commitment to the Falkland Islands." What utter twaddle. Do they really suppose silly statements like that are going to make the Junta shake in their jackboots? What do you think?'

'I think that the Foreign Office know what's going on, but are brow-beaten by Downing Street. Can I get you another pint?'

'Certainly not.' The colonel caught the eye of a serving staff. 'It's all on my tab. What are the options?'

Catesby's eyes glazed over. Repeating the obvious was tedious. 'We either budget to defend the islands or we negotiate a sovereignty deal.'

'Or,' said the colonel, 'we just sit back and let the Argentines take the islands. A bit cowardly, but problem solved.'

The waiter arrived and Catesby stared at the amber liquid lost in thought. When he spoke, it was a mere whisper. 'If she did that, she would have to resign.'

'And that wouldn't be a bad thing. My wife despises the woman. Her ideal solution would be to push the PM down the stairs at Chequers when she's blind drunk.' The colonel smiled at Catesby. 'Must be standard tradecraft for you chaps.'

Catesby didn't answer.

Agency News: 20 March 1982

Argentine Flag Raised on South Georgia

A group of fifty Argentines have landed at Leith Harbour on South Georgia, a dependency of Britain's Falkland Islands colony. The Argentines are thought to be scrap merchants under contract to remove scrap metal from the former whaling station at Leith.

There are no indications of hostile intentions, but an Argentine naval vessel has been reported in the vicinity. The arrival of the Argentines was reported by the British Antarctic survey team located at Grytviken.

The Argentine action has been regarded as a provocation in the ongoing dispute between Britain and Argentina over the sovereignty of the Falkland Islands. The group has been ordered to leave immediately and, in future, to ask British permission to work on the island. The Foreign Office has still not commented on the incident. The only British military presence in the area is HMS *Endurance*, a Royal Navy ice patrol ship with a detachment of forty marines and two attack helicopters. It is not known if the British government intends to dispatch the ship to South Georgia.

Recoleta, Buenos Aires: March 1982

It was the end of the Argentine polo season and Talbot had bounced back over the equator to get ready for the beginning of Northern Hemisphere polo. Once again, Fiona had sole use of the flat. She felt safer making clandestine radio transmissions from there than she did from the polo club – but now the whole business made her sick. At first, the spying had been a bit of a lark – an easy way to collect an extra two thousand quid a year for doing next to nothing. During her first month as a spy in situ, she had read Greene's *Our Man in Havana*. She stole the novel from the university library because she didn't want to attract suspicion by buying a copy – and was careful to hide the book from Ariel. She felt like a female Wormold and that the polo club was her equivalent of Wormold's vacuum cleaner business.

But the spying lark, as Wormold also found out, was no longer a harmless joke paid for by HM's Treasury. Fiona now knew that the Falklands invasion was no longer junior-officer bravado and gossip. It really was going to happen – and the information that she was sending to London might put her fiancé's life in danger. At that moment, Ariel was training at an airbase in the south of the country. His primary mission was to learn how to attack any British ships that dared come south to try to retake Las Malvinas.

Fiona had never felt so torn in her life. If anyone else had ever been in her situation, she would love to meet them and pour out her heart. She knew that she wasn't the only person in history to have slept with the enemy. Or perhaps it was Ariel who was sleeping with the enemy, for she was the foreigner betraying him. He had done nothing to betray her – and never would.

The Strizh radio lay assembled and ready to transmit in front of her on the priceless Tabriz carpet – Talbot only bought the finest. She distracted herself by wondering if Talbot had found the carpet on a polo jaunt to Iran. Oddly, the Russian Strizh radio seemed to go well with the carpet. They both came from the same part of the world. Not all inanimate objects evoke innocence – but somehow the radio did. *I will never judge you. I will faithfully send whatever message you key into my brain. How you use me is your choice.* Fiona stroked the radio and whispered, 'I am not going to use you to betray the man I love. Never.'

Fiona sat back on her firm haunches. Did Ariel love her because she was fit, taut and lively like a good polo pony? Did he ride her like a horse? She giggled. 'I need a glass of wine.' It was an unspoken rule that no one ever drank red wine near that precious carpet, but it was a rule that she was going to break. She found the wine and came back with a large glass. Fiona sat and reflected. *What am I going to do now?* One option was to send an EYES ONLY message to Catesby and explain her dilemma. She would agree to continue to send intelligence to London, but only if it was of no military value and could do no harm to Ariel. A second option was to take Ariel's side – to become a traitor to Britain – and to send false information that would help the Argentines. A third option was to do nothing. In spy parlance, it was called *doing a fade*. Fiona sipped her wine and her father's war-wounded and ravaged face swam up before her. There was a fourth option: accurately and completely report everything. Like him, she could be a loyal and brave British soldier. She closed her eyes and felt her heart pounding. And that's when it happened.

Fiona had been taught to use a gun – a 9mm Browning automatic – during her training at Fort Monckton. There had been some debate about whether to supply her with one via a 'dead drop' – what an apt method, she thought, for supplying a pistol! In the end, SIS decided to leave her unarmed – which was a relief because it meant one less compromising object to hide. But, fortuitously, Fiona was not left without personal protection. The Recoleta flat came with its own Browning automatic – an upmarket 10mm version of the standard SIS weapon with more stopping power and a smoother motion. Talbot's primary concern was being kidnapped – which was why the flat also had a complex locking system. It had even taken the technically adept Ariel a while to get the hang of it.

McCullough had shown Fiona the gun's hiding place: an easily accessible wall plate behind a nineteenth-century New England seascape in the bedroom. As soon as Fiona heard someone unlocking the door she got the pistol. Whoever it was had their own keys. Her first thought was that it was McCullough. But that would have been odd because McCullough never visited without warning her – and would certainly have knocked before she used the keys. If it was her, she would invent some excuse for asking her to wait a moment so she could hide the radio. But the hands at the door were firm and quick and the door was open before Fiona could utter a word.

She pointed the pistol at the intruder who hadn't knocked. His dark Mediterranean features had turned sullen grey. 'Are you going to shoot me?' he said.

'I didn't know it was you. I thought you were on exercise in Río Grande – or on the carrier. I was terrified – which is why I got the gun.'

Ariel answered her with a cold silent stare.

Fiona had begun to tremble. 'Why didn't you let me know you were back?'

'Are you alone?'

'Of course.'

'Then why are you making me stand here and not inviting me in? Have you something to hide?'

Fiona looked at the gun and then handed it to Ariel.

'What do you want me to do with this?' he said.

'Maybe you should shoot me.'

Ariel put the gun on a side table. He gave a wan smile. 'Why, my darling, would I want to do that?'

'I think you already know.'

Ariel followed Fiona into the sitting room and stared at the Strizh radio.

'Are you surprised?' she said.

'Yes, I am. I couldn't believe it was you.' Ariel squatted down and spotted the Cyrillic script on the radio. 'Good god – you're spying for the Russians.'

Fiona gave a faint smile. 'No, that's just a trick – a false flag something they call it. No, I am a British spy.'

Ariel looked almost relieved. He stood up and stared at Fiona.

'Would you like a glass of wine?' she said. 'I opened a bottle of Malbec.'

Ariel laughed. 'You're a British spy, using a Russian radio and drinking Argentine wine.'

'We're a cosmopolitan lot.'

Ariel's face hardened. 'Don't turn this into a joke.'

'You're the one who laughed.'

'It was a laugh of despair and sadness. Okay, I will have some wine.'

As Fiona went into the kitchen to fetch the bottle and a glass, Ariel sat on the sofa with his face in his hands.

She returned with the wine and knelt next to him. 'I'm sorry,' she said and tried to take his hands.

'Don't touch me.'

'I haven't betrayed you. The spying started as a joke for a little extra money.'

'Judas.'

Fiona pulled away.

'I haven't,' said Ariel, 'betrayed you.' He paused. 'Because of what's happening we've had a lot of intelligence briefings – and we were warned about an increase in clandestine transmissions using burster technology.' He gave Fiona a sad smile. 'So you're not the only one. In any case, the intelligence officer did mention a very worrying set of transmissions from Recoleta. He reckoned, however, that it was a banker or a drug dealer or an arms trader – a high-level criminal, as Recoleta is such a wealthy enclave, rather than a spy. Afterwards – and I'm not now going to ask your forgiveness for being suspicious – I spoke to the intelligence officer about the Recoleta transmissions. He showed me a map with a circle drawn on it. They've pinpointed the radio location to within a hundred and fifty metres of this flat. I expect there will be raids in the very near future.'

Fiona filled Ariel's glass.

'If it was you,' he said, 'I decided I wanted to protect you rather than betray you.' There were tears rolling down his face.

'I love you – and will always be yours.' Fiona shifted into English. 'No more fucking secrets!'

Ariel sipped his wine and stared into space.

Fiona shifted back into Spanish. 'I am going to tell you everything.'

'You don't have to.'

'But I'm going to.'

Ariel sat silently as Fiona told the entire story about her spying. She left nothing out.

'And now,' said Ariel, 'there are two practical things that we must do as soon as possible.'

'Of course.'

'We need to get rid of that radio. It's more poisonous than a pit viper.'

From the centre of Buenos Aires it was more than a two-hour drive before they could find a lonely bridge over a river deep enough to ditch the Strizh radio into dark oblivion. As soon as they heard the splash, both of them felt an enormous surge of release – which turned into mad eroticism. The kissing and fondling began even before they left the bridge. They then had wild and unbridled sex in the Ford Falcon that Ariel had signed out from the navy motor pool. As they manoeuvred in the Falcon's tight confines, Ariel whispered, 'When I'm an admiral we'll have a bigger car.'

'Let me suck you,' said Fiona.

'But I want to be inside you too.'

Afterwards, as they lay entwined and scrunched across the back seat, Ariel whispered, 'There is one more practical thing that we have to deal with.'

Fiona began to stroke his penis. 'I want to make love again.'

'That is part of it.'

'What is this practical thing?'

'We must get married.'

'I want that too – you know that.'

'But as soon as possible. If you are my wife, you will have an Argentine passport.'

'Your love is more important.'

'You will have that until the day I die.'

'Don't talk about death.'

'If there is war between our countries, there will be more than death.' He paused. 'There will be suspicions and recriminations too. I haven't said this before, but there are dangerous men in my country's security services. I don't want them to separate us or hurt you. When you are my wife, they would not dare.'

The first thing that Fiona thought about was her parents and sisters. She had dreamed of them being at the wedding, but things were hurtling out of control. She had to make a choice. She turned to Ariel.

'Yes,' she said, 'let's get married as soon as possible.'

CONFIDENTIAL: URGENT

26/03/82
FROM:GCHQ
TO:MOD

ARGENTINE NAVAL DEPLOYMENTS: INTERCEPTED MESSAGES

1 TWO ARGENTINE A-69 CLASS FRIGATES, ARA GRANVILLE AND ARA DRUMMOND, HAVE BEEN WITHDRAWN FROM ANNUAL JOINT SERVICE EXERCISES WITH URUGUAY.

2 COMMANDER-IN-CHIEF OF NAVY, ADMIRAL JORGE ANAYA, HAS ORDERED THE TWO FRIGATES TO PROCEED SOUTH TOWARDS FALKLAND ISLANDS.

3 MORE TO FOLLOW.

CONFIDENTIAL URGENT

27/03/82
FROM: GCHQ
TO: MOD

COPIES EYES ONLY: CABINET SECRETARY, PRIME MINISTER'S PRIVATE OFFICE

IMMEDIATE ARGENTINE MILITARY THREAT TO FALKLAND ISLANDS: LATEST INTERCEPTS

1 THE TWO CLASS A-69 FRIGATES DIVERTED FROM

JOINT URUGUAYAN/ARGENTINE NAVAL EXERCISES HAVE NOW JOINED A FLEET OF SIX OTHER VESSELS (ARGENTINE DESIGNATION TASK FORCE 40). THE GROUP ARE CAPABLE OF UNDERTAKING AMPHIBIOUS OPERATIONS.

2 ANOTHER ARGENTINE NAVAL GROUP OF SIX SHIPS (TASK FORCE 20) HAS BEEN ORDERED TO PROVIDE AIR AND ANTI-SUBMARINE WARFARE COVER FOR TASK FORCE 40.

SECRET IMMEDIATE

31/03/82: 0500 GMT

FROM: GCHQ
TO: MOD, PRIME MINISTER, CABINET OFFICE, CHAIRMAN JIC, FCO

ARGENTINE MILITARY INVASION OF FALKLAND ISLANDS IMMINENT

1 IT IS NOW CONFIRMED BY INTERCEPTED VOICE MESSAGES THAT THE ARGENTINE 2ND MARINE INFANTRY BATTALION ARE EMBARKED WITH TASK FORCE 40.

2 A PLATOON FROM THE 25TH REGIMENT WILL BE ACCOMPANYING THE MARINE BATTALION PROVIDING A TOTAL LANDING FORCE OF 900 MEN AND 20 ARMOURED PERSONNEL CARRIERS.

3 INTERCEPTED MESSAGES BETWEEN INVASION FLEET AND FLEET HQ AT PUERTO BELGRANO SUGGEST CONCERN AT WEATHER CONDITIONS WHICH MAY DELAY INVASION BY 24 HOURS. THE COMMANDER OF

ARGENTINE LAND FORCES HAS BEEN INFORMED THAT THE ELEMENT OF SURPRISE HAS BEEN LOST AND THAT ARMED RESISTANCE SHOULD BE EXPECTED.

4 A SIGNAL HAS JUST BEEN TRANSMITTED (0530 GMT) TO ARGENTINE SUBMARINE SANTA FE ORDERING THEM TO LAND A RECON SQUAD FROM THE BUZOS TACTICOS AT MULLET CREEK.

London: 31 March 1982

Shouting *I told you so* is seldom a good idea. It makes those you are shouting at even more defensive and entrenched. The only other person at the emergency JIC meeting who also had the right to bellow *told you so* was the colonel from DHO. They made the discreet eye contact of conspirators who had been proved right – but still not won. Although military action still hadn't taken place, Catesby did feel a little chagrin that the Defence Minister had heard the news of Argentina's invasion plans before SIS had.

One of the Prime Minister's rare fans in the Foreign Office couldn't resist having a dig at Catesby. 'I'm surprised that your agent in Buenos Aires didn't give advance notice of the invasion – which I believe is now going to take place on Friday, 2 April.'

'Well actually,' said Catesby rustling through his papers, 'if you refer to JIC minutes for the meeting of 12 January, you will see that our agent did warn of such an invasion.'

'But since then, not a specific date; not even a specific month.'

'That is correct.'

'Had your agent not even the slightest inkling that an invasion was in the offing?'

Catesby struggled to control his temper. 'Didn't you hear what I just said? The minutes of 12 January…'

'But that was three months ago.'

Catesby decided to own up. 'Okay. There has, in fact, been a lull in communication from this agent. We have no idea what has happened or whether communications will resume.' It certainly wasn't, thought Catesby, the best time for an agent to dry up.

Catesby did have a very good idea what had happened, but it wasn't one that he could air at a JIC meeting. She had chosen love over patriotism.

Agency News: 2 April 1982
Argentine Military Invade Falkland Islands

An Argentine amphibious force landed near Falklands capital Port Stanley in the early hours of Friday morning. A contingent of Royal Marines engaged the invaders in a fierce fire fight in which at least one Argentine serviceman was killed and others wounded. The Marines were overwhelmingly outnumbered by the invasion force. Shortly after 1 p.m., Falklands Governor Rex Hunt ordered the British troops to surrender. The Royal Marines were taken prisoner and the Argentine flag was raised over Government House.

The Argentine invasion followed months of tension culminating in the recent deployment of Argentine naval vessels off the Falklands. The latest ratcheting-up occurred two weeks ago when a group of Argentine scrap merchants hoisted an Argentine flag over Port Leith in South Georgia – an uninhabited island 800 miles south-east of the Falklands. Questions are being asked as to why the government was caught so unprepared.

Diplomatic ties have been cut with Argentina. There has been an emergency cabinet meeting to make preparations to send a naval task force to the South Atlantic.

Agency News: 3 April 1982
Argentines Take South Georgia After Fierce Battle

A heavily outnumbered Royal Marine garrison finally surrendered after downing at least one Argentine helicopter and inflicting severe damage on a large Argentine warship. It is thought that the Argentines suffered heavy casualties. The number of British casualties is still unknown. The marines, who were prepared to go on fighting, only surrendered when they received news that the Falkland Islands had been taken and there was no hope of reinforcement.

The fierce fighting on South Georgia signals a new level of hostility between the two countries.

Agency News: 4 April 1982
Task Force Ordered South

In a rare Saturday sitting, Parliament ratified the cabinet's decision to dispatch a task force of more than 100 ships to the Falklands. The fleet, led by aircraft carriers HMS *Invincible* and HMS *Hermes* will set sail tomorrow from Portsmouth. The force will also include destroyers, frigates, landing ships and thousands of ground troops.

In her statement to Parliament, the Prime Minister appeared to leave open all options: 'I stress that I cannot foretell what orders the task force will receive as it proceeds. That will depend on the situation at the time. Meanwhile, we hope that our continuing diplomatic efforts, helped by our many friends, will meet with success.' Labour leader Michael Foot agreed that it is right for Britain to take action, describing the invasion of the Falkland Islands as 'an act of naked, unqualified aggression, carried out in the most shameful and disreputable circumstances.' Mr Foot went on to deplore the nature of the Argentine regime:

'We can hardly forget that thousands of innocent people fighting for their political rights in Argentina are in prison and have been tortured and debased.'

Despite near-unanimous cross-party agreement, there were calls for ministers to quit, notably from Tory MP John Stokes. 'In order to save the Prime Minister and the Government, I am afraid that certain heads must roll, including that of the Foreign Secretary and, I very much regret to say, that of the Defence Secretary as well.'

Downing Street: 5 April 1982

It was the only time that Catesby ever met Margaret Thatcher in person. What shocked him most was the provocative glance that she gave him – but he later realised that she was only flirty with underlings like himself and her personal protection officers. Catesby had been sent to Number 10 as a last-minute replacement for Colin Figures, the Head of SIS, who had been called away to do something much more important and urgent than soothe the Prime Minister. It was clear to Catesby that the PM hadn't a clue who he was. She might, in fact, have thought he was a driver or a cop.

The meeting took place in the cabinet room and most of those attending were senior military officers in uniform. Thatcher began the proceedings by praising the Foreign Secretary who had just resigned: 'I had tremendous confidence in Peter Carrington and his loss is a devastating blow for me and for Britain. I have always backed Peter all the way.'

Catesby, like everyone else in the room, stared at the carpet in silence. It was embarrassing. They all knew that Lord Carrington was a thoroughly decent and competent man. The real reason for his resignation was something that the Tory ruling class would never discuss in public. The etiquette was to keep your mouth shut and stay loyal. Catesby looked across the room at Francis Pym, Carrington's replacement. Pym's face was neither stony nor bland: just inscrutable.

Thatcher continued in a voice that someone had once described as a 'perfumed fart': 'I never, never expected the Argentines to invade the Falklands head on. I couldn't believe, even as the reports came in, that they would do such a stupid thing. It was such a stupid thing even to contemplate doing.'

Catesby tried to imitate the Tory grandees by not rolling his eyes or gaping open-mouthed. Thatcher had repeatedly ignored intelligence briefings, press reports, Argentine government statements and all manner of warning bells. There were certainly minor disagreements in Whitehall, but the Prime Minister had been clearly told that there were only two options. One, do a sovereignty deal with Argentina. Two, budget to defend the Falklands with naval deployments in times of tension. Thatcher had chosen to do neither.

Century House, Lambeth, London: 6 April 1982

Catesby was amazed how quickly the Task Force had been assembled, provisioned and dispatched. It just went to show how rapidly a government can pull their finger out when their own survival is at stake – and no expense spared. But Catesby did think it was necessary. He agreed with Michael Foot, a staunch anti-fascist, that it was in Britain's *interest to ensure that foul and brutal aggression does not succeed in our world.* There was, however, a little too much flag-waving for Catesby's taste – and some of the jingoism was a bit silly. Supermarkets were removing Argentine corned beef from their shelves and a patriotic wine shop owner in Chelsea had ostentatiously poured his entire supply of Argentine vintages into the gutter. Hundreds of pounds of excellent wine down the drain! And Whitehall was following suit: Argentine food had been banned from canteens in Government buildings. There was, of course, a logic. You didn't want tabloid journalists catching Government ministers wolfing down Argentine beef. The Argentines were playing the psychological game too. They had offered free colour television sets to the Falkland Islanders for the World Cup. But nothing could make up for the gross Argentine blunder of allowing someone to photograph the Royal Marines as they were forced to lie prone under Argentine guns after they surrendered. It was an image of national humiliation that would rankle the British public and fire demands for revenge.

Catesby didn't normally side with the hawks, but he was certain that the dispatch of a Task Force would result in a peaceful diplomatic solution. Sabre-rattling was, of course, totally ineffective unless it was obvious that you were willing to get blood on those sabres. He realised that the next few weeks were going to be a white-knuckle ride. But the problem with beating war drums was that the noise drowned out just criticism of those who were responsible for the mess in the first place.

When Catesby got to C's office, the door was already open and the chief of the intelligence service waved him in. 'How did it go at Downing Street?'

'The PM was only interested in talking to the military. After a few minutes she waved us away for a private meeting with Admiral Lewin. I gave my briefing notes to her private secretary.'

'Would you like tea or coffee?' said the head of intelligence.

'No thanks,' said Catesby

'Well I'm having one.'

Catesby watched his boss move to the standard civil service tea trolley. The chief had a modest ordinariness which inspired affection throughout the service.

'It's all go,' said C with a slight Midlands accent. 'Never saw anything happen so quickly in Whitehall.'

Catesby was tempted to say *it's because the Prime Minister is desperate to save her skin*, but merely nodded agreement.

'I am sure,' said the head, fixing Catesby with a stare, 'that you know that Mitterrand has pledged us total and unequivocal French support – and, as you are a fluent French speaker, we are sending you to Paris to find out just how unequivocal that support really is.'

Catesby raised an astonished eyebrow. 'To meet the President…'

'No, no, not to meet Mitterrand – although I am sure you would charm him with your wit and learning.'

Catesby frowned. He was never sure when C was being ironic.

'No, we've arranged a meeting for you with the head of the French intelligence service – whom I am sure you will also charm.'

'Is there an agenda?'

'That's entirely for you to decide,' said C. 'But the thing that concerns us most are French weapons systems in Argentina – especially the Exocet.'

Paris: 8 April 1982

The sign outside 141 Boulevard Mortier wasn't particularly welcoming:

ZONE MILITAIRE
DÉFENSE de FILMER
ou PHOTOGRAPHER

But Catesby liked the lack of deception. No one was in any doubt that 141 Boulevard Mortier was anything other than the headquarters of the French secret intelligence service. The building, protected by vehicle barriers and barred windows, was a fortress. In contrast, the SIS HQ at Broadway Buildings had looked like a normal business address. There had been a sign over one entrance describing the premises as the Minimax Fire Extinguisher Company. But it didn't fool anyone – least of all Soviet intelligence officers who regularly drove past with cameras snapping. Like much else in Britain, the supposed non-existence of the Secret Intelligence Service was a polite fiction. And polite fictions that no one questioned were part of the delicate social glue that held Britain together – but was now on the verge of coming unstuck.

The guard behind the bulletproof glass of the entrance cubicle on Boulevard Mortier was a soldier dressed in camouflage combat gear. Catesby told him he had an appointment and handed over his ID. The ID, patently false, described Catesby as a Counsellor Atkinson who was a member of the UK diplomatic mission in Paris. It was part of the game. The person expecting Catesby knew his real name and that he was a high-level spook. The soldier checked a clipboard – and then made a telephone call. He handed back Catesby's ID and said that someone was coming to get him. Clearly, you couldn't have someone like Catesby wondering around the building without an escort – and three minutes later, the escort proved to be none other than the head of the service.

The *directeur général* had a trim moustache and a side parting. He bore an uncanny resemblance to the American author William Faulkner. Catesby half expected to hear him drawling in an American accent from the Deep South. But when the DG spoke it was in the clear crisp French of one of the *vieux polytechniciens* who had run the French state for decades. The École Polytechnique, also known as l'X, was the most elite educational institution in France. Unlike most Oxbridge types, graduates of l'X had a firm grounding in science and technology – which was the principle reason Catesby had come to Paris to meet the DG. Britain needed help in thwarting the lethal Exocet missiles that France had sold to Argentina.

The walk from the entrance to the DG's office involved underground tunnels that were dimly lit and bare. 'You have been here before,' said the director.

'Not recently.'

'Things have changed – and they need to change more.'

Catesby nodded. The DG had been in post for less than a year and had hit the ground running.

'We need to de-militarise and modernise this service.'

Catesby thought it best not to comment. The director's four predecessors had all been army generals who authorised a number of secret operations that were beyond the control of France's elected civilian leaders. The new DG was, in fact, the first head of the service who had no military experience at all. His background was entirely industrial – largely with Aérospatiale, the state-owned company that developed and sold the Exocet.

'By the way,' said the director, 'we have changed our name. We are no longer the Service de Documentation Extérieure et de Contre-Espionnage.'

'That was,' smiled Catesby 'quite a mouthful.'

'Our new name, the Direction Générale de la Sécurité Extérieure, is a little better, but still mystifies the Americans.'

'I believe you spent several years as Aérospatiale's man in Washington.'

The DG gave an enigmatic smile and answered in heavily accented English, 'It was a very interesting time.'

Catesby knew that the Frenchman had been an *informateur informel*, a non-official spy, during his time in the States reporting back to Paris on economic espionage. It probably helped him get his current post.

They reached a staircase and climbed out of the tunnel to the DG's office which overlooked an inner courtyard. The courtyard was laid out in the symmetrical style of a formal French garden with neatly trimmed trees. The idea was to impose order on nature. The borders were bursting into bloom, but with parade-ground precision. While Catesby gazed out the window, the DG shuffled two clerical staff from the office.

'Would you like coffee?' said the director.

'Yes, please.' Catesby was feeling bleary having travelled overnight with little sleep.

The DG opened the door to the outer office and whispered an order.

Catesby had studied a dossier on the new DG before leaving for Paris. It gave the impression that the director was a fierce moderniser and super-innovative technocrat. He was trying to replace the military dinosaurs with a multi-disciplined cadre of economists, engineers and historians. Reading between the lines, Catesby could see that the DG was not a great admirer of President François Mitterrand's more personalised style of rule.

'Have you been informed,' said the DG, 'that France will be supporting European Community economic sanctions against Argentina?'

'We assumed that would be the case.'

'Otherwise,' the DG smiled, 'I am sure you would not be here.'

Someone knocked on the door. The DG said, '*Entrez*.' And a young woman in uniform entered bearing a tray with coffee and petits fours.

As soon as the female soldier had left, the director looked at Catesby and said, 'God…'

At first Catesby was confused, but quickly realised that the DG was referring to President Mitterrand.

'God,' continued the director, 'doesn't want to offend Mrs Thatcher.'

Catesby knew that Mitterrand's other nickname was 'Tonton', Uncle. It was rumoured that those who loved and adored the President called him Tonton. He wondered if those who were more sceptical ironised him as God. It would be good stuff for Catesby's report. Meanwhile, Catesby gobbled two petits fours in quick succession. He was starving. His only breakfast had been a stale croissant at the airport.

'I also think,' said the director, 'that Mitterrand's ideas about women need modernising.'

Catesby raised an eyebrow. It wasn't a point of view that he expected to hear from the French secret service. 'Can you elaborate?' he said.

'At the risk of being indiscreet, I would say – at least in the case of Mrs Thatcher – that the President is on the one hand, condescending, and on the other, intimidated by her. His silly description of her having "the mouth of Marilyn Monroe" and "the eyes of Caligula" proves the point.'

Catesby batted back with an indiscretion of his own. 'I think many of Mrs Thatcher's cabinet ministers also find her difficult.'

'Then they should stand up to her.' The DG tapped on his desk with his reading glasses. 'Your conflict with Argentina should never have happened. It is the result of emotion defeating rationality. De Gaulle would never have fallen into it – that's why he got out of Algeria. We could have won the war, but we would have lost the peace. But I digress. Let us get back to the business at hand.'

'Our concerns focus primarily on the Super Étendard aircraft and the AM39 air-launched Exocets.'

'As well they should. There is very little you can do to defend against an Exocet once it has been launched. The missile skims the sea at only a metre above the water – impossible to pick up by radar. Once the Exocet is under the guidance of its own locking radar system, the Exocet's target – even if it picks up the hostile radar lock – has less than thirty seconds to react.' The director smiled and shifted into English. 'As you say in England, it is a lovely piece of kit.'

'How many have they got?'

'Five – at the moment.'

'Are they ready to be fired from the Super Étendards?'

'Ah.' The DG twirled his reading glasses and went back to speaking French. 'That is a very good question. There are two companies involved. As I said my former company, Aérospatiale, supply the Exocets – but Dassault-Breguet supply the Super Étendards. My colleagues from Aérospatiale have informed me that the detailed work and testing needed to attach the Exocets to the Super Étendards has not yet been completed.'

'How much more work is needed before the Exocets will be operational?'

'I don't know, but I can assure you that no Aérospatiale technicians will be involved – a planned visit by a group of them for next week has been cancelled. But the problem is the Dassault team who are already in place.'

'Aren't they going to be recalled?'

'Of course, but that doesn't mean they will come home.' The director looked hard at Catesby. 'I would like to emphasise that we have been instructed to give you full and complete support – and it is an instruction I am going to obey whatever my personal feelings about God's pro-British policy.'

'It is much appreciated.'

The DG put on his reading glasses and picked up a file. 'The problem with arms embargoes is that they don't work. Getting arms traders to obey trade sanctions is like – how do you say in English, something about shepherding the cats?'

'Herding cats.'

'Thank you. You cannot control arms dealers either because there is too much money involved.'

Catesby stared out the window. The trees in the secret courtyard were unfurling into life. Once again, he realised how much he hated war. Part of him wanted to go straight back to London and grab Thatcher by both arms and shout: 'Just give them the fucking islands – it's not worth it!' But he knew how she would fix him with those cold blue eyes which would suddenly turn soft and understanding. 'I know how you feel, but this is something that must be done.' She knew how to ply the feminine card – and Catesby would feel ashamed of having shouted at her.

'You seem lost in thought,' said the DG.

'Or just lost.'

'So am I,' said the director. 'I cannot understand why the Argentines invaded before the Exocets were fully operational.'

'They misjudged us. They didn't think we would fight back.'

The DG shrugged. 'As I said, the Super Étendard technical team are still in Argentina.' The DG smiled with a hint of satisfaction. 'But fortunately we have an agent informer who is a member of the team. At the moment, there are problems with the missile launchers, but they are being solved.'

'Will they be solved before the task force arrives – in perhaps three weeks' time?'

'Our informer knows we want that information. He estimates four weeks for all of them, but two of the launchers could be ready much sooner – perhaps a week or two. The Exocet is as complex and sophisticated a weapon as it is lethal. In any case,' the DG lifted a folder, 'here is a file for you on the team and what they are doing. As instructed, full cooperation.'

Catesby took the file and opened it up. The first pages contained photos and biographies of all the French technicians.

'The top one,' said the director, 'is the team leader. His colleagues have nicknamed him Pascal because he is a mathematical genius.'

'He'd make a good spy,' said Catesby. 'He looks totally ordinary and anonymous.'

'But sadly, he isn't our informer.' The DG leaned over and pointed to the third photo. 'It's that one.'

'He looks shifty.'

'And I think he is.'

'A reliability problem?'

'No one ever knows until it's too late.'

Catesby picked up the team leader's snapshot. 'On the one

hand, he looks plain. But, on the other, he looks like a man with a secret vice.'

'Ah,' said the DG, 'he certainly has one.'

Catesby's mind raced ahead to honey traps in tango bars. He needed to get on the case. 'I assume the details of his secret vice are in the file.'

'No, they are not.'

'How odd.' Catesby smiled. 'And how unlike French intelligence.'

'Personally, I cannot imagine a vice more boring. I tried it once and found the whole thing totally monotonous – as well as wet and uncomfortable. It mostly appeals to men, but I was seduced into trying it by a very aristocratic Scottish woman. In any case, it did nothing for me – even though the Scottish lady went on and on about how you have to keep trying different techniques.'

Catesby stared at the DG. He didn't know what to say. The Frenchman's frank confession had left him nonplussed.

'In any case, one of the factors that drew Pascal to Argentina was the opportunity to indulge his vice. In fact, it is a bone of contention with the other team members. Pascal is always disappearing for days at a time when he should be working. Apparently, Patagonia is one of the best places in the world for it.'

'He shags sheep?'

The DG looked confused.

'Your reference to Patagonia,' said Catesby, 'seems to suggest that he has sex with livestock.'

'Not as far as I know, but he does go fly fishing. That is his vice. He's obsessed by it and even ties his own flies.'

Catesby tried not to smile or give anything away. It was a 'vice' he shared.

Iglesia Nuestra Señora Del Pilar, Palermo, Buenos Aires: 10 April 1982

The bans had been rushed through owing to Ariel's status as a combat pilot who might soon be required to deploy. Our Lady of the Pillar, a smallish church built in 1734, was packed with the two hundred family and friends who had come to the wedding. The church's name derived from an apparition of the Blessed Virgin who had appeared to Saint James balanced on a pillar of jasper at the time of her Assumption into heaven in AD 40. The original church of that name, the much grander Cathedral-Basilica of Our Lady of the Pillar, was in Zaragoza on the very site where Saint James saw the apparition of Mary. Fiona could not help but wonder how many sailors and soldiers had worshipped at Our Lady of the Pillar in Spain before setting off in the Armada to England. The Buenos Aires version of the church also had an air of departure. It was used more for funerals than weddings as it was located right next to Recoleta Cemetery.

The priest marrying them, Father Bergoglio, was a Jesuit who had a tense relationship with the Junta. He seemed to want to influence them to follow more humane policies, but refrained from opposing them openly. Ariel had described him as *someone who understands power and how to deal with powerful people.* Fiona was immediately struck by Father Bergoglio's obvious intelligence and the deference shown to him – but he was also modest and asked her permission to speak English: 'Two years ago, I spent a few months trying to learn your language at the Jesuit Centre in Dublin, but haven't had much practice since then.'

They chatted briefly about Joyce and Beckett, whom Father Bergoglio had read during his stay in Ireland. Behind the priest's easy charm, Fiona noted a steely conviction that was tempered by something secretive. Thirty-one years later the man who married her and Ariel had become Pope Francis I.

More than half the men attending the wedding, including Ariel, were in full dress uniform. The only person in uniform who wasn't an officer was Ariel's son, Gonzalo, who was a teenage sea cadet. Gonzalo had followed the father he adored into the navy, but was unable to qualify as a pilot because he was short-sighted. Instead, he was training to be a ship's engineer. Gonzalo was proud that he had been assigned to the ARA *General Belgrano*. She may have been an old ship – nearly fifty years of age – but she was a happy ship.

Fiona's father wasn't in uniform, even though Ariel had asked him to be. Major Stewart didn't like the practice, common in the USA and Russia, where former officers dressed up in their uniforms with full decorations for special occasions – or just to show off. Stewart thought that once you had left the military you hung up your uniform for good. The major had tried to make a joke about not being in uniform. He said to Ariel, using his daughter as an interpreter, 'I don't want to be shot or taken prisoner as an enemy soldier behind Argentine lines.' Fiona, fearing that her new husband would not understand English humour, did not give an exact translation.

Her parents' visit to Argentina for the wedding had not been an easy one or a happy one. The suspension of the no-visa agreement between the two countries had made travel difficult. It also gave Fiona's sisters an excuse for not attending. They thought she was doing a 'fucking stupid thing' that would end in tears. If the parents agreed, they kept such thoughts to themselves.

Patagonia: 11 April 1982

When there's a war on, Whitehall can move quickly. Catesby was surprised how swiftly and unquestionably permission for the operation was given. Those who gave the green light knew it was an absolutely essential op that could make all the difference; that could tip the fatal balance.

The flight from Heathrow to Santiago had taken sixteen hours. Catesby was travelling undercover on a Belgian passport that identified him as one of his own cousins; a nephew of his mother who had died as an infant in the Spanish influenza epidemic. The deceased child would have been a few years older than Catesby, but that made the cover more perfect for Catesby looked older than his actual years. It wasn't the first time that he had transformed himself into Jacques Bastin. It was an easy cover legend for Catesby to follow because he had been brought up speaking Belgian-accented French as well as Flemish. It was unusual for a Belgian to be fluent in both languages, but his mother had started life as a barmaid in Antwerp with a Flemish father and a Walloon mother. After the early death of Catesby's English sailor father, his mother had brought him and his sister up as undercover Belgians in Lowestoft. Perhaps she had envisioned returning her family to Belgium or the children becoming translators or North Sea merchants – or even spies.

It is important that agents feel comfortable with their cover identities – and sometimes Catesby felt that he was more Jacques Bastin than he was William Catesby. Jacques was the alternative him who grew up as a European staring across the North Sea at an island and a people that he didn't understand. Jacques admired the British for being polite and good mannered, but they confused him because they didn't always say what they meant. Perhaps, thought Jacques, that was why they had made such a mess of the Falklands: the Argentines didn't understand what they meant either. But there were contradictions of character that Catesby himself found difficult to comprehend. The British were the least militaristic people in the world – and yet their soldiers and sailors had conquered vast swathes of it. 'But,' whispered Jacques in his ear, 'India was full of spices and diamonds and opium – what are you going to loot from *les Îles Malouines*?'

Catesby had hired a Toyota at the airport which had recently been renamed El Aeropuerto Internacional Comodoro Arturo Merino Benítez. Commodore Benítez had founded the Chilean Air Force. Catesby reckoned that rechristening the airport was an attempt by the Pinochet Junta to give the military more national respect. Catesby had been told that the Chilean military – including DINA, the intelligence service – would give him full cooperation if he wanted it, but Catesby turned it down. His excuse was that he didn't want anyone to know about his mission. It was too important to risk a compromising leak. But another reason was that Catesby wanted to distance himself from a junta that had blood on its hands – and may well have killed Nobel Prize-winning poet Pablo Neruda because he had been a close supporter of Allende. All intelligence services are rumour mills. And, even though some of the rumours are 'disinfo' designed to cause mischief and sow mistrust, the one about Neruda's murder had a whiff of truth. The poet suffered from prostate cancer and was visited by an 'oncologist' who gave him a fatal injection. Catesby was certain that the dodgy doctor was a CIA agent who spoke fluent Spanish. It was the one language they were good at.

The Latin American quagmire into which the Falkland blunders had landed Britain was a swamp full of CIA and other Americans. It was their backyard where they could easily play duplicitous games. The additional problem about the Falklands for the Brits was not knowing which side the Americans were on. In truth, they were on both sides – which was another reason why Catesby wanted to keep his visit to Argentina an absolute secret.

The SIS pharmacy had kitted out Catesby with a full

complement of downers and uppers to make sure that he slept on the flight and was fully alert for the eleven-hour drive to Argentina after he arrived. He also had doctors' prescriptions in case the pills aroused the interest of customs officials. You had to think of all the angles when you planned such ops. But undercover secrecy and passing through customs like a normal traveller also meant that Catesby couldn't pack a gun or any other weapon in his luggage. He would have to carry out the hit by hand.

In the end, Catesby had slept so peacefully on the flight that he decided not to take the amphetamines – as they sometimes caused him to hallucinate. The first part of the drive was easy: 500 fast straight miles south down Ruta 5, Chile's main artery and part of the Pan-American Highway. It only became interesting when Catesby turned off east on Ruta 199. It wasn't long before the snow-capped Andes were looming in the distance and the road was no longer paved. The drive to the border pass was stunningly beautiful – clear mountain lakes and pine forests. The first sign that Argentina was just ahead was the Chilean border post with a sign wishing you to return soon – *Vuelva Pronto*. As he slowed down for the Argentine border control, Catesby began to mentally rehearse his cover story in his poor Spanish. He looked around and was surprised that there was no military presence. Odd, considering that Argentina was almost at war and that Chile was turning into Britain's only South American ally. The only person in uniform was a policeman in a booth who seemed more interested in Catesby's car documents than Catesby. He looked at his fake Belgian passport without a flicker of interest and asked how long he would be staying in Argentina.

'About a week,' said Catesby.

'On business?'

'No, I'm on a brief fishing holiday.'

'You've come to the right place, but don't try to take any fish with you back into Chile. They are very strict about any food or agricultural items from Argentina.'

'Thank you for your advice.'

'And another piece of advice: don't ever try driving across this pass in the winter. Very dangerous.'

'I certainly won't.'

The border cop handed Catesby his passport and wished him a *feliz viaje*. Catesby smiled a *gracias* and looked at the road ahead. There were two signs. The first, somewhat faded and weathered, was the standard one of welcome: *BIENVENIDOS A LA REPUBLICA ARGENTINA*. The second was new and glowing, not just with fresh paint, but also with conviction: ***LAS MALVINAS SON ARGENTINAS!*** Catesby felt his bowels twist into a knot. He realised for the first time that he was illegally entering an enemy country as a spy in time of war – and it wasn't just in Hollywood movies where such people were summarily executed. Britain had hanged seventeen German spies during the Second World War – and during the First World War eleven had been shot by firing squad at dawn in the Tower of London.

Catesby's target was staying at a fishing lodge that was part of a 15,000-acre *estancia*. It was only twenty miles from the border, which meant it would be easy for Catesby to 'ex-filtrate' after he had done the job. Catesby regretted that he wouldn't be able to stay longer. The countryside was beautiful, with beckoning rivers and lakes, but Catesby tried to concentrate on remembering his cover story – and how to handle the people who ran the *estancia* if they proved curious and suspicious. He had booked the holiday through a Brussels-based travel agent. The only thing that the *estancia* owners knew about Catesby was that he was a Belgian art dealer named Jacques Bastin – presumably a man of some wealth and culture. Catesby could fake the culture thing having spent years under diplomatic cover as a CULT/AT, cultural attaché, in various embassies. He wasn't, however, sure that more discerning eyes had always been convinced.

Once again, the paramount requirement for an op of this sort was complete secrecy. No one in the British Embassy in Santiago knew that an SIS officer had flown in to carry out a cross-border termination exercise – and no legal advice had been taken either.

Catesby wasn't a lawyer, but supposed that such ops were legitimate acts of war. He had, in fact, done worse – and the swords were still hanging over his head. Only two people knew about Catesby's mission. One was the Foreign Secretary and the other was his boss at SIS. But there was something that bothered Catesby, a nagging doubt – and not just the fact that he hated violence.

The problem was the French. Catesby hadn't told the head of the French intelligence service that he was planning a trip to Argentina to take out the leader of the Dassault team who was showing the Argentine military how to attach Exocet missiles to Super Étendards – but you didn't need to be a genius to work that one out. Catesby had discovered the whereabouts of the team leader from tips, information that the French intelligence chief had passed on from his own grass within the team – and the info was gold dust. Catesby had found out exactly where and when the leader, Pascal, would be staying for his brief fishing break in Patagonia. Apparently, he always went to the same place – not a good practice if you wanted to avoid being assassinated. But Pascal wasn't an intelligence officer; he was an aircraft engineer. When, however, Catesby arrived at the *estancia* – and later, when he experienced the trout fishing – he realised why Pascal kept coming back.

The fishing lodge allowed guests to choose between privacy and sociability – or anything in between. The cabins were set well apart from each other in landscaped gardens, but you were welcome to share communal meals in the *casa* – where Catesby met Pascal, whose first question was not an easy one.

'How did you find out about this wonderful place?'

Catesby winked. 'Ah, that's a state secret.'

'I didn't know that Belgium had any state secrets.'

Catesby gave a forced laugh as he fabricated an answer. 'A few years ago, I visited a tackle shop in London and ended up talking to the proprietor about salmon fishing in Scotland and English chalk streams.' Catesby paused. If the Frenchman asked him which shop, he had the answer. 'In any case, the shopkeeper told me that the best fly fishing in the world was in Patagonia. And so I followed up his suggestion – I'm not interested in trophy-size fish – and found out about this river which seems ideal for the light tackle that I prefer.'

'It is the best fly fishing in the world – and should be a state secret. You have, however, come late in the season. That is why we are the only guests.'

'Have you been here before?'

'Several times. I want to explore every metre of the wonderful river. It runs thirty-eight kilometres from the lake in the mountains to where it joins the plain and flows into a larger sluggish river. You will, by the way, need waders with soles that grip well. Much of the river is fast and treacherous.'

Catesby tried to appear genuinely curious. He didn't want to reveal how well he had researched the river and how its slippery rapids were the ideal place for a termination op that could pass as accidental death. One of the things they teach you at spy school – which, of course, they deny ever having taught – is that assassinations should be disguised as accidents, death by natural causes or suicide. But there are times when suspicion of foul play can be useful. Catesby hoped that Pascal's death would frighten the other members of the technical team into thinking they might be next – and reconsider whether helping the Argentines was a good idea. Catesby wondered if a few anonymous letters might be useful in persuading them to clear off.

The rest of the evening was barbecued beef washed down by lots of Malbec. 'Not a good country for vegetarians,' said Catesby.

'Beef is to Argentina what *frites* are to Belgium.'

'I hope,' said Catesby, 'that we are not on our way to Belgian jokes.'

The Frenchman smiled. 'Three explorers – a Frenchman, a Belgian and an American – are lost in the jungle when they are captured by cannibals.'

'I've heard it.'

'I was only teasing you. Belgian jokes are never very funny.'

'Thank you.' There was one Belgian joke, however, that made Catesby smile, albeit sadly. A Belgian meets a beautiful Englishwoman and asks her for a date. She gets indignant and firmly says, 'Never!' The Belgian replies: '*Bon! Ce soir à neuf heures!*' The misunderstanding summed up Catesby's love life. The idea that spies were glamorous characters with spectacular love lives was far from reality.

'I suppose,' said the Frenchman eying Catesby over his glass of Malbec, 'that with your job you have to travel a lot.'

'Unfortunately that is so; you have to form relationships with museums, curators and collectors – and they don't come to you, so you have to go to them. But the most important skill is spotting trends in taste and the way they affect the market.'

'If I had a lot of money, what would you recommend me to buy?'

The dinner conversation wasn't going the way Catesby wanted it to. The Frenchman was an engineer who, Catesby assumed, had no interest in the arts. Or was he testing Catesby's cover story?

'It depends,' said Catesby, 'on whether you want your art work as an investment or something you desire to treasure and live with.'

'What artist would you choose to treasure – to put on your own walls?'

The question totally nonplussed Catesby. Most of the paintings in his own home were by local Suffolk artists – and mentioning them would be a certain giveaway that he wasn't a Belgian art dealer. He had to play for time while he populated his fictional walls.

The Frenchman gave Catesby a blank stare.

'First of all, I'm a dealer. We don't have personal preferences – although we often rave about a particular artist to complete a sale.' Catesby squinted and scratched his chin. 'My own home? Oddly enough, I like fakes. We often come across them in the trade. They are sometimes more interesting than the real thing and much cheaper to buy. I have several by Han van Meegeren, probably the greatest art forger ever. He duped several high-ranking Nazis included Hermann Göring.' Catesby smiled. He admired van Meegeren and wasn't sure that they should have sent him to prison.

'I suppose,' said the Frenchman, 'we do the same thing when we use fake flies to catch trout.'

'And what flies,' said Catesby, 'should we use to trick the trout tomorrow?'

'I would recommend Blue Duns. I tie my own with cock hackle fibres for the tail, mole fur for the body and grey starling for the wings. Have you got any?'

'I'll check my fly box. I'm not sure I have.'

'Don't worry, I can give you a few. I always bring several extra because they are so easy to lose. Ah, and you must use tiny hook sizes – nothing larger than a size 16. It makes the fishing more of a challenge – and the trout will often ignore anything larger. I once caught a two-kilo brown trout on a 20 – I had to play him for half an hour.'

Catesby smiled with admiration. A size 20 was a mere speck; you needed a magnifying glass to identify what sort of fly it was. Fly fishing was a wonderful sport, but talking about it among non-anglers was a guaranteed way to bore a dinner party rigid. He sometimes did it on purpose.

Catesby slept surprisingly well, not because Malbec was a soporific wine, but because he always did sleep well the night before he was going to kill someone. It was like that in the war as well. It was the night after the action, the killing, that the insomnia came on – and, when sleep did finally come, it was punctuated by nightmares. Perhaps, thought Catesby, the way to cure his chronic insomnia was for SIS to give him a daily list of targets to whack. Each night then would precede a new action and he wouldn't have time to reflect on the previous.

After an early breakfast of *medialunas*, Argentine croissants, and strong coffee they headed for the river. Catesby insisted that they travel in his rented Toyota in return for the Blue Dun flies that Pascal had given him, but the real reason was to make his getaway easier after he had terminated the Frenchman.

It was a beautiful day for a murder. The skies of Patagonia were crystal clear – a perfect backdrop for the Andean condor that Catesby spotted on the way to the river. Murder or no murder, it was a sight that Catesby and his victim wanted to treasure. He stopped the car and they both got out to stare at the magnificent bird. The condor has a wingspan of more than ten feet, the largest of any land bird. This one was almost motionless against the sky – more an icon than a living bird.

'Have you got a camera?' said Catesby.

'Yes, I always bring one to photograph the fish.'

While the Frenchman went back to the car to rummage through his rucksack for the camera, Catesby wondered if he should nick the camera and its film after he had done the deed. It might be a good idea to deprive the Argentine security services of any photographic record of the Frenchman's last movements – and he would also like to have a snap of the spectacular bird.

The Frenchman came back. His camera was an expensive Nikon that he had fitted with a telephoto lens and he began clicking away. Why, thought Catesby, did he need a telephoto lens to photograph dead trout?

'Its stillness,' said Catesby, 'is eerie.'

'He's soaring on heat thermals. They hardly ever flap their wings – and they have some unusual habits. They defecate over their legs and feet.'

'Why?' said Catesby.

'I don't know. Perhaps the evaporation of the faeces creates a cooling effect.'

Catesby was impressed – and a little bored.

'It's called urohydrosis.'

'What is?' said Catesby.

'The habit of excreting over your legs and feet – storks also do it.'

Catesby smiled. Pascal would have been a brilliant dinner party guest.

'Sadly, the bird is an endangered species subject to poisoning and bullets. Many ranchers think the condor is a bird of prey that kills their livestock, but the ranchers are wrong. The condor is primarily a carrion vulture who feeds on the largest carcasses available: guanacos, rheas, alpacas and certainly dead cattle.'

Catesby felt a twinge of discomfort. He didn't like the thought of the condor with its shit-stained claws and legs feeding on the dead Frenchman.

'I think,' said the Frenchman, 'that we had better go to the river. Perhaps the condor will still be there when we come back.'

Catesby nodded.

The rest of the way was a rough unmade road. At first, the countryside was brown and parched-looking – a contrast to the snow-capped Andes in the near distance. The arid landscape disappeared as the road twisted upwards. There were now boulders, ravines and dense forest. Catesby could sense the freshness of the river pouring out of the mountains.

'There is,' said the Frenchman, 'a good place to leave the car – just around the next bend on the left. I think fishermen are the only ones who ever use it – and it's too late in the season for most of them. We will be quite alone.'

Catesby had the eerie sense that the Frenchman was reading his own thoughts. He saw the parking space – shaded by the cover of a conifer tree with low hanging branches – and drove the car on to it.

The Frenchman gestured upwards. 'That's an araucaria tree. It's the oldest tree species on the planet – the araucaria has been here for 200 million years. Its bark is spiked and its needles are sharp – it's a tree that evolved to ward off predators.

Unlike, thought Catesby, yourself.

'But the araucaria also produces large quantities of delicious pine nuts. I'm going to gather some.'

Catesby looked on as the Frenchman removed a plastic box from his rucksack. He placed the box on a large flat rock and began to gather pinecones.

'I don't want to lose time on the river, but it would be nice to have a handful of roasted pine nuts to go with the cooked trout.'

Catesby watched the Frenchman collect the pinecones and then watched him bend over the rock tapping out the nuts. Catesby felt his hand close around a club called 'the priest' which was attached to his fishing vest. The priest was used to kill trout after they had been netted. Catesby stared at the back of the Frenchman's head and wondered if he should do it now;

get it over with. The problem was they were too far from the river. His original plan had been to dispatch the Frenchman near a rapidly flowing cataract to make it look like an accident. The river, however, was nearly a mile away – and there was no way he could drag the body that far over so much rough ground. Catesby loosened his grip on the priest.

'We have enough,' said the Frenchman. 'Let's get fishing.'

It was a difficult hike to the river: dense forest without paths and across steep ravines with rivulets and slippery rocks. It took forty hard sweaty minutes to reach the river, but when Catesby finally saw its clear waters tumbling from the snow-capped peaks of the Andes it was love at first sight. An athletic trout greeted their arrival by somersaulting two feet out of the water.

The Frenchman sat on the side of the bank to take off his walking boots before slipping on his waders. Once again, Catesby wondered if he should get on and finish the job. It would be easy to knock the Frenchman unconscious or break his neck – and then push him into the river. Another trout did a tail-standing jump out of a deep pool. It was a glorious day for fishing. Would it, thought Catesby, make any difference if he killed the Frenchman now or did it after a day's fishing? He was hardly going to be showing the Argentines how to attach Exocets to Super-Étendards while he was casting flies in the middle of a clear Andean mountain stream. And, somewhat self-indulgently, Catesby knew that he would never have another opportunity to fish such a perfect river. Catesby frightened himself. How could he separate the pleasure of fishing from the ugly brutal business that he had been sent to execute? This ability to separate: was there something in him that wasn't altogether normal or human? But he had seen others do odd things in the war. He recalled members of the Maquis offering cigarettes to dead German soldiers and having jokey conversations with their corpses. But maybe that was a way of coping with the stresses of war. Catesby stopped thinking and assembled his fly rod.

'You must,' said the Frenchman, 'use a tippet that is almost invisible. The trout here are plentiful and hungry, but very wary.'

Catesby sat on the riverbank and ran four feet of monofilament leader through the loop on the end of his fly line. Following the Frenchman's advice, he then tied five feet of green monofilament tippet with a breaking strength of three pounds to the leader using a surgeon's knot. You needed supple fingers and a fine touch to be a fly fisherman. The most difficult bit was attaching a tiny Blue Dun fly to the end of the tippet. The tippet was so thin that Catesby could only find it by tracing the line back from the leader.

'Unless,' he said, 'the trout have much better eyes than mine, they won't see this.'

'They have different eyes than you – and better in some ways. Trout can see ultraviolet light and we can't.'

'What about colours?'

'In bright light their colour vision is excellent. In poor light, trout only see black and white.'

'You ought to be a science professor,' said Catesby.

'I used to be, but the money wasn't good enough to pay for my fishing expeditions. Do you need some help?'

Catesby was having difficulty threading the tippet through the eye of the trout fly hook. 'If you hold a magnifying glass over it I think I can manage.'

'No problem, my friend.'

As Catesby threaded the line, he looked at the veins on the back of the Frenchman's hand, which was only a few inches from his own face. He tried not to remember that it was his job to stop the blood from flowing in those veins. Killing was much easier when the target was anonymous. Catesby attached the fly with a blood knot.

'Good,' said the Frenchman. 'Are we ready for the trout?'

'It's either them or us,' said Catesby with a bleak smile.

The water felt cool on the legs even through the waders. The flow of the river was like an electric current. Catesby felt connected to the snow-capped mountains and the condors that hovered over them. The river was about fifty feet wide – just beyond Catesby's best fly-casting ability. The opposite bank was a steep rock wall.

The Frenchman nodded at the cliff face. 'There are deep

pools over there. The deepest are a metre and a half deep. So be careful. I suggest we start further up and work our way down.'

'I'll follow you.'

'We'll take turns fishing downstream of each other.'

Catesby nodded. It fitted in with his plan. He would take out the Frenchman at the end of the day when he was on the downstream leg. Catesby watched the Frenchman as he peeled off line and began his first cast. The line made perfect loops as he flexed his rod with the easy grace of a Javanese dancer. In contrast, Catesby's casting was nervous and too quick.

It wasn't long before Catesby spotted a trout poised in the water with his nose facing upstream. Catesby made a clumsy cast that fell short of the fish. Then another one, which presented the fly directly in front of the trout – who ignored the offering with regal disdain. Catesby made several more casts: some letting the fly drift downstream towards the trout; others across him and twitching tantalisingly past his eyes. Catesby wondered if the trout embraced the spirit of the proud pre-Colombian Tehuelche people and regarded the fly as just another Spanish trick. The previous evening the Frenchman, who was incurably professorial, had given Catesby a little lecture on the history of Patagonia. In the Mapuche language Tehuelche translated as 'Fierce People'. 'If you are so fierce,' said Catesby aloud, 'why don't you attack the bleeding fly?' He then put his hand over his mouth and hoped the Frenchman hadn't heard him speaking English.

Meanwhile, the Frenchman was having better luck. Within the first hour he had landed two brown trout. Catesby looked on with pleasure as the Frenchman battled with the first fish, but stared at him in annoyance when he hooked a second fifteen minutes later. The Frenchman calmly let the fish run and fight until it was tired enough to bring to the net without breaking the tippet. Once netted, he dispatched the trout with two blows from the priest, which echoed hollow through the valley. Catesby had to remind himself not to call the club *un prêtre*; the French simply called the tool of dispatch *une matraque* – a gendarme's cosh.

The Frenchman put the second trout in his creel and waded downstream towards Catesby. 'Shall we go down further and swap positions?' said the Frenchman. 'I seem to be having all the luck.'

'I wouldn't call it luck.'

The new beat was slower-flowing and willow trees shaded the banks. Now it was Catesby's turn. He had a strike on the third cast at the beginning of a slow enticing return. The take was hard and solid and Catesby gave the fish plenty of line without allowing it to go slack completely. The most breathtaking moment was when the trout left the water in a tail-standing leap – madly shaking its head to get rid of the hook. For that aerial second, the line was slack and Catesby thought he had lost him – but it soon went firm again as the fish headed deep. The problem now was an overhanging willow tree with dead, broken branches trailing in the water. Catesby saw what the trout had in mind. He needed to stop him from getting into the shelter of the willow. Catesby overreacted and pulled too hard – and suddenly the line was slack. There was a final flash of the trout's body as he headed for freedom. Catesby retrieved the line and was relieved to see that the Blue Dun fly was still attached. He didn't like the idea of the trout spending the rest of his days with a fly hanging from his lip like the butt end of a gangster's cigarette.

'Bad luck,' shouted the Frenchman from upstream.

The morning continued with more bad luck for Catesby who had two strikes from fish which failed to get hooked, but good fortune for the Frenchman who added two more wild Patagonian brown trout to his bag. They eventually stopped for lunch in the shade of an araucaria tree. Their hostess at the *estancia* had packed them steak and avocado sandwiches seasoned with chimichurri sauce, a Mediterranean tomato concoction with a hint of hot chilli. There was also a bottle of Malbec. The Frenchman uncorked the wine and the echo resounded over the river valley. They clinked glasses and said *santé*.

'What are we going to do with all those fish?' said Catesby nodding towards the Frenchman's creel, which was packed with ice to keep the catch fresh.

'Madame Lynch will cook fillets for us tonight and then she will smoke the others. She keeps most of them for her family and guests, but she sends me some in the post. You know about her famous cousin?'

'No, but her name suggests an Irish connection.'

The Frenchman smiled. 'Surely, you have heard of Ernesto Guevara Lynch, better known as Che?'

Catesby wasn't immune to name-dropping, but this wasn't the time to brag about having actually met Che Guevara. It happened when he was sent to Havana as an undercover negotiator during the Cuban Missile Crisis. And now it was Catesby's job to try to help avoid another pointless war. The thought suddenly hardened his resolve about what he had to do. Catesby remembered a conversation that he had had with Che about his executing a traitor during the revolution. He hadn't pulled the trigger with bitterness or regret, but with the calm necessity of love.

The Frenchman topped up Catesby's wine glass.

'Thank you,' said Catesby. 'Do you suppose Che ever fished this river?'

'He did, as a young boy with this father.'

Catesby felt the ghost of Che wrapping around him and whispering, *Las Malvinas son Argentinas*. He brushed away Che's ghost.

They finished lunch and, as the Frenchman leaned over the riverbank to rinse his wine glass, Catesby looked at the back of his victim's neck and wondered if this was the time to do it. But something stopped him – he wanted to continue fishing. Once again, Catesby took the downstream beat.

The wine and food seemed to have improved Catesby's casting. He was sure that he was managing up to fifty feet. He noticed a place under overhanging willows that had a lot of activity: trout jumping and swirls of water. It dawned on him that lurking under tree branches was a good place for trout to hang out; insects obviously fell from the tree into the water – but it did make casting difficult. It was important not to get your line hung up in the branches.

Catesby was wearing an expensive pair of polarised sunglasses, courtesy of HM's Government, and could see the trout beneath the surface. They were proud, arrogant little bastards – except they weren't little. He imagined the Andean brown trout as courtiers in a Medici palace: smooth, supercilious and cautious. Catesby decided that ten casts to tempt them would be enough; he would then move on. His first cast was an *oh fuck* that landed in the willow. He gave a gentle tug – realising that three pounds of pressure would break the tippet – and the Blue Dun mercifully detached itself. Lucky. The next three casts were too cautious and well short. Catesby imagined that the nearest trout shrugged with disgust: *fuck off, gringo, can't you do better than that?* Maybe the fish weren't Medici aristos, after all. For his next cast, Catesby tried a side arm technique that he had learned from a former Scottish ghillie: *slowly, slowly, don't cast, flick.* Catesby smiled: it was perfect, the leader and fly snaked under the overhanging willow branches. Pure *duende*! Catesby watched as the fly slowly disappeared beneath the surface. He waited; then gave a gentle twitch. There was a swirl of water. He continued to slowly retrieve: two inches at a time, then pausing.

Catesby knew instantly that it was a moment he would never forget. It was 'Zadok the Priest' at full pelt in Westminster Abbey. The trout that had struck the end of his line was more than a fish – he was an epic. Catesby's first sight of him was a dark ripple of back muscle breaking the surface crowned by a dorsal fin. He immediately knew that this proud beast needed all the line he could give him, but realised that any slack would allow him to shake free the fly. Catesby fed the line smoothly but firmly. The trout headed upstream like a steam train bent on destruction – then turned towards a sheer rock cliff that plunged vertically into the river. What Catesby saw next etched itself on the back of his eye. He thought it was impossible for something so big and so heavy to leap so high. For a frozen second the brilliant colours of the trout were silhouetted against the grey rock face. It was as if the fish were trying to scale the cliff while at the same time violently shaking its head to rid itself of the hook.

When the trout came back down Catesby was surprised that

it was still on the line. The fish had already stripped a hundred feet of fly line off the reel and was now taking yards of backing line. The trout then did something unexpected and extraordinary; it started running straight at Catesby. He tried frantically reeling in to stop the line from going slack, but then the trout changed direction and veered downstream. Once again, Catesby had to pay out line to cope with both the weight of the fish and the force of the current – always conscious of the fragile three-pound breaking strength of the tippet line. The race was now on. The trout had decided to do what Catesby feared most.

The river tumbled down a small cataract just downstream of where Catesby was standing. If the trout leapt over that, he would have to follow him. Catesby lifted his rod to apply some pressure to deter the trout, but this wasn't a fish that gave in.

As Catesby had feared, the fish headed towards the cataract as if seeking the distant sea from where his ancestors had come. He watched in awe as the trout leapt over the cataract in one massive bound. Catesby let out more backing line and began to follow. He wasn't going to lose this fish.

The cataract should have been easily negotiable for someone in waders with non-slip soles. Catesby made his way to where the tumbling water looked most smooth. The cataract was a drop of less than three feet. Catesby held the fly rod in his right hand and steadied himself on a rock with his left hand. He squatted with his backside in the water and gently lowered himself over the cataract. It wasn't easy. He was laden with a heavy rucksack and a fish pulling on the end of a nine-foot rod. He felt his right foot make contact with the riverbed and held himself steady against the strong current. *Good, made it*, he thought.

Catesby wasn't sure what happened. He didn't think he slipped, but whatever he had put his right foot on had given way. He shouted a resounding 'Oh fuck!' – and a second later he was flat on his back with a mountain river pouring into his waders. He was surprised at the force of the water and the way he found himself swept along as his waders filled like the ballast tanks on a submarine ordered to dive. He tried to find his footing, but the river was too deep. By now Catesby was beyond caring. Nothing else mattered – not even drowning. Catesby was not going to let go of the rod and the prize trout on the end of the line.

At one point, Catesby's head was under water – but he still held the fly rod above the surface. Instead of panicking, Catesby inwardly laughed. What an odd image. He must look like the Lady of the Lake holding Excalibur above her head. Another thought was an imaginary In Memoriam plaque inscribed: *William Catesby, OBE. Killed by an Enemy Trout in the Line of Duty.* Except it wasn't the line of duty, and Catesby frantically began to kick his waterlogged feet to find the riverbed.

Just as the current had undone him, it almost saved Catesby. The force of the water had swept him downstream to a place where the river was shallower. He felt his feet make contact with a gravelly bottom, but he couldn't stand upright. He heard a voice behind him saying, '*Attendez.*' He was pleased, but not surprised, that his guardian angel spoke French – but the hand that had grasped the back straps of his waders was firmly human. Catesby was relieved: not just that he wasn't going to lose his life, but that he still had the fish.

The Frenchman pulled Catesby backwards to the riverbank while Catesby continued to play the trout. For the first time he thought the fish had begun to tire – but the closer he got him to the bank, the more he began to fight. The battle took another ten minutes. Catesby knew that the fish was finally getting exhausted when he managed to get the trout's head above the water – they don't like breathing air. It wasn't easy to get him into the net – the trout was almost too big to fit. Once netted, Catesby dragged him up the bank and got out the priest to administer last rites. He thumped the trout on the head three times before it stopped twitching.

Catesby looked up at the Frenchman when he had finished whacking the fish. 'I didn't do that to put him out of his misery; I did it out of self-defence.'

The Frenchman looked on blankly.

Catesby took off his waders and sat on the bank to dry out in the strange sun of an autumn that came in April. He spent a lot of time staring at the fish, which weighed in at 2.6 kilos according to the Frenchman's scales – just under six pounds. It was the biggest fish that Catesby had ever caught by rod. The huge cod that he had hauled in long-lining with his uncle and cousin when a boy didn't count. Fishing in an open boat in the North Sea in the winter wasn't a sport, but a grim trade from which Catesby inherited a lifelong fascination with fish. As a boy, he had spent hours wandering around the Lowestoft fish market looking at the usual baskets of herring, cod and whiting – whose faces were as familiar as family. He was endlessly fascinated by the stranger creatures of the deep: gulpers, angels and hatchet fish. Catesby looked at the newly dead trout – still bright-eyed and radiating vivid colour – and then at the snow peaks of the Andes. A love of fish had brought him a long way. Catesby shifted his eyes to the Frenchman whose gracefully looping line reflected the sunlight in perfect casts. Catesby put his hand on the priest. Now was the time to kill. Cold and certain – get on with it.

Catesby pulled on his waders. He decided not to leave his rod behind; the Frenchman might become suspicious if he saw him approaching without it – and a club in his hand instead. Catesby entered the river – *el rio de la muerte* – and felt the current strong against his legs. The Frenchman's face was one of total concentration as he retrieved the Blue Dun fly. Something drew Catesby's eye towards the end of the line. There was a swirl of water next to the fly. The water suddenly broke and the Frenchman's rod bent. *Perfect,* thought Catesby, *when he bends over to net the trout – provided he doesn't lose it – I'll take him then. Hard, just above where the neck joins the skull. And then again if he doesn't fall over. And if he isn't unconscious, hold him under the water until he is. Fuck it if the post-mortem shows signs of foul play. Warning to the others.*

Catesby wrapped his hand around the priest. The Frenchman was playing a good fish, but nowhere near as big as his – as if that mattered. Catesby looked at the Frenchman's face. It was pure bliss in the late afternoon sun. He remembered the funeral of a colleague who had died of a massive heart attack on the golf course just after he shot a hole in one. There were worse ways to go.

'This trout is one hell of a fighter,' said the Frenchman, raising the tip of the rod. 'I'm trying to stop him from getting into the weeds and willow roots.'

Catesby looked on as the Frenchman tried to nudge the fish towards open water. The trout was being awkward. It was a similar situation to the one he had faced earlier, but the Frenchman was handling it with much more expertise.

'He doesn't want to die,' said the Frenchman smiling. 'He must have heard you killing his big cousin.'

There was now a dark shadow on the river. Catesby looked up and saw the condor. He must be hungry.

'Shit,' said the Frenchman. His rod had gone slack.

'You lost him?'

'It is difficult with so small a hook – unless they suck the fly into their gills, as your monster did.'

Catesby was annoyed that the Frenchman had diminished his skill in landing the big trout – and also that the Frenchman had failed to get his hole in one. The time was no longer perfect.

'It has been a wonderful day,' said the Frenchman, 'but tomorrow will be even better.' His face was a picture of contentment and happiness. This was what made him alive. His helping deadly juntas and others glue lethal weapons on to their airplanes was only a means to an end. 'Shall we be heading back?'

Catesby loosened his grip on the priest. The killing could wait until the morning. He would allow his prey another day of bliss.

Dinner at the Lynch *estancia* was a quiet affair. The Frenchman seemed preoccupied and had a book at his side. When Catesby leaned over to pour the wine, he stole a look at the title. It was a volume of *Histoire Naturelle* by the Comte de Buffon, an eighteenth-century aristocrat who helped lead the way to the theory of evolution.

'Are you fond of de Buffon?' said Catesby.

'It's not my book. I found it in Madame's library – I was taken by something inside the front cover.' The Frenchman passed the book over.

Catesby looked at the signature below the pasted-in ownership plate: *Este libro pertenece a* Ernesto Guevara Lynch. He ran his finger over the signature in an act of silent homage.

'That,' said the Frenchman with an ironic smile, 'must have been before he found out that property is theft.'

'Don't you agree?' said Catesby.

'A little bit of socialism isn't bad, but I think that Mitterrand is making a mess of things.'

Catesby shrugged and handed the book back. 'Maybe it's too soon to tell, but as a Belgian I can only comment from the sidelines.'

The Frenchman tapped the book. 'There's an interesting story about de Buffon. Do you know it?'

'I know that he hated cats – and loved dogs.'

'That made him very much a Frenchman of his time – and maybe even today.'

Catesby decided not to express his love of cats for fear it might reveal him as an Englishman operating undercover. As a grown man he had buried a much-loved cat using one of his best shirts as a shroud – and stocked the grave with several tins of cat food to make sure the cat didn't go hungry in the afterlife. Catesby had wept for hours afterwards. It was his most closely held secret – not something he wanted to come out in his annual vetting.

'Are you okay?' said the Frenchman, pouring more wine.

'Sorry,' lied Catesby, 'I was trying to remember something about de Buffon. Le Jardin des Plantes?'

'Correct. He was its first director.'

'It's one of my favourite places in Paris,' said Catesby, telling the truth. He particularly liked the bronze statue in the entrance of a near-naked hunter being eaten by an orangutan. The natural world strikes back. 'But,' continued Catesby, 'I'm still trying to think what this interesting story might be.'

'Actually, it happened after de Buffon was dead. His grave was looted during the revolution. They stripped the lead off his coffin and melted it down to make bullets to shoot other aristocrats. I'm sure Che would have approved.'

Catesby sipped his wine and smiled. The conversation was

taking an interesting turn – and they still hadn't had the main course. Not for the first time, Catesby realised that part of him wasn't British – and how he loved exploring the part that wasn't. It was a side of him that raised eyebrows of suspicion among his staid colleagues at SIS – but made him an excellent spy. The best spies weren't true believers in the cause, but slippery chameleons.

A bell rang in the background. 'I think,' said the Frenchman, 'that your brave trout is about to be served.'

'Madame Lynch is a superb cook.'

'I did,' said the Frenchman with a slight smile, 'give her some suggestions.'

'Was she receptive?'

'She was polite.'

Madame Lynch arrived with a steaming tray. Thick fillets of pan-fried trout with crispy skin topped mounds of fricassée potatoes with chorizo and peas.

'Thank you, madame,' said the Frenchman, 'it looks perfect.'

The Argentine woman gave a weary smile.

'Help yourself to the caper dressing,' said the Frenchman. 'It highlights the flavour and texture of the trout. Cooking a big wild fish like this one is almost like cooking a slab of pork. Having survived so many Patagonian winters in a cold river his firm meat is enclosed in thick layers of fat.'

It was a delicious meal. Catesby was glad he had let the Frenchman live for another day. Otherwise, he would be hot-footing it across the border to Santiago. They ate in silence and the Frenchman went to bed immediately after the *dulche de leche* and brandy.

Catesby slept badly. He woke at three in the morning and tossed and turned until six – when he finally fell asleep again. It was the usual pattern of insomnia that he had suffered from since he got back from the war. The cruel irony was that sleep always returned – soundly and blissfully – just before he had to get up to go to work.

Breakfast was again croissants and coffee. Catesby never drank coffee because it made him too hyper – but he was afraid to ask for tea because, like his love for cats, it might reveal him as an Englishman. The Frenchman seemed in a grumpy mood. He was uncommunicative and poring over a two-day old edition of *Clarín*, Argentina's biggest newspaper.

Catesby finished his breakfast and excused himself by saying that he wanted to load the car with his fishing gear. He also wanted to make sure he had everything he needed for the trip back to Chile. When he saw the car, Catesby stopped himself just in time from issuing a loud cover-breaking *fuck* and shouted *merde alors* instead. The Toyota had a flat tyre – not surprising considering the condition of the roads. He didn't like the scraped-knuckle business of changing tyres, but it wasn't rocket science – so he opened the boot to find the spare. Except there wasn't a spare. This time Catesby suppressed an entire litany of *fucks*. He immediately went into overdrive considering the options. Surely, Madame Lynch knew of local garages – but they were certainly miles away. Ideally, he would also like a spare tyre.

The Frenchman appeared. 'How is it going?'

Catesby explained the situation.

'No problem,' said the Frenchman, 'Madame Lynch can deal with it. I've also had car problems here. The local garage can do anything – they have to in a place as remote as this.'

Catesby gave a tired smile. 'Good.'

'I'll have a word with her.'

'Thanks.' Catesby watched the Frenchman go back into the house and restrained himself from giving the Toyota a good kicking.

A few minutes later the Frenchman reappeared. 'Madame Lynch is sure they can cope with it, but not now.'

'When then?'

'Next week. The garage is closed. The owner's son is getting married to a girl from Buenos Aires; they are away for the wedding.'

'We'll have to find another garage. I can't wait that long.'

The Frenchman turned and was about to go back to the house.

'But,' said Catesby, 'I don't want to miss another day's fishing. Could we go in your car instead?'

The Frenchman smiled. 'No problem. I was going to suggest that myself. I'll start loading my things – and tell Madame to get on with finding another garage.'

Catesby's mind was now devising Plan B. This time no messing about. As soon as they parked the car near the river, he would kill the Frenchman. No time to hike to the river and make it look like an accident. He would drive the Frenchman's car to a town where he could get a bus or a plane to Chile – there were no trains. It was too risky driving the Frenchman's car across the border. The Argentine border guards would be suspicious about him driving a car that belonged to someone else – particularly when they found out that the car's owner was an engineer who was helping the Argentine military attach Exocets to Super Étendards. As escape and evasion ops went, this wouldn't be difficult to pull off.

The Frenchman's car was a large 4×4 and much better suited for Patagonia than the car Catesby had rented. He loaded his gear into it and hoped there was an owner's manual in the glove box. Catesby realised that the dead Frenchman wouldn't be much use at explaining how to deal with the car's lights and indicators.

They drove to the river in silence; Catesby observing the Frenchman out of the corner of his eye and hardening himself for the task. From time to time Catesby turned his eyes to the sky hoping to see the condor again – but it wasn't there. After half an hour the Frenchman broke the awkward silence. 'We'll turn off here,' he said. 'It will be good to work a lower part of the river.'

'Fine.'

'We can get a lot closer to the river in this car.'

Catesby watched carefully as the Frenchman shifted the car into four-wheel drive. He would need to know how to get it back again for normal driving. It had turned into a very bumpy off-road ride. Catesby looked at the countryside: rough, dry and barren. He wouldn't need to hide the body: no one else was likely to come this way.

The Frenchman stopped the car. They were in the middle of

nowhere – except for one lonely araucaria tree. 'This is as far as we're going.'

'How near is the river?'

'You're not going to the river.'

Immediately, Catesby cursed himself for his lack of professionalism and alertness. He hadn't read the signals. If he had been quick enough and observant enough, he would have been able to grab the gun. The Frenchman was right-handed, but being a left-hand drive car he had to reach for the pistol, hidden in the driver's door storage space, with his left hand. A young, alert Catesby would have had grabbed the gun in that moment of awkwardness. But the pistol was now firmly in both the Frenchman's hands and pointed at Catesby's temple.

Catesby closed his eyes and waited for the split second of blinding pain – which would soon vanish into oblivion. On the other hand, amateurs often botched head shots leaving their victims to face a lifetime of disability. Catesby waited three more seconds and then opened his eyes. The Frenchman still hadn't pulled the trigger – which was probably good news. The reprieve might, however, be a temporary one, because the Frenchman wanted information or something else before he pulled the trigger.

'Get out of the car and lie flat on your face. Don't try to run because I am an excellent shot – and, in the unlikelihood that I did miss you, the Argentine Army would hunt you down like a rabid dog. What happens to you next would not be pretty.'

Catesby sensed a negotiation was about to begin and did as he was told – but as soon as he was lying flat, a cold fear shuddered his body. Was he about to be raped? Very unlikely. He wasn't pretty enough – and he was sure that the Frenchman's only vices were fly fishing and food.

'Put your hands behind your back.'

Catesby did so and felt rope loops, which must have been pre-prepared, slide around his wrists and get tightened.

'I'm pleased that you didn't resist. I would have had to shoot you. Now that you're tied up we can have a sensible conversation. You can get up if you like.'

The best Catesby could do was roll on his side so he could face the Frenchman.

'Are you comfortable?'

'More comfortable than if you had shot me.'

'Good. Wait there while I set up the radio.'

Catesby watched as the Frenchman stretched an improvised antenna from the 4×4 to the lonely araucaria tree. He took the radio out of a case and set it up in the rear storage area of the car. Catesby could tell from its matte-black colour and shape – the corners stuck up like four pointy ears – that it was a TAR-224A. It was American-made and standard issue for CIA and US Special Forces units, but several NATO countries also used the TAR-224A. It was a little surprising that the Frenchman had got his hands on one, but not impossible.

The Frenchman made sure the radio was operational and turned to Catesby. 'How much are you worth?'

'Dead or alive?'

'Let's try alive first.'

'If you wanted a decent price you'd have to add a sweetener.'

'Let's just try with your life first. Who should I contact to do the deal?'

'Who do you think I am?'

'You are a British intelligence officer who was sent to kill me.'

'Why do you think that?'

The Frenchman smiled. 'You ask too many questions. Who should I talk to if you want to stay alive?'

'Can you do a phone patch?' Catesby was referring to the procedure by which a radio transmitter was connected to a telephone link.

'Easily.'

'I suggest you contact my wife.'

'Is she rich?'

Catesby laughed. 'If she was, she'd spend the money on a new kitchen rather than rescue me.'

'I think saving your life is going to cost a lot more than a new kitchen – so why do you think she can help even if she wanted to?'

Catesby thought it best not to mention that his wife worked

for MI5. One blown cover was enough. 'She can contact my boss and verify that it is me who is being held hostage.'

'You're not a hostage. You're a bargaining chip.'

Catesby didn't think there was a difference, but wasn't going to argue.

The Frenchman stared at Catesby. 'Your boss is head of British secret intelligence. Why don't you give me his number instead?'

'Two reasons. One: I don't remember it. Two: you would never get through if I did.'

'You're lying. They wouldn't have sent you on this mission without emergency contact numbers and contingency plans.'

The Frenchman was right, but a part of Catesby was still the well-trained and devoted intelligence officer who would rather take a bullet than reveal top-secret procedures. He stayed silent. The Frenchman turned to the radio and began tapping a message in Morse.

Catesby's Morse was too rusty to pick up the gist of the message, but he was surprised that the Frenchman had an accomplice. He closed his eyes – the rough Patagonian earth was hurting his shoulder – and tried to piece things together. He went back over his meeting with the head of French intelligence in Paris. He remembered the spy chief telling him that he had an informer in the Dassault-Breguet team in Argentina. A piece clicked into place. Somehow the informer had twigged that British intelligence were sending someone to Argentina on a covert mission to deal with the team or its leader. Had, Catesby wondered, the head of French intelligence betrayed him? Such betrayals were not unknown. But more pertinently, was the French fisherman working together with the informer? Once again, Catesby remembered MICE. The acronym was drilled into the mind of every trainee intelligence officer. MICE represented the four ways you recruit an agent: money, ideology, coercion and excitement – but the best by far was money. Agents motivated by ideology and excitement were often unpredictable – and sometimes totally off-the-wall. Coercion didn't always work either: sometimes an agent turned brave or ran away or got leaned on by someone harder. But money was golden. Provided you paid the top whack, your agent was sweet and reliable. And that was the beauty of the arms trade. The absence of national allegiances, idealism, principles, personal or corporate loyalty was, in a way, refreshing. Greed was reliable.

The Frenchman called over to Catesby. 'What's your wife's phone number?'

Catesby gave it to him.

'Is that a home or an office phone?'

'It's her home phone.'

'It doesn't sound like you live together. Did she get fed up with your lies?'

'On the contrary, she got fed up with my telling the truth.'

'It often happens that way.'

Catesby laughed. 'Are you offering a marriage counselling service?'

'Men who are passionate about fly fishing do not always make the best husbands.'

'Why don't you ring up Frances and ask her?'

'Your wife and I will have more important things to discuss.' The Frenchman paused and looked at Catesby. 'What if she isn't home?'

'I'll think of something else.'

The Frenchman turned away and began to do things with the radio. Catesby could see that the long antenna turned the TAR-224A into an expensive ham radio. Catesby knew that the radio could send secure Morse messages using a burster device, but wasn't sure it had a voice scrambler. He needed to go on a refresher course. Even if an eavesdropper couldn't decipher the messages, they would know that someone was sending messages from a clandestine radio receiver – and would be able to pinpoint its location. Catesby began to sweat. He was about to express his fears of detection to the Frenchman, but then decided to keep quiet. If he convinced the Frenchman that it was dangerous to use the radio, the logical next step would be to forget about a ransom and shoot him.

'The phone is ringing,' said the Frenchman, 'but no one is answering.'

'She might be in the shower or on the toilet.'

'I thought that Englishwomen didn't shit.'

'You know all our secrets.' But the secret Catesby was most worried about was transmission security. Fortunately, SIGINT – signals intelligence – didn't seem to be Argentina's strong suit. And their com security wasn't good either. GCHQ could read most of their messages.

'Someone's answered,' said the Frenchman passing the handset over, 'you take it.'

Catesby took the handset. It was Frances. She was saying, 'Hello, hello, hello. Who is this?' The problem now was getting her to stop talking. Phone patches are radio transmissions. Only one person can talk at a time. Catesby pushed the press-to-talk button which would elicit loud static in his wife's London phone. He knew that Frances was enough of a professional to twig what was happening.

'Can you hear me? Over,' said Catesby.

'I read you five by. Over.'

Five by, short for five by five, meant loud and clear. He realised that the Frenchman and anyone else listening would recognise his wife as a professional operative.

'I'm making this call under duress,' Catesby laughed. 'I'm in a spot of bother. Over.'

'You sound drunk, William – and it's not even noon. You shouldn't be playing games with radio sets. Over.'

Frances didn't know that he was out of the country. She probably thought he was still in London and cracking up under stress. He tried to sound calm and rational. 'No, I'm sober and not playing a game. You need to get in touch with Colin – and if you can't contact him, try Chris. Believe me, this is urgent. Over.'

Her voice still sounded sceptical. 'What should I say when I do make contact? Over.'

'I'm not sure.' Out of the corner of his eye Catesby could see the Frenchman gesturing for the handset. 'I'm passing you to someone who can give you more information.'

'Allo, 'ave you got zomzing to write. Ovair?'

Catesby groaned. The Frenchman spoke English with what Frances called a *zenk 'eaven for leedle girls* voice from the song made famous by Maurice Chevalier. The Frenchman sounded like an English comedian taking the piss out of a French accent. Catesby feared that his wife would think he was playing a silly practical joke. He didn't hear her reply, but the Frenchman gave Catesby a confused look. Perhaps she had told him to fuck off and he hadn't understood.

'I think,' said Catesby, 'it might be better if you speak to my wife in French. She is fluent.' It wasn't true. Frances spoke French with a strong *rosbif* accent that was just as comic to French ears as the Frenchman's accent to English ones.

The Frenchman nodded to Catesby and continued the conversation in his own language. From what followed, it seemed that Frances was now convinced that she was talking to the real thing. The Frenchman's next words would not have been as convincing or chilling in his accented English: '*Si cent mille dollars américains sont pas dans ...* If one hundred thousand US dollars are not in my bank account by noon, your husband will be dead.'

Catesby knew that his life was hanging by a thread. Her Majesty's Government did not pay ransoms – and, even if they did, Catesby wasn't sure that the number crunchers would agree that he was worth a hundred thousand bucks. Another part of the rational decision-making was: if they did pay up, what assurance was there that they would get Catesby back alive? It happened everyday in the NHS with expensive drugs and ops: would the patient survive and was he worth it? It was a decision in which Catesby's voice counted for nothing.

The Frenchman had walked away to the other side of the 4×4. He was almost whispering and Catesby couldn't make out what he was saying. The Frenchman finally went silent and put down the handset. 'This isn't working,' he said.

'What isn't?'

'I'm not sure your wife understood what I was saying.'

'Perhaps I can help.'

'No, this was all a mistake. I shouldn't have threatened to

shoot you. I should have threatened to turn you over to the Argentine security services – which is what I'm going to do now. That would be easier than explaining your disappearance to Madame Lynch. The officers from the Secretariat of State Intelligence will give a much better explanation and Madame Lynch, wanting a quiet life, will not question it.'

'Che will be rolling in his grave.'

'She's only related to him by marriage – and Señor Lynch died years ago in a riding accident.'

Catesby wondered how the Argentines would deal with him – and whether a bullet would have been better. Meanwhile, his bladder was bursting. 'I need to pee.'

'I'm not going to hold it for you. You'll just have to wet yourself.'

Catesby let go and watched the stain spreading across the crotch of his trousers. How he wished he had killed the Frenchman when he had the chance. Meanwhile, the Frenchman was back on the radio and talking in hushed tones. Catesby couldn't make out the words – or even the language. If it was Spanish, he was toast. Catesby closed his eyes and tried to blot out the world.

He must have fallen asleep, for he felt the Frenchman shaking his shoulder. Catesby opened his eyes.

'Good,' the Frenchman said, 'you're still alive.'

'Is that good for me or you?'

'Both of us, I hope. Your wife has put me in contact with someone who wants to do a deal – but they are not being easy. They are driving a hard bargain.'

'Can I talk to them?'

'Not now.'

The negotiating was fraught and took nearly four hours. Catesby kept staring at the sky, expecting an Argentine helicopter to swoop down at any moment. Surely, the lengthy radio transmissions must have been picked up. Once again, Catesby prayed that Argentine SIGINT was as poor as reported.

In the end, it wasn't saving Catesby's life that swung the deal – he was an expendable pawn – but getting the Frenchman to work for British intelligence. The first step was putting fifty thousand in US dollars into a numbered Swiss account and laundering another fifty into a French account in the Frenchman's own name. But they were only the first payments. The Frenchman wanted another hundred thousand as a golden hello for becoming a British spy – half of which would be paid into the Swiss account before the Frenchman boarded a flight out of South America to London. And all that was cash on the table before the new agent even began to blab. He also expected 'performance bonus payments' for the intelligence he provided – and it was obvious that anything less than six figures would be sniffed at.

The biggest problem was not the money. The few hundred thousand the Frenchman was costing the British taxpayer was chickenfeed compared to the cost of sending the Task Force south. The difficult bit was that he wanted more than money. He wanted things that money couldn't buy – and that many of the filthy rich had tried and failed to buy. The Frenchman wanted a one-mile two-bank beat on the River Test in Hampshire – the most exclusive chalk stream fly fishing in the world – and he wanted it on the Bossington Estate. He knew his stuff.

'Have you ever fished there?' said the Frenchman.

Catesby shook his head. 'If the trout in that stream could speak English, they wouldn't speak to me.'

'Maybe they speak French.'

'If they do, it would be eleventh-century Norman French.'

'I think I can manage.'

'Would you like a Chris Clemes split cane fly rod made from selected Tonkin bamboo?'

'Thank you, but I've already got two.'

The Frenchman turned back to the radio and continued the negotiations, most of which were carried out in French. The DG was an old Far East hand and far from fluent in French. Catesby assumed they were using an interpreter-translator and hoped that the intermediary was security cleared for such a sensitive task. But the annoying thing was that fly fishing was taking up so much time and effort. Doubled agents with simpler tastes were so much easier. Catesby had helped run Oleg Penkovsky, the most prized defector of his time. Penkovsky was happy with booze, nightclubs and prostitutes – and dressing up for photo sessions in the uniform of a British Army colonel to pledge his allegiance to the Queen. Thank god he had never demanded fishing rights.

The negotiations seemed to have switched from English chalk streams to Scottish salmon rivers. Catesby could imagine the look of frustration on the DG's face and the head-shaking of those around him. During a lull, the Frenchman put down the handset and looked at Catesby. 'Have you ever fished in Scotland?'

'I can't afford it,' said Catesby.

'I believe the Junction Pool on the Tweed is the best beat?'

Catesby nodded. It was, if anything, even more exclusive than the River Test.

'Good.'

'I suppose,' said Catesby, 'that you might want Alec Douglas-Home as your ghillie?'

'It would be nice to make the acquaintance of your ex-Prime Minister – and I am sure he is security cleared to discuss sensitive matters.'

Catesby smiled. The Frenchman and his wife had a lot in common. Neither ever picked up his irony or even his sarcasm.

The ex-filtration from Argentina wasn't an easy one. Catesby was sure that crossing the border by car would be too dangerous. Two foreigners in a 4×4 crossing over to Chile at a remote Andean border post in time of war would arouse suspicion and lead to interrogation and phone calls. Catesby wanted to leave by air. The nearest airport – San Carlos de Bariloche – was 150 miles away and there were two weekly flights direct to Santiago in Chile. The disadvantage was that passengers on such a flight were more likely to be under scrutiny, Chile not being Argentina's best friend. The advantage was that it was the quickest way out of Argentina – and Catesby didn't want to hang around.

The drive south to Bariloche along Ruta 40 – sometimes signposted as Ruta de los Siete Lagos, Route of the Seven Lakes – was the most beautiful car ride that Catesby had ever experienced. The landscape was the English Lake District re-scripted and filmed by a Hollywood mogul.

The first sign that there was trouble up ahead was a line of traffic cones in the middle of the road preventing overtaking. The Frenchman slowed down as if he knew what to expect. Catesby looked at him.

'*Les flics*,' said the Frenchman.

The police were wearing orange reflective bibs and directing cars to the side of the road. It was, however, a very beautiful place to have a police checkpoint. The clear blue waters of Nahuel Huapi, the largest of the seven lakes, lapped a pure white beach just below the road and sparkled in the sun.

'It looks inviting, but is a very dangerous place for a swim,' said the Frenchman.

'Why is it dangerous for swimming?' said Catesby.

'Too cold. The surface temperature is only five or six degrees Celsius. Hypothermia.'

Two cops finished with the car in front. One of them had a long braided ponytail, hanging from behind a green baseball cap. Catesby assumed it was a woman, but when the cop turned he had a black beard. The two police approached the car. The other cop spoke to the Frenchman, '*Seguro*.' He wanted the car's insurance documents. The Frenchman had anticipated that and had the papers ready. Ponytail stared at Catesby and said, '*De dónde vienes?*'

Catesby began to explain where they had come from in Spanish. Hearing a foreign accent, ponytail shifted into English – as all foreigners speak English. Catesby could see that ponytail was the sharper and more lethal of the two cops – and he suddenly began to sweat: *had he spoken Spanish with what might have sounded, to the cop's ears, like an English accent*? If so, what would the cop think when he saw that Catesby was carrying a Belgian passport?

'A very beautiful place,' continued ponytail in pretty good English, 'and what were you doing there?'

'Fly fishing for ze trout,' said Catesby, trying to speak English like Jacques Brel used to. He had to smile. The situation was ridiculous as well as dangerous.

'And how good was the fishing?'

Just as Catesby began to answer, the other cop asked for their passports. They handed them over. What happened next was bizarre. As the two policemen examined the passports, they began to talk between themselves in a language that wasn't Spanish. Catesby thought they were speaking an indigenous tongue. On the other hand, the policemen bore no resemblance at all to the indigenous people he had encountered. And then the penny didn't so much drop, as cartwheel into the outer realms of the surreal. The two cops were speaking Welsh. Catesby stared blankly at the nearest mountain and thought of Snowden. The tragic implications sunk in. How many centuries had passed since Welsh-speaking soldiers had faced each other on the field of battle? The thought of the sons of Welsh gauchos and the sons of Welsh miners charging each other with fixed bayonets made him sick. *We must*, Catesby prayed, *stop this war.*

Ponytail looked closely at Catesby and handed him back his passport. 'So you're Belgian, I was trying to place your accent.'

'Do you know Jacques Brel?' said the other cop.

Catesby squirmed. Had he overdone the fake accent? What the hell. 'I love Jacques Brel. Would you like me to sing *Ne Me Quitte Pas*? I know all the words.'

'If you do, I will retaliate with Tom Jones.'

'Never heard of him,' said Catesby laying on the accent.

Ponytail smiled and waved them on.

'We were lucky,' said the Frenchman as he drove away, 'they were provincial police. The ones to watch out for are the PFA, the Policía Federal Argentina, especially Group Scorpion – they wear green berets and military gear.'

The rest of the drive to the airport at San Carlos de Bariloche passed without incident. It was obvious to Catesby that the area was a playground for prosperous Argentines. The snow-capped Andes rose in the near distance and the air was as clear and intoxicating as champagne. There were lots of tanned, healthy-looking types carrying mountain climbing equipment

– professionals from BA whose holiday fun wouldn't be interrupted by a bit of nastiness in the South Atlantic.

'Do you ski?' said the Frenchman.

'I hate winter sports,' said Catesby. 'I'd rather die in the line of duty.'

'This is South America's best place for skiing. Several of my team will be coming here in the winter.' The Frenchman gave a grim smile. 'If your government pays up, I can give you their details – and I am sure you can arrange a convenient avalanche.'

'I don't think the Falklands mess will last until the winter.'

The Frenchman nodded. 'The Argentines are playing for time. They think it is impossible for the British to retake the islands in a South Atlantic winter.'

The remark made Catesby wonder how close the Frenchman had been to his Argentine hosts. He looked at the engineer, who was just as duplicitous as his hand-tied trout flies. 'How, by the way,' said Catesby, 'did you become suspicious of me?'

'How much are you willing to pay for that information?'

'A few days' fishing on a Norfolk chalk stream?'

'Agreed. The Argentines were very upset and disappointed that Mitterrand decided to back Thatcher. The Argentine intelligence service immediately became concerned that the French government would take action against me and my team – and issued a number of warnings. I thought it unlikely, but when you turned up I did consider the possibility that you might be a French intelligence officer posing as a Belgian art dealer. In which case, there was little to worry about. Threats and deals, yes. But a danger to my life, no.' The Frenchman smiled. 'But you gave yourself away.'

'How?'

'When you slipped and fell in the trout stream, you shouted *fuck*. There is no word more unmistakably Anglo-Saxon.'

'I'm not sure that's worth even a single day on a chalk stream.'

'What else would you like to know?'

'How did you get that TAR radio?'

'And what a marvellous piece of technology. The company supplied us with two of them.'

'And how did your company get them?'

'Ah, that is secret. But it's obvious, isn't it?'

'If it's so obvious, you can tell me.'

The Frenchman continued. 'They were supplied by a French government agency. They wanted us to have secure communication with Paris during our deployment.'

Catesby nodded. France's biggest companies and the French state were separated by the most permeable of membranes. The people at the top of both were all products of the same system: École polytechnique followed by a final brush and polish at École nationale d'administration. The French establishment operated at several different levels – and Mitterrand's words of support were only one level.

The airport reception building, in keeping with the winter sports theme, looked like a giant Swiss skiing chalet, but unlike a Swiss resort, was swarming with PFA in paramilitary uniforms carrying FMK-3 submachine guns. Catesby recognised the weapon from an exceptionally tedious briefing about Argentine military hardware. The MoD boffin was particularly impressed because the FMK-3 was a rare weapon of entirely Argentine origin – and hoped that the intelligence services could get their hands on one to test its effectiveness. No one outside the trade, thought Catesby, has any idea how boring the minutiae of espionage can be – but Catesby found it difficult to take his eyes off the FMK-3. The policeman carrying it must have felt Catesby's stare and glared back at him. For a second, he thought the cop was going to swagger over and ask for his ID.

'We're still in time for the flight to Santiago,' said the Frenchman.

'Shhh,' said Catesby. He needed a drink, but knew a strong coffee would be a better idea. Drinking too much alcohol was a serious faux pas in Argentina. Being called a *borracho*, a drunk, was the ultimate social insult – and yet, Galtieri, the head of the Junta, was an alcoholic. The most important lesson that Catesby had learned in thirty years as an intelligence officer was that people and societies were full of contradictions.

'Is something wrong?' said the Frenchman.

Catesby watched the policeman fondle his FMK-3 and walk towards the Santiago ticket queue where he joined other PFA officers. 'We're not going to Santiago,' said Catesby. 'I fancy a double brandy instead.'

The Frenchman shrugged. 'I wouldn't mind going fishing again.'

Catesby looked at the departures board. 'Let's take an internal flight to BA – and plan our next move from there.'

It was obvious to Catesby that the flights to Ezeiza, Buenos Aires' biggest airport, were the most popular and the least scrutinised.

The Frenchman looked at Catesby. 'You know about the massacre?'

'What massacre?'

'It happened nine years ago. Ezeiza was where Juan Perón landed when he returned from exile. He was greeted by more than three million young left-wing Peronistas in a mood of utter euphoria – and then snipers from the right wing of the Peronist party opened fire on the crowd. More than four hundred were killed and wounded.'

It wasn't, thought Catesby, a time for a political discussion – but violence almost always began from the right wing. But when you said this, the rightists shouted you down. There was, however, one thing on which they all agreed – left, right, Peronist and Junta – the Falklands belonged to Argentina. And it wasn't something you could explain to Downing Street.

They bought tickets separately so that they didn't appear to be travelling together. When they arrived at Ezeiza it was midnight. The next flight out of the country was to Rio at 1 a.m. – so Rio it was. The airport departure lounges weren't crowded, but they weren't deserted either. There were a number of police about, but they seemed sleepy and more off guard than the ones at San Carlos de Bariloche. Catesby and the Frenchman kept an eye on each other, but avoided seeming best pals. Catesby yawned and looked at his watch: it was time for a double brandy.

They went through customs and boarded the flight to Rio

without incident. They were greeted at Galeão International Airport by staff and security from the British Embassy in Rio, who had worked out their likely itinerary options and bundled them on a flight to Heathrow with a chunky minder.

Near Iken, Suffolk: Tuesday, 20 April 1982

The safe house for the Frenchman's debriefing was in a remote wooded area between Aldeburgh and Orford. It was also used for safe-house 'interrogations', which were a lot noisier. The house had previously been owned by a trombonist, who was married to a timpani player who often invited Aldeburgh Festival musicians to stay and practise – so the lack of neighbours had a long history of usefulness. The safe house was well stocked with fly-tying equipment – as well as food and fine wine. When not being debriefed or working in the kitchen – the Frenchman preferred his own cooking to SIS catering – he spent a lot of time studying images of sand eels and other sea bass prey. The Frenchman was trying to devise feather and leather versions that he could cast for sea bass in the Ore and the Alde. The SIS was indulgent, for the Frenchman's intelligence info was like a vintage bottle of priceless Château Lafite. You needed to decant it slowly and carefully two days before drinking – and then savour each drop while taking notes.

Catesby gave the colonel from HUMINT a lift to the safe house; he had been chosen as one of the MoD debriefers. Catesby was driving his private car: a purple 1969 Peugeot 404 estate that already had 125,000 miles on the clock when the clock stopped working two years previously.

'Great choice of cover,' said the colonel. 'Who would ever guess a car like this was transporting two senior intelligence officers to a vital top-secret debrief in the wilds of Suffolk. Did you get this piece of shit from Five's disguise department?'

Catesby smiled. 'No, it's mine. I bought it from an old dear in Norfolk after she put her husband in a home. It's a great car – never had any trouble with it.'

'I shouldn't mock. It's probably newer than most of our British Army Land Rovers. By the way, last time I visited our pigeon-eating friend, there were some Spanish-speaking tourists taking photos.'

'Of the pelican?'

'Yes, but it makes you paranoid. In any case, I'm fed up.'

'Why?' said Catesby.

'I wish that I was with the Task Force. I did volunteer.'

'You should have done what I did when I signed up in '42. They originally wanted to put me in the Intelligence Corps. But I didn't want to spend the war in London – so I fucked up the IQ test on purpose and they put me in the infantry.' Catesby smiled as they crossed the bridge over the Deben. They were now in darkest deepest Suffolk.

'And speaking of brains,' said the colonel, 'how did Thatcher ever get into Oxford?'

'Only by accident. Oxford turned her down, but another candidate dropped out so they offered her the place instead.'

The colonel looked suspicious. 'How do you know these things?'

Catesby tapped his nose. 'SIS know everything. I've also seen the docs on her being rejected for a job at ICI. It was obvious that the interviewing panel thought she was mad.'

'It sounds like the knives are out to get her.'

Catesby smiled. He loved Whitehall gossip. 'And what do you know?'

The colonel suddenly seemed reticent. 'The toffs find her difficult.'

'But you're a toff too.'

'Hardly, minor public school and an unfashionable regiment. My wife thinks I'm common.'

'Who finds her difficult?' said Catesby.

'My wife?'

'No, Thatcher.'

'I don't want to give you names.'

Catesby felt mildly irritated that an army officer below his own pay grade was playing the ultimate Whitehall insider. He wondered if the colonel had been part of the military's plans to replace Heath during the Three Day Week and later Harold Wilson. 'By the way, were you part of that military coup business?'

'No, but I know three people who were.'

'Who were they?'

The colonel rattled off three names, then added. 'But I'm sure you already knew.'

'I did.'

'I thought so.' The colonel smiled. 'Otherwise, I wouldn't have told you.'

'Are we now on the same side?'

'Which side is that?'

'Avoiding unnecessary war.'

'I've only seen Northern Ireland.'

'Bad enough,' said Catesby. He knew the colonel was understating what he had actually experienced.

'What,' said the colonel, 'was the worst thing in your war?'

Catesby saw a recurring image of Oradour-sur-Glane after the massacre. He was the only British officer to have seen the burned remains of the 642 victims of the SS atrocity – three-quarters of whom were women and children. 'I'd rather not say.'

'Sorry.'

'You mentioned,' said Catesby, 'that the toffs find her difficult.'

'You ought to recruit my wife to find out more. She's related to everyone – and knows all their secrets.'

'Any foreigners?'

'No, only British.'

'Then I'll have to pass her on to Five – except that I suspect she regards them as common too.'

'She does.'

Catesby frowned. 'The class system and its petty snobberies have poisoned our country.'

'Thatcher would agree. It's a tune she loves to play.'

'It's a false tune that rankles.'

The colonel smiled.

'We're going in circles. Who are these grandees that your wife knows who are slagging off the PM?'

'One is a very senior member of the government. I can't tell you who he is because he's related to my wife and she swore me to secrecy. The gentleman in question is the ultimate in decorum, calmness and genteel courtesy. But after a meeting in Thatcher's private office in Downing Street he said, "If I have any more trouble with this fucking stupid petit-bourgeois woman I'm going to resign."'

'I thought he said that on the way to the meeting.'

'Touché,' said the colonel.

'Her man-management skills – and there are only men in her cabinet – are non-existent.'

'Have you heard the latest about her and Mitterrand? In fact, that's one of the reasons why I've been sent – by the Secretary himself – to ask questions at this debrief.'

Catesby was concerned about how far out of the loop he appeared to be. A week away from London at a time like this meant you were no longer match fit. But he wasn't going to swallow his pride completely. 'Yes, I did hear about it. What do you think are the key points?'

'Obviously, Thatcher threatening to use nuclear weapons against Argentina if the French don't provide full cooperation.'

Catesby turned pale. 'I am sure the submarine commanders would refuse to obey orders.'

The colonel shook his head. 'The navy are strange – but I'm pretty sure the Americans would block access to the GPS satellites that we need for targeting. But the threat rattled Mitterrand.'

Britain's 'independent' nuclear deterrent was a myth, but apparently the French President didn't realise it. Catesby wanted to know more, but didn't want to give away how little he did know. 'For points of comparison, can you tell me what you've heard?'

'I was only briefed at all because they want me to question your French chap about the Exocet self-destruct codes.'

'Could you please start from the beginning?'

'Someone must have told Thatcher that Exocets have secret codes that either blow them up in mid-air or disable their guidance systems. It's a safety feature in case the Exocet accidentally homes in on the presidential palace instead of an enemy ship. So Thatcher – probably fortified by a whisky or three – rings up Paris and tells Mitterrand that unless he gives her those secret codes she might have to nuke Buenos Aires.'

'Fucking hell.'

'I know.'

'Did he give her the codes?'

'I don't know. If Mitterrand did so and it became known, it would obliterate French arms exports. Who's going to buy French weapons if the French can wreck them at the point of use?'

'So your job is to find out whether we can do it with the codes that we may or may not have?'

'That's it.'

'Good luck.'

The best thing about the debriefing was the secluded Suffolk location bursting with spring and birdsong. The second best thing was the Frenchman himself. Unlike Soviet defectors, who usually had big egos, he didn't need to be the centre of attention. The Frenchman, a perfect example of Enlightenment reason, was only interested in the money – and fishing rights. There was no preening, no posing – no wild claims – just a calm business-like approach to answering questions as accurately and truly as possible. If he didn't know, he said he didn't know.

One of Catesby's jobs at the interview was to act as an interpreter-translator. At times, however, he asked the Frenchman to answer in English to assure the non-French speakers that his translation wasn't putting a slant on things. The first good news to come out of the briefing was that the Argentines only had five AM38 Exocets, the air-launched version; the bad news was that the air-launched Exocets had already been married up to the Super Étendards and were already capable of being used.

'The problem at first,' said the Frenchman, 'was that the launch systems on three of the Exocets did not function. But we located what was wrong and solved the problem. We also developed a way of testing the missiles to see if all systems were functioning properly.' The Frenchman flashed a proud smile. 'Remember we are not missile specialists. None of us ever worked for Aérospatiale and learned all the secrets of the Exocet. We are Super Étendard experts. In other circumstances, our two companies would have worked together – but, nonetheless, we managed to discover the dark secrets of the Exocet.'

Catesby was impressed by the cool professionalism of the Frenchman, but could see that the others may have regarded him as the grinning spawn of Satan.

'We also,' continued the Frenchman, 'showed the Argentines how to carry out pre-launch checks to make sure everything is functioning to perfection. When you only have five of those precious missiles you don't want to waste one.'

An officer from naval intelligence gave the Frenchman a flinty-eyed stare before saying, 'Can you tell us anything about Argentina's deployment of MM38 Exocets?'

The Frenchman began to answer before Catesby could translate the question. 'The MM38 is the ship-launched version of the Exocet. You probably know more about Argentina's ship-to-ship missiles because you, Britain, supplied Argentina with the Type 42 destroyers on which they are deployed.'

The naval officer didn't blink. 'On which other ships are the MM38s deployed?'

The Frenchman spread his hands. 'I can't say for certain. I am an aircraft engineer.'

A member of the Foreign Office intel team, fastidiously groomed and lofty in manner, chimed in. 'Is it not possible to glue these ship-to-ship things to aircraft?'

There was an almost audible groan from everyone else in the room. It was an incredibly stupid question.

'The MM38,' said the Frenchman, 'is a very large and bulky missile that is more than twice the size of the air-launched Exocet. It is fired from a large ribbed weatherproof container that is mounted on ships. Totally impossible to adapt to a Super Étendard or any other attack aircraft.' The Frenchman seemed to realise that the FO type had made a fool of himself, and came to his aid. He raised a finger, 'Ahhh, but…'

'But what?' said Catesby wanting to move on.

'Our Argentine technicians have, however, succeeded in mounting the MM38 Exocet on the back of flatbed trucks – so the ship-to-ship Exocet could be used as a mobile land-based missile and hit British ships approaching the islands. Accomplishing this involved overcoming some very difficult engineering problems and also reprogramming computers. We were very impressed by the skill and ingenuity of the Argentines.'

The naval officer looked concerned and scribbled a note.

'May I say something about British attitudes?' said the Frenchman.

'Please do,' said Catesby. He sensed that the Frenchman was probably going to annoy many of his colleagues, but thought they needed to know a few home truths.

'I have a friend,' said the Frenchman, 'who is a very senior French diplomat.'

'His name, please,' said Catesby.

The Frenchman gave the diplomat's name. Catesby knew him slightly. The diplomat was not a big fan of 'les Anglo-Saxons'.

The Frenchman continued. 'My friend describes Britain as having the arrogance of a superpower, but without being a superpower. Arrogance leads to hubris, and hubris – as the Ancient Greeks well knew – leads to downfall.'

Catesby winked at his colleagues and translated the words with a hint of bored irony to appease those who hadn't picked up the French original. But the Frenchman's next words were ones that Catesby endorsed.

'Many of your countrymen have a deep contempt for the people of South America. You think the Argentines are baboons from an undeveloped country. Sure, they have economic and political problems – but in terms of engineering and technical skills the Argentines are first rate. The Argentines have been working with advanced planes and missiles for eight years. They have not been held back by lack of skill or knowledge, but by lack of equipment and resources.'

The most senior person present was Cecil Parkinson, Chairman of the Conservative Party and a Thatcher favourite, who was also a member of the War Cabinet. The party chairman had the perfect grooming of a very upmarket car salesman. Parkinson nodded sagely at the Frenchman's last words and added, 'So we must stop them from getting those resources.'

Catesby smiled and wanted to congratulate Parkinson for having so gracefully jumped through the hoop of the bleeding obvious – but held his tongue.

The colonel from Defence Humint now pitched in. 'Can you tell us about the Exocet's secret codes – the ones that order a mid-air diversion, cancel an attack or enable a self-destruct?'

The Frenchman looked pleadingly at Catesby who slowly and carefully translated. The Frenchman shook his head and answered in English, 'The Exocet is fire and forget.'

'Can you elaborate on that?' said the colonel.

'That is the reason why the Exocet is so lethal. Once it is launched, you can do nothing to alter its flight or targeting. At first, it is blindly propelled by the inertia of its rockets – like a rock hurled by a medieval catapult – and, at this point, is just as dead and numb as that rock. The Exocet's brilliant brain – its radar – only switches on at the end of its flight. The missile now drops to sea level – literally skimming the waves at one to two metres above the surface. Owing to the radar horizon,' the Frenchman glanced at the naval officer, 'partly dictated as you know by the curvature of the earth, it is impossible to detect an incoming Exocet until it is less than 6,000 metres from its target. The missile is now travelling at 1,134 kilometres per hour and locked on its prey. This means that the target has less than thirty seconds, in most cases less than twenty, to take countermeasures – an almost impossible task.'

The colonel looked closely at the Frenchman. 'Many similar missiles have command-destruct codes – as you well know.'

'In fact,' said the naval officer, 'most anti-ship Exocets also have command-destruct codes.'

'You are, commander, mistaken. The air-launched Exocets do not have command-destruct systems. At least, not the ones presently in service. Such a system would add too much weight to the missiles.' The Frenchman spread his hands. 'And it would defeat the very raison d'être of these deadly missiles. The Exocet was specifically designed to be deaf and blind to countermeasures.' The Frenchman smiled. 'We live in a world where security breaches are not uncommon – and where secret codes do not always remain secret – and those who designed the Exocet were well aware of this.'

Catesby suppressed an urge to shout *bravo* as he finished translating. Secrets were a more valuable currency than gold bullion. If he were in the arms business, he *would* build missiles with command-destruct systems – and then sell the secret destruct codes to all the enemies of the people he sold the missiles to.

The party chairman stirred uneasily. 'I think,' he said, 'this might be the right time for a little break.'

What Parkinson really meant was that he wanted the Frenchman and a few others to leave the room. The security goons came in and led the Frenchman away. In the end, there were only six people present, including Catesby and the colonel.

Parkinson gave the colonel a look that combined irritation with embarrassment. 'I think that we have strayed into an area of confidentiality that ought to have remained confidential.'

'I was,' said the colonel, 'asked to pursue the matter by...'

'I know, but I don't think we should pursue the matter any further.'

Catesby kept a straight face, but was enjoying every minute of it. You didn't have to be psychic to read between the lines. Basically, Thatcher makes a late-night telephone call to Mitterrand after half a bottle of whisky and threatens a mini-nuclear holocaust if she doesn't get the secret command-destruct codes for the Exocets – someone having put a bee in her ill-informed bonnet that such things existed. Mitterrand does everything possible to pacify her – and agrees to hand over the codes, which he doesn't, of course, have on his bedside table in the Élysée Palace. In the cold light of day, things look a lot different – but a panicky MoD had already dispatched the colonel to find out more. It was, Catesby well knew, the way that governments functioned. Professionals often had to deal with political masters who didn't understand the details, but thought they did. It was also obvious that the party chairman was embarrassed by the PM and wanted to sweep the incident under the table.

The Frenchman and the others were invited back into the room and the interview shifted on to the heart of the matter: how Argentina was trying to get more Exocets and other weapons too. Catesby knew that on this subject the Frenchman was literally worth his weight in gold. The first gem was the Argentine Naval Procurement Office in Paris. SIS knew that such an organisation existed, but assumed it was located in the Argentine Embassy in its rather drab building in the rue Cimarosa. During the flight from Rio, the Frenchman had already informed Catesby of the Naval Procurement Office's clandestine move to 58 avenue Marceau, a tree-lined avenue that was a better address than the embassy's. The avenue Marceau premises were shared with a bogus German shipping company – staffed by German-speaking Argentine nationals – and an equally bogus soybean export business.

As soon as the Frenchman had finished his account of the Argentine Naval Procurement Office, Cecil Parkinson, as the only member of the War Cabinet present, asked for another recess. This time the only persons left in the room were the most senior FCO official, Catesby and Parkinson.

'This is a matter of urgency,' said the party chairman, looking at Catesby. 'I think you'd better get hopping.'

'The matter,' said Catesby, 'is already being dealt with. Both French intelligence services are providing full cooperation.'

'Which ones?'

'The DST,' continued Catesby, 'and DGSE. The DST, Direction de la Surveillance du Territoire, are responsible for surveillance in France itself. It's their turf and they don't want DGSE elbowing them out of the way.'

'I am well aware of the difference between the two agencies.'

Catesby suspected that Parkinson had never heard their names before, but hated being patronised or shown up.

Parkinson put on a weighty frown. 'What really concerns me

– and surprises me – is that we haven't been informed of these developments.'

Catesby knew that a detailed minute had been sent to the War Cabinet and had seen the Cabinet Secretary's acknowledgement, but the minister obviously hadn't read it. 'As we all know,' said Catesby with false emollience, 'the situation is fast moving. I am sorry the document hasn't reached you yet – and will make sure that such communications are dispatched with the greatest urgency.'

The party chairman nodded. 'Can you fill us in on the latest?'

'The DST broke into the roof space of avenue Marceau late at night to create a horrendous water leak. They arrived the next morning disguised as plumbers – along with our man in Paris and an SIS technician – to install bugging equipment in the Argentine offices. It was done with the utmost professionalism and GCHQ is already monitoring all their communications as well as office conversations. So far there has been no encryption GCHQ have been unable to break.'

'It sounds like,' said the FCO official, 'signals security isn't an Argentine strong point.'

'The security issue that concerns me,' said the minister, 'is having the French so intimately involved. They are duplicitous.'

Once again, Parkinson seemed peeved to be out of the loop. 'What positive actions have SIS carried out so far?'

'At the moment, the operation is still surveillance and monitoring.' Catesby paused and looked at the minister. 'We haven't killed anyone because we haven't been authorised – and no one has requested it either.'

The Foreign Office official came in. 'There are diplomatic factors. We shouldn't take lethal action on French soil without the permission of the French as it could end further French cooperation – and killing the Argentines could make a peaceful resolution, of which there are still hopes, impossible.'

'Killing,' said Catesby, who didn't entirely agree with the FCO official's assessment, 'may well be a necessary option, but at the moment it is more important to use surveillance to uncover the international networks that the Argentines are trawling to buy more Exocets.'

'Which,' said the minister, 'is the overriding reason for this interrogation.'

'Interview,' corrected Catesby. 'And I believe the financial team have already arrived and are ready and waiting.'

'Well let's get cracking,' said the minister.

Catesby gave a weary smile. Two things that the British excelled at were war and financial transactions – not national traits of which to be overly proud. And the mess in the South Atlantic was testing these skills to the limit.

When the interview recommenced, the panel was augmented by a team from HM's Treasury accompanied by two vetted and trusted bankers. This is when the Frenchman really began to prove his worth. He unravelled a web where so-called legal banking dipped in and out of a financial underworld whose ethics would have shamed the Mafia. Well, maybe not shamed them *that* much, for the Mafia were also deeply involved – but as good Catholics they probably confessed their transactions as sins before going to Mass and taking communion. And, assuming the Mafiosi's confessor was a worldly priest, the involvement of the Vatican Bank made absolution easier to grant. It was at times like this that Catesby felt a certain unease. On his mother's side he was European and Catholic – and, owing to whatever twist of ancestry, he bore the name of an English traitor who died trying to return England to Rome. Catesby's feelings alternated between pride and self-loathing.

The Frenchman's revelations confirmed suspicions that Catesby had always had about an Italian connection. The language and the country were beautiful – but the scandals and conspiracies were ugly. At the heart of the corrupt web, as always, was P2 – Propaganda Due.

P2 was a pseudo-Masonic lodge, later expelled by the Masons, that had been founded in 1945. It was, in Catesby's view, an organisation aimed at secretly perpetuating the regime that had ended when Mussolini and his entourage were hung upside down on meat hooks from the girders of a half-completed Standard Oil petrol station in Milan's Piazzale Loreto. Some claimed that P2 was a 'shadow' government pulling the strings of the 'official' government. But who could really know? The most impressive – and sinister – aspect of P2 was its cult of secrecy. It was more closed and secret than any state intelligence agency that Catesby had ever encountered. In preparation for the debrief, Catesby had got the SIS woman in Rome to cable him a list of known P2 members – even though it was an impossible task. The previous year the Italian police had raided one of the homes of Licio Gelli, thought to be master of the P2 lodge, and discovered a list of 970 members that included former prime ministers, heads of intelligence services, newspaper editors, television executives, bankers, judges and thirty-one generals. Catesby wasn't sure they were all P2 – maybe what the cops found was Gelli's address book. But once again, who knows?

But SIS Rome – who sometimes went around disguised as a nun, stoking a laddish fantasy or two – had uncovered some gems. The best was that the niece of P2 boss Gelli was married to the head of the Argentine Naval Procurement Office in Paris. It wasn't, however, a gem that he was going to share with everyone at the debriefing. Catesby already had a plan in mind that would either require a Clause 7 Authorisation from the Foreign Secretary – or, more simply, be another 'deniable op' where people closed their eyes and kept their mouths shut. Probably the latter.

The other gems from Rome included the extent to which P2 activities had extended into South America – especially Argentina. Argentine P2 members included an ex-president and several senior members of juntas. The influence of P2 was also apparent in the 'Dirty War' and in the ruthless conduct of Triple A – the Argentine Anticommunist Alliance. It occurred to Catesby that P2 might have been using Argentina as a practice ground for trying out techniques – such as control of the media and violent suppression of trade unions – that they might one day use in Italy.

The next part of the debrief echoed *bancos*: Banco Ambrosiano, Banco Andino and Banco Central Reserva. When you're willing to dish out between seventy and eighty million US bucks for Exocets you can't carry the cash in a suitcase. Secure transfers of huge sums were one of the reasons why bankers got paid enormous salaries. The art of such deals was making sure that neither buyer nor seller got shafted. You don't want to hand over the money until you've got the keys and are ready to drive away your shiny new Exocet. And likewise, you want to make sure the bucks are banked before you hand over the keys. Catesby suppressed a smile, for unlike the bankers, his job was to totally fuck up those transactions and make sure everyone got shafted.

There was another hour of intense questioning and note-taking. The Treasury guys and their banker pals – one ex-Treasury and one ex-SIS (he gave Catesby a warm wink) – were squeezing the Frenchman for every recollection and name and even faces without names. The party chairman finally looked at his watch and said it was time for a break – it was nearly two o'clock.

Catesby milled around, eating an egg and cress sandwich and drinking a cup of tea. He didn't like the juggling act of eating standing up and making light conversation. Food and talk were best consumed sitting down. Catesby found himself standing next to the ex-SIS colleague who now worked for a merchant bank.

'Lots of dosh?' said Catesby.

'Basic's about the same as C's salary.' C was the head of the intelligence service. 'But have to pay my own pension out of that.'

'Poor you. I can see the hardship and poverty in your eyes.'

'Oh, not at all,' said the spy-turned-banker, 'it's the bonuses that count.'

'And how much are they?'

The banker put a finger to his lips. 'Can't tell you. It's confidential – they don't want jealousy and resentment among colleagues. Bad for morale.'

'Ah, come on. Give us a clue.'

The banker winked. 'On a good year, two to three times basic.'

'So you're worth three Cs.'

'But he has a lot more fun and mystique.'

One of the Treasury types beckoned for the banker with a barely detectable raised eyebrow – as if he feared the banker was becoming contaminated by talking to an impoverished pleb from SIS.

'See you later,' said Catesby. He needed fresh air. Catesby looked at his watch. There was time. It was only a brisk ten-minute walk.

Iken was one of Catesby's favourite places. The view from the churchyard was pure coastal Suffolk – a place where sheep, heath and woods were licked by the tides. It was coming up to high water and the vast glistening expanse of filling river stretched to the dark woods of Blackheath. But it was magic at low tide too, when the gleaming mud flats were bird-loud with dunlin, redshank, peewit, mallard, big lumpy shelduck, strutting oystercatcher in their evening-dress plumage – and curlew. Catesby had often sailed the river and anchored there for the night. The sound of the curlew – 'curr-leek-leek, cur-leek-leek-leek, cu-r-r-r-r-leek' – always meant that he had finally come home. Catesby gripped the top of the church wall. 'No one,' he said, 'can ever take this from me.' Then he laughed. He remembered a childhood friend who had also loved the place. They had once cycled there on a glorious summer's day when they were teenagers. The friend looked out over the river from the churchyard and pronounced, 'This is where I want to be buried. I want to hear the waves lapping around me, the sound of the wind and the calls of the birds.' The friend was now lying in a Commonwealth War Grave 6,000 miles away.

Catesby sensed someone behind him in the churchyard. For a second he thought the ghost of his friend had squeaked over from Asia. When he turned around he did find himself looking at a soldier, but one who was still alive. It was the colonel from HUMINT.

The colonel covered his embarrassment with a nervous smile. 'I wasn't following you. I just now realised it was you standing there. Sorry, you look like you want to be alone.'

Catesby smiled back. 'Not particularly – you haven't broken the spell.'

'I love this place too. I suppose we're fellow spirits.'

'Not everyone likes it. Suffolk is an acquired taste.'

'My wife,' said the colonel, 'despite being born here and coming from an old Suffolk family, still hasn't acquired the taste. She says Suffolk is for loners who prefer their own company – and that the people are shy, sly and reclusive.'

'We're not sly – but we do retreat into our shells.'

'Do Suffolk people make good spies?'

'We're good at watching and listening, but not friendly and charming enough to get people to open up.'

'But you've been very successful.'

'I learned to be a good actor – to hide what I really think and believe.'

'Not a very nice way to live.'

'It isn't – which is why I don't do it all the time.'

'Hiding what you really think,' said the colonel, 'is obviously the key to success in Whitehall. The frightening thing is that no one's standing up to Thatcher even when she's wrong. The key to success is to agree with her every whim. It's a game that I'm going to stop playing.'

'How are you going to do that?'

'I'm going to resign my post as chief of HUMINT and volunteer for frontline service.'

'You've missed the boat – they've already sailed.'

'If I can cadge a flight to Ascension Island I can catch up with them.'

'I doubt,' said Catesby, 'that you'll see any action.'

The colonel looked disappointed. 'Why's that?'

'No one is going to be stupid enough to let this thing escalate into a full-scale war. In the last resort, the Yanks will pull the plug.'

'You think it's all sabre-rattling?'

Catesby looked out over the river glowing in spring sunshine and thought of his dead friend. 'I hope so – for all of them.'

When the debriefing recommenced there were two more bankers present who had swapped careers in SIS for big money in the City. One came from an old Roman Catholic family and had recently been knighted into the Sovereign Military Hospitaller Order of Saint John of Jerusalem of Rhodes and of Malta. As Catesby rose up the ranks in the intelligence service he became aware that many senior officers were prominent Catholics – and that his name, far from being a hindrance, was an advantage. The Knight of Malta had once buttonholed Catesby in an empty corridor and whispered, 'You are one of us.' Catesby had faked a knowing smile and nodded – not having a clue who 'us' were. He feared that he was about to receive an invitation to a party involving black leather masks and strange rituals.

The rest of the session was devoted to squeezing every remaining drop of info out of the Frenchman – and also going back over questions that he had already answered. Interrogation sessions – and this had turned into one – always returned to the same questions long after, sometimes years after, the interrogee had already answered. If you were lying you had to have a flawless memory. That was how they had broken Blunt. The chairman finally thanked the Frenchman for his 'cooperation' and the security guards came in to lead him away.

The next part of the meeting was sharp and quick. It was clear that the War Cabinet wanted action immediately.

ARA *General Belgrano* near Tierra del Fuego: Tuesday, 20 April 1982

It was the first time that Gonzalo and the other eighteen-year-old sea cadets realised they were really at war. When the siren sounded, calling them to battle stations, they knew it wasn't a drill. The radar room had detected an unknown ship – and there was no report of an authorised ship in the area. Because of the tense situation, Buenos Aires had put out a warning that all merchant shipping and fishing trawlers must regularly report their positions to avoid being mistaken for enemy vessels.

The captain ordered the *General Belgrano* to close in on the ship and the gun crews to prepare for action. It was a polar autumn night, but the silhouette of a blacked-out ship soon appeared on the horizon. The fact that the unknown ship wasn't showing navigation lights created more suspicion. The captain ordered a five-inch gun to fire an illumination round which burst above the vessel and bathed it in unearthly light. It was obvious that the vessel wasn't a warship, but a merchantman. The ship was ordered to stop and did so immediately. At the same time, the merchant skipper turned on, not just his navigation lights, but every available deck light and his ship soon looked like a seagoing Christmas tree. It transpired that the ship had experienced engine trouble and was two days behind schedule. After a stern warning, the *Belgrano*'s captain let the merchantman proceed on its way.

Gonzalo had an aptitude for engineering, encouraged by his aviator father, and had been assigned to the engine room. Gonzalo's battle station duties required him to squeeze between hot and noisy boilers and shout out readings from various dials and gauges. During one exercise, when the *General Belgrano* had fired a fifteen-gun broadside, the ship had shuddered so severely that he thought there had been a terrible accident and that he was going to die. He later realised that it was just the recoil of the guns thrusting the cruiser a metre or two sideways.

Despite the cramped, sweaty conditions, Gonzalo loved the comradery and dark humour of the boiler rooms. The officer in charge warmed to him and called him Gonzalito – as did his own father. The *Belgrano* was a happy ship with a great sense of solidarity. But as every one of the cruiser's 1,093 crew well knew, they were on a serious mission. Gonzalo remembered what he had been told during one of their first exercises: 'We are not going to a football match, we are going to war. Do not stop carrying out your battle station duties, whether it's loading ammunition or tending the boilers, to look after the wounded. That's the job of God and the medics.'

As he lay down on his narrow bunk, Gonzalo felt a sense of completeness. He liked being valued as part of a team – and, at his age, the prospect of war seemed a romantic adventure of glorious heroism and bonding with other brave men. He also felt happy that his father had remarried. Even though it was odd that he could soon be fighting his new mother's kith and kin. He didn't love Fiona more than his birth mother, but she was more fun to be with – and so good at sport. She always beat him at tennis, but also provided useful coaching tips. Instead of losing six-love, he now lost 6–3 or 6–2 – and once had even taken a set to tie-break! Some of the other sea cadets, the cruder ones, sometimes teased him about having a mother who was so young and beautiful – but, when Gonzalo examined his own conscience, he was sure his thoughts were pure.

Rome: Friday, 23 April

It was just before midnight when the ex-SIS officer, now banker, arrived at the Vatican. He was there for a meeting with the cardinal who headed the IOR, the Instituto per le Opere di Religione, also known as the Vatican Bank. The IOR was located in the Nicholas V Tower, which was clearly the ugliest building in the Vatican. The tower was a low, squat building of grey stone that seldom felt a ray of sunlight, even at noon. Two Swiss Guards in helmets with scarlet plumes and breastplates stood sentry on either side of the heavily bolted entrance door. The hard expressions on their faces suggested their presence was more than a matter of ceremony. The banker presented his credentials as a Knight of Malta – a white cross and his ribbon of rank – and uttered the passwords, '*Tuitio Fidei et Obsequium Pauperum.*'

The Swiss Guard saluted and answered, '*Ave Crux Alba.*'

The second guard saluted and opened the heavy door. The banker walked into a dimly lit foyer. There was another Swiss Guard sitting at a desk. He wasn't in armour, but did have a Heckler & Koch MP5 submachine gun close at hand. 'May I be of assistance?' he said.

The banker explained his business.

The Swiss Guard picked up a phone and spoke in muted Italian. The guard sat stony-faced as if waiting for an answer.

A minute later there was a murmur and the guard said, '*Sì*.' He hung up the phone and turned to the banker. 'His Eminence will see you now.'

The banker was directed up a spiral staircase to an office that occupied the top of the tower. The banker was married to an art historian. Although he took a keen interest in her work, his opinions were usually sniffed at. As soon as he entered the office, he recognised the painted panels behind the cardinal as fifteenth century – and guessed that they might even be by Fra Angelico. The banker would have loved to tell his wife about the rare masterpieces in front of him – and was certain she wouldn't have sniffed and dismissed – but he realised that his meeting with the head of the Vatican Bank was too secret to share with even his nearest and dearest.

The cardinal was in full rig: a black cassock trimmed in scarlet, a similarly trimmed shoulder cape, a broad scarlet sash, a gilt pectoral cross and a scarlet skull cap. He stood up and extended his left hand. The banker bowed low, whispered, 'Your Eminence,' and kissed the gold Episcopal ring proffered to him.

The cardinal sat back down and glowered at the banker. When he spoke, the mystique of ecclesiastical grandeur was broken. The cardinal not only had an American accent, but the kind of accent you heard in gangster films. He had, in fact, been brought up in a rough area of Chicago. The cardinal was tough and streetwise – and had once helped save the previous Pope's life when the Pontiff was attacked by a man with a knife.

'I believe,' said the cardinal, 'that the people you represent have sent you here to make a complaint.' He paused and glared over arched fingers. 'I think I know what it is, but I'd like to hear it from you first. And why don't you sit down – I don't like all this ceremony stuff.'

The banker lowered himself into a stiff white upholstered chair. 'We are concerned about letters of credit that the IOR has extended to,' the ex-SIS man took a document out of a folder and handed it to the cardinal, 'this bank.'

The cardinal put on his reading glasses and examined the document. 'How did you get this?'

'Letters of credit would be pointless if they were completely confidential. Several copies are in circulation.'

'This should not have been put into circulation – not at this time.'

'I think the person you are dealing with is unreliable – and also desperate.'

The cardinal gave the banker a hard stare. 'The world of money has always been unreliable – and if people chasing money weren't desperate, the system wouldn't produce wealth.'

The banker decided not to debate the point. He knew the cardinal was skating on thin ice in his own job – and in some ways just as worried as the banker that he was trying to bail out.

'I have, your Eminence, brought other documents that you may want to look at. The bank in question is technically insolvent.'

The cardinal frowned and stretched out a huge paw of a hand. He was a big, powerful man who looked more like a rugby prop forward than a priest.

While the cardinal was looking at the documents, the banker studied the paintings adorning the wall behind his desk. He was now certain that they were by Fra Angelico, who had been a very different priest from the cardinal. Angelico, the truest of believers, even managed to combine the mystical with the financial. One of the paintings shows the Pope entrusting the Church's treasury, represented by a leather purse of gold coins, to a hallowed saint. The banker suddenly twigged why the paintings were in the cardinal's office. The images told the life of Saint Lawrence – the cardinal's predecessor as Vatican banker. In the middle painting, Lawrence is dispensing the Church's wealth to the poor. A legless man sits on the ground in front of the saint; a blind one is feeling his way to Lawrence with a stick and a number of orphans are milling about. The final two paintings are dark and ominous. Lawrence is being tried and martyred by being laid out on a red-hot gridiron heated by burning coals. According to legend, Lawrence is said to have joked, 'I'm well done on this side; you ought to turn me over.' Which is why Lawrence is the patron saint of both cooks and comedians. Was, thought the banker, the cardinal fearing his own martyrdom?

The cardinal looked up from the documents. 'This doesn't tell me anything that I don't already know.'

'Then why don't you withdraw the letters of credit?'

'Because there are things that you don't know about – that will make this bank one of the most solvent in Europe.' The cardinal frowned and took off his spectacles. 'Who sent you here? Your bank or the British government?'

'To be frank, both.'

The cardinal remained silent and frowned at the British banker. The sound of organ music and Gregorian chant began to drift in from an open window.

'What lovely music,' said the banker.

'Not if you hear it all the time.' The cardinal got up and closed the window. 'It's the Benedictines. We can do without their racket.'

The banker stared at the cardinal. He could see that gentle persuasion and good nature were not going to appeal to His Eminence.

The cardinal stared back. 'You can't run a Church of 1.2 billion members on Hail Marys alone.'

'You can't run a bank with no assets, other than letters of credit written by yourself.'

The cardinal turned flinty-eyed. 'The bank has recently received a secured loan of 270 million dollars.' He touched the file that the banker had just given him. 'In fact, you refer to that loan in your own documents.'

The banker smiled. 'The loan came from a subsidiary bank owned by the bank in question. You can't loan money to yourself and call it an asset.'

'The loan, as you probably know – otherwise you wouldn't be here – is underwritten by solid cash from another source.'

Both men knew what and who they were talking about even though they weren't naming people or institutions. The Vatican Bank had long been using a dodgy banker called Roberto Calvi and an even dodgier Sicilian investor – who was now serving a prison sentence in the USA – to invest Vatican Bank money in South America. The funds were siphoned through companies registered in Luxembourg to disguise the Vatican's investment in tainted deals involving dictators and the Mafia. The cardinal regarded himself as a good and loyal Catholic who was looking after the best interests of the Church, but the investments were not something that he wanted the Pope to know about it. He wasn't sure that the Holy Father would agree that you can't run the Church on Hail Marys alone.

The banker could see they were reaching a stand-off and didn't want to push things too far. If he did, the cardinal would dig his heels in and refuse to cooperate. The banker hoped to show the cardinal where his chances of survival best lay. The bottom line was that the dodgy Italian bank was being used to disguise the origins of the Argentine money that was being dangled on the international market to buy Exocets. If the source of the money was revealed, the deals would be in violation of the European Community's ban on trade with Argentina. The arms dealers and bankers – even though they knew where the money was coming from – needed a fig leaf to enable them to plead ignorance to avoid a jail term or a big fine. It had to be what the intelligence world called a 'deniable op'.

The banker smiled. 'I am, Your Eminence, most grateful that you have taken the time to meet me and listen to my case. If you have any questions, I am at your service.'

The cardinal stared into space, chewing on the end of his spectacles. After a long minute he finally said, 'Why on earth does your government want to hang on to those barren islands? I cannot imagine there's much of a market for guano and coarse wool.'

'It's not about the islands. It's about the Prime Minister's survival. She is a ruthless woman who will stop at nothing. The only possibility of a peaceful solution, which we as good Catholic followers of Aquinas are trying to arrange, is for the Argentines to back down.'

'Yeah, sure.'

As the banker got up to take his leave, he gave a last glance at

The key to the success of the operation was the SIS woman Rome. She spoke fluent Italian and hoped her fake persona uld be convincing. It was not just a matter of posing as the fe of an Argentine admiral – that was the easy part – but also etending to be the niece of P2 boss Licio Gelli. SIS Rome had searched her role well and could gossip about many of the ople that the Italian aristocrat would have known socially. In ct, she had met several of them at embassy receptions as well s undercover and knew their style.

SIS Rome checked her clothing as she walked to the hotel oom. She had the sizzling sexuality that women often don't chieve until the age of fifty and was expensively fragrant too - the sort of woman you would expect to find on the arm of a unta admiral. At precisely the agreed moment of rendezvous she knocked on the door. A voice responded in Italian-accented German. For a second, SIS Rome thought about answering in Italian-accented German, but decided not to risk it and answered in Italian instead.

The door opened. The dealer from the Middle East was smiling. SIS Rome was momentarily taken back by how handsome he was. He spoke Italian with only a slight accent and had the easy grace and manners of a prince. Rome entered and was greeted by the Italian aristocrat racing driver who was slightly less handsome, but charmingly languid. Both men were dressed in sleek Italian suits with flapless pockets, the type of tight-fitting suit that can only be worn by slim men with flat stomachs. Neither man wore a tie and both were looking at SIS Rome with much flattery. They were younger, but clearly regarded her as one of them. Rome was pleased that she had chosen her own clothes with care. She was wearing a black slip dress and velvet Miu Miu pumps with discreetly jewelled buckles. She felt pleased, but also uneasy to be desired by younger men – and she could see that desire, that lust, in their eyes.

'My husband,' she said, 'is slightly delayed – typical of Carlos. We haven't eaten all day and he is ordering a light snack – champagne and lobster – which we hope you will share with us. It is good to talk and do business with food and drink.'

Fra Angelico's St Lawrence. His face was one
and serenity, even as he was roasted alive.

Left alone, the cardinal was not serene. Th
choices; only bad ones. The nightmare began
of Luciani in 1978. What had the College of
thinking! The man was clearly not *papabile*? Iro
supporter had been Cardinal Sin of the Philippi
ballots before the white smoke went up. And Lucia
as Pope John Paul I, was dead thirty-three days la
shortest papacies on record. Thank goodness tha
had discovered his body had passed on the note t
on his bedside table – without telling anyone. The
never discovered who had supplied the new Pope
of names. The note had been quickly burned, but i
alive and stirring. There was scandal at the heart of

Hamburg: Friday 23 April

It was also midnight when Catesby turned up at th
Hamburg. The real heroes of the sting op were the e
pers at GCHQ. The bugging of the Argentine Naval P
Commission in Paris had provided an open sesame
network of arms dealers and bankers who were also bu
surveilled. The two dealers Catesby was meeting in H
were experienced floggers of arms who had successfull
sanctions all over the globe – and were also on MI5's ra
smuggling guns to the IRA. One of the dealers was an
aristocrat addicted to fast cars and ski jumping. Illega
trading also fed his need for adrenalin highs, but the
was useful too. The other dealer was a charming opera
Middle Eastern origin who carried four different passport
sting involved using stolen Argentine passwords and encry
methods. The two dealers were certain that they were mee
the Argentine admiral who was head of the Naval Purcha
Commission and his Italian wife – even though they had n
met either in person.

'How kind of you, signora. Please have a seat.'

Rome lowered herself into a gilt chair and crossed her legs with a silken swish.

'I am sure,' said the Italian, 'that we have met before.'

SIS Rome tried not to show her nervousness; she suspected that might have been true – in which case she risked having her cover blown. She tried to avoid sparking the Italian's memory by pretending to have attended social events where she *hadn't* been. 'It must have been,' she said, 'at the Sala Bianca. It was a gorgeous show, but nothing that I personally would wear – even if Carlos had been so generous.'

The Italian shook his head. 'No, I didn't go to the show – it must have been someplace else.'

'But I was there,' said the Middle Easterner. 'As odd as it may seem, I love women's clothes. I would love to have been a fashion designer, rather than…' he made a dismissive gesture, 'a dealer in this sordid trade.' He looked at his Italian colleague. 'It is, you must admit, a business without grace or beauty.'

The Italian suddenly snapped his fingers at Rome. 'I know where I saw you. It was at Selena's wedding – and what a lovely wedding it was. You must know Selena – she's related to your uncle.'

SIS Rome forced a smile to hide her panic. She had, in fact, been at the wedding, but not as a guest. The wedding had taken place at the Basilica of Santa Maria in Trastevere and had been one of the social events of the Italian year – an event where high life mixed freely with low life. SIS Rome had gone to the wedding undercover as a nun. Part of her cover job was tidying up and directing people to pews. The two genuine nuns on duty, accustomed to Church secrecy and silence, had shown little interest in who she was. SIS Rome calmed down. It was impossible that the Italian could have remembered her in nun's habit. She had worn no make-up and tried to look as dowdy as possible. Her job had been to surreptitiously photograph the many low-lifes present – especially the drug dealers, the money launderers and the Neo-fascists. The Americans always appreciated shared info about drug dealers – even though some of them had long worked for the CIA.

'I am sure I saw you there,' persisted the Italian.

'I would love to have been at Selena's wedding. We did send presents, but at the time it was impossible to leave Argentina.'

'Ah,' said the Italian with a note of scepticism, 'it must have been one of your beautiful cousins.'

SIS Rome looked at her watch. 'Apologies again for Carlos, I am sure he should be here any minute.' But Rome was really thinking *where the fuck is Catesby*!

The conversation shifted to 'mutual' Italian acquaintances – including the film director Luchino Visconti who had been safely dead for six years. As SIS Rome spoke to the Italian aristo arms dealer, she realised how much Visconti had got right in his films. The Italian aristocracy were moping around in a swamp of bored cynical disillusion – which can be very attractive. Many had no values, other than manipulating situations to sustain what was left of their power and wealth. Some of them had turned from leopards into jackals – but were still beautiful. Rome sank deeper into her cover story. She could play the game too.

She leaned forward and touched the Italian gently on his wrist. 'I want you to do well out of this deal.' She smiled. 'We are both Italians and I still love my country.'

The Italian felt something stirring and nodded.

'Carlos,' said SIS Rome, 'tells me everything. He says that you are offering the Exocets for one million dollars each including delivery. He may complain about the price, but I am sure that he can pay even more.'

The price, in fact, was irrelevant. SIS Rome was trying to create a mood of trust and confidence to safely waste time while she was waiting for Catesby and his partner.

The night manager was proving a real pain in the arse. She had spotted Catesby and the ex-SAS soldier pushing a trolley laden with champagne and a silver service towards the lift. They were both dressed in tailcoats as upmarket catering staff, but clearly not staff belonging to the hotel.

'Excuse me, please,' said the manager with a look that could curdle cream. 'What are you doing?'

'We are delivering a meal to room 423,' answered Catesby in fluent German – hoping that his German was more convincing than his blond wig and fake goatee.

'That is not allowed.'

'We were given permission,' lied Catesby, 'by the duty manager.'

'I am the duty manager.'

'I mean by the day shift manager.'

'I am sure that is not true.'

Catesby smiled blandly. 'Perhaps I was misinformed by my manager.'

'This is totally unacceptable. Our guests are only permitted to consume food and drink provided by the hotel.'

Catesby smiled. 'Can you show me that rule in writing? I have never seen it posted in any of your hotel rooms.'

'How do you know that?'

'I have,' Catesby lied again, 'served many of your guests on other occasions – and read the house rules posted on the back of every door.'

The manager turned scarlet and looked as if she was about to explode. 'The rules are written down in the hotel agreement and every hotel guest agrees to them. If you like, I will find you a copy.'

'Good. You go find a copy and we will serve our guests in room 423.'

The manager wasn't going to let them out of her sight. The argument continued for another five minutes. Catesby began to get restless and thought about asking the manager if they could discuss the matter in the privacy of her office – where they would overcome her, gag her and tie her to a chair. But she was tall and athletic and it wouldn't be easy.

Finally, the manager threw down the gauntlet. 'I am going to have security eject you from the hotel.'

At that moment the lift door next to Catesby and his accomplice opened. 'Good,' said Catesby, 'we will meet them in room 423.'

They pushed the trolley into the lift and as soon as the door closed Catesby pushed the button for the fifth floor.

'I thought we were going to the fourth floor,' said the ex-SAS man.

'You don't think I gave her the correct room number.'

'I am impressed, sir.'

'I hope room 423 isn't a honeymoon suite.' Catesby felt his stomach twist into knots. The argument with the manager was no longer amusing – nor was his joke. What they were about to do was serious and sickening.

SIS Rome was running out of small talk and she felt her cover story as a niece of Italy's most notorious *éminence grise* and the wife of an Argentine naval officer was starting to curl at the edges. The Italian had made some comments about her supposed uncle to which she was unable to reply. Once or twice she had spotted a shadow of doubt crossing his forehead. SIS Rome looked at her watch and expelled a hiss of frustration. 'I'm getting hungry,' she said, 'I wonder what's keeping Carlos.'

On cue, there was a knock on the door. The Middle Easterner got up to answer it. As he opened the door, Rome saw Catesby's inhospitable face and a serviette folded awkwardly over his left arm. She couldn't imagine someone who looked less like a catering industry professional. She knew instantly it was going to go wrong – but maybe it was just her nerves. She looked at Catesby and said, '*Finalamente!*'

Catesby answered in German, 'There was a problem with the bill – your husband's credit card.'

The Italian laughed and said in rapid Italian, 'Well, I'm glad we found out about this in time. I think we had better drink the champagne before they take it away.'

SIS Rome gestured for Catesby to come in and said in fake bad German, 'All need a drink.' Catesby, looking less like a caterer than ever, passed champagne flutes around, lifted the magnum out of the ice bucket and sent the cork bouncing off the ceiling. The Italian shook his head and laughed. Catesby just about managed to fill the flutes without spilling. The Italian proposed a toast to *successo* and they all lifted their glasses. At the same time, Catesby lifted the huge silver lid off the food tray – but there wasn't any lobster.

The ex-SAS man grabbed the gun and fired in one motion. The discharge of the Browning 9mm was muffled by the long silencer – which was the rationale for the long covered food tray. It had been agreed to take out the Italian first for he, as a racing driver, probably had quicker reflexes. The bullet entered his right eye and exited behind his left ear, splattering the cushions behind him with blood and brain. Meanwhile, Catesby picked up a second Browning with silencer and aimed at the other dealer – but not quickly enough. The Middle Easterner turned and ducked. Catesby's bullet deflected off his right shoulder blade before lodging in his left lung. He was still alive, but the ex-SAS man delivered the *coup de grâce*. The double killing had taken less than three seconds. It took three more seconds to fling around a kilo of cocaine – courtesy of Scotland Yard's seized property section – with a street value of Catesby's annual salary. The purpose of the coke was to confuse the police investigation.

Four seconds later all three of them were racing down the service stairs towards the ex-filtration cars which were parked outside the laundry chutes. The ex-SAS man was in charge of the guns, which they were not to leave behind. He carried the weapons in a smart leather shoulder bag,

The cars were waiting in the service bay with their engines running. The ex-SAS man, still wearing his disguise, got in the first car without saying a word or even giving a glance of comradeship. Catesby wondered if he would recognise him without his disguise. He was the ultimate cold professional. SIS Rome and Catesby shared the same car, but could not speak as it was a UK Eyes Alpha Need to Know Only op, and the driver, although a vetted and trusted SIS operative, didn't need to know any details other than the picking up and dropping off. The drive to SIS Rome's safe house in the suburbs of Hamburg was silent. That's the way these ops were. No blubbing or emotional feedback. Do it and get the fuck out.

Catesby's flight back to the UK wasn't from Hamburg International, the huge air hub that caters for millions of passengers, but from a small private one, Flughafen Hamburg-Finkenwerder, which was located south of the Elbe and south-west of the city. The single airstrip seemed surrounded by water – or that's what Catesby remembered of it from the post-war years. He recollected surreptitiously flying agents in and out – a lot of whom were total shits. Some of them were ex-Nazis trying to erase their pasts by touting intelligence to the occupying powers. Some were power-crazed opportunists posing as freedom fighters – and some were Soviet double agents also posing as freedom fighters. A handful, however, were genuine idealists who wanted to rescue their homelands from occupation – but they tended to get ground up in the melee. But mourning – or secretly rejoicing – for agents who met a sticky end was a waste of time and emotional energy. The best way to survive as a British spy, as Catesby realised after several harsh lessons, was to focus entirely on the UK's own intelligence needs and to ignore all other agendas. He was trying to apply the same principle to the Falklands mess – which had nothing to do with a clash of ideologies or a struggle for world dominance, but everything to do with the survival in power of a handful of key players. The lack of idealism wasn't refreshing, but did create clarity.

The plane that was taking Catesby to England was a private executive jet with six passenger seats. He didn't know who the plane belonged to and he didn't recognise four of the five passengers – although two looked familiar. The only passenger he did recognise was an ex-SIS officer now a merchant banker. The two made brief eye contact, but there was no further communication. Everyone on the plane had their own jobs, and those jobs were all need-to-know-only. The flight was going to be as silent as the car journey after the hotel killing. The only communication was from the pilot who informed the passengers that the flight time to Stansted in Essex was one hour and forty minutes. It was only then that Catesby found out where he was going.

Catesby managed to fall asleep for an hour on the jet – so he wasn't completely dead when he got to Stansted. There was no passing through customs and all were whisked away to cars. Catesby recognised his driver as a Signal Corps lad on loan to SIS. There were no other passengers. Catesby tried to make small talk about football – Ipswich were having a fantastic season under Bobby Robson and were battling Liverpool for the First Division championship – but the driver had no interest in football. Dawn was breaking over the Thames when the driver dropped Catesby off at his flat in Pimlico.

Catesby let himself into the dark basement flat – where sunlight was a rare event that lasted mid-morning for ten minutes on a bright day. He found the brandy bottle and the morphine tablets. Two tabs and a good swig should do the trick.

When he woke up four hours later, he was refreshed – and, when he left the bedroom, he even found a ray of sunlight percolating through the barred front window. After caffeine and toast he would be strong enough to face a meeting with C at Century House. There would, of course, be no report-writing. You don't leave a paper trail for 'deniable ops'.

The view from C's office on the tenth floor looked over the Thames towards the Palace of Westminster. If his watch was broken, C could glance at Big Ben to see the time. Catesby's office faced glumly north over Waterloo Station, but he could see the Tower of London in the middle distance – a dark reminder of *Honi soit qui mal y pense*. Was there, he thought, another country anywhere in the world that had such a national motto? The literal translation, *Shame on whoever thinks it evil*, is bad enough, but the implied meaning even worse: *Don't even think about it or we'll kick your head in*. Catesby wondered if the motto was where Orwell got the idea of 'thought crime'.

C got up from behind his desk and went to a table where there was a kettle and cups. 'Tea, coffee – or a beer or whisky if you like.'

'Thank you, sir, tea would be fine.'

'Ordinary builders' tea?'

'Fine.'

C brought over two mugs of tea. 'Let's sit down.'

The two men sat in standard civil service office chairs, stiff but with armrests. Their backs were to the Houses of Parliament. The ordinariness made Catesby feel relaxed. C was a grammar school boy from a solid West Midlands background and was lacking in pomposity.

'I already know,' said C, 'that the op was successful.'

'We tried,' said Catesby, 'not to leave any fingerprints, but the German cops aren't stupid.'

'The FCO, aside from the Foreign Secretary, have been kept in the dark. Nonetheless, the FCO have been warned to deal with diplomatic consequences – and there will be some, even if the protests are behind closed doors.'

Catesby smiled and said, 'It won't be the first time our diplomats have had to smooth ruffled feathers for an incident they know nothing about.'

'But it isn't something they like to do. The Germans,' continued C, 'readily agreed to an arms embargo against Argentina, but their position is, let us say, equivocal. Argentina is one of their biggest trading partners and they don't like British forces being diverted from their NATO roles. There is also the problem of German public opinion, which loathes British jingoism. Basically, do you think we got away with it?'

'The two biggest problems in keeping this op deniable are the night manager, who clearly knew something was fishy and that we weren't ordinary criminals carrying out a hit, and the sheer professionalism of the operation. There might not be enough evidence to convict, but there aren't any other suspects. So, frankly, we haven't got away with it.'

'Any ideas on how we can calm things down and keep the Germans onside?'

'We need to lean on the BND.' Catesby was referring to the Bundesnachrichtendienst, the West German Secret Intelligence Service.'

'How?'

'The sweet way would be to give them more access to GCHQ – they always want that. But the more effective way would be to dangle the files we have on the BND's illegal phone-tapping and their illegal spying on journalists. I don't know how you do that in a sweet way – maybe smile a lot and talk about what a great football team they have.'

'Who compiled these files?'

'I did – a bank account for a rainy day.' Catesby told C how to find them in the Registry. It was easy to deal with C on issues like this. He didn't seek to break rules, but he had a clear appreciation of damage limitation. The idea, as suggested by Catesby, was that blackmailing the BND would put pressure on the *Aussenministerium,* the foreign ministry, which in turn would put pressure on the Chancellor's office – and that somewhere along the line the *Polizei* would lose their enthusiasm for investigating the killings in the Hamburg hotel.

C nodded and sipped his tea. 'By the way, you don't take sugar? I forget to ask.'

'Only with coffee.'

'Any other options?' said C.

'Only our files on the Chancellor.'

'Did you have any part in composing those files?'

'No,' said Catesby, 'but I have seen them. There's not much dirt, but after the Brandt scandal there are still raw nerves – and the German right-wing press would pounce on it.'

'That,' said C, 'would be the nuclear option.'

It was, thought Catesby, a dirty business. The Secret State had too much power and influenced too many agendas. And it was impossible to speak out. If they couldn't shut you up, they locked you up – and smeared those around you. Truth was a bright but fragile bird, whose neck was easily wrung.

'The Italians?' said C.

'What about the Italians?'

'You just killed one.'

Catesby smiled bleakly. 'Blackmail doesn't work with them.'

'The FCO are worried about Italy. Half the population of Argentina are of Italian origin and the press are not on our side. The Italian government are dragging their feet over economic sanctions – and putting on a lot of pressure for a negotiated settlement.' C paused and looked at Catesby. 'Never before have we been in a situation where covert action had to take into account so many diplomatic issues. The nightmare, of course, is Spain – where the press are utterly delighted by Galtieri's invasion of the Falklands. This happens just at a time when delicate negotiations are taking place over Gibraltar – and also Spain becoming a member of NATO and the EC.'

'Our ships in Gibraltar,' said Catesby, 'are obviously a sabotage target.'

'I don't think Downing Street understands how wide-ranging this conflict could be – or how many fans Argentina may have.'

Catesby sipped his tea.

'By the way,' said C, 'the Foreign Secretary will be seeing you in the morning. He will probably be a bit jet-lagged as he's just getting back from Washington.'

Catesby finished his tea and took his leave.

Catesby's stepchildren, twins Geraldine and Peter from his wife's wartime liaison with an airman, came around that evening to cook him a vegetarian meal. He was pleasantly surprised to see them, but pretended he wasn't. It was part of the family banter. 'Why are you here on a Saturday evening?' said Catesby. 'Don't you have any friends?'

'Mother sent us around,' said Peter, 'to check on your drinking.'

'How kind of her.'

'But,' said Geraldine, 'I nicked a bottle of good burgundy from one of my rich clients in case you've already drunk your store cupboard dry.'

'How perceptive you are about my habits.' Catesby looked at the bottle. It was a very fine red and not cheap. 'How fortunate you are to have clients of taste as well as wealth. Otherwise, of course, they wouldn't have hired you.' He looked at his stepson. 'Poor Peter, on the other hand, only represents clients who are destitute victims of the capitalist system.'

Geraldine gave a loud theatrical yawn. The fact that she was a successful and well-paid architect as well as a member of the Socialist Workers Party was an irony that Catesby had played too often. Her brother, by no means destitute himself, was a barrister who specialised in human rights cases. The twins were, in fact, exactly the sort of people that their mother, an MI5 officer, got paid to spy on. That was, however, an irony that Catesby left alone.

Geraldine gave Catesby a hug. 'We do worry about you.'

'I know you can't talk about your job,' said Peter, 'but you must be under a lot of stress.'

'We're paying the price for Thatcher fucking up.' Catesby kept quiet about secrets, but not his opinions.

Both the stepchildren were excellent cooks – as was Catesby when he had the time or interest. Food and wine were an important way to relax – something that he had inherited from his mother. He hated the culture of rushed meals and everything piled on one plate. It was the biggest cultural difference between him and his British half.

The twins worked more amicably as a team when cooking together than at any other time. It was difficult to see which one had chosen what. It began with goat's cheese and sesame seeds in filo pastry for which Catesby opened a bottle of Pouilly Fumé. 'I'm not sure it goes,' he said.

'It doesn't matter,' said Geraldine. 'This meal's a bit of a lash-up of what was left in our fridges.'

The next dish was spinach timbales served in ramekins, followed by a conversational pause. 'How are Catherine and the kids?' said Catesby to Peter, knowing it was a fraught subject.

'They're returning from Malawi in ten days' time.'

'And Catherine's parents?'

'I'll have a full report when she gets back.'

Catesby sensed that it was something Peter didn't want to talk about. His Malawian wife was an economist and her parents were political activists. Once again, Catesby breathed a hidden sigh of relief that he had nothing, absolutely nothing, to do with the African desk at SIS.

The main dish was an aubergine charlotte. It looked like something out of a chic cookery magazine. Catesby was impressed. 'Only an architect could have designed that and only a barrister could have negotiated the perfect harmony of the layers.'

'I think, Will,' said Geraldine, 'you are going over the top.'

'But I'm going to open the burgundy to go with it.'

'There's also a green salad and plebeian rice for the workers,' said Peter.

Catesby closed his eyes and sipped the burgundy. It was a moment of heaven, but he knew it wouldn't last. The arguments would soon begin. He was their much-loved stepdad, but also a decorated member of the hated 'state repressive apparatus'. But the opening gambit wasn't one he expected.

'By the way, Will,' said Geraldine, 'in case the Security Service surveillance report still hasn't crossed your desk, I am no longer a member of the Socialist Workers Party.'

'I didn't know, but thanks for telling me so I can pass it on.' In a way Catesby was disappointed. He didn't want to think the children were going to follow the tired pattern of people becoming less radical as they became older and more successful.

'And could you also pass on,' said Geraldine, helping herself to a generous portion of Aubergine Charlotte, 'my reasons for resigning?'

'Which are?'

'Sexism and misogyny.'

'I'm not surprised,' said Catesby.

'Then why didn't you pass on the details?'

'Because I didn't know the details.'

'Then why did you say you're not surprised?'

'Because I was trying to be supportive. In any case, spying on the SWP is more your mother's turf.'

'Why are you bringing her into it?'

Peter raised a calming hand. 'Don't take it out on Will, Geraldine.'

'I'm not sure,' said Catesby, 'I understand what's going on.'

'I'm moving out of the flat,' said Geraldine.

'You must do what's best for you and ignore everyone else.' He long suspected there had been relationship problems – even though Geraldine was very secretive about her love life. She was a complex and confused person. 'I'll be putting her up in Islington,' said Peter.

'But only until Catherine and the kids come back,' said Geraldine.

'At least,' said Peter, smiling, 'you've found a new party.'

Catesby took a spoonful of 'workers' rice' to bulk up the aubergine. He wondered if Geraldine had become a 'tankie' and signed up with the CP. 'May I ask which party?'

'The Labour Party.'

'Good god,' said Catesby, 'I thought they had sold out the workers. Look at Peter's MP.' Catesby was referring to Michael O'Halloran, who had defected to the Social Democratic Party the previous year.

'Things are moving on in North Islington,' said Peter. 'We're going to replace O'Halloran with the chair of the constituency party, a guy named Jeremy Corbyn.'

Catesby looked at Geraldine.

'It wasn't an easy decision,' she said, 'but Corbyn's convinced me that you can be a socialist and a member of the Labour Party. He's even convinced Tariq Ali to join.'

Catesby smiled. He was glowing inside, but didn't want to make a point of it.

'So,' said Geraldine, 'why don't you say stuff the pension and join up too?'

'I don't know,' said Catesby, 'it's a difficult question and don't think I haven't thought of it before.' There were, of course, things he couldn't tell the children about – like the Sword of Damocles that constantly swung over his head. A lifetime of toxic loyalties, illegal ops, betrayals and lies had left him vulnerable. A principled resignation from SIS wouldn't mean an impoverished retirement hoeing his vegetable patch in Suffolk, but a long sentence in the Scrubs – if not something worse. For the time being, Catesby was going to walk the tightrope – not just out of fear, but also in the hope that he could do something good for his country as a tricky insider.

Geraldine continued to stare at Catesby. 'Can anyone imagine anything more stupid than sending that Task Force south?'

'The Junta aren't exactly sweetness and light. They've summarily executed tens of thousands of their own people.'

'If the Argentine government is so awful, then why did the UK government sell arms to them up to the day they invaded?'

Catesby smiled. 'You are obviously well informed. And the answer, Geraldine, is that the UK government is totally amoral when it comes to making money by exporting arms. But, one could argue, some of the evil profits made by the weapons exporters are paid in taxes which pay for schools and hospitals.'

'But most of those profits go into the pockets of fat-cat tax avoiders.'

'You don't have to tell that to Will,' said her brother. 'He's on our side.'

'I was,' said Catesby, 'playing devil's advocate. And the devil would also argue that helping the UK's chronic balance of payments deficit is another reason for arms sales.'

'Oh, I know,' said Geraldine stifling a fake yawn. 'I've heard it all before: this-is-the-way-things-are-in-the-real-world.'

'I suppose,' said Catesby, 'what they should really say is: this-is-the-way-things-are-in-the-world-that-we-the-ruling-class-have-created. Okay?'

'Despite what Peter says, I'm not sure, Will, what side you are really on.'

'I'm on your side. But it's not something I can actually get up and declare in the middle of a Joint Intelligence Committee meeting.'

'But,' said Geraldine, 'you're in favour of sending the Task Force.'

Catesby squinted. 'We had to respond to the use of force, especially by a bad guy – and the UN Security Council also calls for a complete withdrawal of Argentine forces.'

'But also for an immediate cessation of hostilities between Argentina and the UK.'

'You have done your homework.' Catesby smiled. 'But the resolution you referred to, 502, also gives us the option to invoke Article 51 of the UN Charter – which means we can use military force under the right of self-defence.'

Peter laughed. 'I thought I was the lawyer in the family.'

'I could have done law,' said Catesby, 'but I didn't lose my Suffolk accent fast enough to get called to the Bar.'

'You're avoiding the question, Will,' said Geraldine. 'How much killing is the Task Force going to do to recover a post-colonial remnant to which our claim is dubious and ambiguous?'

Catesby frowned. 'The Task Force is serious sabre-rattling.'

'But they will resort to war?'

'Sabre-rattling isn't serious if you rule that out.'

'So you're willing to kill people to get back those islands?'

'Me personally, no. It's not my decision.' Catesby took a long swig of the fine wine, which he should have slowly savoured. His head began to spin. In the early hours of that very same day he had participated in the extra-judicial execution, some would call it murder, of two arms dealers. He tried to hide his hand tremor and nausea.

'Are you all right, Will?' said Peter.

'Too little sleep, I'll need an early night.'

'We won't keep you up.'

'There isn't going to be a war.' Catesby spoke firmly and stared into the distance. There was an uncomfortable silence around the dinner table. Catesby broke it by offering more wine.

'Why are you so sure?' said Geraldine.

'Because no one could be that stupid.'

'Not even Thatcher?'

'She's not the only player,' said Catesby. 'And even if she and Galtieri decided on a drunken punch-up, the Americans wouldn't let it happen. There's no way that Washington is going to let two of her most important allies go to war. The Argentines beat up communists in South America and we stare them down in Northern Europe.'

The twins nodded, but neither seemed totally convinced.

Catesby looked at the kitchen clock. 'Oh my god, we're missing it!'

'Oh no,' said Geraldine, 'we were hoping you had forgotten!'

'Don't worry,' said Catesby. 'We'll finish eating first. Even in these circumstances house rules apply. No food in front of the television.'

Peter looked at his sister. 'Eat slowly, Geraldine.'

The family knew that Catesby rarely watched television, but agreed that what he did watch was appalling. Catesby, in turn, accused them of being snobs. *The Eurovision Song Contest* from Harrogate was nearly half over when the plates were finally cleared. One of the reasons Catesby loved the programme was Terry Wogan. He liked Wogan's relaxed attitude and the way he always seemed to be gently and affectionately taking the piss. Catesby fantasised about Wogan chairing the Joint Intelligence Committee and bringing some sanity to Whitehall.

Catesby's favourite for the 1982 Eurovision was the Luxembourg entry, 'Cours après le temps', which had a line or two that brought a lump to his throat: 'Cours san regarder ceux qui sont tombés'. The most surreal was the Portuguese girl group who dressed up as the Four Musketeers. He also couldn't understand why the Finnish entry, 'Nuku pommiin', got *nul points.* But Catesby did think it was right that Nicole, a seventeen-year-old schoolgirl from Germany, won the contest with 'Ein bißchen Frieden', 'A Little Peace'. The lyrics didn't ask for much: just sun, cloud and birds on the wind – and a little bit of peace. But no one was listening.

Buenos Aires: 24 April 1982

Fiona had begun to understand why military wives often turned to drink. It could be so boring and lonely. Because of the Falklands crisis, Ariel was away most of the time practising dangerous manoeuvres. She had begun to hate the islands with a passion – and the selfishness of the leaders who wanted to fight over them. Part of her wished that she could still communicate with Catesby. She would tell him that the conflict was one of massive cultural misunderstanding. The Argentines mistook the quiet languid manners of the British for weakness and decadence – and had no idea that the British are a warlike people who love the occasional brawl. The British, on the other hand, had no idea of the national passions that those bleak offshore islands ignited in every Argentine. Nor were they aware of the bravery and professional competence of Argentina's pilots. Part of Fiona, with marital pride, wished that she could transport Ariel to the MoD HQ in Whitehall so that she could shout at the admirals and generals: 'Tell Thatcher that this wonderful man is a fierce and highly skilled warrior who will kill your sailors and sink your ships.' But she knew that she would come across as a besotted wife and no one would listen.

Fiona poured herself another glass of Malbec. Now that her mother-in-law was in bed with her rosary beads, she could indulge herself. Besotted wife that she was, she knew that her marriage could turn out to be an awful mistake. The problem with love and passion was that it meant taking risks. Her sisters, who thought she was just stupid, didn't realise this. Fiona knew there were problems, but was sure they would navigate a way through. She hoped that someday Ariel would leave the navy and devote his life to horses and polo. In fact, he would probably make more money out of that than he did as a pilot. In her dream world, she saw them having children and spending half the year in Argentina and half in England. She missed her family – and, since the invasion, long-distance telephone calls had become difficult. She still wrote letters, but careful ones because she feared they would be read by the intelligence service.

Fiona put an Edith Piaf record on the phonograph. The singer had also fallen in love with a military man, in Piaf's case a beautiful Foreign Legionnaire who was killed in North Africa and buried under *le sable chaud.*

Except, thought Fiona with a shiver, Ariel's resting place wouldn't be under the hot sand, but underneath a cold sea.

Chevening House: Sunday 25 April 1982

It was the first time that Catesby had ever been to Chevening, the Foreign Secretary's grace and favour country residence. Not that Catesby, from darkest, deepest Suffolk, regarded a place so near to London as country. But, he had to admit, it was an impressive pad. The house had been designed by Inigo Jones and begun around 1620 to replace a dilapidated medieval manor. The estate consisted of 3,000 acres including a lot of woodland, so you wouldn't realise that you lived in the suburbs.

Catesby had been picked up at nine in the morning from his flat in Pimlico. The car was an unmarked BMW with a driver in plainclothes from Special Branch. The fact that the Met's top-end cars were now Bimmers instead of Jags struck a worrying note in Catesby's residual patriotism. And he couldn't remember the last time he had seen a cop on a British motorbike. But still, they were about to go to war to keep some sparsely inhabited, and largely uninhabitable islands, 8,000 miles away. To make small talk, he turned to the driver from Special Branch: 'What do you think of this motor?'

'It goes like shit off a shovel, but the gears are stiff.'

Catesby didn't carry on the conversation. Cars bored him senseless. They were all pieces of polluting excrement that ate money and space. In any case, the BMW did go like shit off a shovel and they were at Chevening House in less than an hour.

The final approach to the house was well-raked gravel that gleamed pinkish beige in the watery morning sun. The drive had been designed as a sweeping circle so that coachmen could drop off their guests for grand balls and then head off out of the way. There was a grassy bit in the middle with a fountain. Catesby was surprised so few cars were parked on the drive. He counted six. Catesby's driver dropped him off at the main entrance without saying a word. The house was a work of art and symmetry. The clean classical lines anticipated the Age of Enlightenment by a hundred years. What Catesby liked most about the architecture of the period was its lack of religious purpose and sentiment. The original owners may have been stupidly rich, but the first steps towards justice were clarity of thought.

Catesby walked into the entrance hall. There was hardly anyone about – but those who were carried important-looking document folders and wore strained faces. The only two that Catesby recognised were the head of the FCO's South America Department, whose importance had grown hugely in the past few weeks, and the FCO's Permanent Undersecretary of State. The FCO Perm Sec was the civil servant who headed up the Foreign and Commonwealth Office and was one of the most distinguished-looking mandarins that Catesby had ever seen. Catesby thought he could have got the job on looks alone.

Another distinguished-looking gentleman approached Catesby with a clipboard. Catesby was pleased that he was wearing his best Marks & Spencer's suit.

'Good morning, sir,' said the clipboard person. 'May I please have your...'

Catesby didn't answer. He took the clipboard and scribbled his name and time of arrival on the list. He left the box for 'organisation' blank.

The clipboard person nodded knowingly. He knew that blank meant Secret Intelligence Service. 'Would you mind waiting in the library until the Foreign Secretary is ready to see you? Would you like tea or coffee?'

'Tea, milk no sugar.'

The library had two sofas, armchairs and eighteenth-century escritoires scattered around – and, of course, shelves full of leather-bound books that were for display and not for reading. Catesby chose an armchair next to a side table so he wouldn't have to balance his tea on his knees. The tea was delivered by an unsmiling servant without a hint of deference. He couldn't understand why there were slices of lemon neatly arranged on the tray as he had clearly said tea with milk – but decided not to make an issue of it. Rules are rules.

Catesby was pleased to be left alone so he could scratch and yawn as much as he liked. He looked at the ornate scrolling on the ceiling. After you had been in a few of them, British stately homes had a boring sameness. If, he thought, you wanted to impress your rich colleagues, why didn't you build something different and original? Catesby closed his eyes and felt sleep coming on – but he didn't want to be caught snoring, so he opened his file to prepare for his meeting. The problem was he hadn't a clue what he was preparing for or what the Foreign Secretary wanted.

The silence was eerie. Catesby was surprised that Chevening House was so empty in the middle of a national crisis. He tried to focus his eyes on the documents in front of him, but the underlying reason for the Falklands crisis pulsed through the pages in block capitals: the personality of the PM. She had a total lack of flexibility and an inability to take advice. The only advice she listened to was what she agreed with in the first place. Another problem was her belief that if you ignored a problem long enough, it would go away. The do-nothing option.

Catesby sipped his tea and thought back to the meeting in Switzerland in August 1980. It was the time he had provided intelligence cover for a foreign minister's secret meeting with his Argentine counterpart. The two had hammered out a one-hundred-year leaseback agreement – a face-saving deal for the Argentines which would have ended the dispute. After Thatcher rejected that option, the only alternative was to budget for defending the islands. But the PM rejected that too and continued to implement plans to cut the size of the Royal Navy by a third. The final straw had been announcing that the ice patrol ship, HMS *Endurance*, the UK's only naval presence in the South Atlantic, was going to be withdrawn and scrapped. The PM had wrongly derided the ship as useless. If the Junta had been waiting for a signal that the UK would do nothing about an invasion, this was it. Catesby remembered that Foreign Secretary Francis Pym, whom he was about to meet, had formerly been Secretary of State for Defence and had been sacked for opposing the spending cuts. How ironic, thought Catesby, that Pym was now tasked by the PM with sorting out a mess that could have been prevented if she had taken his advice a year ago when he was Defence Secretary.

The library door opened and a man in a frock coat announced, 'The Foreign Secretary will see you now.'

The office was on the first floor and had two tall sash windows overlooking gardens in early spring flower. Catesby could see the complicated Chevening maze over the Foreign Secretary's hunched shoulders. Pym was clearly tired after jetting back and forth across the Atlantic.

The Foreign Secretary sat at his desk in profile without making eye contact. He was an eloquent man, but had an inner shyness – a characteristic of many war heroes. Pym had been decorated for taking over command of his company after the OC had been badly wounded. Catesby didn't know all the details, but knew the Foreign Secretary had shown courage and leadership in the middle of blood and chaos. He was renowned for coolness and patience – not always qualities that the PM fully appreciated.

The Foreign Secretary looked at Catesby over the rims of his reading glasses. 'We're sending you to Peru via Washington. I've talked to Colin about it.' Catesby was a bit surprised to hear his boss called by his first name. 'Time is precious so you will have to leave today. I thought of putting you on the same RAF VC 10 that brought me back – but it would be better if your arrival was less conspicuous. So we are putting you on a commercial flight.'

Catesby felt a tremor go down his spine.

'I haven't given Colin all the details about your role, because I still don't know all the details. You will find out more in Washington.' The Foreign Secretary paused, then carried on in a quiet and cautionary voice. 'You realise, of course, that dealing with the Americans requires the ability to listen carefully and some degree of shrewdness. There are, how should I say, a variety of views.'

'I understand.' Catesby didn't have to say more. Both men knew there were many in Washington who would like to see Britain fall flat on its face and get kicked out of the Western Hemisphere.

'You have, I believe, operated as a backchannel diplomat before?'

'Yes.' Catesby smiled. 'It worked that time.'

'Otherwise we might have turned into nuclear ash.'

'I was only a messenger boy.' Catesby was referring to the darkest days of the Cuban Missile Crisis when he had ping-ponged back and forth between Havana, Washington and London.

'Harold Macmillan was a very shrewd PM who knew how to make deals in secret.'

Catesby wondered if the reference to Macmillan was a criticism of Thatcher. He was surprised that Pym, always so reserved and enigmatic, had let his mask of loyalty slip.

'We have not,' continued the Foreign Secretary, 'given up on a peacefully negotiated settlement – even though military action is imminent.'

Catesby looked puzzled.

'Have you been briefed?'

'I'm not sure, Foreign Secretary, to what you are referring.'

'Even as we speak, an operation is underway to retake South Georgia.'

Catesby was surprised that he hadn't heard about the operation, but could understand the need for total secrecy. The military had their heads down and were going for it. South Georgia had been in Argentine hands for three weeks. The vastly outnumbered Royal Marines had put up a brave fight before surrendering.

'Assuming that our forces are successful, it is hoped that the Argentines will be convinced of our determination to pursue full military action to recover the Falklands.'

Catesby sat in silent reflection. As a former infantry officer, he couldn't think of anything worse than fighting over the glaciers of South Georgia. 'We hope that the action will focus the Junta's mind on a peace deal.' The Foreign Secretary paused and lowered his voice, almost as if speaking to himself. 'None of us want war.'

Catesby was certain that Pym's 'us' referred to the members of the cabinet who had experienced war at first hand. He suspected that the cabinet was divided along those lines. Catesby looked out the window at the morning mist rising over the gardens. It was as if Chevening and Chequers, the Prime Minister's grace and favour country residence, were the seats of rival barons.

The Foreign Secretary hunched deep in his chair. Catesby noticed he had an unusual ability to curl up within himself. But just as Pym seemed about to disappear into a brown ball, he reappeared. 'Your job in Peru will be to convince the Argentines that they can't win. My job is to help them save face.'

'And in Washington?'

'As I suggested, to listen and to learn the latest. By the way, the Americans will provide you with useful contacts in Peru. We can't negotiate a peace deal without Washington's help.'

'I assume that Washington is putting pressure on the Junta.'

Pym gave his most lugubrious smile. 'But mostly pressure on someone else.'

Catesby's theory of rival baronetcies gained more credence.

'But we also need to make the Argentines think that their chances of winning a war are nil.'

'Even if they're not nil?'

The Foreign Secretary stared into space, the weight of office evident. 'Our biggest trump card is stopping them from getting additional Exocets – and all praise to you and your SIS colleagues for what you have done so far.' Pym looked closely at Catesby. 'What do you, personally, think their chances are of getting more Exocets?'

'That's a nightmare question to ask an intelligence officer. We don't like to provide risk analysis when we have so few facts.'

'But have a try.'

'I would say fifty-fifty.'

'You have to convince the Argentines that those chances are a lot less than fifty-fifty. When you get to Lima you will be meeting diplomats as well as intelligence officers. But it's not enough to convince them alone that the chase for more Exocets is futile; they have to convince Galtieri and the Junta.'

'There's a lot more at stake for them than us – and that's going to make the bargaining more difficult.'

'Indeed, that's the biggest problem. If the Junta lose power, a lot of them are going to face prison sentences for human rights abuses.'

'Which they deserve.'

'I couldn't agree more – but if we don't provide the means to a soft exit they won't have anything to lose. They'll fight to the bitter end and there will be no peace deal. As you know, peace and justice are not always served on the same plate.' The Foreign Secretary went silent again.

Catesby didn't know whether he should interrupt or not. He looked at the hunched and gloomy Pym and wondered what demons were leaping and mocking in his mind.

The Foreign Secretary stood up and walked over to the window and stared out. 'There are children in the maze. They seem to be doing much better than we did.'

'You've tried it?'

'Yes, it was just after Peter Carrington became Foreign Sec. He invited me and my wife for high tea and showed us around. Valerie and I tried the maze and we both got hopelessly lost. We had to be rescued by the head gardener. That, by the way, is top secret. If it ever got back to the PM she would never let me live it down.' The Foreign Secretary turned and faced Catesby. 'And what you will be doing in Washington and Peru is also top secret. You are not to share anything with anyone – not our ambassadors and not even dear old Colin. You will report directly to me and to no one else.' The Foreign Secretary gave a weary smile. 'Apologies for sounding like a regimental sergeant major, but these peace negotiations are a matter of great sensitivity.'

'I understand.'

'Good.'

Catesby sensed it was time to go. 'Thank you, Foreign Secretary. Is there anything else?'

'We haven't got much time. We need the deal signed and delivered within a week – nine days at most. Otherwise, the guns will be blazing.' Just as Catesby turned to leave, the Foreign Secretary spoke again, 'By the way, you will be picked up by the Americans. They will be looking after you.'

Catesby made his way out of Chevening House to the waiting car where he found the Special Branch driver reading *The Ego and the Mechanisms of Defence* by Anna Freud. The driver put the book down as soon as he saw Catesby and gave an embarrassed smile. 'Not the usual reading for a cop, but I'm doing an OU degree in psychology.'

'Interesting?'

'Yeah, it is. Anna Freud is mostly a child psychologist. But I'm not sure that most of us ever get beyond being a child.'

Catesby smiled, but considered it best not to say what he thought.

Agency News: 25 April 1982

Royal Marines Retake South Georgia

The message signalled to London from the commanding officer of British forces was brief and dramatic: 'Be pleased to inform Her Majesty that the White Ensign flies alongside the Union Jack in South Georgia. God Save the Queen.' Following seven hours of air assault and ground-fighting, the island is once again in British hands only twenty-three days after the Argentine invasion. No British casualties have been reported and the Argentine forces surrendered after only limited resistance. Margaret Thatcher, besieged by questioning journalists outside Downing Street, had only one comment to make: 'Just rejoice at that news and congratulate our forces and the Marines.'

The operation began at 1100 hours GMT when Royal Navy helicopters attacked the Argentine submarine, *Santa Fe*, which was moored in the harbour of South Georgia's capital, Grytviken. The submarine was raked with machine-gun fire and rockets. There is still no news of her eighty-five-man crew, but the submarine is smoking, leaking oil and badly listing.

At 1500 GMT, Royal Marines and SAS soldiers were landed on the island by helicopter. After a two-hour battle, British forces had taken complete control of the island from the Argentine garrison.

Chevening House: Midnight, 25 April

As soon as he was informed that the retaking of South Georgia had been a success, the Foreign Secretary knew he was going to have to telephone his Ambassador in Washington. The Ambassador was the ultimate Englishman and well known for his unaffected, rumpled charm. Americans loved him. He had the most disarming smile in the British armoury. It was impossible to disagree with him – at least, in his presence. The Foreign

Secretary appreciated the value of Nicko, as the Ambassador was called by intimates, but didn't always know how much to confide in him. Nicko Henderson's job was to get the Americans on Britain's side and to keep them there. It was not an easy task.

The Ambassador must have been waiting for the call because he picked up the secure voice phone as soon as it beeped.

'Good evening, Foreign Secretary.'

'How are you, Nicko?'

'Very pleased about South Georgia – and that there were no British casualties.'

'But there will be. You can't do these operations without losing people. In fact, we've just heard that a helicopter crewman has been lost in a crash at sea.'

'Sorry, I didn't know.'

'Nothing to do with South Georgia. It was an accident involving a Sea King from *Hermes*.'

The Ambassador gave a respectful pause – and remembered the Foreign Secretary's chronic pessimism.

'In any case,' continued the Foreign Secretary, 'how do you think South Georgia will affect the chances of a negotiated settlement?'

'It certainly shows the Americans that we are determined to go to war if necessary. I don't think it will change the position of the anti-Brit faction, but it might strengthen the hand of the pro-Brit faction in getting Reagan's still reluctant support.'

Pym stirred uneasily: Nicko wasn't answering the question he asked.

Not only a charmer, but a mind reader too, the Ambassador continued, 'As for the chances of a negotiated peace deal, I don't think our retaking South Georgia will make much difference. The big problem is getting through to Galtieri, who is usually drunk and not always completely rational.'

The Foreign Secretary frowned. The drink flowed freely in Downing Street too.

'I am sure that Haig realises this – and therefore is not optimistic about a negotiated settlement. In fact, he's starting to convince his colleagues that the chances of a peace deal are remote – and that a US tilt towards the UK is the only option.'

Pym hunched in his chair and stared at the wall. It wasn't the same message that Alexander Haig, the general turned US Secretary of State, was giving to him. How ironic that Haig had referred to a former British Foreign Secretary as a 'duplicitous bastard'.

'We need,' said the Ambassador, 'to win in Washington if we are going to win in the South Atlantic.'

'What are the obstacles?'

'Splits in the White House and the Pentagon – and Reagan trying to be friends with both sides. Jeane Kirkpatrick continues to loudly rally the pro-Argentine faction. She had dinner at the Argentine Embassy on the evening of the invasion. But the US military are a problem too, even if they are less vocal.'

Pym frowned. The notoriously anti-British Kirkpatrick was US Ambassador to the UN – a place where Britain needed friends. 'But,' said Pym, 'I thought Haig, as a former general, would convince the military to follow his lead.'

'The US military are not renowned for falling into line behind their leaders. West Point and Annapolis create big egos. The first problem is that many in the Pentagon don't think that we can pull it off so far from home – and don't want to taint their reputations by supporting a losing side. Vietnam still rankles. The other problem is that many top-ranking US military have close personal relationships with the Junta. A week ago the commander in chief of the US Atlantic Fleet tersely informed me that Admiral Jorge Anaya was his son's godfather. I think we can see where his sympathies lie – and he's not the only one.'

Pym continued to stare at the wall. Suddenly the wallpaper peeled back and there was the image of a burning tank in Italy. He closed his eyes and when he opened them again the wallpaper had mended. But when he resumed speaking his voice was dead. 'Continue working for American support. You are doing a splendid job.'

Northern Virginia: 26 April 1982

It was 6 p.m. in Washington when Catesby's flight touched down at Dulles Airport in northern Virginia, but 11 p.m. in London. It was going to be a twenty-nine-hour day. Catesby had fortified himself with a few stiff brandies on the flight – which was probably a mistake as well as unprofessional. He was travelling on a diplomatic passport which meant he was quickly whisked through customs to his waiting minder, a tieless man in his thirties with long curly black hair who was dressed in a smart suit of Italian cut. Catesby felt deliciously light-headed in the spring air, slightly warmer than London, as he was led to a car. He didn't recognise the make, but the American called it 'a metal turd'.

After his bags were stowed in the 'trunk', Catesby made the usual tired Brit faux pas of getting in on the wrong side. 'You can drive if you want to?' said the American.

'No thanks.'

They swapped around and the American stuck out a slim artistic hand. 'My name's Luc, spelt with a c. I'm a flunky on the Seventh Floor.'

Catesby recognised the reference. The Seventh Floor was the floor in the State Department building where the Secretary of State and the senior staff had their offices.

'We're putting you up in a safe house near Manassas. Nice place. We use it for undercover VIPs and high-level defectors. Nobody will bother you – and if they do, tell them to fuck off.'

Catesby looked closely at the American. He was what some people would call pretty – but a prettiness that was deceptive. For a second he felt unease; he wondered if he had been picked up by someone who wasn't what he said he was. In fact, the driver's looks and dress had a suggestion of something Argentine.

As if reading Catesby's mind, the American reached for his jacket pocket and said, 'I should have shown you my ID.'

'No problem.'

'No, no, have a look.'

Catesby took the card. It was a normal photo ID enclosed in

plastic. He checked Luc's date of birth: October 1942. He was older than he looked. And the place of birth: Washington, DC. He was obviously a born DC insider; probably came from a family of them. He handed the card back.

'Tell us what you need,' said the American, 'booze, babes – don't worry about honey trapping – we'd never do that to a British ally. We could even conjure up some Colombian marching powder – but be sure to flush what you don't snort down the toilet.'

'A bottle of good wine would be nice.'

'Tinto or blanco.'

'Tinto.'

'Actually,' said the American sounding a bit British, 'you can have whatever you want from the drinks cupboard. It's well stocked – and there's some very nice tinto made by gringos. Europeans who are snooty about Californian wine have never tasted the stuff. I'll show you the best bottles of Napa Valley Cabernet Sauvignon. In blind tastings Californian wines often beat the big-name Bordeaux estates.'

Catesby gave a tired smile. Overwhelming military and economic power weren't enough: they had to produce the best wines too. Catesby found himself humming 'La Mer'. There are some things money can't buy.

It wasn't a long drive. In less than half an hour Luc turned off the main road on to a lane that twisted and weaved through woodland. Ten minutes later, they arrived at a gated entrance. Luc got out of the car, keyed a password into the electronic lock and the gates hissed open.

'Don't worry,' said Luc as he drove in and the gates hissed closed behind the car, 'there aren't any neighbours.'

The safe house was 1950s modern. What Catesby most liked were the lake views through an eighteen-foot wall that was entirely glass window. It brought the outside in, which was what the architect intended. The use of big bright stone slabs and ornate banisters reminded Catesby of the type of British bungalow that many of his generation aspired to – if they had the money. They wanted to escape the dark cramped Victorian terraces of their past.

'What do you think?' said Luc.

'It's okay, but I prefer old houses. My own home was built in 1490.' Catesby smiled. 'Two years before Columbus discovered Cuba.'

'You have to get used to the new. That's what America is about. The Russians who stay here love it.'

Catesby's eye caught a life-size painting of a nude. Its rough edges and colour complemented the stonework. 'That painting certainly fits in.'

'Thanks. That's why I lent it to them.'

'You collect art?'

'Not on my salary. No, I didn't buy it. I painted it.'

Catesby realised that Luc's duties went beyond giving him a lift from the airport.

'I spent a year at the Slade when my father was stationed in London. Derek Jarman was a classmate of mine – he's a film-maker.'

'I know,' said Catesby, with an irritated smile.

'Of course – you would know.' It was Luc's turn to smile. 'Your diplomatic cover was often cultural attaché. And no apologies for looking up your records – just like you will look up mine as soon as you get a chance. In fact, I'll even give some extra details. A few years ago, Derek made a punk version of Shakespeare's *Tempest* and asked me to play Ariel. I wasn't particularly flattered – because I think Derek had his own agenda and I've always been straight which, I agree, can be a bit of a bore. Which is why I paint: I want to escape the conventional part of myself.'

Catesby tried not to be a patronising Brit. The great thing about Americans is that they love to talk about themselves. They weren't a people who liked to keep personal secrets secret. He didn't want to stop Luc's flow.

'And after the Slade?' said Catesby.

Luc beamed. 'I joined the US Army. I'm pretty sure I'm the only ex-Slade student to have served in Vietnam – but they are such a weird lot you can never be certain.'

'Why?'

'Why what?'

'Vietnam.'

'As an artist, I wouldn't have missed it for anything. Vietnam was the ultimate psychedelic experience. You didn't even need drugs.' Luc paused. 'This is getting kind of ironic. My job is finding out about you and I keep telling you about me.'

'It's a good technique to get the other person to reveal.'

'So I've heard. Would you like some grub?'

'I am hungry.'

In the end, the safe house wasn't as well stocked with food as it was booze. But Luc managed to rustle up a spaghetti bolognese with lots of Napa Valley Cabernet Sauvignon.

'Okay,' said Luc between mouthfuls, 'I know you're not going to tell me why they sent you, but it's pretty fucking obvious it has something to do with the mess in the South Atlantic.'

'Good guess. Who is it that wants you to report on me?'

'The Secretary of State.'

'You said you were a mere flunky.'

'But I'm Al Haig's flunky. We go back a long way.'

Catesby stared at Luc. He didn't look the sort, Slade and all, who would be an intimate of General Haig.

'Does that surprise you?' said Luc.

'Frankly, yes.'

'What you don't know about me is that I am god's own fucking bureaucrat, fixer and staff officer. I saved Haig's bacon in Vietnam and I'm still saving it now.'

'What was your job?'

'I started off in 1966 as an infantry platoon leader in Big Red One, that's the First Infantry Division. I did a pretty good job and later became a staff officer in Haig's battalion. At the end of my tour, when I was due to be sent back to the States, Haig asked me to extend for another six months and I agreed – and just after that the shit hit the fan.' Luc took a long sip of wine and went silent.

'What happened?'

Luc shrugged. 'Who knows? The infantry companies at Ap Gu were completely pinned down and I'm sure that the commanding officers couldn't see what the fuck was happening. It was Haig's decision to fly in and take charge on the ground. He knew that we couldn't win a traditional infantry battle with rifles and bayonets – so he had our soldiers dig in and he called in massive air and artillery support. In the end, we had seventeen killed and a hundred wounded, but we killed nearly six hundred of them.'

'How many weapons did you capture?'

Luc smiled. 'You're right to be sceptical. We captured fifty weapons.'

'So 550 of the troops you killed were unarmed?'

Luc gave a non-committal shrug.

'And what,' said Catesby, 'was your role in all this?'

'My job was advising and supporting Al Haig – and making sure that he got the recognition that he deserved.' The American gave a sly smile. 'I'm sure you know how these things work.'

Catesby didn't reply.

'It ended up with Haig winning the Distinguished Service Cross – second highest bravery award after the Medal of Honor – and his getting promoted to brigade commander. Westmoreland, of course, loved him.'

Catesby tried not to show his feelings. He rated Westmoreland, who commanded the American military in Vietnam, as history's stupidest general – and there was a lot of competition when it came to stupid generals. But the worst thing was that Westmoreland hid and falsified statistics to justify his failed strategy to his civilian bosses in Washington.

'Of course,' continued Luc, 'back in '67 body count based on massive use of air and artillery was the latest craze – and Haig's success at Ap Gu was just what Westy wanted to hear.' Luc paused. 'From what I've found out about you, you had a good war too – parachuted into occupied France with SOE. Weren't you in F Section with Violette Szabo?'

'Can we talk about something else?'

'Fine. I've noticed that a lot of Brits don't like talking about what they experienced in the war.'

'Not all. Some write books about it.'

'And you don't approve?'

'Only if it's important history or good literature.'

'Don't worry. I respect your not wanting to talk about it. But my job, like yours, is to find things out and report back. Al Haig says that his counterpart, Foreign Secretary Francis Pym, never talks about what happened to him in the war either. Any idea why? Is he traumatised?'

'I don't know. You'll have to ask him.' Catesby smiled. 'But maybe it's because Mr Pym is a reserved and modest gentleman.'

'And Al Haig isn't?'

'You're better positioned to answer that yourself.'

'Okay and I will. Al is a very dignified man, who usually knows how to behave, but sometimes sticks his foot in his mouth. Like last year when Reagan took a bullet.'

Catesby nodded without smiling. Luc was referring to the incident that took place while Reagan was undergoing emergency surgery. A flushed and sweating Haig announced to reporters in the White House, 'I'm in charge here.' Ignoring the basic constitutional fact that the Secretary of State was fourth, not first, in line to follow an incapacitated President.

'It was,' whispered Luc, 'an utter PR disaster. Haig made it sound like he had staged a *coup d'état*.'

Catesby couldn't help noticing that Luc's voice had begun to sound more and more British. Perhaps it was a legacy of his time in London – or he was imitating Catesby's own way of speaking. He realised that Luc was the sort of chameleon that alternately flattered and sabotaged in the shadows of power.

Luc poured out the remains of the wine and held up the empty bottle. 'More of the same?'

Catesby nodded. 'Yeah, it's good stuff – smooth and velvety.'

'Everything that Haig isn't.' The American got up to find another bottle of the Californian red.

'It sounds like you're not very fond of your boss.'

Luc popped the cork and looked at the wine. 'Liking or not liking has nothing to do with this game. Haig is still my ladder to the top – just as General Douglas MacArthur was Haig's ladder when he was a young officer in Japan and Korea. Al was only twenty-five when he became aide to the chief of staff and used to give daily briefings to MacArthur. Haig never commanded a battlefield unit in Korea, but still chalked up three medals for valour.' Luc smiled. 'It's who you know.'

'Why are you telling me these things?'

'Because I want to help Haig. If you and your British colleagues understand more about him, you can avoid misunderstandings – and stop him fucking up.' Luc folded his hands around his wine glass as if he were warming a chalice. 'There is a plot to get rid of Haig, but it's too soon for me to take sides.' Luc laughed. 'He's still trying to recover from the Orlando Tardencilla fiasco which only happened last month.'

Catesby hadn't a clue, so he said, 'Remind me.'

'We would love to prove that Cuba is behind the guerrilla war in El Salvador – even if they're not. The El Salvador Army, in a rare moment of competence, managed to capture a nineteen-year-old guerrilla fighter named Orlando Tardencilla. Of course, the Salvadorans tortured the fuck out of the kid and got him to say that he had been trained in Cuba. To jazz up his tale, Orlando said he'd been to Ethiopia – even though he didn't even know that Ethiopia was in Africa. It was kind of funny, but Haig didn't get the joke and had the kid flown to Washington for a press conference to prove that Cuba was fomenting communist revolution in Latin America. And, by the way, I advised him against it. As soon as Orlando got in front of the cameras, he admitted that he had made up the story to escape being tortured and had never been to Cuba. The rest of the game was damage limitation.'

Catesby refilled his wine glass.

'The problem with Al Haig – well, one of many problems – is that he thinks he is the only person who can solve a problem. The way to deal with this is to feed him ideas in such a way that he thinks they are his own ideas. He also doesn't know how to relax and he over-schedules. We once had a trip to Europe that included back-to-back summits. None of us got more than three hours sleep a night. The most embarrassing thing was Reagan falling asleep while talking to the Pope – an incident that was televised around the world.'

Catesby felt a wave of pessimism engulf his brain. Haig was the mirror image of Thatcher: an insomniac who had all the answers.

'You look worried.'

'No,' said Catesby, 'I look totally hopeless.'

'Cheer up. The thing to remember about Haig is his unbridled ambition. He likes to take over things. He doesn't get drunk on booze; he gets drunk on power. He loved being in charge during the dying days of the Nixon regime – and he wants to be in the White House again. But this time as President.'

'And you want to be beside him?'

Luc laughed and shook his head. 'It's not going to happen. Haig is too brittle and totally lacking in charm. However, I still want him to succeed while my cart is hitched to his chariot. But if he doesn't, I don't want to be seen as one of those who wielded the knife.'

Catesby smiled. The wine was going to his head. 'You are, Luc, such a wonderful person.'

'Washington is a nest of vipers – but some of us have a nice side that isn't completely false.' He nodded towards the portrait of the nude woman. 'I'll tell you about her later – but one more thing about Generalissimo Haig.'

'Go on.'

'He'd love the Nobel Peace Prize. He could pin it up on the wall next to his Distinguished Service Cross – a nice balance.'

Catesby stared at the nude portrait. 'How do you reconcile being an artist and a bureaucratic shit?'

'No problem. They both require careful observation and creativity.'

'She looks athletic,' said Catesby.

'I would say gamine.'

'Did you meet her at the Slade?'

Luc smiled and took a sip of wine. 'No, I met her at a polo match in Virginia. A lot of rich dudes and dudettes. Her father is an arms dealer who has never heard a shot fired in anger – but, in his defence, he is a fearless and magnificent polo player. In any case, after a lot of champagne we went back to my pad in Georgetown.' Luc paused. 'I won't go into the details, but it didn't work.'

Catesby was intently listening – and hoping that the flash-bulbs going off in his brain weren't showing through his scalp. The first flashbulb primed when Luc mentioned 'polo match' and then went off at 'arms dealer'. It was always odd how key pieces of intelligence arrive unsolicited.

'I hope,' said Luc, 'I'm not boring you.'

'Not at all. It's fascinating.'

'Are you being ironic or just polite?'

'Actually, I'd like to know what happened next.'

Luc laughed. 'Nothing happened. She put her clothes back on and went home. She was very sweet. As she left she put her hand on my cheek and said, "It's not your fault. It's me, the way I am."' Luc got up and went over to the painting. He ran his finger over the portrait's left arm. 'It was obvious why it wasn't working – but she was so beautiful. Her arms were so graceful – like a ballet dancer's. In fact, she had once trained as a dancer, but preferred running and tennis.'

'But you obviously saw her again.'

'Of course. She became my regular model. I photographed, sketched and painted every square inch of her body and caught her in a thousand poses. I've catalogued them. I have 231 photos, drawings and paintings of her. One day we were going through them together and she said something that was kind of peculiar – but maybe there wasn't anything to it.'

'What?'

'She said I could make a lot of money – in her words, "one big fucking pile of filthy bucks" – by selling them to her father.'

'Why don't you?'

'I'm saving them for a rainy day.'

'Does she have any of them?'

'Fourteen. I haven't given them to her – I've *lent* them. That's what artists do – and we never get them back.'

'What does she do with them?'

'I don't know. Maybe she gives them to her girlfriends – or maybe not.'

'Do you still see her?'

'I haven't seen her for two years. She fucked off to South America – but I occasionally get a letter or a card. She's taken up scuba diving and wants me to do a portrait of her underwater.' Luc helped himself to more wine and whispered, 'Andalucía.'

'Southern Spain. Have you been there?'

'No, but McCullough, that's her name, suggested we could meet there in a few weeks.'

Another flashbulb went off in Catesby's brain. *Gibraltar.*

Chevening House: 26 April 1982, 5 a.m. BST

The Foreign Secretary was fully dressed except for a tie. It was early and he didn't want to do a Churchill by conducting business from bed in his pyjamas. Also, to make the urgent call, he had to be in his office for that was where Chevening's only secure voice phone was located. It was midnight in Washington, but it was essential that he speak to Haig.

Pym spoke first. 'Good evening, Al. Thank you for taking this call so late.'

'It isn't late. I'll be up for another three hours.'

'One of our negotiating team has already arrived and will be ready for briefing whenever you are.'

'We've put him in the diary for the morning. Your communication is welcome now that the imminence of hostilities has taken place.'

Pym was certain the Secretary of State was referring to the retaking of South Georgia. It wasn't always easy translating 'Haig-speak' into English. 'I hope,' said Pym, 'that our show of force in South Georgia won't make the Argentines less likely to negotiate.'

'On the other hand, it might persuade them that Britain can still rule the waves – and that they have to negotiate.'

Pym winced at Haig's transatlantic echo of British jingoism. He lowered his voice as if the fine Georgian furniture of Chevening House was eavesdropping. 'The problem…'

'The problem,' interrupted Haig, 'is finding a moment when Galtieri is sober enough to listen to reason.'

The problem, thought Pym, *is that you won't keep quiet and listen.*

'As you were saying, Francis.'

Pym lowered his voice to a whisper. 'The unwillingness to negotiate is not just an obstacle we face in Buenos Aires, but one we face in London as well.'

'I know only too well. She isn't easy.'

Pym ignored the comment about the Prime Minister. 'The best way to go down the diplomatic route is very quietly.'

'You mean secretly.'

'Those are your words, Al. I have no secrets from the Prime Minister.'

'Are you going to send her a transcript of this telephone conversation?'

'I would,' purred Pym, 'if she wasn't too busy to read it.'

'I know what you're saying. She doesn't understand the price of refusing to compromise. Her stance could cost you a lot of international support.'

The Foreign Secretary silently nodded. The words from the previous day 'totally' and 'unacceptable' were still ringing in his ears. It didn't just apply to the Falklands, but to the PM's attitudes about everything else. The concept of give-and-take was something she regarded as synonymous with total surrender. Pym had recently listened with embarrassment at a European Community summit while the translator struggled for a polite rendering of the words of an exasperated French official who described the UK leader as *un enfant gâté qui casse ses jouets.* Sitting next to the PM, Pym thought it best not to suggest something about toys being chucked out of a pram.

'If,' said Pym, 'we can bring Argentina to the table…'

'We must convince them that they can never win a war against Britain.'

Which, thought Pym, is why he had dispatched Catesby.

'But,' continued Haig, 'they must have some sort of face-saving fig leaf. Now listen, the path to a peaceful settlement leads through Peru.' For the next fifteen minutes the American Secretary of State laid out his plan while the British Foreign Secretary stared at the wall.

The White House: 26 April 1982

When Catesby woke up that morning in the safe house, Luc was gone – but the dishwasher had been emptied. If he ever got over McCullough, Luc would make a good husband. Catesby made a cup of tea and looked out over the lake in the dawn light. The best of America was water and trees. He didn't understand the fascination many British had with the deserts and canyons of the American West. Someone was knocking at the door. Catesby looked at the clock; they were early. He opened the door and found a US Marine in full uniform: white trousers and red-trimmed blue jacket. He gave a snappy salute and said, 'Good morning, sir.'

Catesby, still in his dressing gown, returned the salute by lifting his cup of tea. 'Good morning.'

'I am here, sir, to take you to the White House for your meeting.'

'Well, I'd better get ready then.'

Ten minutes later Catesby had brushed his teeth and was wearing a regimental tie that he had bought especially for the trip. The Marine held the door open to the back seat of a gleaming Lincoln Continental sedan – the hardtop version of the car Kennedy had got shot in. Half an hour later as they drove into Washington, Catesby wondered if there had been a case of mistaken identity. Shouldn't he be going to the State Department building in Foggy Bottom? He leaned forward to speak to the driver. 'I believe my meeting is with Secretary of State Alexander Haig.'

'That is correct, sir.'

'Thank you.'

Catesby sat back and smiled: another insight. Haig's self-importance preferred the grandeur and pomp of the White

House to the workaday dullness of the modern State Department building. But when they arrived there was little pomp. Haig had been relegated to a 'situation room' in the White House basement with no natural light. The thing that fascinated Catesby most was a white, bolted steel door. He wondered if it led to the nuclear bunker of last resort.

The Secretary of State began. 'I was discussing the situation with Francis Pym last night and explained in no uncertain terms that this is the last roll of the dice for a negotiated peace settlement.'

The American paused to light a cigarette. Catesby wondered if smoking was a good idea for someone who had recently had a triple-bypass heart operation. In fact, triple-bypasses seemed – like cosmetic surgery for Hollywood stars – a must-have operation for high status Americans. Henry Kissinger had just had one as well.

'The Peruvians, as you will soon find out, are being very helpful. Only they can present the Argentines a pot pour wee of fig leaves that Buenos Aires may sniff and decide to accept.'

Catesby was baffled. He assumed the Secretary of State was referring to a pot for pouring urine – then he realised that it was the way Haig pronounced *potpourri*! But Haig's mispronunciation, suggesting a dish full of dried and pointless fig leaves, was a better metaphor.

'Mr Pym,' said Catesby, 'assured me that you would be providing a list of contacts for me in Peru.'

The Secretary of State gave him a sharp look, as if Catesby's tone wasn't sufficiently deferential. Haig drew deep on his cigarette before answering. 'You will be staying at the Ambassador's residence in Lima. I'm sure you already know that.'

'No, I didn't know.' Catesby was surprised that Pym hadn't told him.

'I am sure you will find Frank and Dolores most hospitable – and very helpful.'

Catesby frowned. He couldn't think of any senior dip named Frank who was married to a Dolores. 'There must have been a change of posting of which I am unaware.'

'What are you talking about?' said Haig with irritation. 'There hasn't been any change of personnel in Lima.'

'Then our Ambassador is still Charles Wallace.'

Haig stared at Catesby as if he were the dimmest cadet in the officer intake. 'I wasn't talking about the *British* Ambassador, I was talking about the *American* Ambassador.'

'My apologies for forgetting that Britons are not the only players.'

'I don't think it's a habit that we can cure.'

Catesby thought it best not to reply. He knew it would be undiplomatic to ask Haig if he was referring to the Prime Minister.

'You'll be impressed by Frank. He speaks fluent Spanish and is a direct descendant of the conquistadors. His family settled in New Mexico centuries before it was called "New" – and Frank knows Latin America like the back of his hand. Very respected too.'

Catesby gave a false smile of thanks. He had to put aside his personal feelings of dislike and use Haig for what was required. But who was Haig supposed to be helping? Pym, Thatcher, the British people? And what was it that he, she or they wanted? A military victory or a peace deal?

'Frank has a close and excellent relationship with President Belaúnde Terry, who could be the most important player in negotiating a peaceful settlement.' Haig paused to light a new cigarette from the stub of the last one.

'What in your view, Secretary of State, are Peru's interests in this situation?'

Haig waived his cigarette like a dismissive wand. 'I'd rather keep my powder dry on that one. But I have arranged a briefing for you that will cover that subject. As soon as you leave here you will be reporting to Foggy Bottom for that briefing.'

Catesby was tempted to remind Haig that he wasn't a junior staff officer in the US Army, but displaying personal and national pride would not be constructive at the moment.

'Your briefing at State will be led by Vernon Walters, who I believe you've met before.'

Catesby suppressed a smile. General Walters, now an ambassador-at-large, was an odd character. Catesby had first met Walters at a NATO conference in Paris. Both of them were helping as interpreters for confidential conversations where a non-vetted professional interpreter would be inappropriate. The thing that most impressed Catesby about Walters was his skill as a linguist – which surpassed that of most professional interpreter-translators. What disconcerted Catesby about General Walters wasn't his right-of-centre politics – standard for the turf – but his personality. Something just didn't add up.

'The best way to a negotiated settlement,' said Haig, 'is for all sides to see the situation with perfect clarity. The Argentines must realise that they are a third-rate military power that, despite the bravery of their best soldiers, sailors and pilots, could never win an armed conflict against the UK. It would be suicidal. But,' Haig paused and took a long reflective drag on his cigarette, 'people do commit suicide for a variety of reasons.'

As Catesby watched Haig continue to smoke, he wondered if the Secretary of State had any sense of irony.

The American gave Catesby a sly look. 'This isn't for general dissemination, but if necessary we may tilt to the UK. We're not going to do another Suez on you.'

Catesby, who thought Suez had been a combination of arrogance and stupidity, kept silent. In 1956 Washington had pulled the plug on the pound sterling to reverse Britain's attempt to regain control of the Suez Canal after Nasser's nationalisation. It was the end of the UK as a world power – and proved that banks can be more powerful than tanks. Catesby looked up and saw the Secretary of State staring at him. He wondered if the American was waiting for him to say *thank you.*

'You were,' said Haig, staring at Catesby's regimental tie, 'in SOE during the war.'

'Yes – largely because I speak French.'

'Then you know what war is like.'

Catesby was tempted to answer *and so do the people of My Lai.*

'I can assure you,' said Haig, 'that we both want peace.'

Part of Catesby believed him. Maybe the American was more fucked up than he looked.

The black Lincoln Continental that chauffeured Catesby to the State Department building at Foggy Bottom was the same model as the earlier one, but the Marine driver was shorter and more talkative. He told Catesby that he was three weeks too late to see the Washington cherry blossom display – which was 'downright purdy'. The driver also made a great show of dropping Catesby off in front of the colonnades at the main entrance. The Marine gave Catesby his second smart salute of the day as he held the car door open. Catesby felt he was the Crown Prince of Ruritania – and was tempted to ask the Marine if he could hire him, dress uniform and all, for dinner parties in Suffolk.

Catesby was also treated with deference when he got inside the building. He wondered if a 'be-nice-to-the-Brits' memo had been issued. He was escorted to the hallowed Seventh Floor by a refined woman with a transatlantic accent. Before taking him to Walters's office, she showed him around the Treaty Room Suite, a blue oval reception room with Ionic columns. She spread her hand grandly. 'All of the paintings and furniture, which date from the early years of the Republic, are on loan from their owners. No tax dollars have been spent.'

The deference ended, however, as soon as Catesby met General Walters, who greeted him in French. '*Bonjour, Monsieur Catesby.* I think it's best that we speak French as you say that I speak English with the accent of a gangster from the Bronx.'

'*Vos renseignements,*' answered Catesby, '*sont manifestement faux.* I would never say such a thing – and it isn't true.'

Walters switched to English. 'It was a joke, Catesby, don't you understand irony?'

Catesby smiled and shook hands. The real irony was that Walters did sound like a gangster from the Bronx.

'Have a seat, Catesby.'

Unlike the elegance of the Treaty Room Suite, the office was functional, with thinly padded chairs made from curved beech laminate.

Walters began. 'The Argentines are drinking in the Last Chance Saloon – Galtieri, of course, would drink in any saloon. In fact, he was pretty drunk the day before they invaded the Falklands and told me they were going to do it. Well, I'm sure that nothing I would have said would have made any difference or stopped the invasion – so I didn't say anything.'

Catesby was sure that Walters was sanitising what had taken place, and wanted to know more. 'Didn't Galtieri even consider the possibility that Britain would respond militarily?'

Walters smiled. 'He said that the South Atlantic weather would make the British so seasick that they wouldn't be able to fight.'

The telephone rang and Walters turned away to answer it. Catesby tried to eavesdrop, but the Ambassador-at-Large was speaking rapid Spanish in hushed tones – and had lost his American accent. Once again, Catesby was puzzled by the enigma that was Vernon Walters. Walters was the son of a British businessman and had grown up in France and England. The young Walters had been a boarder at Stonyhurst, a posh school for Catholics run by the Jesuits, but hadn't retained a trace of an English accent or British manners. But even more unusual, at least for Catesby who guzzled hospitality champagne at embassy bashes and conferences, was that Walters kept himself to mineral water. Nor did the unmarried American smoke or womanise. Catesby, of course, suspected hidden vices and made the obvious enquiries, but found nothing. He came to the conclusion that Walters was a devout Roman Catholic, *un moine-soldat*, a latter-day Knight Templar. Interpreting the machinations of such a person was impossible. The Vatican, who supported revolutionary groups and reactionary juntas in Latin America, made the plots fomented by Moscow Central almost transparent.

Walters put the phone down and looked at Catesby. 'Tom Enders is going to join us.'

Catesby felt a grim foreboding. It was like a priest telling you that he had just invited Satan in for a chat. Enders was the ultimate Ugly American. He wasn't ugly to look at. In fact, he was tall, handsome and elegant. But Enders was a gung-ho hawk who had played a key role in Nixon's secret bombing of Cambodia. He was now Reagan's chief advisor on Latin American affairs and had ordered Jimmy Carter era diplomatic appointees 'to stop going on about human rights'.

Enders came in without knocking. He didn't shake hands or acknowledge Catesby's presence. If a 'be-nice-to-Brits memo' had been issued, it hadn't reached Enders's office.

'Al,' said Enders, looking at Walters, 'just told me that you're going to Peru.'

'It was on the cards,' said the other American, 'but hadn't been confirmed.'

Catesby found Enders's physical presence intimidating. He was an athletic mountain climber who was dressed smartly in expensive Savile Row blue pinstripe. At least Britain was still good for suits if you had the cash. Catesby felt mousy and invisible in Marks & Spencer grey.

Enders turned to Catesby. 'I won't mince words. We have never been happy about the British refusal to discuss sovereignty. Constantly ignoring a problem does not mean it will go away. Your government's stalling tactics provoked Argentina to take action.'

Catesby put on an expression that he hoped was a total blank. It wasn't his job to get into an argument with a senior American official. There were, however, many in the Foreign Office who believed that Enders had given the Junta a green light to invade by telling them that the UK would not respond and that the USA would remain neutral. Enders was being proved wrong on both accounts – and yet he was a man who Haig described as having 'a massive brain'. Catesby disagreed. Being bad never works if you are also stupid.

'But,' said Enders, 'that's clearly water under the bridge. The biggest problem now is that the British do not understand the Argentine character or the situation. You stereotype them as hot-blooded impulsive Latinos, which they are not. You mistake dignity for machismo.'

Catesby nodded. Enders wasn't completely stupid. 'Any guidance would be most appreciated.'

'That, obviously, is why you are here.'

Catesby didn't reply. Enders' reputation for being blunt and cold was well deserved.

Enders suddenly shifted into Spanish. '*¿Que tan bien...* How well do you speak Spanish? It doesn't matter if it's Castilian.'

Catesby stumbled through an answer in Spanish explaining that it wasn't his best language, but that he could get by.

'I suggest then that you save your Spanish for waitresses and taxi drivers.'

Despite their difference in size, Catesby wanted to headbutt the American and watch the blood flowing from both nostrils of his broken nose. But he had to remember that he was a backchannel diplomat on a sensitive mission and not a drunk Lowestoft trawlerman confronting his wife's lover in a pub. Maybe, thought Catesby, we know more about machismo than the Americans realise.

'You should know,' said General Walters, 'that many of the Argentine negotiating team meeting you in Lima have been on training courses in the USA. Their English, if not always fluent...'

'Will be,' said Enders, 'much better than your Spanish.'

'You ought to know, Tom,' said Walters in a conciliatory tone, 'that Mr Catesby is an outstanding linguist.'

'But, like most British, he knows little about the situation in Latin America.'

Enders's tone was grating and obnoxious, but Catesby bit his tongue and smiled blandly. To keep calm he ran a piece by Miles Davis through his head: *so what, so what, so what, SO WHAT...* There was an America that Catesby loved, but Enders and Walters were not part of it.

'One of the Argentine negotiating team,' said Walters, 'is an officer from the Secretaría called Horacio Spinoza.'

'Cool name,' said Catesby.

The two Americans stared at their visitor. They hadn't a clue what he had meant.

Meanwhile Catesby was trying hard not to tap his foot in rhythm with the Miles Davis piece that was going through his head. He wondered if he had time to visit a DC jazz club before he jetted off to Lima. But he knew he didn't. Catesby's brain reluctantly lifted the tone arm off the Miles Davis record that was playing in his mind. The music was gone and he was back with the squares.

'Yeah,' said Catesby, 'I recognise Spinoza's name from our files on SIDE – which, admittedly, are probably far less extensive then yours.' The Secretaría, as the Americans preferred to call the Argentine intelligence service instead of by its initials, was not only involved in foreign intelligence, but also in domestic repression.

'What do you know about Spinoza?' said Enders.

'Only that he shares the name of a Dutch philosopher.' Catesby thought it best to leave out the fact that the SIS files on Spinoza cite his role in liaising with an American professional assassin and the use of car bombs. Spinoza was a dangerous man.

'Horacio Spinoza,' continued Enders, 'keeps a low profile and little is known about him outside the Secretaría. You will find no photographs of him and no biographical details. Spinoza is not a coward, but he wants to protect his family.'

It was obvious, thought Catesby, that Spinoza was a man with enemies who required personal protection for himself and those around him.

'He loves his three daughters,' said Walters, 'beyond belief – and protecting them is almost an obsession. Spinoza joined the Secretaría when he was eighteen and has never known another life – outside the service and his family. But you would never think so.'

'Horacio,' added Walters, 'is great fun to be around – not at all institutionalised by years in the service. He is charismatic, charming and loves a good laugh.'

Catesby smiled. The people who interrogated Hermann Goering had also found him charismatic and full of laughs.

Enders stared hard at Catesby. 'I'll give it to you straight from the shoulder. We don't want Galtieri and his Junta to fall from power. They are very valuable allies to America. Unfortunately, if it comes to a full-scale war, it is almost certain that your country will win and that the Junta will fall. We don't want that. Our primary job is fighting communism in the Western Hemisphere. We had a lot of bleating from the Carter administration about human rights – and now we hear echoes of that same bleating from across the Atlantic. If Latin America becomes communist, there won't be any human rights at all – and the rot could cross the Río Grande. The very survival of civilisation could be at stake.'

Catesby kept a blank face and tried not to show his own feelings. Would a largely Spanish-speaking, mixed-race Western Hemisphere with free health care, education and social equality really be such a bad place? He didn't think so, but Americans like Enders regarded the prospect as hell on earth – and would support murderous juntas and deploy nukes to stop it ever happening.

The Marine driver who had been sent to fetch Catesby from the State Department wasn't alone in the Lincoln Continental. There was a smartly suited civilian in the back with slick black hair. The civilian was wearing horn-rimmed spectacles and going through a file on which he made notes with a thick fountain pen. As soon as the driver saw Catesby approaching, he jumped out of the car to hold the back door open with one hand as he saluted with the other. The VIP treatment was a soothing balm after his ordeal in the Ambassador-at-Large's office.

When Catesby glided on to the fine leather of the back seat, the other passenger extended his hand and introduced himself. Except for the President, Catesby had now met all the top team.

The American pressed a button and a thick panel of glass slid into place separating him and Catesby from the driver. They were encased in a soundproof cocoon. 'I hope,' said the American Defense Secretary, 'that you found today's briefings useful.'

'Enlightening.'

'They are a variety of views in the Administration. Al is trying to straddle both fences. I think it's pretty obvious which side of the fence you have just heard from. Some of the Enders faction are more fools than fascist – but I think Tom is more fascist than fool.'

Catesby was taken aback by the frankness of the American. Sometimes such indiscretion was a ploy to get the other person to do the same. So it was better to ask questions rather than give anything away. 'What about the President?'

The Secretary smiled. 'He delegates. In other words, he lets us squabble among ourselves.'

'You mean he's lazy.'

The American continued to smile and pressed an intercom button to speak to the driver. 'Can we take the long way to Tango Five and give our visitor a tour of the Mall and the memorials?'

'Yes, sir. Will do, sir.'

The Secretary took his finger off the intercom to restore the sealed cocoon. He turned to Catesby. 'Washington is beautiful in the spring. But you've come too late for the cherry blossoms.'

'So I've been told. But it is very different from London.'

The American nodded. 'London's a working town with banks, businesses, docks and industry. Washington was designed and laid out as a capital – and is nothing else. Washington's only industry is government. In London you can get away from it. Here we can't.'

Catesby stared out the window at the geometric perfection of monuments, greensward, reflecting pool and the white Capitol Building looming over it all. No imperfections like the messy mud of the Thames at low tide or the untidy horror of pigeon-eating pelicans in St James's Park.

'I know,' said the American, 'that you are going to Lima as a backchannel diplomat – a personal secret emissary of the British Foreign Secretary.'

Catesby laughed. 'I wouldn't describe myself as anything so grand. I'm a lowly member of a team trying to secure a last-minute peace deal.'

'You are too modest. But I hope you don't rate your chances of success too highly. Your mission is what American football players call a Hail Mary Pass – a desperate long forward throw in the dying minutes of a game to snatch victory from defeat. They seldom succeed.' The American paused and stared at Catesby. 'And speaking of Hail Marys, there seem to be a lot of Roman Catholics involved in this business.'

'What do you mean?'

'Walters, as I'm sure you know, was educated by the Jesuits in England and is still a devout Catholic.'

Catesby nodded.

'Al Haig,' continued the Secretary, 'is another one. He doesn't flaunt his Catholicism as openly as Walters, but it is still there – and, I think, influences Al's taste for conspiracy. Haig's brother is a prominent Jesuit – and a lot brighter than Al – but I don't know what role he plays. There were a lot of warring Jesuits fighting behind the scenes during the last months of Nixon's White House.'

Catesby stared out of the window at the Washington scenery which scrolled by like a US Information Agency PR film. They were now passing the Tidal Pool and the Jefferson Memorial.

'Would you like to comment?' said the Secretary.

'I always thought Jesuit conspiracies were part of an English tradition. Your stealing that from us is like putting on Shakespeare with American accents.'

The American laughed. 'You British sneer at us as vulgar. It's weak revenge for having lost power. And it is all about power – that's why the Jesuits have shifted their focus from London to Washington.'

Catesby shrugged. 'I'm sure you're right.'

'By the way,' said the American, 'has no one ever commented that you share the name of the leader of the Gunpowder Plot?'

Catesby's eyes glazed over with boredom and annoyance.

'I can see from your expression that they have.'

'It's a joke that wore thin decades ago.' Catesby smiled. 'By the way, I had a classmate named Fawkes and his parents ordered him not to speak to me.'

'Very wise advice.'

'Tommy Fawkes also came to a painful end. His tank brewed up in Normandy. He burned to death.'

'I served in the Pacific during the war. None of us who have seen combat want this thing to end in a war.'

'But…'

'But it will be war.'

'Why?'

'Because we're coming down on Thatcher's side regardless. If necessary, we'll give her another aircraft carrier. Supporting our closest NATO ally is more important than Argentina.'

Catesby noted that the US Defense Secretary had said 'Thatcher's side' and not 'Britain's side' – but he didn't want to make an issue of it. 'You mentioned earlier,' said Catesby, 'that the President lets you squabble among yourselves. How can you be sure that you're going to win the argument?'

'Because Haig is an idiot – a narcissistic buffoon.' The Defense Secretary smiled. 'I'm surprised that you hadn't noticed.'

'It would be undiplomatic for me to comment.'

The American laughed. 'I can't imagine anyone being more undiplomatic than I have just been. But this is an off-the-record conversation. Nonetheless, it would be useful if you repeated my words to Al Haig. He would expand, turn purple and his triple-bypass would explode. You'd have to mop up what was left – and we wouldn't have to worry about him any more.'

'It's my turn to be frank,' said Catesby. 'I don't know why you are telling me all this. My boss, the UK Foreign Secretary, is sending me to Peru to try to persuade the Argentines to accept a peace deal. I am personally and professionally committed to carrying out those instructions.'

The Defence Secretary gave a patronising smile.

'Actually,' said Catesby turning flinty-eyed, 'what you are doing is inciting me to treason.'

'Perhaps your boss, the UK Foreign Secretary, is the one committing treason.'

Catesby stifled an impulse to shout *fuck off.*

'You must,' said the American, 'be either blind or stupid if you can't see what is going on. Pym wants to get rid of Thatcher. If he and Haig can stitch together a peace deal behind her back, your Prime Minister will have to resign.'

Catesby looked out the window. They were crossing the Potomac where a single sculler was pulling against the tide.

'And who,' continued the American, 'would be the next Prime Minister? None other than Francis Pym.'

'I've had enough,' said Catesby. 'You are insulting a person of great integrity and character.'

'Would you use the same words to describe Prime Minister Thatcher?'

Catesby didn't answer.

'It is well known,' said the Defence Secretary, 'that you are a left-wing cuckoo in the British intelligence nest. You detest Mrs Thatcher and would do anything – including keeping a murderous Junta in power – to get rid of her.'

'Tell the driver to stop and let me out. I can find my own way to your fucking safe house.'

'Don't worry,' said the American, 'I'm getting out now – you can have the car to yourself.'

Catesby looked up. A severe grey concrete building of four stories loomed above them. There was a busy traffic of people entering and leaving a columned entrance – more in uniforms than in suits. Catesby realised they had arrived at The Pentagon. The American left the limousine without a word or a glance.

The glass separating Catesby from the driver remained in place, but his voice came through on the intercom. 'My instructions, sir, are to take you to the address where you spent the night. Is there any change to them?'

'That's fine.'

Catesby blankly regarded the countryside of northern Virginia. At first there were motorways and suburban sprawl; then pleasant rolling countryside with more trees than England. Pleasant indeed, but he sensed a poison that curdled the natural beauty of America. He longed to be home in Suffolk.

The US Defense Secretary's words rankled in his ears – as home truths often do. He detested Thatcher, but it was a feeling that he – and many other senior figures in Whitehall and even in her own cabinet – had to hide behind stony faces or cold smiles.

She had an obsession with tidiness that was toxic – and, unlike Ted Heath with his music and sailing, she had no hinterland. Her pastimes were not books or art, but cleaning her shoes and scrubbing the bottoms of washing-up bowls. When that tidiness extended to governing a country, it destroyed harmony and public services. And it wasn't just those on the Left who detested her: the One Nation Tory toffs couldn't stand her either. Well-born Tories were not Catesby's natural allies, but they were when it came to Thatcher. The American Defence Secretary may have been lying about Francis Pym, but it was a cunning lie festooned with trappings of plausibility – as are the best lies.

Catesby had been an atheist since the age of fifteen – and often bragged, 'I lost my faith when I found my brain.' But the effects of a Roman Catholic childhood still dogged him, like the practice of making 'an examination of conscience'. It was a habit that often led to depression, self-reproach and indecisiveness – which was where he found himself now. Catesby knew that the Argentine Junta was a brutal regime that ought to be overthrown. So why not by Thatcher and her Task Force? Answer one: it wasn't the job of a foreign power to do so; it was the job of the Argentine people themselves. Answer two: bloodshed. Catesby had seen war close up and hated it. So, he suspected, did Francis Pym and others like him in the government. Of course, not everyone who had been in battle hated war – some came back from the battlefield thirsty for more blood. Catesby considered them a sick minority – but they, in turn, regarded the war-bloodied doves as weaklings. Answer three: bloodshed again. The worst-case scenario, as described in a top-secret memo from the MoD, was more than three thousand British dead. The memo didn't evaluate Argentine losses. If Argentina suffered a similar number of casualties, that would amount to more than three dead service personnel for every Falkland Islander. You don't fight a war when the losses are so disproportionate to what is gained. But, apparently, this was an argument to which Thatcher refused to listen. Basically, risking six thousand dead would be a price worth paying for her to stay Prime Minister. Power was a poisonous drug.

Catesby closed his eyes and felt a wave of relief sweep over him. The examination of conscience was over. He was going to do everything possible to help bring about a peaceful settlement.

Palermo, Buenos Aires: 28 April 1982

Ariel had managed to get his mother-in-law out of the house – to an evening with mothers and grandmothers knitting jumpers and balaclavas for soldiers on the freezing Malvinas – so that he could have time alone with Fiona.

'You mustn't worry, my darling,' said Ariel, 'the Junta are going to chicken out.'

'How do you know?'

'The army are putting pressure on Galtieri – and that leaves Anaya standing alone. My guess is that he will give in too.'

'How do you feel about that?'

'My feelings are mixed.'

The US Ambassador's Residence, Lima, Peru: 28 April 1982

The sound of gunfire was familiar to Catesby's ears. He was certain that the shots came from military-type rifles. There were, fortunately, no machine guns or heavier weapons involved. The Ambassador and his wife were not at all disconcerted.

'This happens from time to time,' said Ambassador Ortiz sipping his mint tea, 'but nothing to worry about.'

'Do you suppose, Frank,' said the Ambassador's wife, 'it's that new group that Manolo was telling us about?'

The Ambassador arched an eyebrow. 'You mean, Dolores, the Sendero Luminoso? I very much doubt it. They are still struggling to form a base in the countryside. I think those shots were from the EGP, just to announce that they're still here.' The Ambassador glanced up at Catesby, 'EGP stands for Ejército

Guerrillero Popular – the Popular Guerrilla Army – but I'm sure you already knew that.'

Catesby smiled. The manners of the Ambassador and his wife were very soothing. The couple could have been dispatched by Central Casting in response to a director's request for 'refined and genteel Americans'. At any moment Catesby expected them to break into a Fred Astaire dance routine. But the couple were certainly not East Coast types. The Ambassador was a Spanish speaker from New Mexico and very proud of the fact that his ancestors had arrived there in 1598 – 'twenty-two years before the *Mayflower* gringos stepped on to Plymouth Rock.'

'Have a top-up of Jerez,' said the Ambassador refilling Catesby's glass. 'The reassuring thing about gunfire in Latin America is that it is almost always inaccurate – sometimes a statement rather than an attempt to kill.'

The Ambassador's wife had politely joined Catesby in a pre-prandial sherry, but didn't require a top-up.

'I can't remember the first time I came under fire,' said the Ambassador, 'because I was only one year old. My father was working for a firm in Mexico City when a rebellion broke out. He put my mother and me on a train to San Antonio which was attacked. She later told me we had to lie on the floor to escape the bullets.'

Catesby thought about mentioning that he had once been on a train between Lowestoft and Norwich that had been strafed by a Messerschmitt, but he didn't want to interrupt the Ambassador's flow. He was a man who clearly liked being a raconteur.

'You have to remember,' said the Ambassador, 'that Latin America is the Wild West superimposed on sixteenth-century Spain – and many of the ruling families still derive from the Spanish nobility and speak pure Castilian. You will meet two of them this evening.'

Catesby gave an ironic smile. The sort that was always lost on Americans. 'Unfortunately, I didn't pack formal dinner dress – but I'm sure our embassy could find me some gear.'

'I don't think that will be necessary.' The Ambassador eyed up Catesby. 'But if it were, I think we're about the same size and you could borrow one of mine.' The Ambassador was of unusually slight build for an American.

'How generous of you.'

'But it won't be necessary this evening.' The Ambassador looked at his watch and then at his wife. 'What time are Manolo and Isabel arriving?'

'They should be here already.'

The Ambassador said, 'Oh dear,' and winked at Catesby.

Catesby knew that the wink was cryptic, but didn't know why.

'I hope your room is comfortable,' said the wife rather obviously changing the subject.

The gunfire began again and sounded nearer.

The Ambassador smiled at Catesby. 'They must know you're here – but I assure you they are not Argentine. In fact, it might be the Shining Path lot, after all.'

'Sendero Luminoso,' said Catesby to show that he twigged the translation.

'Indeed. They are a Maoist group who model themselves after the Communist Party of Nepal. Their leader says the revolution will cost a million lives.' The Ambassador's voice had turned sombre and serious. 'Three months ago Shining Path executed two teachers in front of their students. They are also involved in drug dealing – mostly cocaine smuggling from Colombia.'

Catesby detected a note of self-justification in the Ambassador's voice.

'I am going to check on things in the kitchen,' said his wife getting up, 'and the shooting seems to have stopped.'

'I am sure,' continued the Ambassador as soon as his wife had disappeared, 'that you know Jimmy Carter sacked me after less than a year in post when I was Ambassador to Guatemala.'

'I didn't know that,' lied Catesby. He did know, but the reasons were muddled.

'I was undermined by a series of anonymous leaks to journalists and the lobbying of so-called human rights activists.'

Catesby nodded and remained silent. He didn't want to start an argument with his host.

'Dealing with a military government,' continued the Ambassador, 'is a difficult balancing act. Sure, the Guatemalan leader, General Romeo Lucas García, was a bit heavy-handed.'

Catesby tried not to laugh. 'Heavy-handed' was a gross understatement to describe Lucas García's murder of labour union leaders, students, professors and former government officials.

'I managed to persuade Lucas García to tone down his policies towards those he perceived as opponents. As an award, I arranged a goodwill visit by a US Navy destroyer – for which I was castigated. I reported that government-sponsored violence was decreasing – but the Carter gang in Washington didn't believe me and claimed the violence was getting worse. Utter nonsense.' The Ambassador reached for the bottle. 'I think I'll join you in a little Jerez. You know I came very close to resigning from the Foreign Service. Fortunately, I had friends in the State Department who advised me to await the outcome of the 1980 presidential election. It was wise advice and Reagan appointed me Ambassador here – quite a promotion from Guatemala.'

Catesby could see that under his smooth and polished exterior Ambassador Ortiz had a brittle ego.

'What you must realise,' continued the Ambassador, 'is that Latin America possesses a natural ruling class who are neither junta generals nor communist revolutionaries. They are the descendants of the conquistadors. I must admit that I am a great admirer of sixteenth-century Spain.'

Catesby stirred uneasily as he remembered a visit to the Kunsthistorisches Museum in Vienna. He had stood transfixed before Pieter Bruegel's *The Procession to Calvary*. The hundreds of faces and figures depicted could have been modelled on his own peasant ancestors. Among them is a woman in mourning who could be his own mother. Who is she mourning for? Could it be one of the men who is being whipped and carted to execution by the scarlet-coated soldiers of Habsburg Spain who ruled the Low Countries at the time? Catesby had vowed once again as his eyes brimmed with tears that he would always be on the side of the oppressed and of the peasants. This wasn't a thought he could share with the Ambassador who so admired those conquerors.

'Are you all right?' said the Ambassador.

'No, I'm probably a little jet-lagged.'

'But you don't get that from travelling north to south.'

'It must be something else then.'

'Here's to a peace agreement,' said the Ambassador raising his glass.

Catesby clinked glasses. 'Cheers. But not everyone in Washington is as enthusiastic.'

'It's no secret that the administration is split from stem to stern with those who want to tilt to Argentina and those who favour Britain. But it shouldn't be a matter of tilting, but of rational common sense.' The Ambassador leaned forward and lowered his voice to a whisper. 'Mrs Thatcher has no idea how dangerous this is. A planeload of Cubans has just arrived in Buenos Aires offering military assistance to the Junta – not their usual alliance partners. And the Soviet Union is also poised to jump in. Suppose a Soviet submarine sank one of your aircraft carriers? How could anyone prove the sub wasn't Argentine?'

Catesby frowned. It was a nightmare scenario that, as far as he knew, hadn't been considered by the War Cabinet.

'I think someone's arrived,' said the Ambassador.

The residence was an enormous mansion. The voices and doors opening and closing were muffled by distance.

'I'd better give you a quick briefing. The Prime Minister's wife is Isabel – and has some difficulties.'

It was the first time that Catesby realised that he would be dining with the Peruvian PM, Manuel Ulloa, and his wife. But the PM wasn't the top man. He was an appointee of President Fernando Belaúnde Terry – but still someone to reckon with.

'There are problems with…' The Ambassador looked up towards the door. 'Excuse me, Dolores wants to have a word.'

Catesby found himself alone and helped himself to more Jerez – which was very fine indeed. He was beginning to enjoy himself. He loved dinner parties that went tits up and this one certainly was heading in that direction. He was also pleased that he was billeted with the American Ambassador – the surroundings were much more palatial than anything the British mission could offer. It was, however, very odd to be turned over to the Yanks for bed and grub. Catesby wasn't sure whose idea it was. Had he been kidnapped by the Americans? Or was it at the request of the Foreign Secretary? He could, however, appreciate the negotiating tactic. If the Argentines saw Catesby arrive arm-in-arm with pro-Argentina Americans, they may take what he had to say more seriously.

Being alone gave Catesby the opportunity to take in the vast sitting room. The design was neither subtle nor consistent. There was a grand piano next to a stuffed alpaca bedecked in ribbons. The ceilings were very high and hung with massive gold chandeliers. All the windows opened on to balconies – where presumably the Ambassador and his guests would be easy targets for a Shining Path sniper, but if they stayed inside the sniper's aim would be frustrated by heavy, green velvet curtains that spilled over the floor. The best furnishing was a huge carpet woven into the geometric patterns of traditional Inca design. Catesby's rumination was interrupted by what sounded like a woman shouting and crying. A moment later, the Ambassador came back in.

'It looks like you've been casing the joint,' the Ambassador said in a mock-gangster accent.

'I've been admiring your alpaca.'

'He was a present from a Quechua-speaking group. There are more than four million Quechua speakers in Peru. I can get by. I'm not fluent – but I do speak it much better than Che did.'

'Guevara?'

'That's the one. Terrible person – how annoying that he is hero to so many young. In any case, Che couldn't speak Quechua at all which is one of the reasons that he was captured and executed in Bolivia. He was unaware of what was going on around him.'

'Well,' said Catesby, 'I'd better start taking lessons.'

'Touché. What do you think of the decor?'

'I'm still taking it in.'

'Very diplomatic answer. Dolores thinks it's appalling – but it isn't cheap. My predecessor was very sheepish about it and said during the handover, "Well, it didn't cost as much as an aircraft carrier!"'

'But maybe it did cost as much as one of ours.'

The Ambassador shrugged. 'Well, my naval attaché does say that *Hermes* and *Ark Royal* are a bit long in the tooth.'

The sound of distant women's voices was audible, but the words weren't. The crying and shouting had stopped.

'I think,' said the Ambassador, 'we are going to be eating a little later than planned. It looks like you're ready for a top-up?'

'Thank you.' Catesby held out his glass.

'Isabel is Manolo's third wife – I think she is number three.'

Catesby finally twigged that Manolo was a diminutive for Manuel.

'Manolo's reputation as a playboy is no secret: the gossip columns are full of his trysts with models and heiresses. In some ways, it enhances his popularity and status as a serious politician and businessman. Remember this is Latin America.' The Ambassador lowered his voice. 'But it doesn't always mean domestic bliss.'

Catesby nodded to pretend he knew more than he did. He wondered what all this had to do with hammering out a peace deal with the Argentine Junta – but then he remembered that the world of power was a ball of twisted silk. You can't pull one thread without tightening or loosening the rest of the tangled web.

The Ambassador's next words confirmed Catesby's thoughts. 'Isabel, by the way, is Argentine, but considers herself Spanish. In fact, she has or had a title. Isabel's previous husband was Vicente Sartorius y Cabeza de Vaca, 4th Marquis de Mariño – which made her Marquise of Mariño. I don't believe divorce invalidates your right to bear the title. Isabel found Vicente quite a handful. He was an Olympic bobsledder and finished fourth place in the '56 Winter Olympics in Cortina. He liked living fast and taking risks.'

'And Isabel's luck doesn't seem to have improved with Prime Minister Ulloa?'

'It has nothing to do with luck. These people are thoroughbreds – and so is Isabel. Their very lives are part of a dangerous game – which is why they love polo and off-piste skiing.'

Catesby faked a nod of approval. His stepdaughter referred to such people as 'Eurotrash' and 'gilded scum'.

There was a gentle knock on the door and the Ambassador said, *¡Pase por favor!*

A woman with Andean features entered. The conversation was in Quechua and Catesby immediately thought the Ambassador had been too modest about his fluency.

'Dinner,' said the Ambassador, 'is ready to be served, after all – the difficulties seem to have been resolved. Since there are so few of us, we will be eating in the family room. In fact, we only use the banqueting room for grand occasions.'

Catesby found Isabel, aka La Marquise de Mariño, a little scruffy and looking older than her forty-two years. She wasn't wearing make-up and was dressed in jeans and a jumper – and with her faded brown hair looked very Home Counties English. Her manner was unpretentious and Catesby warmed to her. The conversation bounced back and forth between Spanish and English. Isabel seemed to prefer to discuss her marital difficulties in her first language, but spoke fluent English in an accent that was more British than American – adding to the illusion that Isabel came from a nice place in Surrey.

Isabel looked at Catesby with hurt, washed-out grey eyes. 'Manuel was so looking forward to meeting you and regrets that he had urgent business to attend to.'

'I was looking forward to meeting him too, but am sure we will meet in the near future – and please convey to your husband my fondest regards.' Catesby knew that he was crap at playing HM's diplomat and knew the words rang hollow in his mouth. He also saw Isabel's face recoil in pain at the words *your husband* and wished that he had chosen a different phrase.

She changed the subject. 'Have you been assigned to Lima before?'

'No, I am not a Latin American specialist, but recent events have called all hands to the pumps.'

'What an interesting metaphor. It must derive from England's maritime heritage.'

'I suppose so.' An image of a sinking aircraft carrier flashed across Catesby's brain.

'You must,' said the woman, 'get to know Lima before you leave. It is a fascinating city.'

Catesby detected something cryptic in her tone, but his thoughts were interrupted by the food. The first course was *ceviche,* Peru's national dish, and served with Californian Chardonnay.

'The fish,' said the Ambassador, 'is called *corvina*, I'm not sure what it's called in…'

'Sea bass.'

'Thank you, Isabel, but the fish isn't cooked, it is marinated in lime juice and hot chillies.'

The fish was served with crunchy kernels of maize, crisp onions and sweet potato. It was delicious and Catesby joined Isabel in gulping down the Chardonnay. The next dish was something called *cuy.*

'At first,' said the Ambassador's wife, 'I couldn't believe it – but I have become a convert.'

The Ambassador looked at Catesby. '*Cuy* is roast guinea pig.'

'Ah,' said Catesby, 'they must be related to coypu – we have lots of them in Suffolk.'

'A near relative,' said Isabel, 'but the coypu is much larger – they are native to my Argentina.'

Catesby thought it best not to say that the Suffolk coypu were a serious environmental problem. It would be like blaming Argentina for that too. After escaping from fur farms, the coypu damaged wetlands and destroyed crops. But its Peruvian cousin was scrumptious.

The rest of the dinner party passed off calmly with polite conversation and some excellent Argentine Malbec from Mendoza.

Catesby was impressed by how much Isabel could put back without appearing the least affected. She did, however, seem nervous and tense, as if something was missing.

It was just before midnight when Catesby made his apologies for bed. He was in the sitting room with the Ambassador and slowly nursing a brandy; the Ambassador was back on mint tea. The muffled voices of Isabel and Dolores came from a side room. Catesby had the impression that Isabel was staying the night.

'I'll show you to your room,' said the Ambassador.

'Thank you, but I'm sure I can find my own way.'

A few seconds after Catesby left the sitting room he realised that he had overestimated his navigation skills. He ended up on the wrong staircase; the one that led to the servants' quarter. As he retraced his steps, something weird happened. It was Lou Reed. Someone was playing Lou Reed's *Transformer* on a phonograph. The track was 'Perfect Day'. He followed the sound of the music to a half-opened door. He surreptitiously glanced inside – and wondered if the Ambassador had laced his brandy with LSD. The furniture was pushed back and they had kicked off their shoes. Dolores and Isabel were dancing. Catesby pinched himself. Was it possible that a fifty-something woman dressed in twinset and pearls could be bopping to Lou Reed? Catesby tiptoed away and found the correct staircase.

As usual, Catesby slept well for the first part of the night; the bad dreams and the insomnia usually kicked in at about half past two after the soporific effect of the booze wore off. But in this case, it wasn't the nightmares that woke him up. Someone was sitting on the side of his bed. He reached out and found a silky thigh.

'Sorry to disturb you.' It was Isabel's voice; now sounding more American than British. 'I hope you can help me.'

Catesby looked at the luminous dial on the clock on his bedside table. It was half past one. He smiled and replied, *¡A sus órdenes!* In the circumstances, 'At your service,' seemed the appropriate answer. But he knew that what she wanted was more complex than a bed partner to compensate for betrayal and loneliness.

'My husband keeps me under surveillance – so I can't get what I need.' She turned on the bedside lamp. 'It's a form of torture.'

Catesby was struck by the paleness of her face and the way her hands were shaking. 'What do you want me to do?'

She explained. It wasn't complicated, but it was dangerous. Part of Catesby's job was doing 'risk/benefit evaluations' – but they were difficult when human beings and human needs got in the way. One voice in Catesby's head said *don't*. Another voice said *fuck the rulebook, do it*. The second voice won. As soon as Catesby agreed, Isabel reached into the pocket of her dressing gown and produced first a map, and then a huge roll of US greenbacks. 'I've counted it,' she said. 'There are four thousand dollars here. Don't haggle and don't pay him a cent more.'

As Catesby walked through Miraflores, the city's most fashionable district, he realised that Lima was a place that never slept. It was 2 a.m. and many of the restaurants were still full – including the one nearest the rendezvous point. It hadn't been an easy job to pull off – and it was far from finished.

Catesby's first hurdle had been dealing with the US Marines in camouflage uniforms and armed with M-16s who guarded the Ambassador's residence. Leaving the compound wasn't a problem, but getting the Marines to agree to let him back in was. The NCO in charge looked at Catesby's diplomatic passport and scratched his head. 'This is kinda unusual, sir, we don't normally let people in after midnight and before six.'

'I've been called away on a confidential matter and won't be gone longer than an hour – or two.' In truth, Catesby didn't know how long he would be gone – and if he was coming back.

The Marine returned Catesby's passport. 'I think I understand. But you'll need a password to use on the entrance gate intercom – and also some personal verification. What was the name of your first pet?'

'We didn't have any pets.'

'How about the name of your kindergarten?'

'I didn't go to kindergarten – but you can have the name of my first school, Roman Hill Primary.'

'That'll have to do.'

'Good.' Catesby was certain that there was no urban guerrilla in Lima wanting to gun down the US Ambassador who spoke in an English accent and could name any school at all in Lowestoft.

As Catesby set off into the night, there was another problem. There were two men in a car keeping watch on the entrance to the Ambassador's residence. It looked like Isabel hadn't been making it up. Her Prime Minister husband did keep her under surveillance. Catesby's worry now was that they would follow him instead. As he walked past the car he kept his eyes focused ahead. You mustn't ever look behind to check if you're being followed – that gives the game away. When Catesby knew he was out of sight he bent down to stroke a stray cat that brushed against his leg. The cat allowed him to make an unobtrusive turn around for a counter-surveillance check. He hadn't, unlike the cat, grown a tail. The dank night air had sobered Catesby and he realised that what he was doing was stupid. It then began to drizzle. Cool clarity descended with the rain and Catesby realised there was another problem. What if the cops stopped him and they found four thousand dollars worth of Class A drugs in his possession? Oh, shit. The British Ambassador would love that one. And would he lose his pension? Catesby was about to turn back when he remembered Isabel's face and her shaking hands – and her pleading voice. One of Catesby's weaknesses was that he was a sucker when it came to people who were fucked up – even when it was their own fault.

The rendezvous point was easy to find, but spooky as hell. Isabel's supplier either had a sense of humour or a sense of history. The Huaca Pucllana was an ancient ruin pulsing defiant darkness against the bright lights of modern Lima. The ruin was the remains of a pyramid constructed of clay and adobe steps. Catesby assumed that the steps had been fashioned so that priests could take sacrificial victims to the top. It was pre-Inca and dated from AD 200. No one knew exactly what its function had been, but Huaca Pucllana was a local protection god and the grounds of the pyramid were a sacred place. Catesby felt uneasy placing his feet on the ancient steps and waited where Isabel had marked an X on her map.

It wasn't long before Catesby saw a walking shadow emerge from the ruin – and wondered if Huaca Pucllana was in the mood to protect him or sacrifice him. The shadow approached closer and was wearing a traditional poncho. There was enough light from nearby street lamps to distinguish a face with Andean features and damp black hair. He spoke Spanish with a clear accent that was easy to understand. It sounded like the voice of a professor.

'I believe,' he said, 'that you are from Isabel.'

'Yes.'

'I like her very much. She is the victim of a bourgeois lifestyle and a cruel ruling class.'

They were not the words Catesby had expected to hear from a drug dealer.

'I trust you have brought the money?'

Catesby nodded as he felt the thick roll of notes in his coat pocket.

'You realise that the money isn't for me, but for the revolution?'

Catesby was speechless. A sky full of pennies began to drop. He, a senior officer in Her Majesty's Secret Intelligence Service, was being asked to hand over a four-thousand-dollar contribution to a Maoist guerrilla movement as part of a drug deal. There was a limit.

'No,' said Catesby, 'I don't have the money. Trust me. Hand over the drugs and you'll get an extra two thousand tomorrow.'

The Shining Path guerrilla laughed. 'I don't mind you lying, but I do mind you insulting me by suggesting I am stupid.'

'I wasn't…' Catesby didn't finish the sentence. The semi-automatic pistol pointed at his midriff looked like a Makarov 9mm. He wondered if it was the Chinese-made version, the Type 59. In any case, all Makarovs had the Star of Revolution embossed on the handgrip.

'If you hand over the money, I will give you the drugs – and there won't be any problem or ill feeling. If you don't give me the cash, I will kill you and take the money off your dead body

– and keep the drugs to sell to another messed-up bourgeois. Meanwhile, Isabel may well die of withdrawal symptoms. You cannot fault my logic.'

Catesby nodded and handed the drug-dealing guerrilla all four thousand bucks.

The guerrilla in turn gave Catesby a packet tightly wrapped in plastic.

'Thank you,' said Catesby beginning to back away.

'Hang on. There's something else – a present for you.' The guerrilla reached into his pocket and, with a slight bow, presented Catesby with a small red book. Two seconds later he had disappeared into the shadows and Catesby was alone with Huaca Pucllana and the remains of his pyramid.

The drug packet was heavy for its size and made Catesby's coat pocket droop as if he was concealing a gun. He squinted at the gift the guerrilla had given him. It was obviously Chairman Mao's 'Little Red Book', but the title was written in a language that Catesby didn't understand – probably Quechua. For a second he was tempted to read aloud a few quotations for the benefit of Huaca Pucllana's ghost, but didn't think his pronunciation would be recognisable by any Quechua speaker alive or dead.

Catesby found Isabel sitting on his bed. She was shaking and chewing her nails. She was in a state. She took the drugs without a word and disappeared into the ensuite bathroom to shoot up, snort or both. Catesby lay back on his bed and began to doze. When Isabel came back into the bedroom she was 'normal'. She lay down next to Catesby.

'I want you to hold me,' she said. 'No sex, just hold me.'

They both slept soundly. When Catesby woke up it was half past five. At first, he wasn't sure who the other person was – but then remembered.

'You snore,' she said.

'I hope it didn't keep you up.'

'Not much. The odd thing is that your snores don't sound like you at all. It's almost as if your sleeping body is inhabited by someone else. Manuel doesn't snore at all. He grunts and the grunts are the real him.'

'What about your other husband?'

'Vicente used to cry. He had nightmares that his bobsled was leaving the track at high speed and tumbling down the mountainside.' Isabel paused. 'I'm going to go now. We are, how do you say, boats that passed in the night?'

'Ships.'

'Ah, that reminds me. You're here because of something to do with Las Malvinas.'

'Or the Falklands.'

'Last time I was in BA I heard something interesting. It was at a party and some of the Junta were there – and one was very drunk and joking about doing a deal trading polo ponies for some sort of missiles, you know the kind that go whizz and bang.'

'Exocets.'

'That was the word.'

'Anything else?'

'Yes, something to do with a very rich American named Talbot. I've met him. He is a very detestable man, but very handsome and an excellent polo player.' Isabel smiled. 'I'm sorry I can't tell you any more. That is all I remember, but Manuel always tells me that gossip is useful – and sometimes gold dust for a statesman. I must go now.'

Catesby watched her dark silhouette through the door. He knew that he would never see her again – and it didn't really matter. They had been useful to each other and that was that.

When Catesby finally met the Peruvian Prime Minister he thought it best not to mention his nocturnal grunting. Or to ask Dulce, who seemed to be the PM's companion, if she had noticed it too. They had ended up in a nightclub called Terrazas del Oeste which overlooked the yacht club and the Pacific Ocean. It was an exclusive club and Catesby knew he would never have got past Pollito the doorman (who, despite his name, was anything but a cute small chicken) if he had not been with the Prime Minister.

Another name that amused Catesby was Dulce. He was tempted to ask if her surname was Et Decorum Est, but doubted that anyone would pick up the reference to Owen's poem. And the joke wouldn't have been that funny – or respectful, considering that battle was looming on the horizon. Dulce was a model – and, apparently a highly successful one, who could have got into the nightclub on her own. Things between her and the PM seemed fraught. Catesby guessed it was because he wasn't treating her with the respect she rightfully deserved. The problem with adultery, as Catesby well knew, is that you betray both your lover and your spouse.

The fourth person in the PM's nightclub party was Horacio Spinoza, the Argentine intelligence officer who needed convincing that a peaceful settlement was the only way out for the Junta. Even though Spinoza had been involved in murder and brutality, Catesby found it difficult not to like him. Horacio Spinoza was a charmer with perfect manners – and a great dancer. He spun Dulce around the floor first in a rumba and then a Brazilian samba.

'He is,' said the Prime Minister nodding towards Spinoza as he deftly paced the downward dips of the samba, 'the ultimate professional – and has the respect of the Junta.'

Catesby made a mental note to suggest to C that ballroom dancing be part of the training programme for SIS entrants. Catesby often found himself feeling lumpy and gauche in social situations that didn't require guns, bribes or blackmail.

Dulce and Spinoza finally came back to the table and the Prime Minister poured them more champagne. Catesby noted that the PM's mood towards Dulce had changed. He was now oozing wit and charm. The next piece was a slow waltz and the Prime Minister led his mistress back on the dance floor. Catesby could see that the charm was part of a calculated move to leave him alone with Spinoza.

'It is,' said the Argentine offering Catesby more champagne, 'a complicated situation.'

Catesby accepted the champagne, but wasn't sure whether Spinoza was referring to the Prime Minister's love life or the Falklands.

'Have you met Isabel?'

'Very briefly,' said Catesby wanting to get on to the weightier matter.

'She has problems – and Manolo, although a warm and wonderful man, is not always an easy husband.'

'How does he fit into things – politically?' said Catesby trying to shift the focus.

'Manolo is snake-charmer-in-chief for the President – and totally loyal to Belaúnde. Their careers are closely linked.'

'Which one of the two has more influence with your country?'

The Argentine smiled. 'You are asking a very loaded question – even though the answer is obvious. President Belaúnde, of course – and Peru is our best friend in South America. Part of the reason is geopolitical. We both need an ally against Chile – and another reason is personal chemistry. Fernando Belaúnde and Manolo are old world aristocrats. The Junta admires their style.' The Argentine raised his champagne flute. 'Now what are you going to tell me?'

'Thatcher is vindictive and dangerous – and will never admit that she is wrong.'

Spinoza gave a smug smile. 'That was my analysis too – but many in the Junta did not believe me. They thought she was weak – and when she announced she was scrapping *Endurance*, the last Royal Navy ship in the Southern Ocean, they thought it was a signal that the UK would not defend Las Malvinas.'

Catesby gave a comradely clink of his champagne flute against Spinoza's. 'Don't you think we told her that too?'

'And she didn't listen?'

'Of course not. But I haven't started on the secret stuff yet.'

Spinoza leaned forward.

'Thatcher is widely despised within the government and civil service – but covertly.'

'But she must have her supporters?'

'I didn't say she hasn't. They tend to be people like her – or those who want to get promoted or are afraid of losing their jobs.'

'But what about in the military?'

Catesby was tempted to remind Spinoza that the UK wasn't like South America – although coups weren't impossible.

'I think,' said Catesby, 'her biggest support might come from the navy. The admirals are the ones most afraid of budget cuts and want to prove their worth.' Catesby paused and wondered if Spinoza was wired up, but surely he couldn't be if he had been dancing so vigorously. If, however, the conversation was being recorded, it would be evidence for treason. But it was too late to stop now.

'Who are Thatcher's enemies?'

Catesby gave a broad grin. He remembered the tittle-tattle of Whitehall gossip that undermined the Prime Minister. Someone in the Foreign Office had surreptitiously circulated her Christmas card list which included Saddam Hussein and Libyan leader Muammar Qaddafi. The Qaddafi card had been addressed to 'the Leader of the Great First of September Revolution'. No one in the FCO had pointed out to her the inappropriateness – or the fact that both dictators were Muslims who didn't celebrate Christmas.

'The people,' said Catesby, 'who hate Thatcher most are trade unionists and those on the Left.'

'But they have been deposed.'

Catesby smiled bleakly. 'But she is also widely despised within her own party – and even her own cabinet.'

'Yes.'

Catesby looked at Spinoza, whose eyes were so full of eager curiosity that he almost felt inclined to defend Thatcher.

'A number of upper-class Tories loathe Thatcher because she is "common". She comes from a petty bourgeois background and lacks grace, good taste and manners.'

'She sounds the opposite of President Belaúnde.'

Catesby suppressed a sigh. He could see that Spinoza agreed with the Tory toffs.

'Many in Thatcher's cabinet,' continued Catesby, 'also find it difficult to deal with a woman in a position of power.'

'But they are fine with Queen Elizabeth?'

Catesby was momentarily confused. He had forgotten that

foreigners didn't always realise that the Queen was simply *the* Queen.

'That's a different situation,' said Catesby.

'Queen Elizabeth knows how to behave?'

'I would think so.'

Spinoza sipped his champagne. 'I am glad we have met – and it is always lovely to come to Lima.'

'But you think we might be wasting our time?'

Spinoza shrugged. 'Tell me more about Thatcher.'

Catesby knew it would be a waste of time to say how wrong it was to look down on Thatcher because of her social class or gender, but how important it was to oppose her policies and her brainless bullying. So he went straight to the point.

'The best way to get rid of Thatcher is a peace deal. She needs a war to save her premiership.'

Spinoza stared through his champagne flute at the dance floor. The waltz was over and the Peruvian Prime Minister and his mistress had joined another couple at their table.

'I think,' said Spinoza, 'that Manolo wants to give us more time alone – so that you can convince me that Argentina would lose a war against Great Britain.'

Catesby gave a wry smile. 'How did you guess?'

'It's not exactly, how do you say, missile science?'

'Rocket science.'

'Although, in this case, missile science might be more appropriate. I am sure that you are responsible for what happened to the Exocet dealers in Hamburg.'

Catesby maintained a discreet silence.

'In any case, my friend, it is not me you have to convince, but the Junta.'

'If we meet again, I can provide documents.'

'That would be useful – but what you must realise is that Galtieri thinks he is facing a lose-lose situation, which is why he is drinking even more than usual. Losing the war would certainly bring down the Junta, but so would any peace settlement that didn't give Argentina sovereignty over Las Malvinas.'

'So it's hopeless.'

'No, not completely. President Belaúnde is a genius who can work miracles – and we love the Peruvians. If we have a chance to win the war; it would only be with their help.'

Spinoza had just clarified what Catesby had long suspected. The Peruvians could be arms suppliers as well as peacemakers.

'There is,' continued Spinoza lowering his voice to a whisper, 'one personal favour that I would like to ask of you.'

'I hope I can help.' Catesby knew that it wasn't a request, but a condition.

'If the Junta falls, I will be in danger – but that doesn't matter. What does matter is my family. I want to protect them and their future.'

It wasn't the first time that Catesby had heard that line. It usually came from Soviet or Warsaw Pact double agents who wanted to defect – and most of them weren't worth the deal and didn't get it. It was a hard game.

'I would like,' said Spinoza, 'a promise of political asylum for myself and my family in Great Britain. Can you give that?'

'Yes,' lied Catesby. He didn't have the authority to make such an offer, but thought he could wing it.

'I will want something in writing.'

'Of course.'

'Where shall we meet again?' said Spinoza.

'You know Lima better than I.'

'Are you a Catholic?' said the Argentine with a slight smile.

'I was brought up as one, but I gave it up.'

'Maybe a visit to the Cathedral of San Juan Evangelista will restore you to the One True Faith.'

Catesby wasn't altogether sure that the Argentine was being ironic, but replied, 'I doubt it, but I'll take the risk.'

'Let's meet there at midnight. We can discuss things in the shadows. I'll meet you at the tomb of Francisco Pizarro.'

The British Embassy, Lima: 30 April 1982

Because he had been keeping a low profile, it was Catesby's first visit to the embassy and he wasn't greeted with deference. His first problem was convincing the person on the reception desk, a Peruvian national, that he was a British government official even when he flourished his diplomatic passport. After an internal phone call, conducted in Spanish, Catesby was invited to sit down and wait for someone. Twenty minutes later, a languid Second Secretary turned up with his hands in his pockets and took Catesby to his office.

'Coffee?' said the Second Secretary.

'Tea please, milk no sugar.'

The diplomat turned to a sideboard and switched on an electric kettle.

Catesby looked out of the window at a courtyard with towering palm trees.

'Unfortunately, the Ambassador can't see you at the moment – I know that he would have liked to have had a word. There is, as you can imagine, a lot going on. Would you like a briefing on the latest – bit of a bombshell, actually.'

'A bombshell for whom?'

'Not for us, for the Argies. The Americans have abandoned neutrality and tilted in our direction.'

Catesby raised an eyebrow in feigned surprise. He had already been told this was likely to happen during his car ride with the US Defense Secretary.

'Haig,' continued the Second Secretary, 'gave up his shuttle diplomacy yesterday.' The diplomat picked up a telex from his desk and smiled. 'This is marked SENSITIVE and EYES ALPHA. Apparently, Haig's exact words were: "It was a fucking charade. These guys were diddling me."'

'I assume "the guys" are the Junta.'

'The problem is a lack of leadership. Everyone in the Junta down to the bag carriers seems to have a veto.'

'I suppose,' said Catesby testing, 'my being here might be a waste of time.'

The Second Secretary replied with a knowing smile.

'So,' said Catesby, 'what exactly does "tilt" mean? Are the Yanks going to lend us an extra aircraft carrier or two?'

'Good Lord, no. Nothing, in fact, other than some intelligence – which, as you know, they have already been supplying covertly. The Americans are not generous. Basically, the "tilt" is symbolic – and there are some in DC who blame Argentina for the failure of Haig's peace negotiations.'

Catesby wondered if the failure could be blamed on Haig's ineptness as well.

'The important thing,' said the Second Secretary, 'is that the "tilt" gives us the green light to commence hostilities without the Americans frowning.'

Catesby shrugged and finished his tea. 'So that's it?'

'Probably – but that's still a chance. Have you a view?'

Catesby did have a view. But he wasn't going to share it with the Second Secretary who was asking questions beyond his pay grade.

'The current view around here,' continued the Second Secretary undaunted, 'is that the peace settlement is a broken machine, but we're going to let President Belaúnde have a go at repairing it before we take it to the dump.'

'I need to send a cable to London. I'd like to use your cipher facilities.'

The Second Secretary nodded to a machine with a keyboard. 'Would you like to use my Noreen? It's a bit ancient and they say we shouldn't use it for UK EYES ALPHA – but no one's ever broken the Vernam cipher as far as I know.'

'Ah, I was hoping for…' Catesby was searching for a tactful way of saying *privacy without you looking over my shoulder.* Just then someone knocked on the office door.

'Just a second.' The Second Secretary got up and opened the door a crack. Catesby caught a glimpse of the Peruvian receptionist who had given him a rough time when he arrived at the embassy. She was very good-looking. There was a whispered conversation in Spanish. The Second Secretary returned to his desk to gather a few things, then looked at Catesby. 'I'll be gone an hour or so. Please make yourself at home and help yourself to tea or coffee.'

'Thank you.'

'If you have any trouble with the Noreen, the Comm Centre is in a secure room on the next floor. In any case, you'll have to take the tape there for sending to London. Good luck.' The Second Secretary turned and left for his siesta assignation – or maybe they were just friends.

Catesby, now alone, went over to the Second Secretary's desk and sat behind it. He was tempted to, but wasn't going to go through it looking for secrets or love letters. What Catesby wanted was headed embassy stationery and an example of the Ambassador's signature. He soon found both. He then took the cover off the Remington electric typewriter which rested on a pull-out shelf of the desk. The Remington was covered in dust. The Second Secretary obviously didn't do much of his own typing.

Catesby inserted the headed letter paper into the typewriter and took a deep breath. A forged letter signed with an ambassador's forged signature was more than enough to get him dismissed from the service, but, hopefully, not enough for a prison sentence. 'Fuck it,' whispered Catesby to himself, 'this could be a matter of war or peace – and I've done worse.' He smiled. 'And how the fuck are they going to prove I did it?' He began typing: *Dear Señor Horacio Spinoza, I would on behalf of Her Majesty's Government like to offer you, your wife and three daughters complete and unconditional political asylum in the United Kingdom...*

As soon as Catesby finished the letter, he sealed it in an envelope and put it in his breast pocket. He then went over to the Noreen which also had a QWERTY keyboard. He remembered not to encrypt the 'message indicator' before switching the machine into the 'on' mode. Catesby didn't put anything into his report that he didn't want the Embassy or the Foreign Office to know. Unfortunately, it was nearly impossible to communicate directly and securely with the Foreign Secretary alone. That would require a secure voice telephone that he would probably have to borrow from the Ambassador himself.

The Comm Centre, where Catesby handed over his encrypted tape, looked more modern and technologically advanced than he had expected. He wondered if it had been updated at the beginning of the Falklands crisis. There would, obviously, be no excuse for top-secret cables not getting through to London quickly and securely.

The Basilica Cathedral of Lima: 30 April 1982, Midnight

The cathedral both frightened and confused Catesby. What was such an ancient pile of European religious ornamentation doing in the New World? It was as if a space ship had lifted the massive sixteenth-century basilica out of Spain and dropped it in Peru to impress the natives. But it was also a reminder that South America had been colonised long before North America. The construction of the cathedral had begun in 1535 – nearly a century before the *Mayflower* pilgrims had set off for New England.

The outside of the cathedral was garishly illuminated – as if someone had forgotten to take down the Christmas lights. The large central gateway, La Portada del Perdón, 'The Door of Forgiveness', was bolted. So Catesby slipped in through a side entrance with his sins intact. The inside of the cathedral was dark except for flickering pools of candlelight. Catesby had arrived a few minutes early so he could do a recce before meeting Spinoza and see who else was hanging around in the dark corners. And there were a lot of them – fourteen side chapels.

The basilica was a vast emptiness devoid of human life, but pulsating with candles and fear of retribution. The only people about were midnight nuns re-lighting candles and the usual lonely ones looking for refuge. Most of the side chapels were completely dark or dimly lit. The Chapel of the Immaculate Conception was, however, an exception. Located in the middle of the left-hand wall of the cathedral, the chapel was brightly illuminated by tiers of candles. At first, Catesby felt an ancestral urge to make the sign of the cross as he approached – the voodoo was in his DNA. But as he got closer the pious impulse disappeared and he found it hard not to laugh. The ornamentation of the chapel vaulted from baroque grandeur into pointless ostentation. The ugliness was breathtaking. The ghosts of the Inca architects who achieved grandeur through simplicity and triangles must have been sneering at the vulgarity of the newcomers. It was then that Catesby realised that he was not alone and slunk back into the shadows.

The dark-suited figure bowed in prayer looked too large to be a Peruvian. Catesby thought he knew who it was. He moved to the side to catch a profile of the face. He had guessed right. It was General Vernon Walters, more than ever the soldier-monk. Catesby wasn't surprised that Walters was in Lima, but wondered what strings the American was pulling. His face was puffy, but pious – and Catesby knew that his prayers were as sincere as they were pointless. What, thought Catesby, was he praying for? Peace or forgiveness? After a few minutes the American rose and made the sign of the cross.

Catesby remained hidden in the dark and waited until the footsteps retreated and he heard a door close. Catesby continued his journey around the cathedral to his rendezvous at the tomb of Francisco Pizarro. The conquistador's life was the stuff of legend – and like many legends was full of violence and brutality. Pizarro grew up illiterate, the bastard son of a Spanish Army officer and a poor woman – and went on to conquer Peru after capturing and murdering the Incan emperor, Atahualpa. Pizarro kept the enormous ransom he had been given for Atahualpa's release – and later took Atahualpa's child wife as his own and impregnated her. Winner takes all. He later quarrelled with a fellow Spaniard, a long-time friend and comrade-in-arms, and had him executed too. The son of Pizarro's murdered comrade eventually gained revenge by storming a dinner party. Pizarro managed to kill three of his attackers before being stabbed in the throat. He died painting the sign of the cross on the floor with his own blood and calling for Christ to forgive him – which, thought Catesby, entitled him to a tomb in Lima's cathedral.

The tomb of Francisco Pizarro was as brightly lit as the

Chapel of the Immaculate Conception. Catesby felt neither awe nor curiosity as he stood before the conquistador's coffin. He had known many violent and ruthless men in a career that spanned nearly forty years – and he had himself committed acts of violence. It wasn't glorious – or even that interesting – just squalid and traumatic.

Catesby sensed someone at his elbow. Still thinking of Pizarro, he reached for an imaginary sword – only to find he was unarmed and vulnerable.

'Sorry if I startled you.'

Catesby turned to find Spinoza, who was broadly grinning.

'I am sorry I am late,' said the Argentine. 'There were some last-minute cables to deal with at our embassy.'

'Good news, I hope.'

'Not the worst news.' Spinoza smiled and nodded at the tomb. 'You found the Great Conquistador.'

'His ghost met me at the door.'

'Did he say anything?'

'No, but his hand was very cold.'

'Ah,' said the Argentine, 'then it wasn't him.'

'How do you know it wasn't him?'

'Because they never found his body. That coffin only contains his head.'

Catesby wasn't going to argue the metaphysical point of whether ghosts required more than a head in the nearest coffin to appear fully bodied. Instead, he referred to a tangible being. 'By the way, I nearly ran into General Vernon Walters. He was praying in a side chapel.'

Spinoza looked bemused.

'Did you know he was in Lima?'

Spinoza remained silent.

'In any case,' said Catesby, 'I've got some documents that I hope you will copy and send to Buenos Aires.'

'What are they?'

Catesby reached into his pocket and passed over a bulging brown envelope. 'They are a rational and logical plea for a peaceful settlement.'

'Do you mind if I look at them?'

'Please do.'

Catesby looked on as Spinoza opened the envelope and slid out the papers. He had to squint to read the print in the candlelight. The Argentine pursed his lips and frowned. Catesby could sense Pizarro peering over Spinoza's shoulder and shaking his head: *Don't believe them. It's a perfidious British trick.*

'How can we be sure that this information is correct and true – and not a bluff?'

'I would think that your own knowledge of the networks involved would verify the authenticity of the information.'

Spinoza smiled wanly. 'The English know a lot about banks and bankers – and the defection of the French engineer was a serious blow.'

Catesby interpreted the comment as a tacit admission that Argentina's attempt to buy more Exocets had been thwarted. Several of the documents that he had handed over were a cool account of what had happened in Hamburg, Paris, Rome and Zurich. The intention was to convince the Junta that they would obtain no more deadly missiles by either love or money. Another set of documents revealed that SIS had busted a large number of Argentine intelligence agents and sources. The final packet was a frank assessment of the UK's prevailing military might in the South Atlantic. Catesby wondered if they had provided *too much* secret information to convince the Junta that war would mean certain defeat for Argentina and that a face-saving peace deal was the only option.

Spinoza gave Catesby a sly look as he folded the documents into his jacket. 'Is there anything that you would like to add – that isn't here in writing?'

'Thatcher will never admit that she has made a mistake.'

'Galtieri is the same.' Spinoza smiled. 'At least, he won't make that admission in public.'

Catesby sensed that any flexibility, any chance for peace, would have to come from the Argentines.

'But you seem to have forgotten something. We are taking a far greater risk than Thatcher or her government. If the Junta falls, we don't go into cosy retirements serving on boards of big companies and playing golf – we face jail or firing squads.'

'You think the Junta will fall if it accepts a peace settlement?'

Spinoza shrugged. 'I don't know all the details of President Belaúnde's peace plan, but I think the chances of the Junta surviving if they accept it may be no better than fifty-fifty.' Spinoza looked closely at Catesby. 'My help, as I explained before, comes at a price.'

Catesby reached again into his coat pocket and handed over the final envelope. He watched the Argentine open and read the forged letter offering political asylum in the UK.

'Good.' Spinoza smiled. 'I've checked. An ambassador does have the right to grant asylum. Thank you for arguing my case.'

Catesby glanced at the tomb behind the Argentine. 'I'm not sure you could have trusted this offer if it had been given by Francisco Pizarro.'

'You could have trusted Pizarro if he had something to gain – and Britain has much to gain by avoiding a costly war.'

The glass coffin containing Pizarro's remains continued to draw Catesby's attention. Four nubile women, one bare breasted, were carved from black marble and knelt in mourning next to a plaque inscribed: *Aquí Yace El Marquez Gobernador Don Francisco Pizarro Conquistador Del Peru Y Fundador De Lima.* He noted that Pizarro had been seventy years old when he was hacked to death at the dinner party. Not a bad innings for someone who lived by the sword.

'You seem in a reflective mood,' said Spinoza.

'You spend a lot of time watching people, don't you?'

'It's part of our interrogation training.'

'And do you ever learn more about yourself than you do them?'

'It's why I go to confession.'

For the first time Catesby noticed his own face reflected in the glass of Pizarro's coffin. He was shocked by how aged and ascetic he looked – and lonely too. But it was time to stop self-indulging and get back to the job.

'What,' said Catesby, 'are you going to do now?'

'I'm going back to the embassy to give them a debrief on our meeting and await further instructions – and I will strongly put the case for my returning to Buenos Aires.'

'Would you be able to see Galtieri personally?'

'I hope so. It depends on how sober he is – but he might be as it's a national holiday and he will have to give speeches.'

Catesby remembered and smiled. 'Happy May Day.'

'*El Día Internacional de los Trabajadores* is an important holiday in Argentina regardless of the government. Everyone must love the workers.'

Catesby decided not to comment on Thatcher's view of the workers.

'I must go now,' said Spinoza. He paused and stared straight into Catesby's eyes. 'You know there is blood on my hand, but will you still shake it?'

Catesby reached forward and took the Argentine's hand. They stood for a moment in the flickering candlelight and then parted in silence.

It was now half-past one in the morning. Catesby was in the Comm Centre at the British Embassy and had begun to compose a cable reporting on his meeting with Spinoza. Once again, he wished he could use a secure voice facility to talk to the Foreign Secretary directly and confidentially.

The only other person in the centre was the Night Duty Officer, a female Third Secretary who was one of the FCO's best Spanish and Portuguese linguists. She was looking at a UK EYES ALPHA cable that had just arrived. 'Oh shit,' she said in Estuary English.

'What's wrong?' said Catesby.

'I've got to fucking wake up the Ambassador. He's the only one allowed to decrypt and read it.'

'Poor you.'

'And I am sorry, but you'll have to leave the Comm Centre. We're not allowed to leave anyone in here alone with an EYES ONLY cable even if it hasn't been decrypted.'

Catesby perched himself on a chair outside the Comm

Centre. There was a table with teabags, sugar, an electric kettle, but no milk. He settled himself with a black tea and a two-day old edition of a newspaper called *El Comercio.* Twenty minutes later the Ambassador arrived, smartly suited but without a tie, and gave Catesby a curt nod as he disappeared into the Comm Centre. The Ambassador came out ten minutes later bearing a decoded printout in his hand.

'Nice seeing you again,' said the Ambassador extending a hand.

Catesby couldn't recall having ever met the Ambassador, but replied in the same vein.

'Things are starting to get very interesting,' said the Ambassador, flourishing the cable.

'I hope I can be of use.'

The Ambassador gave Catesby a shrewd look. 'How did your meeting with the Argentine intelligence officer go?'

'It was very cordial. I carried out my instructions and handed over the authorised documents.'

'What did he say?'

'He hopes to go to Buenos Aires today and thinks he might wrangle a meeting with Galtieri.'

'Did he ask for anything in return?'

'No,' lied Catesby.

'The next forty-eight hours are going to be very delicate.'

Catesby could see that the Ambassador was not going to give anything away. 'What should I do now?'

'Get some sleep – and come back in six hours.'

The Great British Gazette: 1 May 1982
RAF Vulcan and Navy Harriers Hammer Argie Airfields

Argentine occupying forces were caught napping as British aircraft launched a pre-dawn surprise attack. The attack was intended to prevent the Argentines from landing supplies or attacking the British Task Force as the ships close in on the islands. A Vulcan, swapping nukes for conventional bombs, carried out the longest bombing raid in history – an epic return flight of 8,000 miles! The unexpected pounding of Argie airfields and facilities by the Vulcan, was followed up by carrier-based Harriers that pummelled Argentine fuel and ammunition dumps with 1,000-pound bombs and 30mm Aden canon shells. The Harriers then made a second sortie scattering cluster bombs over the heavily cratered airfields to make repairs either impossible or very dangerous. The Argentines retaliated with anti-aircraft fire, missiles and Mirage fighters. The Ministry of Defence has confirmed that no British aircraft were shot down. A single Harrier sustained slight damage to a tail fin which has now been repaired.

A statement from British Task Force commander, Admiral Sandy Woodward, confirmed that the mission was a success. Woodward went on to say: 'We didn't want this fight, but we've shown our colours and this is our day.'

Lima: 1 May 1982

The US Marine guards at the American Ambassador's residence were now familiar with the comings and goings of the mysterious British visitor. Catesby, for his part, felt uneasy being the guest of a foreign power. But it wasn't the first time in his career that he wasn't totally certain who he was working for. At least the pawns on a chessboard are colour-coded as to their allegiance.

When Catesby woke after a fitful sleep filled with anxiety dreams, only the servants were stirring. He had two cups of tea and gobbled a croissant as he penned a thank-you note for the Ambassador and his wife. Even spies have manners, however rudimentary. He then packed his things, for intuition told him that he wouldn't be coming back. A Marine summoned a taxi to take him to the British Embassy.

This time there was no nonsense or ID checks at the reception desk. After a brief enquiry using the internal switchboard, the receptionist said, 'The Ambassador will see you now.'

Catesby was impressed to see that the Ambassador looked even sharper and more spruce than he had in the middle of the night. The key to high rank was endurance and little need for sleep.

'It's all kicked off,' said the Ambassador. 'That's what the cable was about. They wanted to give me time to prepare a briefing for President Belaúnde – which I have just done.'

'I assume that fighting has begun.'

'Indeed. The RAF has just bombed the airfield at Port Stanley and adjacent Argentine facilities. It was an aerial tour de force. The Vulcan had to be refuelled seven times.'

'Too early for a damage assessment?'

'The actual damage isn't the important thing. The purpose of the Vulcan raid was to give the Junta a show of British military might and prowess.' The Ambassador smiled. 'We are still in the realm of diplomacy.'

Catesby could tell from the Ambassador's tone and body language that he wasn't going to say more. He was one of those British mandarins who are the soul of discretion and take secrets and revelations to the very grave. The Ambassador was part of the glue that kept the establishment from falling apart. It was a trait that Catesby admired, but not one that he possessed himself.

'Are there any further instructions regarding myself?'

'Can you remind me of your codename?'

Catesby told him.

'Thought it was you.' The Ambassador handed a teleprinted strip across his desk.

'Thank you.' Catesby stared at the decoded message: TRAVEL TO WASHINGTON DC ASAP. REPORT TO UK EMBASSY FOR FURTHER INSTRUCTIONS.

Casa Rosada, Buenos Aires: 1 May 1982, 6 p.m.

The first thing that Horacio Spinoza did when he got to the Pink House, the Presidential Palace, was to go for a pee. Despite being well known to the staff as a senior intelligence officer, Spinoza was followed to the toilet by a security guard in polished jackboots, wearing a tasselled helmet and carrying a sabre. The purpose was more to impress than to protect. He couldn't imagine the sabre would be much good against an assassin wielding an automatic rifle. But the state of the toilet gave Spinoza more worries about his country than the pointlessness of having security guards in ceremonial uniforms. The toilet was filthy and didn't flush. The floor was damp with pee. The urine soaked a pile of shredded documents which, he assumed, was meant to be toilet paper. It was the sort of toilet one would find in the most wretched slum – and yet it was at the pinnacle of Argentine state power. Spinoza prayed, for the sake of his country's honour, that the Super Étendards and their Exocets were in a better state than the Presidential lavatories – and that the pilots were in a better state than General Galtieri.

When Spinoza arrived in the Salón Norte, the elegant conference room where meetings of state take place, he was relieved to see that Galtieri was sober – or at least appeared so. The Head of the Junta was poised in the centre of a long table which seated forty-six – but on this occasion only ten places were occupied. By Junta standards, it was an intimate meeting. Galtieri was flanked by Jorge Anaya, the Head of the Navy, and Nicanor Costa Méndez, the Foreign Minister. Spinoza wasn't privy to the Junta's most private discussions, but he suspected that Anaya was the war party while Costa Méndez represented the peace settlement option. It was as if Galtieri was trapped between good and bad angels. Spinoza was pleased to see that both angels had copies of his report and the documents that Catesby had passed on. The interaction between the two was interesting.

Costa Méndez looked past Galtieri at Anaya. 'You were certain that the US would remain neutral.'

Anaya replied, 'And you were certain that Britain would accept a sovereignty deal.'

'The situation, gentlemen,' said Galtieri trying to sound more sober than he was, 'has moved on. We are here to discuss the current military situation which is evolving quickly.'

Anaya sighed deeply. 'The British bombing raid was a propaganda ploy. One plane dropped twenty-one bombs – and only one bomb hit the runway. The damage will be repaired by tomorrow morning.'

'The bombing raid,' said the Foreign Minister, 'was more aimed at British public opinion than at our airfields on Las Malvinas. Thatcher is getting her people in the mood for war – and the raid will also strengthen support from the Americans.'

Anaya frowned and shook his head.

'Don't shake your head, Jorge, look at the statistics. You have nine surface ships and the British have forty-four – plus at least two nuclear submarines in the area.' The Foreign Minister lifted the documents provided by Spinoza. 'And the intelligence assessments are dire.'

Galtieri, bleary-eyed, looked across the table at Spinoza. 'Would you like to say something, Horacio?'

'The documents given to me by the British intelligence officer in Lima are obviously intended to influence our decisions, but the information and assessments are, sadly, accurate ones. Our ability to obtain Exocets and other advanced weapons has been seriously thwarted by British and French intelligence.'

Anaya frowned at Spinoza – and Spinoza felt it. Anaya, as commander-in-chief of the Argentine Navy, had been responsible for the failure of the Argentine Naval Procurement Office in Paris which had its cover so easily blown.

Costa Méndez could see that tempers were getting frayed and remembered that there were members of the Junta who didn't always behave in a rational manner. It wasn't easy being a career diplomat in a room full of military professionals with much blood on their hands – a majority of whom also knew the invasion had been a mistake and their backs were against the wall.

'At the first sign of failure,' said Anaya, 'Washington will ditch Thatcher – just like they ditch other allies in trouble. Never trust the Americans.'

'They have,' said the Foreign Minister, 'already provided the British with satellite intelligence, fuel supplies, the use of the US airfield on Ascension Island and have promised to lend them a US aircraft carrier if necessary.' Costa Méndez gave a wry smile. 'But you are right, the Americans do ditch allies – and we are one of them.'

Galtieri was clearly bored with the squabbling. He looked across the table at Spinoza, whom he trusted. 'Is there anything, Horacio, that you would like to add?'

'The most revealing intelligence insights from the British agent were not the ones that are written down, but what he said and implied?'

'Which are?' said Galtieri.

'The British government is split at the very top.'

'What proof is there of this?' said Anaya.

'There is never written or recorded proof of such things,' broke in the Foreign Minister, 'just as there are no records of our own disagreements.'

Galtieri tapped his fountain pen. He needed a drink.

'A peace settlement,' said Costa Méndez, 'no matter how generous to the British, would see the end of Mrs Thatcher as Prime Minister.'

'And what good would that do?' said Admiral Anaya.

'It would mean that we would be dealing with a more reasonable British Prime Minister who would offer…' What Costa Méndez really wanted to say was *a face-saving way out of the mess*, but instead said, '…offer a way of avoiding a war that we would surely lose.'

There was an uneasy silence, which was broken by a naval officer who had close ties to the ESMA torture centre. 'This meeting is about treason. There is no peace settlement that would leave Las Malvinas in our hands. It would be the end of us – and the end of Argentine dignity.'

An army officer spoke up. 'I totally agree. We need to reinforce the Las Malvinas garrison with commandos and marines from the border with Chile – and, if necessary, fight to the last man.' The officer gave a sly smile. 'But there is an advantage to peace talks and letting them drag on. Every day gets closer to winter and will make British operations more difficult and an amphibious landing impossible.'

'I am sure,' said the Foreign Minister, 'that the British have already considered that. The deal that is being offered would need to take effect immediately – or war would be inevitable.'

'We are being too soft,' said the ESMA naval officer. 'What nonsense giving the Las Malvinas kelpers colour televisions to watch the World Cup. They should be interned – and next time the British bomb the islands, we execute one kelper for each bomb dropped.'

Several embarrassed faces looked away. The naval officer was a minority of one. The Junta realised that what they did in secret to their own people was not something they could do to British citizens in the full glare of global publicity.

'Let's have a vote,' said Galtieri. 'How many say we should start again on negotiations for a peaceful settlement?'

Anaya shook his head. 'Not through the Americans.'

'No,' said Galtieri, 'this time it will be negotiated by our best friends and closest allies in South America, the Peruvians. Okay? How many in favour?'

Galtieri abstained and Spinoza was unable to vote because he wasn't a Junta member. In the end, there were five votes in favour and three against.

Galtieri kept a straight face. 'I will speak with Fernando Belaúnde this evening.'

HMS *Conqueror* 57°29'S 64°34'W: 1 May 1982, 2000 Hours Zone Time

Diary of Bellman First Class Weapons Stowage Compartment

We have sailed many months, we have sailed many weeks,
(Four weeks to the month you may mark),
But never as yet ('tis your Captain who speaks)
Have we caught the least glimpse of a Snark!

Our submarine's library is not very extensive, but I am pleased to see it contains one author who knows what is going on in the South Atlantic. I wonder if he stowed away as a lark. After reading Alice *and* Looking Glass *(twice), I began to think that Lewis Carroll is hiding in the shadows – and laughing at us – and now I am sure he is.* The Hunting of the Snark *is exactly what we are doing.*

We finally spotted the Snark this morning. We knew she was there because we had picked her up on sonar the evening before. The captain ordered us up to periscope depth and started having a look just before 1000 Zulu Time – and there she was. The Snark wasn't alone: she was with two destroyers and an oil tanker that was replenishing her precious fluids. Snarks don't live on air alone.

I'm the only one on the sub who calls her a Snark; the others refer to her as the General Belgrano. *But the important thing is whether or not this Snark is a Boojum!*

But oh, beamish nephew, beware of the day,
If your Snark be a Boojum! For then
You will softly and suddenly vanish away,
And never be met with again!

Boojums, of course, are highly dangerous. But is the Belgrano *a Boojum? Her main armament are fifteen six-inch guns that can hurl 120-pound shells – but their maximum range is only thirteen miles. Very unlikely that* Belgrano *can get that close to a Royal Navy ship without being taken out.*

Is this why we didn't sink her this morning? Because

Belgrano *isn't really a Boojum? Or because she was outside the Total Exclusion Zone – the TEZ?*

Ah, that's the interesting thing! There's a rumour – shhh – that we can attack Boojums outside the TEZ, but no one else. The most obvious and notorious Boojum is the aircraft carrier, Veinticinco de Mayo. *Whereas the* Belgrano *Snark can only hit ships visible on the horizon to the naked eye,* Veinticinco de Mayo*'s planes can strike ships that are 400 miles away. Unfortunately, we still haven't seen that monster Boojum. But if we do, say some of the sub's jokers, wouldn't it be wonderful to sink the* Veinticinco de Mayo *on the 25th of May.*

The other Boojums are enemy submarines – which may or may not be attacked outside the TEZ. In any case, any attack outside the TEZ needs the consent of Fleet Headquarters in Northwood – which, I assume, was denied this morning.

I have to admit that I am frightened – not just for myself and my fellow crewmen – but also for other sailors.

O hear us when we cry to Thee
For those in peril on the sea!

The Government Palace, Lima: 1 May 1982, 2300 (Lima time)

President Fernando Belaúnde wasn't alone when he made the final preparation for his critical phone call to the Casa Rosada in Buenos Aires. The Peruvian Foreign Minister, Dr Javier Arias Stella, the Prime Minister and several aides were present. Belaúnde respected Javier as a fellow professional and a Renaissance man. The Foreign Minister was someone who, like Belaúnde himself, had a distinguished career in a totally different sphere from politics. Belaúnde had been one of Latin America's most eminent architects before entering politics; likewise, Dr Javier Arias Stella was a world-renowned pathologist.

Belaúnde turned to the physician. 'Have you had a chance to do a medical analysis?'

'I have given your request some thought, Mr President, and I have decided that medical confidentiality extends beyond one's own patients.'

'I am not surprised that you take that point of view, Dr Arias Stella, and I respect your professionalism.' Belaúnde paused and smiled. 'So I have invited someone else to give a psychological assessment – an acquaintance from the United States.' Belaúnde turned to one of the aides. 'Could you ask him in, please?'

The American had two different faces. One face belonged to the horn-rimmed-glasses-wearing academic who had a PhD in clinical psychology. The other face was that of a hard cynical CIA officer who had played a key role in the Project MK/Ultra mind-control experiments. He had spent a lot of time in Honduras overseeing experiments that were too controversial to trial in the USA, which was why he spoke good Spanish. When the American began speaking, it was in the reasoned tones that went with his academic face.

'From a Freudian perspective, the most striking aspect of the British Prime Minister's personality is lack of warmth towards her mother and strong identification with her father. When recounting her early years, she has never once referred to her mother. The biographical details which she supplied to *Who's Who* refer to her as being the daughter of Alderman Alfred Roberts of Grantham, "a practical man who taught her the importance of hard work and a free market".'

'Why?' said one of President Belaúnde's military aides. The aide was clearly unimpressed by psychological profiling.

The American shrugged. 'We can only speculate as to the reasons for paternal identification and the lack of maternal bonding. I would suggest breast denial in her infancy.'

The Foreign Minister, himself a doctor, whispered, 'Oral frustration.'

'Exactly,' said the American, 'and oral frustration can lead to competitiveness, belligerence and extreme aggression in adult life. Mrs Thatcher also seems to have a strongly anal-retentive personality. This is probably the result of harsh toilet training as a toddler. It forms an adult who can be very stubborn and who is also obsessed with tidiness and frugality.'

'In summary?' said President Belaúnde.

'The British Prime Minister,' said the American, 'has a highly authoritarian personality and views the world – including those close to her – with hostility and suspicion.'

The military aide looked at the American with a frown. 'You haven't mentioned Thatcher's alcoholism.'

'Thank you for your report,' said Belaúnde, cutting his aide short. The president wanted to end the discussion lest it shifted to Galtieri and his alcoholism – not something he wanted to discuss in front of a CIA agent.

As soon as the American was gone, Belaúnde passed the psychological report to an aide and told him to forward it to Buenos Aires. He wanted Galtieri to have no illusions about his opponent in London being reasonable.

An aide wearing headphones spoke up. 'We are now, Mr President, connected to the Casa Rosada – and General Galtieri is on the telephone.'

'Good evening, President Galtieri,' said the Peruvian President.

'And good evening to you, Dr Belaúnde,' said the Argentine acknowledging his fellow leader's doctorate in architecture, 'but it is morning here.'

'We are two hours behind you in Lima – which means we have had more time to work on the peace proposal. It is a seven-point plan.'

'I am ready to record so can you read it to me.'

Belaúnde read the proposal. The important points were an immediate ceasefire and mutual withdrawal of forces. The Argentine forces on the Islands would be replaced by a 'contact group' composed of Brazil, Peru, West Germany and the USA.

'I have my doubts, Doctor, about the United States.'

'And Britain has its doubts about Peru being part of the group. We thought it was a matter of balance: one friend each.'

'But if necessary,' said Galtieri in a hushed voice, 'we could change these two members of the contact group?'

'Yes, it wouldn't be a sticking point.' Belaúnde paused. 'I hope, Mr President, that you realise how much effort and passion my government and our friends have put into this peace plan. It is the last chance to avoid a bloodbath that would deeply hurt us all.'

'The bloodbath has already begun. We were very shocked by the British air raid on Port Stanley – we suffered fifty casualties.'

Belaúnde was pleasantly surprised by Galtieri's tone of voice. He sounded sober and thoughtful.

The Argentine President continued. 'We've had several meetings in the last few hours. The consensus among the generals is that we should avoid all-out war and negotiate a settlement. The last nut to crack was Admiral Anaya, as you know the most hawkish of the Junta, who has now rescinded our fleet's attack orders. Our ships have now been ordered to return to port.'

'That's good news. We want to be able to celebrate the end of this conflict – even though your soldiers and sailors are fighting so bravely and so professionally.'

Galtieri sounded very tired. 'It is nearly 2 a.m. Can we talk again tomorrow – I mean later today.'

'Are the conditions acceptable?'

'I have heard your message, Dr Belaúnde, and I thank you and warmly embrace you on behalf of Argentina. You will have my answer later this morning – after we've slept.'

'But first, listen. This peace plan is very recent – only a few hours old – and less elaborate than the one that preceded it. If we don't have a simple and unambiguous formula, the Pym peace mission could fail. The US State Department needs to know your reaction within the hour.'

'You haven't given us a lot of time, Dr Belaúnde. We will call you in a few hours. And a thousand thanks to you and the Peruvian people – and the lasting gratitude of the Argentine people.'

'Thank you, Mr President.'

Belaúnde put the phone down and looked at the Prime Minister. 'What do you think, Manolo?'

'He can't say more than he already has without getting the peace plan ratified by Costa Méndez and the Junta. Now that

Anaya is in favour of negotiations there shouldn't be any obstacles. Galtieri, of course, still wants a stylish and face-saving exit – which Thatcher may well sabotage.'

'The Junta needs to act quickly.' Belaúnde folded his hands and stared into space. 'The key to success is Francis Pym. I don't know what or how he thinks, but, if I were giving Pym advice, I would tell him to get this deal signed, delivered and publicised before Thatcher even knows about it.'

'You mean a fait accompli behind her back,' said the Prime Minister.

'I hope he is capable of it.'

Washington DC: 1 May 1982, Midnight (Eastern Daylight Time)

Catesby was picked up from Washington National Airport by the SIS Intelligence Liaison Officer from the UK Embassy. It was one of SIS's most senior overseas postings and was usually given to officers destined for high places – as was Kim Philby when he held the post. Unlike Philby, the current holder was sound and loyal, but reminiscent of his predecessor, the liaison officer was the archetypal Englishman in name, looks and manners. Like the Ambassador himself, Digby Wrangham was a languid Brit straight out of Central Casting. It was as if the Foreign Office and SIS wanted to impress and reassure the Americans with Hollywood images of 'Englishness'. Catesby couldn't imagine London sending an ambassador to the US with a Geordie accent or blunt Yorkshire directness.

'How did it go?' said Wrangham.

'On or off the record?'

'The latter sounds more interesting.'

One of Catesby's skills was imparting unclassified and harmless information as if it was top-secret intelligence and the height of indiscretion. It was a way of getting the confidence of others without giving anything away. It worked with the liaison officer.

Wrangham gave a conspiratorial smile. 'Haig's been bouncing around like a toddler on Christmas morning. He thinks the Nobel Peace Prize is under the tree and has his name on it.'

'What's the latest?'

'According to GCHQ – and, by the way, we're getting copied in on everything – the telephone lines between Lima and the State Department have been hot and hopping.'

'They've broken the codes?'

'Not necessary. Haig and Belaúnde have been talking in the clear.'

For some reason Catesby wasn't very happy about the lack of security.

Wrangham continued. 'It looks like Galtieri is on the verge of accepting the peace plan. There's still wrangling about a word or two and who will replace the Argentine troops in the Falklands as peacekeepers. At the moment, it looks certain that West Germans and Brazilians will form two of the groups.'

Catesby smiled. 'The football games will be fantastic.'

'Ah, and that's where you come in.'

'As a ref? I'd have to give an extra goal to the West Germans to make up for 1966.'

'No, but they want you to do some liaising.' Wrangham reached into his pocket and passed over a telex printout. 'This is from C.'

Catesby read the paper. Request that Dir/LatinAmerica liaise with FIS chief at FRG Embassy as well as other relevant officials and report to HOM on feasibility of FRG participation in Contact Group. It took him a second to remember that Dir/Latin America was one of his job titles – and that FIS was the English equivalent of the BND, the Bundesnachrichtendienst. Basically, he was being instructed to go to the West German Embassy to liaise with the Federal Intelligence Service chief of station about West Germany's likely participation in a Falklands peace deal.

Catesby turned to Wrangham. 'Is the BND bloke still Gerhard?'

'Afraid so.'

'He isn't that bad.'

'His sense of humour takes a bit of getting used to.'

'Indeed,' sighed Catesby.

The West German Embassy was as much a national stereotype as was the mock-Georgian British one. The German Embassy was strikingly modern: all glass and steel. The liaison meeting took place in the office of the military attaché where newly printed maps of the Falkland Islands were spread out on a long glass table. Gerhard looked smug and pleased with himself as a West German First Secretary gave an account of the Peruvian Peace Plan and the role that West Germany might be asked to play.

Catesby could see that the German intelligence officer was either about to pee himself or was bursting to speak. 'Would you like to say something, Gerhard?'

'Don't you find it amusing?'

'Don't I find what amusing?' said Catesby with a stern stare.

'Is it not amusing to think that the Falkland Islanders would prefer to have German troops patrolling their streets than Argentine ones?'

Catesby gave a steely frown.

Gerhard pointed at the map. 'Perhaps you should rename the main islands Jersey and Guernsey?'

Catesby saw that none of the Germans found the joke funny, but it was better than most of Gerhard's – and bleakly ironic. Catesby looked at his watch. It was now past three in the morning.

Someone knocked on the door and a young diplomat, the Night Duty Officer, entered and had a whispered conversation with the First Secretary who then said, 'There's been a telephone call from the White House.'

Everyone around the table was too seasoned to be impressed. The White House was a big office building with a lot of telephones.

'It was from Haig's office.' The First Secretary continued in a tone that balanced scepticism and optimism. 'The message is that the Argentines have accepted the peace plan – but we'll have to wait and see for confirmation.'

'And,' said Gerhard, 'it takes two to tango.'

Catesby exchanged a glance with the First Secretary and was certain that the German was thinking the same thing. It was too early for the Junta to have discussed and approved the plan. Someone in the US Secretary of State's office, probably with a prod from Haig himself, was trying to hurry the West Germans into preparing to be part of the Contact Group.

'*Let's look on the bright side*,' sang the military attaché in English. He was an unlikely fan of Monty Python.

Once again, Catesby felt he had passed through the Looking Glass.

'I think,' said the military attaché switching back to German, 'that we should have a drink – even if it is too soon to celebrate.' The military attaché went over to the office fridge and took out a bottle of *Sekt* as someone else passed around long-stemmed glasses. When the cork was popped and the glasses charged, the German officer raised his glass: 'To peace in the South Atlantic!'

As Catesby echoed *Zum Frieden im Südatlantik* and drank the dry sparkling wine, he sensed something ominous and otherwise.

Catesby was on his way out of the West German Embassy when he was stopped by the Night Duty Officer. 'The Ambassador would like to see you.'

Catesby was surprised that the Ambassador wanted to see anyone at five o'clock in the morning, much less himself. But Peter Hermes was an unusual man who had been whacked by the folly and tragedy of twentieth-century Germany. His father had been a member of the Reichstag who had been imprisoned for being anti-Hitler in the 1930s. Hermes's father was locked up again in 1944 and sentenced to death on suspicion of having been part of the von Stauffenberg plot to kill Hitler. Fortunately, his wife managed to get his execution delayed until the Soviet Army overran Berlin. Meanwhile, Peter Hermes, whose two brothers had already been killed on the Eastern Front, was captured by the Russians and held as a PoW for five years.

The Ambassador greeted Catesby in English – and Catesby continued speaking English for reasons of courtesy, for his own German was much better than the Ambassador's English.

'I wanted to tell you,' said Peter Hermes, 'that my government is committed to West Germany becoming part of the Peruvian Peace Plan Contact Group.' The Ambassador smiled. 'I've just telephoned Bonn. The Chancellor doesn't know it yet, but the Foreign Ministry will soon inform him.'

'Thank you for telling me.' Catesby realised that the Ambassador had played a flanker – and that Chancellor Helmut Schmidt wouldn't be able to rescind his decision. 'Have you, sir, informed London?'

'Yes – and I've also sent a copy of the cable to your Ambassador here in Washington and also to the US Secretary of State.'

At the time Catesby didn't realise the significance, but evidence that a peace plan was on the cards was quickly stacking up.

Ambassador Hermes stood up. 'I want to show that Germany is now a force of peace and progress.'

Catesby well knew that Peter Hermes was passionate about restoring his country's image. It was an obsession with him.

The Ambassador leaned forward to shake Catesby's hand. 'I hope we are on the road to peace and friendship.'

Dawn was breaking when Catesby arrived at the British Embassy. The clean morning light was supposed to show the architecture at its best. The Embassy was the only building in the States that had been designed by Sir Edwin Lutyens – the same architect who had designed the Cenotaph. It was clear to Catesby that Lutyens' brief had been to design a building that impressed Americans – but it didn't impress Catesby. The Embassy was supposed to look like a grand old English country home, but Catesby had never seen an English house or building that looked anything like it. The ludicrous Ionic columns belonged more to a set of *Gone With the Wind* than anything British.

Fortunately, Catesby's business didn't require him to sully the Lutyens' edifice with the soles of his dirty and cynical spy shoes. The modern office block, where most of the embassy's day-to-day business was transacted, was sufficient. A bleary-eyed Third Secretary checked Catesby's ID and entered him in the logbook before showing him to an office with an electric typewriter. Catesby occasionally glanced up at a scowling photo of Winston Churchill as he typed out his report. He suspected that there had been another Churchill behind the bluff iconic image: one formed and haunted by the close battle he had seen as a young man, including being overrun and seeing a fellow soldier hacked to death a few feet from himself. Catesby wondered what Churchill would do in the South Atlantic: escalate into 'war war' or continue to 'jaw jaw'?

As soon as Catesby had finished his report, he took it to the Comm Centre and then collapsed in an armchair in the corridor. He started reading a newspaper and then fell asleep. He didn't know how long it was before a young female diplomat shook him awake. Her smile was very warm – and for a second Catesby thought he had died and gone to heaven.

'Director Catesby,' she whispered.

He was pleased to see he hadn't been demoted and said, 'Was I snoring?'

'Only a little, but a message for you has just arrived.' She handed him a teletext.

Catesby read the words of the message signed by C without fully understanding the context: RETURN TO LONDON IMMEDIATELY FOR DEBRIEF AND WELL DESERVED LEAVE. The message dovetailed with two other questions that had been in the back of Catesby's mind. Why had there been no further cables from the Foreign Secretary and why had the British Ambassador been ignoring him? *Had,* Catesby thought, *he become an embarrassment who knew too much and was being kicked into the long grass?*

Chequers: 2 May 1982, 10 a.m.

It was love at first sight. The Prime Minister fell in love with Chequers the very first weekend she stayed there. In many ways, it was more modest than the government's other grace and favour country houses – only eleven bedrooms – but she loved the combination of homeliness and discreet grandeur. She also liked being able to play the role of a thrifty household manager. One of her first economies was turning off the heating for the indoor swimming pool, which cost more than four thousand pounds a year to heat. So anyone going for an early morning exercise dip would be greeted by a bracing North Sea chill.

She hadn't slept well – if at all. Even the whisky lacked its usual soporific effect. One of the problems had been the late-night telephone calls from Washington and Lima. Ten in the evening in DC was three in the morning in London – and she wasn't always certain that Haig and the others realised that. The fact that she was a legendary Iron Lady who survived on only three or four hours sleep a night had its drawbacks. But it was a bright spring morning now and the coffee had kicked off a delightful adrenalin high.

The Prime Minister was sitting in the Hawtrey Room and admiring the tidiness. The Chequers staff were so much more fastidious than the ones in Downing Street. Number 10 was, in fact, a bit of a tip. She could never regard that place as home. It was a Whitehall office building full of untidy civil servants in suits that needed a dry clean. But at Chequers everyone and everything had its precise place – and there was never any dust behind the portraits on the wood-panelled walls. She knew, because she checked. And although she seldom read newspapers, she was pleased that they were ironed and arranged like guardsmen on parade.

Someone knocked on the door. She knew who it would be and purred, 'Come in.'

The War Cabinet member who entered, Cecil Parkinson, was Thatcher's favourite. The son of a railway worker, Parkinson came from a background even more humble than her own.

Of the members of the War Cabinet, Parkinson was the one whose judgement she trusted most. The Prime Minister valued his confiding warmth and political acumen. She kicked off her shoes and folded her feet under her thighs. She felt silky and feline.

'An unsettled night,' said Thatcher. 'A lot of distracting noise from Washington and Lima.'

'Any developments from yesterday morning?'

Thatcher frowned. 'Belaúnde has put his proposals to Galtieri – and they have not been rejected.'

'It sounds like the air raids on Port Stanley have concentrated minds.'

'But this is not the result we wanted.'

The party chairman smiled and thought, *But what result did you expect?* He admired the PM, but could see she needed guidance as well as loyal support.

'And Haig is laying on the pressure again.'

'Any word from the President?'

'Reagan is a weakling.' Thatcher's contempt for the US President was often aired in private, but airbrushed and hidden in public.

'And what about Francis?' said Parkinson raising an eyebrow.

'Just a brief cable to say that he's arrived in Washington and will be meeting with Haig this morning. I'm glad he's not here today. He always seems hunched and sheepish.' Thatcher was not a big fan of her Foreign Secretary. 'His caution saps our resolution. If Francis Pym had his way he would have us sign a conditional surrender.'

The party chairman nodded agreement with the PM's assessment, but refrained from openly criticising his colleague.

Thatcher looked at Parkinson and knew that she could always rely on him. It was impossible to make such changes in the middle of a crisis, but when it was all over she would like him as her Foreign Secretary – and perhaps one day would anoint him as her successor.

'I talked to Cranley Onslow this morning,' said Parkinson

Thatcher puckered a brow. Onslow, second to Pym as Minister

of State for Foreign Affairs, wasn't one of her favourites either. She loved the story about how Onslow had been surprised in his bath by communist guerrillas when serving as a Consul in Maymyo, Burma. The guerrillas demanded typewriters, money and Onslow's Purdey shotgun. The pink and dripping Consul handed them over, but asked for a receipt so that he could claim for loss of the priceless Purdey.

'And what,' said the PM, 'does Cranley have to say?'

'He seemed reluctant to say anything. I had to press him and he admitted that the Foreign Office knows all about the latest peace proposals.'

'Do they know more than we do?'

'I believe so.'

'That is totally unacceptable.'

'I completely agree, Prime Minister.'

'We must make sure – perfectly sure – that no announcement is made that implies that we have agreed to these peace proposals, that they have been formally presented to us...' The Prime Minister paused. 'Or that we even know of their existence.'

An hour later, the Chief of Defence Staff, Admiral Terence Lewin, and First Sea Lord, Admiral Henry Leach, arrived at Chequers. In the absence of Admiral Lewin, who was on an official visit to New Zealand, Leach had been acting Chief of Defence Staff when news of the Argentine invasion reached London. It was Leach who convinced the Prime Minister that it was possible and vital for a Task Force to retake the Falklands. In turn, Thatcher dubbed Admiral Leach her 'knight in shining gold braid.' The rest of the War Cabinet soon followed. The only member not present was Foreign Secretary Francis Pym, but he would be informed of any decisions made. On this occasion, the War Cabinet was augmented by Leach as well as Admiral John Fieldhouse, operations commander at Northwood HQ, and the Foreign Office Permanent Under-Secretary. All of them would be staying for lunch at Chequers – and the morning meeting had an air of informality. Denis Thatcher began serving pre-lunch gin and tonics as soon as everyone had assembled.

'Any more news about that aircraft carrier?' Thatcher was referring to the Argentine *Veinticinco de Mayo*, which was everyone's biggest worry.

'Still no further sightings, Prime Minister,' said the admiral in charge of operations, 'and it's not likely that we will see her again in light of the information that we've just had from GCHQ.'

Thatcher remembered the phone message, but hadn't quite taken in its significance at the time. There was so much going on.

Chief of Defence Staff Lewin spoke up. 'Argentine signals security is practically non-existent. We managed to break all their codes from early on. The entire Argentine fleet has been ordered to return to their home bases. The instruction was sent at 0700 our time.'

The PM reflected for a second and tried not to show her anger. It was part of the pattern. They were conspiring behind her back. 'They think they can cut and run.'

Admiral Lewin, assuming that the PM was referring to the Argentine Navy, replied, 'There appears to be a complete change of heart since yesterday when Anaya ordered his fleet to attack.'

Operations Commander Fieldhouse chimed in, 'The movements of their cruiser, the *Belgrano*, may well reflect this pattern. Yesterday she was heading east as if part of a possible pincer movement...'

'And why wasn't she sunk?' said the Prime Minister.

'Because she was outside the Total Exclusion Zone.'

'But,' said the PM, 'there wouldn't have been any problem about attacking that aircraft carrier of theirs outside the Exclusion Zone.' The decision about the carrier had been endorsed at a War Cabinet meeting the previous morning – just before Pym had jetted off to Washington.

'As we mentioned yesterday,' said the operations commander, '25 *de Mayo* constitutes a far more serious threat to the Task Force. The carrier's A-4Q Skyhawks could hit our ships from more than 400 miles away. *Belgrano*'s six-inch guns are indeed lethal, but only have a range of thirteen miles.'

'Excuse me, Admiral,' said the party chairman, 'you had begun to comment on the *Belgrano*'s movements.'

'HMS *Conqueror* has been tracking the *Belgrano* and the two destroyers accompanying her for thirty-six hours. Although the battle group has fastidiously remained outside the TEZ at all times; they were, according to yesterday's reports from *Conqueror*, on an easterly course that could have been interpreted as hostile intent.'

'Ah, but,' continued Parkinson pointing a finger, 'we still don't know whether the *Belgrano* battle group has followed what, according to GCHQ, is Admiral Anaya's latest order to change course and return to port.'

'It would be very unusual for a subordinate commander to disobey a direct order from headquarters.' Admiral Fieldhouse smiled. 'I don't believe *Belgrano*'s captain is Lord Nelson.'

'When will we know for certain that the *Belgrano* is heading back to port?'

'*Conqueror*'s next scheduled contact with Northwood is 1500 hours. Submarines have to stay hidden for most of the day which makes continuous communication impossible.'

'I think,' said the Prime Minister, 'that we have to make a decision now.'

Willie Whitelaw, the oldest member of the War Cabinet, suddenly stirred. He was someone who had seen war at close quarters. He became second-in-command of his tank battalion after he saw his predecessor killed directly in front of him. The PM looked at him, 'You want to say something, Willie?'

'What sort of decision, Margaret?'

The PM stared at her older colleague whom she respected. 'We need to instruct our submarines – and all of the Task Force – to sink Argentine warships wherever they find them. The Total Exclusion Zone should no longer be used by the Argentines as a way of avoiding battle.'

There was a hush in the room.

The First Sea Lord exchanged a long glance with the former tank officer. Both of them had seen the horror of battle and both had lost their own fathers in war.

Admiral Fieldhouse broke the awkward silence. 'There is, Prime Minister, a military logic to such a course of action. If Argentine naval units are allowed to return to their bases unscathed, they would be able to sortie out again to cause damage. I would recommend once again that the rules of engagement be changed so that any Argentine warship can be sunk anywhere on the high seas.'

There was another silence. The weight of the impending decision was palpable and irreversible.

'I think,' said a member looking up over his reading glasses, 'we have to consider diplomatic repercussions which could outweigh any military advantages.'

The PM shook her head. The comment clearly annoyed her. 'The time for diplomacy is past.'

Attorney General Michael Havers weighed in. 'There could be legal implications.'

Thatcher sighed. 'We'll consider those when and if they arise.'

Whitelaw, who was usually credited with understanding the Prime Minister best, could see that her head was down and she wouldn't be deterred. He turned to Admiral Fieldhouse. 'Could you please tell us more about the two destroyers escorting the *Belgrano*?'

'They are called *Hipólito Bouchard* and *Piedra Buena*. Their most dangerous armament are ship-to-ship Exocet missiles with a range of thirty-five miles.'

'So they are more of a threat to the Task Force than the *Belgrano* whose main guns, you said earlier, only have a range of thirteen miles?'

'In some situations that may well be…'

'I don't see the relevance of this conversation,' interrupted the Prime Minister. 'In any case, lunch will soon be served – Scottish salmon and Welsh lamb – and I would like to send a message changing the rules of engagement without further delay.'

'I totally agree,' said Parkinson, making eye contact with the Prime Minister.

'Now,' said the PM, making a decisive chopping gesture with

her right hand, 'is there anyone here who does not agree that we should instruct the Task Force to disregard the Total Exclusion Zone and to sink any Argentine vessel that may prove a present or future risk to our ships?'

No one spoke up, but four War Cabinet members replied with grim stares.

'Good.' She turned to the operations commander. 'Can you relay that message immediately?'

'Yes, Prime Minister.'

The PM then turned to the Foreign Office Permanent Under-Secretary. Her face glowed with grim satisfaction. 'And can you let Francis Pym know about this decision as soon as possible?'

'I will make sure, Prime Minister, that he is apprised of it immediately.'

'Good,' said the PM. 'It's now gone past one o'clock and time for lunch.'

HMS *Conqueror*: 56°47'S 61°19'W: 2 May 1982, 1030 Hours Zone Time

Diary of Bellman First Class Weapons Stowage Compartment

We've received a very confusing set of signals which has everyone scratching their unwashed pubes – and the boat is getting a bit pongy. There are only five showers for a crew of 101 – and, likewise, five toilets.

During a briefing after a NATO exercise I once heard a disgruntled American admiral moan, 'If you haven't got communications, you haven't got shit.' And he was a surface officer. The problem with being on a submarine is hardly ever knowing what the fuck is going on. In order to communicate we have to rise to periscope depth to receive and transmit messages via the fleet satellite on our UHF aerial – and the satellite may only be in position once or twice a day.

The first message we received today was a real

what-the-fuck-was-that-about. Total confusion reigned. It was the cancellation of an order to sink the Belgrano *– but the original order to sink her was one that we never received. The second message, however, cancelled the cancellation:* DISREGARD SIGNAL 159 RESCINDING INSTRUCTION TO ATTACK CRUISER BELGRANO. PERMISSION NOW GRANTED TO ATTACK BELGRANO. PROCEED TO DO SO IMMEDIATELY.

Well blimey, we'd better act fast; otherwise, she'll get away. About four hours ago, the Belgrano *completely changed course – a complete 180-degree turn – and she is now heading due west back to port. We reported this change of direction back to Northwood HQ and the Task Force commander, but our instructions are still to attack the ship – even if she remains outside the Total Exclusion Zone. It appears that the Snark has turned out to be a Boojum after all!*

For England expects – I forbear to proceed:
'Tis a maxim tremendous, but trite:
And you'd best be unpacking the things that you need
To rig yourselves out for the fight!

Now, what should we be unpacking? The wizard Tigerfish torpedoes which can follow a ship even if she takes evasive action? Or the old-fashioned Mark 8s which can only go in a straight line but carry bigger warheads?

Government House, Lima, Peru: 2 May 1982, 0800

President Belaúnde had just finished talking to the US Secretary of State and it was now time to telephone Galtieri. Belaúnde looked at the clocks on the office wall. It was now 10 a.m. in Buenos Aires, 11 a.m. in Washington and 4 p.m. in London. The fact that the Americans and the British put their clocks ahead an hour for 'summer time' added to the time zone differences and confusion. *Is it not odd,* thought Belaúnde, *that the Anglo-Saxons, who pride themselves on empirical thought, somehow think that moving their clocks forward means that they will have an extra hour of daylight?*

An aide interrupted the president's thoughts. 'We now, Mr President, have a telephone connection with the Casa Rosada.'

'Are you ready to record?'

'Yes.'

'And please prepare English transcripts to pass on to the British Ambassador and to Washington.'

'Yes, sir.'

Belaúnde picked up the phone. 'Good morning, President Galtieri, and warmest wishes to the people of Argentina.'

'And a warm greeting to you, Dr Belaúnde. Here it has been a busy night and early morning. Our naval units are now withdrawing and we have discussed the peace proposal in depth.'

'I am pleased to hear that.'

'But,' said Galtieri, sounding a bit slurred, 'I am now passing the phone to the Foreign Minister who will continue the negotiations with my government's total backing.'

The next voice that Belaúnde heard was one of refined tone and manner. Nicanor Costa Méndez, who came from a patrician Argentine family, was the only civilian member of the Junta. For years he had been a Catholic nationalist and fierce anti-communist. Belaúnde knew that Costa Méndez felt deeply betrayed by the United States and was now seeking the aid of Cuba and other communist countries. But the Peruvian President knew that this wasn't something they could discuss in a recorded telephone conversation.

'The good news, President Belaúnde, is that there have been no more belligerent actions since yesterday's bombing by the British. This is an excellent sign and suggests that the British are pausing to negotiate.'

'By the way,' said Belaúnde, 'I've just spoken to Haig.'

'What did he say?'

'He said that Britain is objecting to Peru as a member of the Contact Group.'

'Good,' said the Argentine. 'In that case, we object to the Americans being part of the group. That means we are even: one each.'

'I warned Haig that you might take this line and he thinks that it is a fair compromise that the British would agree to. I believe that Canada and Mexico would be acceptable substitutes.'

There was an upbeat lilt in Costa Méndez's voice. 'Yes, that would be agreeable.'

'The important thing is that the Americans be eliminated from the Contact Group.'

'That is correct – and without the US involved there will be no problem.'

Belaúnde nodded. He could see it was a question of bruised national and personal pride. Costa Méndez felt the Americans had let Argentina down – and they had. It was now, Belaúnde realised, for Peru to take the place of the USA as a peacemaker. Ironically, the peace plan was very close to the one the Americans had last proposed – which is why insiders were now calling it 'Haig in a poncho'.

'So,' said Belaúnde, 'I believe there is only one more issue to resolve – which boils down to a single word.'

'Yes,' said the Argentine in English, 'we cannot accept that *viewpoints* of the Islanders be part of the wording in the peace agreement. It means the same thing as wishes.'

Belaúnde knew that *viewpoints* and *wishes* were not synonymous, but wasn't going to argue the point.

'How would you feel,' said Belaúnde replying in English, 'about *aspirations* of the Islanders?'

'Perfect. Aspirations would be fine.'

Belaúnde smiled. Diplomacy was a funny game. In fact, *aspirations* was closer in meaning to the dreaded *wishes* than *viewpoints*. But the word *viewpoints* had been suggested by the British and Costa Méndez had to show that Argentina was not going to be dictated to by the British.

'Is then,' said Belaúnde, 'the peace proposal acceptable?'

'Yes,' said the Argentine, 'the job is nearly finished. You can take it as certain that the Junta will accept these proposals when they meet early this evening.'

'What time are they meeting?'

'About 7 p.m. – and they will make a formal public announcement of acceptance within an hour of that meeting.'

Belaúnde calculated the time difference between Lima and Buenos Aires: that could be another seven hours.

'I wish,' said the Peruvian president, 'that the Junta could meet sooner.'

'I'm not sure that is possible.'

'In that case,' said Belaúnde, 'would you have any objection if I transmitted this news and a transcript of our conversation to the British Ambassador and to Haig?'

'None at all. By all means do so. As I said, the Junta's acceptance is at this late stage a mere formality.'

'Thank you, Foreign Minister, and my warmest greetings to the people of Argentina.'

Foggy Bottom, Washington DC: 2 May 1982, 10 a.m. (Eastern Daylight Time)

Francis Pym had never been in a more embarrassing position. He was faced with one of two choices: treason or duplicity. An hour earlier he had received a telephone call from London on a secure voice line in the British Embassy. The news was very bad. Part of him wished that the American NSA had eavesdropped and managed to break the codes, but spying on allies at a time like this would have been an unforgiveable breach of etiquette. In any case, if Al Haig had found out, he would have come into the breakfast meeting with all guns blazing. Pym was certain that the Americans didn't know. Haig sat behind the table smoking and drinking strong coffee as if he was Master of the Universe and everything was going to plan.

Treason or duplicity? Of course, it was going to be duplicity. Pym knew this was the only option. It was totally unthinkable and unacceptable that he could reveal secret military plans to a high-ranking official of a foreign country – even if that country was Britain's closest ally.

The duplicity had, in fact, begun the evening before. Pym had assured Haig that Britain was not going to further escalate military action and would do nothing more than enforce the Total Exclusion Zone. However, just before flying to Washington the previous day, Pym had been at the meeting where it had been decided that the *Veinticinco de Mayo* could be attacked and sunk outside the Exclusion Zone.

But now, twelve hours later at the breakfast meeting with the US Secretary of State, Francis Pym had far more to hide. He wondered if he was a good enough actor to pull it off. At Eton he had played oboe in the school orchestra, but never ventured on the stage otherwise.

'Have a look at the offerings,' said Haig stubbing out his cigarette and waving his arm at a sideboard heaving with American breakfast.

'I think I'll only have toast and tea – and maybe a poached egg.'

A white-coated Filipino served him. Non-stop eating was an occupational hazard of the diplomatic trade. As soon as they were finished the breakfast meeting, they were off to lunch at the British Embassy.

'We are pleased,' said Haig, 'that there has been no follow-up to the bombing raids on Port Stanley airfield.'

'Our purpose,' said Pym with a straight face, 'had been to concentrate minds.'

Haig had nodded agreement: 'You seem to have succeeded. Belaúnde tells me that the Junta are much more receptive to the peace plan.'

Pym sank deep in his chair as the US Secretary of State recounted the latest progress on the Peruvian president's peace initiative. He was shamefully aware that he was the only one in the room who knew that a British nuclear submarine had been given permission to stalk and destroy an Argentine cruiser with a crew of more than 1,100. And what could he, Francis Pym, do about it? If he told Haig, Haig would explode and have a transatlantic rant at Thatcher. The peace plan would then be dead. Pym hoped that somehow the *Belgrano* would evade the submarine and make it back to port – or at least escape being sunk long enough for the peace plan to be ratified and made public. If that happened, Thatcher's order to sink the ship would probably remain a secret forever – or maybe not.

Pym sank even lower in his chair and hoped that Alexander Haig couldn't read minds. He was sure he couldn't. Haig was too full of himself to even read someone else's thoughts in block capitals on a page. Meanwhile, Pym tried to read Thatcher's mind. He well knew that she regarded most of the old-school British ruling class as sentimental noblesse-oblige fools and weaklings – himself being a prime example – which is why she preferred people like Parkinson. And how odd it was that she had studied science, because she ruled by intuition rather than by cold analysis. But she could read and touch the public mood – and jingoistic war fever was rampant in Britain. Thatcher knew that a peace deal would go down like a damp squib with her main support base. A general election was just over a year away. Thatcher needed to sink the *Belgrano* to stay in power.

The Secretary of State suddenly broke into Pym's reflections. 'Apparently, Admiral Anaya was the last to crack. He has ordered Argentine naval units back to port – and our satellite surveillance confirms that this is true.'

Pym looked away with a blank stare.

HMS Conqueror: 54°21'S 59°37'W: 2 May 1982, 1900 Zone Time

Diary of Sailor Shit-Scared Weapons Stowage Compartment

The adrenalin rush and sense of exhilaration is all gone. None of it seemed real until it actually happened. We had our normal Sunday lunch of roast pork and spuds with pie and/or ice cream for pud. And immediately afterwards, when we started the serious stalking stuff, it still seemed as normal as the traditional Sunday roast. I'm sure I wasn't the only one who had to pinch himself to remember that it wasn't a dream – or another exercise or a sabre-rattling bluff – but something that was real and meant real death to others. (I wish that I didn't keep repeating that word 'real' – but it keeps echoing in my brain).

The first bit was fun: a cat and mouse game that we had often played before with Russian and American ships. The best place to stalk a target is directly beneath her propellers. The ship cannot hear the submarine with her sonar because of the noise of her own engines. So there we were: less than fifty metres beneath the Belgrano*'s hull; less distance than a goalkeeper's clearance kick.*

When everything was ready we dropped back into a position from where we could attack. We had decided to use the Mark 8s – World War Two torpedoes for a World War Two ship. We decided to attack Belgrano*'s port side because both escorting destroyers were on her starboard side. The plan was to fire a fan of three torpedoes at slightly different angles. This means that the target cannot escape even if she sees them coming. A manoeuvre to avoid one will steer into the course of another.*

The first shiver went down my spine when I heard the order for number one, two and six tubes to stand by – and another shiver when I heard: 'Tube bow caps open.' Shit, we are actually going to fire the fucking things! Then the strongest shiver: 'Fire number six.' The first sound was the mechanical growl of the hydraulic ram driving the torpedo out of the tube and into the water – and then the whirring of the torpedo's own motor as it launches itself towards the target. And then after a three-second interval: 'Fire number one.' Three more seconds: 'Fire number two.' Each order followed by the same deadly launch noises. The first voice I heard afterwards was a stunned whisper: 'Fucking hell. We've actually fucking done it.' Followed by a quavering voice: 'How long to impact?' The periscope then went up again and that's when we heard the first explosion, quickly followed by another.

This was when disbelief disappeared and the adrenalin kicked in. A lot of people started shouting: Fucking hell, we got her! Wow, we've really bloody done it. Hey, sir, did you see the torpedoes hit?

The exhilaration dissipated fast. It was only a few minutes before reality kicked in. The periscope came down and we were running for our lives. We were heading east at 23 knots when we heard two explosions. Were they depth charges and were we soon to join the Belgrano *in a watery grave? I had a premonition of our bones mingling – dead sailors together.*

Two hours after the attack we heard more explosions. Someone, a happy chap, suggested they might be anti-submarine ordnance dropped by aircraft. The worse thing is not knowing – trapped under the sea in a cocoon of unknowing.

I am now lying in my bunk once again reading Lewis Carroll's Hunting of the Snark *– because I want to find comfort and lightness.*

They returned hand-in-hand, and the Bellman, unmanned
(For a moment) with noble emotion,
Said, 'This amply repays all the wearisome days
We have spent on the billowy ocean!'

In the midst of the word he was trying to say,
In the midst of his laughter and glee,
He had softly and suddenly vanished away—
For the Snark was *a Boojum, you see.*

But Carroll provides no comfort, only bleak sarcasm. Each word is like a sharp finger jab in the chest. I can almost feel Carroll's ghost grabbing the book from my hands and snapping it shut. And hear his disproving, stammering Oxbridge voice: You, you, thought this was a game … a game. You've now sunk a ship … s-sunk … and k-killed. Killed how many?

Government House, Lima, Peru: 2 May 1982

President Belaúnde was ready and well prepared for the press conference – and pleased to see how many of the international press had crowded into the Golden Hall. The hall was both imposing and magnificent. Its gilt ceiling was hung with a galaxy of gold and crystal chandeliers. The walls were decorated with Louis Quatorze mirrors. There were marble columns and marble tables. On the central table was a statue of Duke Emmanuel of Savoy, who had won the battle of St Quentin in 1557. The bronze-sculpted Duke frowned down at a gold antique clock – a reminder, no doubt, of the importance of time in the events of men. Belaúnde looked at the clock as it chimed 4 p.m. It was time to begin.

'Before you ask any questions, I would like to say that we now have a document that will lead to an immediate end of hostilities. The agreement is a fair one and does not represent a surrender, or even a backing down, for either Argentina or Great Britain. As I speak, President Galtieri is presiding over a meeting that will decide the final text. We are in direct and constant contact with Buenos Aires and Washington, where the British Foreign Secretary is in discussion with Secretary of State Haig. I would also like to mention that the President of the United States has thanked us and supports the proceedings.'

Belaúnde pointed to one of the journalists who had put up his hand.

'When, Mr President, are the full terms of the agreement going to be published?'

'They will be published tonight. I am not able to give you all the terms in advance, but there is one point, the first point, which is no longer under discussion and that is Point One – Immediate Cessation of Hostilities.'

As soon as the press conference was finished there was a rush to the exits as journalists headed for telephones and teleprinters. As the Golden Hall emptied, a senior aide came up to President Belaúnde. The aide didn't yet know the news, but his face was etched with concern.

'Mr President, Secretary of State Haig would like to speak to you – and he says the matter is important and urgent.'

'I'm coming now. We must phone him back immediately.'

'We don't need to phone him back,' said the aide. 'The Secretary of the State is still on the telephone waiting to talk to you.'

Tachbrook Street, Pimlico, London: 3 May 1982

Owing to a delayed flight and time differences, Catesby hadn't tumbled into bed until 3 a.m. He had only woken once during his alcohol-drugged sleep – almost a record – and was quite refreshed when he finally got out of bed at eleven. As it was a glorious spring morning, Catesby decided to celebrate his day off and feeling of well-being by going for a run along the Embankment. The Thames sparkled in the sun and there were rowers and scullers on the Putney side of the river. Britain was once again at peace. The last thing Catesby had seen before he boarded the plane at Dulles Airport was an Associated Press breaking-news headline on a kiosk: FALKLANDS LATEST! PRESIDENT OF PERU ANNOUNCES THAT BRITAIN AND ARGENTINA WILL DECLARE AN END TO ALL HOSTILITIES. Catesby tried to buy a copy of the newspaper, but the dealer said the print copies still hadn't arrived. As Catesby reached the end of his run and turned off the Embankment he was glowing with healthy sweat. It was as if all the evil he had experienced over the past weeks had turned into perspiration and was now being expelled from his body. Perhaps he would even drink less – but then something caught his eye. It was a newspaper on the top rack of the local newsagent:

The Great British Gazette: 2 May 1982

SUNK YA!

British submarine holes Argie cruiser. The 13,000-ton *Generalissimo Belgrano*, the second biggest ship in the Argentine fleet, is reported to be sinking. The Argie cruiser was poised to attack the Task Force when it was torpedoed by a British nuclear submarine. Armed with fifteen six-inch guns and Sea Cat missiles, the *Belgrano*

> posed a deadly threat to our ships. Our lads, flying helicopters armed with Sea Skua missiles, also spotted and sank an Argentine patrol boat and damaged another.
>
> The British military build-up continues apace. The *QE2* has been called into service to carry 3,000 infantrymen to the South Atlantic. Two ferries and a container ship, *The Atlantic Conveyer*, have also been requisitioned.

Catesby blinked in utter disbelief, then turned around and ran back to the flat.

His first impulse after he let himself in was to telephone C and shout, *What the fuck!* But after staring at the phone for a few seconds, he realised it would be pointless. In fact, he doubted if C or anyone in SIS had a clue what had happened. He was certain that the attack had been carried out without the knowledge of the intelligence service. They had been played for fools. Catesby began to shiver as his sweat coagulated and chilled. He needed to shower. Catesby tuned into the BBC one o'clock news as he buttered his toast for a late breakfast. Why, he thought, do we need an intelligence service when you only have to buy a newspaper or turn on the radio? In this case, the voice of the newsreader intoned classic BBC cool and non-judgemental neutrality. *It is now confirmed that the Argentine cruiser, torpedoed yesterday by a British nuclear submarine, has sunk. The* General Belgrano, *with a crew of about 1,100, was struck by two torpedoes from HMS* Conqueror. *Owing to the state of the sea, thirty-five-foot high waves and freezing conditions, the chances of anyone being found alive are slim. The Ministry of Defence has acknowledged that the* Belgrano *was outside the 200-mile Total Exclusion Zone at the time she was attacked. When asked whether the sinking was justified, the Defence Secretary replied: 'The* General Belgrano *was a threat to our men and therefore it is quite correct that she was attacked by our submarines.'*

Catesby turned off the radio and whispered to himself, 'What a shitty fucking thing to do.'

That evening he had a pub meal with his stepson, Peter. It was less than forty-eight hours since the *Belgrano* was torpedoed, but Peter and the other human rights lawyers in his chambers were already questioning whether or not it was a war crime.

'What do you think, Will?' said Peter over his bangers and mash.

'I'm not a lawyer – you are.'

'But you must know some details.'

'It looks bad.'

Peter lowered his voice. 'Would you ever consider providing any details?'

'It's too soon for me to say.' Catesby paused and dropped his voice. 'You know I could go to jail for that sort of thing.'

'The system is rigged against truth.'

Catesby laughed so hard at the understatement that the other diners stared.

'Are you okay, Will?'

'No, Peter, I am out of my fucking mind. We are now going to have a war that could have been easily avoided – and a lot of young men of your age are going to get their faces and genitals burned off. And yes, the Prime Minister is a war criminal.'

Aeronaval Base, Río Grande and South Atlantic: 4 May 1982

Ariel still didn't know the fate of his son. The rescue effort continued to pick up rafts full of frozen survivors forty hours after the sinking. It was difficult for Ariel to think of anything other than the son he loved more than life itself – and his commanding officer had given him the option of not undertaking the mission. But Ariel had chosen to go through with it because he knew he was the best pilot available. No one else had spent as much time practicing refuelling techniques and doing mock launches of Exocets.

The enemy's position had been last reported 390 miles north-east of the base at Río Grande. The long distance meant that Ariel's Super Étendard would have to rendezvous with a KC-130H Hercules Tanker for mid-air refuelling. The skills needed were those of both a racing driver and a polo player. The refuelling was accomplished by inserting a probe into the tanker's drogue – which resembled a giant shuttlecock. Unless the pilot had a very steady hand to control a plane buffeted by air turbulence, the probe rivets would shear and the fuel valve would break off – and the mission would be cancelled. It was like threading a needle in a gale. Ariel was all concentration as he approached the drogue which danced horizontally and vertically in the turbulence. He needed to make his approach at less than walking speed. If you closed too quickly the drogue could shatter the cockpit canopy and injure or kill the pilot. The best approach was from below and behind the drogue – never level with it. As Ariel got closer, he watched for transverse oscillation on the hose behind the drogue. Not too bad, he thought. Slowly, steady, slowly – contact! Good, no amber light for misalignment and the fuel is flowing.

Fully fuelled, Ariel flew on. The target was 240 miles away. They kill our sailors; we kill theirs. The weather had turned: visibility was less than 1,000 metres – and far less at sea level, which was dense fog. The conditions were perfect; it meant they would never see it coming.

Ariel switched on his radar. This was the tricky bit because the enemy could now detect his presence on their radar and take countermeasures. The target immediately appeared on the screen – just forty miles away. Ariel launched the Exocet without a second's delay. Once released, the missile was its own boss. It would drop to the sea surface and skim the waves – completely undetectable by radar or eye – until it hit the ship. It was Ariel's turn to hug the waves. He flew back to base unmolested.

Agency News: 4 May 1982

HMS *Sheffield* Hit By Argentine Missile

The HMS *Sheffield*, a Type 42 destroyer, is ablaze and adrift after having been struck by an Exocet missile launched by an Argentine fighter-bomber. It is not known how many of the ship's crew of 268 have survived. The *Sheffield* caught fire when a French-made Exocet missile penetrated deep into the ship's hull. The subsequent blaze released a poisonous plume of smoke which engulfed the vessel and forced the crew to abandon ship. A major rescue operation is underway in the South Atlantic.

The news was announced on television by Ministry of Defence spokesman, Ian McDonald, who said that HMS *Sheffield* was 'in the course of its duties within the Total Exclusion Zone around the Falkland Islands'. The exact position of the 4,100-ton destroyer remains secret.

It is thought that two Exocets may have been fired by Super-Étendard fighter-bombers; one missed and the other hit the *Sheffield*. The Exocet is the most advanced of anti-ship missiles. It is not known how many Exocets the Argentines have in their possession.

The attack came two days after the Argentine cruiser *General Belgrano* was sunk by a British nuclear submarine. An Argentine diplomat based in Washington said that the destruction of the *Sheffield* was 'justified after the massacre that the English have done shelling our men and our ships'. A diplomatic solution to the Falklands dispute now seems highly unlikely.

Century House, Lambeth, London: 4 May 1982

Catesby and all of his senior colleagues had been summoned to an emergency meeting with C even before the news of HMS *Sheffield* had been officially announced and broadcast. It was late afternoon when C's deputy telephoned. 'We've lost a ship. So you best get over here pronto. The details will be released soon, but keep it hush until they are.'

All the faces at Century House were glum and haggard – they were a reflection of MoD television spokesman, Ian McDonald, who was fast becoming a minor celebrity for his lugubrious tones. The meeting began with a briefing by an officer from naval intelligence dressed in civilian clothes.

'We now,' said the naval officer, 'have a full casualty report. There were twenty officers and ratings killed and twenty-six wounded. A number of the dead were killed by the initial impact, but most of them were asphyxiated as they burned, trapped below decks. The Exocet's warhead did not explode – and the lack of an explosion may have made things worse. The un-spent missile fuel caused a fire which spread through the *Sheffield* and ignited her own diesel supplies. Unfortunately, there was no water to fight the fire as the missile had fractured the ship's fire water main. The fire became so hot that deck and bulkhead paint blistered and melted the boots of the sailors who were trying to contain the blaze. Eventually, HMS *Arrow* and HMS *Yarmouth* came alongside to fight the fire. The water being sprayed on the *Sheffield* became a hazard in itself as it immediately boiled and bounced back in people's faces. I would like to conclude by saying that no government official or member of the public should be under the illusion that Argentina is a pushover with a weak military machine. This is not going to be an easy war.'

C looked at Catesby. 'Are we sure they had only five Exocets?'

Someone interjected. 'Which means they now have only three left. Apparently, they fired two in the *Sheffield* attack. There were two Super Étendards involved.'

'Our primary source of information for the number of Exocets is the French engineer that we recruited.' Catesby was referring to his erstwhile fly-fishing pal. 'Perhaps we should interview him again.'

C looked pained. 'Our French friend is no more. His body was found in the River Tweed this morning. We are, of course, slapping D-notices all over the place – and Five and Special Branch are already on the case. It looks like we will be able to keep it out of the press – at least until the Falklands crisis is resolved.'

'Cause of death?' said Catesby.

'We still don't know. In any case,' continued C, 'the game as far as we are concerned is preventing Argentina from getting more Exocets – no expense or ruthlessness spared – and the War Cabinet is completely behind us.'

The rest of the meeting was devoted to strategy and planning. Catesby joined in with vigour and provided a list of countries who might be persuaded to covertly supply the weapons – as well as financial vehicles to provide the funding – and routes any Exocets procured might follow on their way to Argentina. The meeting ended after midnight. Later, as Catesby lay tossing and turning in the dark watches of the night, he was haunted by the conversation he had had with his stepson. Was he a two-faced liar, who put on one face for his colleagues in SIS and another face for his stepchildren and left-wing intellectual friends? In his heart of hearts, Catesby genuinely did despise the Prime Minister and everything she stood for, but in reality he was prepared to take great personal risks and use all his skills to carry out secret missions that would assure Argentina's humiliation and keep Thatcher in power.

He got up and poured himself a brandy. You couldn't survive as a spy if you didn't know how to cope with inner conflict. And Catesby always found some justification to cling to. If the Junta got more Exocets and those Exocets sunk a British carrier or two, it would not end the war and the Task Force would not come skulking home. Thatcher – with, at first, the roused-up people of Britain behind her – would continue fighting. The war would become a *cause célèbre*, but might – after a few thousand casualties – eventually divide the country. And god knows what Thatcher would do next. Catesby wouldn't put it past her to use nuclear weapons. The best solution – and the one with the least loss of human life – would be for Britain to win the war as cleanly and as quickly as possible. What was wrong with him?

Why did he always need moral justifications? Catesby put his drink down. He had a job to do.

Palermo, Buenos Aires: 8 May 1982

Fiona hated the marital home. It was large, comfortable and well decorated – but it was a tomb. At first, it had been the tomb of Inés, Ariel's dead wife, but now it was the tomb of Gonzalo as well. The presence of both permeated the very fabric of the house. Ariel had once said of Inés, 'I don't miss her because she has never gone away.' And as soon as Fiona moved in, she could see why – and immediately felt like an interloper who was violating the private space of Inés. It was still her house – the colours of the rooms, the pictures on the walls, the furniture, the bedding, the arrangement of storage jars in the kitchen – everything belonged to Inés and was patiently waiting for her to return.

The only ray of sunshine in the Tomb of Inés had been Gonzalo, still called 'Gonzalito' at the age of eighteen. Fiona loved him, not so much as a stepson, but as the younger brother that she never had. He was so unlike his father: bespectacled, bookish and ironic. Sometimes they joined together to poke gentle fun at Ariel – sometimes making up fake quotes from classical Spanish authors or creating bogus authors. And now, gentle, loving, funny Gonzalito had joined his mother in the shadows.

The past week had changed from the hell of not knowing to the sheer hell of believing and not believing. After it was confirmed that Gonzalo was not among those who had survived the sinking of the *General Belgrano*, Ariel became convinced there had been a mistake and ranted at his colleagues at Naval Headquarters. He accused the rescuers of incompetence and shouted that they had not provided a comprehensive list of all the survivors. When Ariel came to accept that his son was not among the 770 living or twenty-three dead that the rescue ships and aircraft had plucked from the freezing sea, he became oddly calm and focused. Ariel now knew that his only son – the tender and kind Gonzalito who was not made for war – had perished, trapped below the decks in a hell-scape chaos of blackness, scalding steam and rushing water. Among the survivors that Ariel had talked to in Ushuaia was a friend of Gonzalo's. The friend wept as he recounted the terrible screams and pleading from the wounded and dying – and the awful realisation that there was no way to reach them in the mangled sinking steel.

The marital home was not just a tomb of unbearable grief. It was also a place of bitterness and resentment. The mother-in-law's snake-like eyes followed Fiona everywhere – silently comparing and criticising.

Buenos Aires: 10 May 1982

This time the meeting wasn't a scruffy café, but a very fine townhouse that had been commandeered by the Junta. Official visitors entered the building through heavy wooden double doors facing the street. Unofficial visitors, such as SLIME and the urban guerrillas, arrived clandestinely through a back entrance. The meeting venue was a large sitting room on the first floor with a marble fireplace and boiserie walls. The curtains were drawn.

The deal had largely been brokered by SLIME with the tacit approval of the First Directorate. Tacit means: *If it goes wrong, we didn't know anything about it and you're fucked.* Intelligence services of all nationalities have a lot in common.

At first, SLIME hadn't been happy that the American woman was going to be part of the team sent to Gibraltar. But on reflection, it seemed an excellent idea with credible cover – an American woman and her Argentine boyfriend on a skin-diving 'vacation' in Southern Spain. And an old pal of the boyfriend tagging along because he was a former diving instructor who was giving them lessons. In return for the cooperation and underwater demolition skills of the urban guerrillas, the Junta were releasing a number of suspected guerrillas from detainment and granting Mateo an amnesty for anything he had done or not done in the past. It was a good deal – and winning back Las Malvinas was one aim that Mateo and the Argentine Left shared with the Junta.

The highest-ranking Argentine was Admiral Jorge Anaya, second only to Galtieri in the Junta. Anaya began the meeting by emphasising the need for complete secrecy. 'And,' added Anaya, 'if you are captured, we will deny all knowledge of you.'

'Who, then, are we working for?' said Mateo.

'You are,' said Anaya raising his chin, 'Argentine patriots working alone – out of love of country and national pride. You might want to say that you were seeking revenge for the sinking of the *General Belgrano*.'

'It is important,' said a more junior naval member of the Junta, 'that you do nothing to embarrass Spain.'

Marco, the member of the underwater sabotage team who was a diving instructor, had a fit of the giggles.

'What is it that you find so amusing?' said Anaya

'You don't want to cause problems for the football team,' said Marco.

There was an uneasy silence. The World Cup was due to begin in Spain in a few weeks' time – and it looked likely that two of the participating countries would still be at war. Argentina had won the tournament in 1978 and it was important to the Junta that they did well again – and not put the host country in an awkward situation regarding the Argentine team.

'Yes, that is one of many reasons why there must not be any links at all between this operation and the Argentine government. If you succeed in sinking a British warship it must be seen as an act of patriotism carried out by the Argentine *people* and not the Argentine *government*.'

SLIME responded to a nod from Anaya. 'Our own contribution to people's struggle against Western imperialism will be limpet mines with timed detonators. The mines are Italian ones, so no link either to Argentina or Soviet Union. They will be sent to Spain via diplomatic bag. You will be instructed when and where to pick them up.'

Marco smiled. 'Not easy items to disguise as normal holiday diving equipment.'

'The purpose of this operation,' said Anaya, 'is to prove to the world that the people of Argentina are united and angry – and that there are no safe havens for British ships.'

Casa Rosada, Buenos Aires: 12 May 1982

The fact that the President had met him, however briefly, convinced Talbot that his proposal was receiving serious consideration. The chat with Galtieri was warm and welcoming. The President, who did not seem particularly sober, admitted that he wasn't *much of a polo fan* and *preferred football.* Which, thought Talbot, augured well. Fortunately, he wasn't making a bid to buy Diego Maradona in return for what he was offering.

As soon as the presidential formality had ended, Talbot was taken to an office by the general everyone called Loco. Unfortunately, Loco was a polo fan and was going to be a tight negotiator because he knew what was at stake. The two were alone in the office.

'How many ponies?' said Loco.

'Ten ponies for the first Exocet; twelve for the second; fifteen for the third – and twenty ponies for every Exocet after that.'

'Who chooses them?'

'I do.'

Loco scribbled some figures on a notepad. He understood the American's commercial logic. Talbot would accept fewer ponies for the first Exocet because those ponies would be the very best of Argentina's playing and breeding stock and therefore more valuable. Loco frowned and shook his head.

'Well,' said Talbot, 'then it looks like you're going to lose the war and I had better be going.'

'And you and your team,' said Loco, 'can then continue to lose matches with your own overpriced nags.'

Talbot remained silent and gave the general a stony stare.

'I thought,' said Loco, 'you came here to negotiate, not dictate.'

Talbot laughed. 'I thought you guys were the dictators.'

Loco didn't seem to get the joke.

'What are you offering?' said Talbot.

The negotiating was long and hard. In the end, it was six ponies for the first missile, ten for the second and fifteen ponies for all additional Exocets. The ponies would be embarked on planes and ships for America as soon as the Exocets arrived in Argentina. Although Talbot didn't mention him by name, he was sure that his friend in North Africa would be obliging. But the more immediate matter was choosing the best ponies. He had a telephone call to make.

It had been, thought McCullough afterwards, an unexpected and odd telephone call – and she was surprised that her father was in Buenos Aires. He only came for the polo season.

'I've heard,' said Talbot, 'that your English friend has married Ariel Solar.'

'You've heard, Daddy, because I told you.'

'So you did. In any case, I would love to have a little talk with Señor Solar.'

'It might be difficult. Ariel, as you might have forgotten, is a naval aviator and is currently busy fighting the British – and his son was recently killed. So, Daddy, it might not be a brilliant time to have a talk.'

'Please extend my condolences.'

'How unlike you – have you been taking politeness pills?'

'Don't be mean.'

'If you like,' said McCullough, 'I'll have a word with Fiona.'

'Tell her she's a nice piece of ass.'

'It sounds like you've used up all your politeness pills.'

'And it sounds like you've used up all your sense-of-humour pills.'

'It isn't funny. What the fuck do you want?'

'I wanted some advice from Ariel Solar on buying Argentine polo stock.'

'I am sure they would only sell you rubbish.'

'Maybe things have changed.'

McCullough paused. There was something in her father's voice that was a giveaway, but if she pursued it he would clam up. 'Any more news,' she said, 'from the Master of the Universe?'

'I'm bored with the universe.'

'Maybe, Daddy, you need a new game.'

'Maybe I've got one, honey. See you later – and I won't be needing the apartment. I'm staying in a hotel.'

As McCullough put the phone down, she remembered once again the basic fact of her life. Everything she had – every glass of champagne, every pair of shoes and every plane ticket – was paid for by war.

She picked up the phone again. McCullough thought it best to tell Fiona about the conversation. She didn't trust her father.

Recoleta, Buenos Aires: 20 May 1982

The precious two days' leave had gone too quickly. Ariel now had to return to flying duties at Río Grande. They decided to spend the days in the Recoleta flat because Fiona wanted to get away from the censorious eyes of the mother-in-law, who, among other slights, had never let Ariel and Fiona share the same bedroom. At first, it would have been an insult to her daughter's memory and was now compounded by the death of Gonzalo. Although the mother-in-law had never said as much, it was clear that she believed sleeping together during a time of mourning was wrong – even though both Ariel and Fiona longed for the comfort and closeness. There was another factor. The casualty rate among pilots was mounting and every night they spent together might be their last – and somehow the shadow of death increased their longing and sensual need.

The flat was separated from the marital home in Palermo by the cemetery – a place that Fiona loathed. Her favourite walk was through the Plaza Francia, a quiet park where families picnicked, children played on swings and artisans sold hand-knitted clothing and mate gourds. But Ariel preferred rambling through the Recoleta Cemetery with its tumbling baroque mausoleums and statues of dead generals. Fiona found the cemetery ghoulish, but she liked the thousands of cats that swirled around it. Although Ariel wasn't a Peronista, he liked visiting Eva Perón's tomb to 'make sure she was still there'. Fiona noted there were always fresh flowers.

'If,' said Ariel, 'Thatcher attacks Buenos Aires with nuclear weapons, Eva's body will be the only one that survives untouched. Her crypt is five metres underground and protected like a nuclear bunker.'

'Do you really think that could happen?'

'The woman is a monster who has no respect for human life.'

'Do you want revenge?'

'Yes – but it is also about pride and dignity.'

Fiona blinked away a tear. Hearing him talk like that was unbearable because he meant and believed every word. Her husband was from another century.

'Let's go back,' she said.

Afterwards they lay like spoons and she could feel his heart beating against her shoulder blade. As she relaxed she looked at the paintings on the walls. There was one of a nineteenth-century American clipper ship in full sail. And next to it, a later one of an early steamship still equipped with auxiliary sails. They were family heirlooms – the actual ships had been owned by McCullough's ancestors.

She could feel Ariel stirring. They would make love again. She had lost count of orgasms for both of them. Perhaps he needed it so much because he knew that everything was finished – not just between them, but between him and life.

One of the things that Fiona liked most about Talbot's flat was that none of the paintings or photographs depicted men in uniform. Unlike other old money families, McCullough's were proud that not a single relative had been killed or wounded in battle. Some had served, but reluctantly. As McCullough explained, 'My family's business wasn't making war, but selling weapons and bombs for other people to make war. As my dad always says, "We are a family of draft-dodgers who make arms for idiots to kill each other – and oh how the money rolls in!"'

Later that evening, Ariel cooked a carbonada and opened a bottle of Malbec. Fiona watched him bent over the chopping board, wearing one of Talbot's silk dressing gowns. She hoped he wouldn't get grease on it – and then reproved herself for thinking like a wife. He was barefoot and Fiona looked at the black hairs on the back of his calves.

A hush descended when they began to eat. Fiona knew that Ariel was often silent at mealtimes, but she wanted to talk. 'Please say something.'

Ariel fixed her with his dark eyes. 'Where are the apostles? Did you forget to invite them?'

Fiona raised her voice in anger. 'This isn't our last supper! And you're not Christ.'

'But maybe you are Judas.'

Fiona slammed her knife and fork down and jumped up from the table. 'How dare you!'

Ariel got up and put his arms around her. 'I shouldn't have said that. My brain is all over the place.'

She kissed him. 'I forgive you a million times. You feel nervous and tense.'

'I'm worried about flying a Skyhawk again.' He paused. 'But I shouldn't be. It's just that I got used to the SUE and all its quirks.'

Fiona knew that 'SUE' was Argentine military slang for the French-made Super Étendard that carried Exocets.

'You love flying, don't you?'

'Not as much as I love you.'

'Let's run away, to Spain – or the South of France.'

'I have a sense of honour.'

Fiona tried not to smile – but was also close to tears.

Ariel put his hands on both sides of her head and looked into her eyes. 'You don't understand, do you?

'No.'

'I discovered my destiny when I was a child of three. I can still see it clear and vivid as the too-bright colours of a summer's day. My mother had taken me to the sea. A lone silvery plane flew low over the beach and then out across the sun-sparkling water. The sea, the endless sky, the height and the eyes of an astonished child who had discovered his destiny in a single burning moment. I have never turned back.'

Fiona refilled his glass with wine.

'I must be clear-headed in the morning. You have to decide about life and death faster than you can blink your eye.'

'What time are you leaving?'

'They're sending a car for me – very early in the morning, at five. I'll try not to wake you when I get up.'

'I'll be up with you – to make your coffee and breakfast.'

Ariel smiled. 'Just coffee. They will give me something to eat on the flight to Río Grande – it takes four hours.'

The base was near the southern tip of Argentina. When Ariel took off to attack the British fleet, he would be closer to Antarctica than he would be to her.

'I wish that you were flying a SUE instead of a Skyhawk.'

'Why?'

'Because you said that SUEs are much safer.'

'We share the risks – and the sacrifices. You see we only have two Exocets left – and the Skyhawks are much better for attacking the ships with conventional bombs. Also, we don't want to lose the SUEs because we will need them when we get more Exocets.'

'I want this war to end – I don't want any more deaths.'

'I can understand the way you feel – but things have gone too far.' Ariel gave a weary smile. 'By the way, remember that message you gave me from McCullough about her father wanting to trade Exocets for polo ponies?'

'She didn't actually say that. She guessed that was what he was doing.'

'Well, it's true – and the Junta think it's a good idea.' Ariel grinned. 'So I may never ride a world-class pony again.'

They made love once more that night – long and slow. Fiona no longer cared whether she became pregnant. Like Ariel's flying missions, it was a roll of the dice – and you accepted the outcome. It was, somehow, exhilarating not to be in control of events. Maybe that was the appeal of war.

Ariel's departure was subdued and understated. He drank his coffee and then packed his bag. He was wearing a simple khaki uniform with no medal ribbons, only his pilot's wings and a round blue shoulder patch that read ARMADA ARGENTINA AVIACION NAVAL. Fiona was still in her dressing gown.

'It's best you don't come down with me,' he said.

'Why?'

'Because I want to remember you in all your perfection. Take your dressing gown off.'

Fiona let the gown drop to the floor.

'You are perfect – and you are my wife, till death do us part.' He reached out to touch her abdomen. 'I hope there is a baby in there.'

They kissed – and once again Fiona prayed it wouldn't be for the last time. He left the flat and she listened to his parting steps – which sounded oddly squeaky on the marble floor of the corridor. She went to the window and watched until he appeared in the street. The driver, also in naval uniform, saluted and took Ariel's bag. She watched until the driver turned left on Avenida Santa Fe – in the direction of the cemetery. Fiona felt a cold chill run down her spine.

Agency News: 21 May 1982
British Forces Land On Falklands

At 0440 hours Falklands time, sixteen landing craft began to carry troops ashore at San Carlos Bay, sixty-five miles west of Port Stanley. The first troops to land were from 2 Para and 40 Commando. By nightfall, 3,000 British troops and 1,000 tons of supplies were ashore. Although British ground forces encountered little resistance, there were fierce air attacks on British ships providing cover in Falkland Sound. A Type 21 frigate, HMS *Ardent*, was disabled after repeated attacks by Skyhawks and Daggers. An order was finally given to abandon the defenceless frigate. It is reported that at least twenty-two sailors on *Ardent* lost their lives. Several other Royal Navy ships were hit by bombs and cannon fire and suffered casualties, but are still providing air cover.

It is now clear that the fighting spirit and aggression of the Argentine air force and naval air arm have been underestimated. Argentine planes were seen attacking below mast height and dodging between ships. Their pilots continued to attack despite heavy losses. It is reported that at least thirteen Argentine aircraft were shot down. The losses account for nearly half of the planes deployed in the attack.

San Carlos Bay: 24 May 1982

Ariel checked the three Mark 82 500-pound bombs before he climbed into the cockpit. He made sure the suspension hooks securing the bombs to the plane were the correct distance apart and that the arming wires ran free. He knew there was a problem with the fuses and the ground crew were working on a solution. If you released the bombs from too low an altitude, there wasn't time for the fuses to arm and the bombs didn't explode when they hit the ships. But if you released from a sufficient height for the bombs to arm, you got picked up on the radar and shot down. It was difficult to get the right balance.

The flying time to the British ships was exactly one hour. Ariel flew low, skimming the waves so that British radar would not be able to pick him out against the land profile of the islands. He would only rise and expose himself during his bombing runs.

Ariel felt nothing when he saw the grey outline of the ship he was about to attack. He didn't imagine the men inside it or the lethal danger it posed to him. He felt neither exhilaration nor anger – only a certain cool detached confidence. It was like stroking a ball through the uprights in a polo match. The mind wasn't part of it – only a trained body responding to training, experience and instinct.

He pulled the stick as he approached the ship and the Skyhawk rose. He reached out towards the armament release panel with his left hand and tripped the ARM switch; he counted the seconds – the bomb needed six seconds of flight to arm. When he reached eight seconds he saw the orange flash behind him and heard the explosion. The whole time he was rolling and twisting to avoid anti-aircraft fire, but now the fire was concentrating on the second Skyhawk. He watched his colleague release his bomb. It hit the ship, but there was no explosion.

Ariel climbed and turned for his second bombing run. Smoke was pouring out of the ship. He knew that one more would finish her off. He released the bomb, calmly and perfectly – but didn't see its impact. All his attention was on the dark pencil shape approaching him from six o'clock. He knew there was no way he could outrun a Sea Dart missile, which flew at twice the speed of sound, but thought he could turn a tighter circle – it was an evasive manoeuvre called the 'tactical egg'. But it didn't work.

Ariel was surprised he was still alive and conscious after the missile impacted – and miraculously the engine was still running. But he found there was no elevator trim and the rudder was gone. The Skyhawk was haemorrhaging fuel. Ariel pulled the yellow ejection seat handle between his legs.

When Ariel awoke he was in the sea. He had been knocked unconscious by the ejection. His life jacket had inflated automatically. Despite the fact that the water temperature was five degrees Celsius, almost as cold as the seas around Antarctica, Ariel was comfortably warm. He knew that his flight suit, when wet, turned into a waterproof anti-exposure suit. The suit was designed to keep a pilot alive for at least six hours. The next part of the downed pilot drill was to get in the life raft which was strapped to the pilot's buttocks. Ariel reached behind and pulled the ring to inflate the life raft – but nothing happened. The carbon dioxide cylinder wasn't working. He tried blowing it up by mouth, but that didn't work either. Ariel removed two bottles of water and the chocolate survival rations from the uninflated raft and stuffed them between his life jacket and his body. Things could be worse.

For a while, there were explosions in the distance, but then silence. Ariel was out of sight of land, but began to swim towards where he thought was the nearest land. At first the exertion kept him warm, but the anti-exposure properties of the flight suit don't last forever. When he stopped swimming a slight chill began to creep in. Ariel looked at his watch: he had been in the water for three hours – and there was still no sight of land.

The despair didn't set in until it began to get dark. The chill was turning into cold; uncomfortable, but not unbearable. It was overcast and there was going to be neither moon nor stars.

Ariel felt the moment that the adrenalin rush of battle finally left his body. He could almost see it dissolve into a mocking mist as it blew away laughing into the sky. The excitement of battle was an age-old trick to lure the young to death.

What came next was self-contempt. What a fool he had been. There was no reason to be freezing in the South Atlantic – he could be back in bed with Fiona. He began to realise how much he loved her. Why had he been tricked into such a dangerous career that was now going to cost him his life? There was nothing, nothing that was more important than staying alive. Las Malvinas no longer mattered – the war was a joke. The Junta, the military, the Church – they were all idiots or con artists.

The cold was now penetrating. Ariel passed in and out of

consciousness. He no longer had a desire for warmth or the comforts of a woman's body. Just sorrow and regret for his dead wife and his dead son. In the end, he began to cry out for his son over and over again: 'Gonzalito, Gonzalito, Gonzalito, Gonzalito…' His tears warmed his cheeks before the cold waves splashed them away. His final gesture was to try to undo his life jacket, 'Gonzalito, I am coming for you now. It won't be long…' But his hands were too numb.

There comes a point when the body stops trying to keep itself warm – the eyes dilate and the heart rate slows. Ariel was drifting into oblivion and felt no need to stop it. Indeed, it was good. He became giggly and there were a series of hallucinations – somehow he and Gonzalo were both young boys on a beach with his mother. Gonzalito was exactly as he had been at the age of eight. His son had become his younger brother. A silver plane flew low over the beach and both boys looked at it in wonder.

Ariel died an hour before dawn.

Agency News: 25 May 1982

Argentine Air Attacks Sink Three British Ships And Damage Others

Two Royal Navy ships, HMS *Antelope* and HMS *Coventry*, have been sunk following attacks by Argentine Skyhawks. The frigate *Antelope* was lost when an attempt to defuse two unexploded 1,000-pound bombs tragically failed. The explosion killed the Royal Engineer staff sergeant who was trying to make the bombs safe and badly wounded another member of the bomb disposal team. HMS *Coventry*, a Type 42 destroyer and sister ship to HMS *Sheffield* which was lost three weeks ago, was hit by four 1,000-pound bombs. Two of the bombs exploded, ripping a huge hole in the ship's port side and starting a fierce fire. *Coventry* finally capsized with the loss of twenty-one of her crew. In the days before her loss, she had shot down several Argentine aircraft.

In a separate attack, the container ship *Atlantic Conveyor* was hit by an Exocet missile fired by a Super Étendard. The Exocet was the same type of missile that destroyed HMS *Sheffield*. Eight crew from the *Atlantic Conveyor* are still unaccounted for. Among them is her skipper, Captain Ian North.

Palermo, Buenos Aires: 26 May 1982

Fiona was stunned and heartbroken, but not surprised – and was already yearning for the understated English way of dealing with death. She knew she had to dress in black to receive the endless procession of uniformed officers bringing their condolences – and play the role of a dignified war widow. The worst bit was the set speeches about Ariel's *bravery* and *unswerving sense of duty* and *love of country*. A number of relatives also emerged from the woodwork – ones she had never met before and who had boycotted the wedding.

There was no body, so there would not be a Catholic funeral – but an officer from CANA, Comando de Aviacion Naval Argentina, assured her that there would be a memorial service for Ariel – *and the other fallen heroes* – when hostilities had terminated. Fiona wasn't looking forward to it, but would fortify herself with strong drink even if it did mean telling senior officers what she really thought of their stupid fucking war. Now that Ariel and Gonzalo were gone, she felt her links to Argentina unbinding like silk threads in a candle flame. She realised how much her commitment to Argentina was the result of one man: a man she had so passionately loved – and still loved. She so wished that there was a body that she could kiss and cover in flowers. Snowdrops – the symbol of winter breaking. And that lovely week when the still full-blossomed snowdrops and the twittering calls of the goldfinches overlapped. She wanted to gather baskets full of snowdrops from her parents' garden and pour them over Ariel's body. But it was too late. The snowdrops had been gone for months – and her father would now be earthing up the first early potatoes. She felt unbearably homesick and the tears poured out.

Fiona knew that the evening alone with the mother-in-law was going to be the worst – and she was right. The house reeked of emptiness and lost lives. The mother-in-law's eyes were full of unspoken hatred and blame: *You killed my daughter and my grandson. And my daughter's husband too – you were never his real wife. You are* una puta, *a whore who doesn't belong here. I should burn the sheets that you slept in.*

It was midnight when the others had left and they finally spoke alone. The mother-in-law's impenetrable dark eyes stared at Fiona over the candle flame as she sipped a bowl of mate. Her first words were, 'You will inherit nothing. This house is mine.'

Fiona kept a straight face. 'I understand.'

'But I am a generous woman – and you can live here as long as you like.'

'That is very kind of you.'

'I am glad you realise that.'

A smile almost struggled through Fiona's grief, but she repressed it. The mother-in-law was oblivious to irony.

The mother-in-law stared into space. 'Ariel is now gone to join Inés and Gonzalito where they will be together again and happy for all eternity.'

For a second Fiona's grief disappeared and she wanted to pour the bowl of mate over the other woman's head.

The dark eyes returned to Fiona. 'I will leave you now. I am going to bed. But you can stay up.' She nodded towards a cabinet. 'Help yourself to drink. I know that you like alcohol.'

As soon as the mother-in-law had gone, Fiona poured herself a glass of wine. She wiped a tear away and raised her glass. 'I still love you, husband – and always will.' She then found a pen and writing paper.

Dear Mummy and Daddy,
I tried to phone but couldn't get through. Ariel is dead. My heart is broken and I NEED YOU. I am so lonely and so homesick and need you so much. I feel again like that girl of twelve who wrote to you from France – and I know I'm using the same words I did then. I am SO homesick and so lonely and NEED you SO MUCH. I was such a cry-baby then – but you never blamed me and were never angry

and drove all that distance to come and get me. And as soon as you were there everything was all right again – and I completed my exchange like a big girl and you had a little holiday in Normandy. And you never had a cross word – only BIG HUGS. Well I'm not a big girl now – and how I NEED you…

Fiona paused to wipe her tears away. Some of them had fallen on the letter. Just like that letter from France. When she was home for Christmas during her first year at Cambridge, her father had shown her the letter which he had kept as an heirloom and confided for the first time, 'The tear stains on your letter come from all three of us.'

Fiona picked up her pen again: *I love you. And NEED YOU and NEED YOU. PLEASE, PLEASE, PLEASE…*

Vejer de la Frontera, Spain: 27 May 1982

The idea had first come to Catesby from an officer in NID, the navy's intelligence division who asked, 'Has anyone considered all the Franco fascist dingbats in Spain with a grudge about Gibraltar? Now stirred up, of course, by what's going on in the South Atlantic – and wholly on the side of the Argies. Easiest thing in the world – just like the Italians did in World War Two – slip over the side of a fishing boat with a bag full of limpet mines and *bang*.'

It was something that Catesby had thought about. He had even discussed the matter with an officer from CESID, Centro Superior de Información de la Defensa, Spain's intelligence service. The CESID guy was helpful and reassuring. 'We keep an eye on those types and know who they are. We want a return to democracy – and I assure you there is *nada*.' It was obvious to Catesby that what Spain and her security services also wanted most was a non-eventful World Cup and a smooth transition to NATO membership. The current mood music was *don't rock the boat* – and a corollary to that was *if anything untoward does happen, sweep it under the carpet.* Which was exactly, thought Catesby, what was happening now. The incident of the police impounding a hire car with limpet mines would never reach the press. And it had nothing to do with 'Franco fascist dingbats'.

Catesby had been alerted to the situation by the SIS officer in Madrid – who had heard about it from his American counterpart as the incident involved 'a US citizen'. Catesby flew to Seville where he got a lift to Vejer de la Frontera with the SIS officer from the Madrid Embassy.

'I hope we get there in time,' said SIS Madrid, 'the Spaniards want to see the back of the suspects as soon as possible. The plan is to take them to Madrid and then fly them on to the Canary Islands under police custody – where they will be placed on a flight to Buenos Aires.'

'What about the American?'

'I'm not sure what they are going to do with her. She's quite a hero. She deserves a medal.'

'What did she do?' said Catesby.

'I think I'll let Rowe tell you the story. I wouldn't want to detract from his American eloquence. In any case, he has a full transcript.'

Rowe was CIA Head of Station in Madrid. Catesby knew him slightly, but he had a reputation for being a colourful character who was covertly pro-British.

'By the way,' said the man from Madrid, 'CESID are out of the loop. The whole thing is being handled by the Spanish police, the Ministry of the Interior – and the Prime Minister personally. In fact, the PM is flying them to Madrid in his own plane. There is a lot of stuff at stake. Basically, the Prime Minister doesn't want to annoy us or Argentina – and he's good at walking tightropes.'

Catesby nodded agreement. There had been a coup attempt the previous year when two hundred heavily armed members of the Guardia Civil had stormed into the Congress of Deputies just as the Prime Minister was being elected. The King went on television to denounce the coup and it collapsed less than twenty-four hours later. Catesby hated it when Brits stereotyped

Latins as impulsive and reckless. Few British had any idea what happened behind the scenes in Whitehall – or how close Britain had come to a coup in the 1970s.

'So,' said Catesby, 'what were these people up to?'

'I'm not sure – the Spanish are being close-lipped. But it seems, according to Rowe, that they were planning to swim across the bay from Algeciras to Gibraltar in the middle of the night, attach the limpet mines and their timers, and then swim back. Easy peasy. We should have seen it coming.'

Catesby wondered if his contact in CESID had been intentionally complacent. The world of intelligence is a looking glass wilderness of distorted shapes pretending to be truth.

'What about,' said Catesby, 'your phone taps on the Argentine Embassy?'

'They discovered the taps.'

'With outside help?'

'I believe so.'

Vejer de la Frontera was a white Moorish hill town of narrow winding streets that had been built by the Moors as a fortification in the eighth century. Catesby was taken by its bleached austere beauty – even the police station fitted in with the architectural genre. A senior officer – too senior to be normally stationed in Vejer de la Frontera – greeted them and ushered them into a side office.

'Can I offer you coffee?' said the policeman in his best charm-school voice. 'Or perhaps tea, since you are British?'

They both declined.

'Thank you for coming all this way, but there are no British nationals involved.'

'But,' said Catesby, 'British national interest may be deeply involved.'

'Ah,' said the policeman with a broad twinkling smile that left nothing to doubt.

Catesby beamed back with a smile equally devoid of concealment. He found it hard not to like the Spanish cop. His British equivalent would have kept a ludicrously straight face.

'Yes,' said the Spaniard, 'I see what you mean. But I can say nothing – and I am sure you know why I can say nothing.'

'Are the suspects,' said Catesby's colleague, 'still being held here?'

The policeman spread his hands. 'I can't tell you that either.'

Someone knocked on the door and the policeman told him to come in. It was Rowe, CIA Head of Station.

'Hey guys, great to see you!' The American turned to the policeman. 'Permit me, Pablo, to get these nosey Englishmen out of your hair.'

'They are very fine gentlemen. I adore the English.'

'Then you must adore warm beer, insipid tea, boiled cabbage and duplicity.' Rowe looked at Catesby and his colleague. 'Why don't you come back to my hotel for a drink and a chinwag?'

'Sounds good,' said Catesby.

'Come on then, *vamos hombres*!' said Rowe hustling them out.

The American's hotel was a short walk away from the cop station. It wasn't the type of hovel that British spies usually end up in, but a tasteful period piece furnished with antiques and hung with Andalucían art.

'Nice pad,' said Rowe, noticing Catesby's envious eye. 'It's one of the perks of being a spook for the world's only superpower – the Sovs, of course, are fucked and getting their asses kicked in Afghanistan. By the way, I wish I could show you the view from the roof terrace. At night, you can see the harbour lights of Tangiers blinking away in the distance. But I can't take you guys up there in case you get taken out by an Argentine sniper.'

'But,' said Catesby, 'our ships are safe.'

'I don't think so. How many have been sunk so far? What are you guys trying to prove?'

Catesby decided not to mention Vietnam. The World's Only Superpower could be thin-skinned.

'But, as usual,' said Rowe, 'the USA is standing by to bail out plucky little Britain if things go wrong.'

'We would,' said Catesby, 'like to interview the American woman who was part of the demolition team.'

Rowe gave a strained smile. 'Are you crazy? The Spaniards would go bug-fuck if I did that. In normal times, that wouldn't matter, but Spain is becoming a member of NATO and a democracy – and we want to keep things nice and smooth.' Rowe paused. 'But the important thing is that I would get recalled to Langley to have my young ass reamed out. No way.'

'I told my colleague,' said SIS Madrid, 'that you were a man of principle.'

'Hey, I can do without the British sarcasm.' Rowe smiled to show he had the upper hand. 'In any case, our young *gringa* is an interesting case – and is certainly a spirited filly that no one should mess with.'

'Can you, at least, tell us her name?' said Catesby.

'Can you, at least, wait a fucking second,' said Rowe. 'Okay, no more messing around. By the way, it's getting hot. Would you guys like a couple of *cervezas*?'

'That would be lovely,' said Catesby.

'*Lurvely*,' echoed the American as he got the beer.

Madrid winked at Catesby.

'In my experience,' said Rowe, 'secret ops usually go wrong for one of three reasons: because someone is fucking stupid, because someone has a big mouth – or because someone is too horny. And in this situation it was the latter – and your ships in Gibraltar are safe because this *hombre* was horny with the wrong *chica*. They were an interesting threesome.' The American laughed. 'Not that *that* was ever on the cards. The leader, can you credit it, is a Jesuit priest – of the ascetic, asexual variety – no horny problems with him. The *chica* – a *very* attractive and athletic young lady – is, I would guess, more inclined to Sappho than Adonis. Nothing wrong with that – my ex-wife went that way and we get along better since she left. Are you following me?'

Catesby nodded. He could see that behind the crude American bluster Rowe was quite a civilised person.

'Now,' continued the American, 'the third member of the party, the one who calls himself Marco, was a horny bastard who didn't understand that *go fuck yourself* really means *go fuck yourself.* The unwanted touching began soon after they arrived in Spain. At first, it was an *accidental* stray hand against a breast or thigh – which accelerated into butt fondling. She didn't like it and slapped his paws away.' Rowe paused to gather his thoughts. 'Marco is a good-looking guy with a sense of power and entitlement – who doesn't understand boundaries. It's a pity some girl's older brother never kicked the shit out of him. In any case, yesterday was the final straw. It was a hot day and our young woman was wearing a skirt. They were taking turns driving and it was her turn. Marco was sitting next to her and probably thought *what can she do to stop me?* So he put his hand up her skirt. She, of course, went berserk and started screaming – waking up the Jesuit in the back.' The American reached for a file. 'I'm going to read from the transcript.'

'Sure,' said Catesby.

'This is her. *I pushed his hand away and drove the car off the road. He shouted in his crap English: "Why you do this? I only grab your pussy. All women like that – something wrong with you."*' Rowe shook his head. 'You can see where this is going. She refused to drive any more and he took over. She swapped places with the priest in the back seat – and started plotting. An hour later, they pulled into Vejer for lunch. As soon as they got to the restaurant, our brave young woman said she had to go to the bathroom. Instead, she went to the proprietor and told her to call the police because she had been sexually assaulted. And that was the end of *Operación Palmones* – Palmones was the beach they were going to swim from.'

'And what happened next?' said Catesby.

'When the cops arrived she told them to search the car: *you'll find something very interesting.* And, of course, they discovered military-issue scuba gear and two 25-kilogram limpet mines. But rather than have the shit hit the fan, the Spanish authorities want to quietly flush it down the toilet. No charges of any kind – including sexual assault – are going to be pressed.'

'And how does the American woman feel about that?'

'She's livid.' Rowe picked up the transcript. 'This is her again: *Anti-imperialism is no excuse for ...* and here she mocks Marco's accent ... *pussy-grabbing.* She goes on: *Assaulting women doesn't mean you're a revolutionary; it means you're an asshole.*'

Catesby frowned.

'And that,' said Rowe, 'kicked off an ideological screaming match. The Jesuit guy shouted that Marco wasn't *a real revolutionary but a double agent who sold out to the Junta* and so on.' The American paused. 'But the really interesting thing is our American woman and who her father is. His name is Talbot...' Rowe's voice dropped as he whispered the surname.

'Fucking hell,' said Catesby.

Rowe smiled broadly. 'Now here is where I'm going to do my British friends one fucking big favour. And please keep it quiet. If word of this gets back to Langley, I would be spread-eagled over the director's desk and reamed with an 800-mil oil-drilling bit – and, as they say in the Foreign Legion, *sans Vaseline.*' The American stood up and handed a file to Catesby.

'Thank you.'

'You will find in there complete transcripts of all the interviews – but, what may be important to you, a top-secret Agency bio of our friend Talbot. I am sure you will find it useful reading.'

Agency News: 29 May 1982
British Paras Win Land Battle

After a bitterly fought battle, British soldiers from 2 Para overcame an enemy force that outnumbered them by three to one. The action took place at Goose Green near the remote settlement of Darwin. The victory leaves British forces in effective control of more than half the island of East Falkland. The battle, which took place one week after the landing at San Carlos Bay, was a costly one. The commander of 2 Para, Colonel Herbert Jones, was killed while personally leading the assault. British losses totalled eighteen killed and more than sixty wounded. A British helicopter was also downed in the fighting. Argentine casualties number approximately fifty killed, 100 wounded and 1,000 captured.

North Norfolk: 30 May 1982

Fiona was sitting in an armchair in the garden office with Wandapuss purring on her lap. The cat was in seventh heaven at being reunited with Fiona.

'Your father,' said Catesby, 'called to say you wanted to see me.'

'I missed the goldfinches, but you don't see them so much this time of year because of the foliage and because they are breeding. Late autumn is better when they are foraging for seeds.'

Catesby sat down on a cane chair.

'But,' said Fiona, 'the dawn chorus is wonderful this time of year – and Daddy is going to take me to hear a nightingale on the marshes.'

Catesby looked away. He and his wife had listened to a nightingale on a Suffolk marsh the night they had got engaged. He often wondered if she had fallen in love with the nightingale instead of him. He heard a noise coming from Fiona. He looked at her. Her shoulders were heaving as she wept.

'Is there anything I can do?' said Catesby. 'Perhaps I should leave.'

Fiona wiped her eyes. 'I'm just a big cry-baby.'

'No you're not. You've been through hell.'

'Who hasn't? Look at Daddy, look at his mangled face.' Fiona turned her eyes to Catesby and laughed. 'And now you're crying.'

Her words had touched a hidden grief. Catesby blew his nose and wiped his eyes. He then smiled. 'Okay,' he said, 'it's a competition. Let's see who's the biggest cry-baby – and I bet I win.'

'You've made me feel better – you're just like Daddy.'

Catesby felt a lump in his throat. It was the nicest thing anyone had ever said to him.

'By the way,' said Fiona, 'I'm still getting three hundred and thirty-three pounds a month paid into my bank account.'

'You deserve it.'

'Maybe I deserve to be locked up for treason.'

'No, not at all.' Catesby wondered if he had spoken too loudly.

'You sound angry,' said Fiona.

'I am angry. This isn't the first time that there has been a war between two villains in which the young and innocent died – and it won't be the last.'

'When Ariel's son was drowned, I wanted to bomb Britain.'

'Thatcher committed a war crime.'

Fiona looked up surprised. 'How can you continue to do your job?'

'I don't know – but I'm worried about the alternatives.'

'You mean,' said Fiona, 'the war dragging on and on and more people being killed and maimed.'

Catesby nodded. 'It's a cruel choice. I suppose it comes down to maths.'

Fiona suddenly sounded cool and rational. 'My father and I had a long talk about this. He didn't convince me. I convinced myself – and that's why I wanted to see you.' She paused. 'And that's why I'm going to tell you everything.'

They talked for two hours. Catesby didn't want to call it a 'debriefing', but that's what it was. The most interesting piece of intelligence came at the end – and Fiona threw it in almost as an afterthought.

'The night before Ariel died, I had a telephone call from McCullough. It was a bit bizarre – even silly.'

At the mention of Talbot's daughter, Catesby's ears pricked up. 'Go on.'

'McCullough said that her father wanted Ariel's help in choosing Argentine polo ponies. I was more than a little cross. I reminded her that Ariel was a pilot on active service risking his life every day – and that he didn't have time to look at polo ponies.'

Catesby felt the sudden exhilaration of an artist who had finally found the key. His brain was on fire. It all made sense. The vertical lines of the crossword were the Vatican bankers and the horizontal lines were Talbot's secret CIA biography – and the polo ponies were the final cryptic clue.

The Cabinet Office, Whitehall: 2 June 1982

Since hostilities had broken out, JIC meetings were shorter and more focused. Everyone had a lot to do in their own departments and wanted to get cracking. Catesby, for his part, was anxious to get on with the polo-ponies-for-Exocets deal which now seemed almost certainly true. The most urgent things were tracing the money trail and finding likely suppliers. He wasn't prepared when JIC began with a solemn turn. The DCDI, Deputy Chief of Defence Intelligence, began by asking the chairman if he could make a statement. You could have heard a pin drop.

'I am sorry to say that John, who often deputised for me before he bravely volunteered to join 3 Commando Brigade, has been reported missing in action and presumed dead. The helicopter he was flying in was lost over the sea. There is no chance that anyone survived the crash.'

Catesby forced himself to concentrate on the meeting and the agenda items. He reported the latest information on the Exocet denial operations. 'On the one hand,' he said, 'we need total secrecy about what we are doing and what we have discovered. On the other hand, we need to make discreet enquiries from international bankers. It is a difficult combination.'

When the meeting was over, Catesby walked across Whitehall to St James's Park and sat on the bench facing the lake from where they had often observed the pelican. The bird was now squatting with his eyes shut. Catesby looked at his watch. He couldn't stay long; he was meeting an ex-SIS banker in twenty minutes for a chat about clandestine financing in the illegal arms trade. Catesby didn't realise he was making a fool of himself until he heard a passing child.

'Mummy, why is that man crying?'

'Shhh.'

It was time to go.

Agency News: 8 June 1982

British Landing Ships Bombed and Set Ablaze

The RFA *Sir Galahad* and the RFA *Sir Tristram*, ships that are part of the Royal Fleet Auxiliary, were attacked by Argentine Air Force A-4 Skyhawks while preparing to disembark soldiers from the Welsh Guards. The attack, which took place at Fitzroy Cove south-west of Port Stanley, claimed the lives of fifty-four soldiers and crewmen. Another forty-six were badly wounded, mostly from burns. Royal Navy helicopters were seen manoeuvring in thick smoke above the burning ships to winch survivors to safety. In terms of casualties, the bombing at Fitzroy is the worst single incident inflicted on British forces so far in the war.

Port-Vendres, France: 13 June 1982

It was, thought Catesby, difficult not to be impressed – or horrified – by the *11e bataillon parachutiste de choc*. They were the hardest soldiers Catesby had ever seen. They subsisted on a diet of zinc masonry nails washed down with liberal quantities of red wine vinegar. They did ten hours of callisthenics with weights every day, followed by ten-mile runs in full combat gear. At least, they looked like they did.

The *11e choc* were stationed in a thirteenth-century castle, complete with drawbridge and a Knights Templar seal above the entrance gate. Their expertise included maritime commando missions and they were the 'military action arm' of DGSE, the French secret intelligence service. A perfect fit for what Catesby requested – and the director of DGSE, who had put Catesby on to the French engineer helping Argentina, was still obliged to show the British 'unequivocal support'.

Catesby felt a little guilty about enjoying himself so much during an important mission that meant life or death. A couple who were old friends of his wife had a holiday flat overlooking the harbour at Port-Vendres which, fortuitously, was the perfect observation point. Borrowing the flat for a short break also provided the perfect cover story. Catesby and his wife gilded the cover legend by visiting the town's excellent seafood restaurants and doing a Charles Rennie Mackintosh tour. Mackintosh, a Scottish artist with Suffolk connections, had spent a year in Port-Vendres painting watercolours of the harbour and sea – which, in fact, incorporated some of the very places the Exocet-bearing boats might land their lethal cargoes. How ironic, thought Catesby, that Mackintosh had been arrested in Suffolk in 1914 on suspicion of being a German spy. The Walberswick locals had mistaken his Glaswegian accent for a German one. When he was spotted repairing a lamp in his home, he was reported to the police for signalling enemy ships. As Catesby gazed across the Port-Vendres harbour entrance with a pair of binoculars from the very spot where Mackintosh had set up his easel, he said to his wife, 'We wouldn't get away with this in Walberswick.'

Catesby reported to the *11e choc* castle HQ twice a day for updates and secure communication with London and GCHQ. What they knew for certain was that the missiles were coming from Libya and would be disembarked somewhere along the French coast between Sète and the Spanish border – a long stretch to cover. The messages from London were screaming urgency: NEED TO BE STOPPED AT ALL COSTS: AUTHORISED TO TAKE ANY ACTION. Nerves were strained to breaking point. Two days ago, HMS *Glamorgan* had been hit by a shore-launched Exocet that killed thirteen crew.

The urgent messages from London had been followed by more useful ones from GCHQ. They had intercepted signals and telephone calls that suggested the Exocets had already embarked from Libya and were being carried in a small coaster that would be calling in at Tunis to pick up a cargo of summer fruit. Catesby assumed the missiles would be hidden among the melons and pomegranates. GCHQ had also picked up several other messages – some of which were contradictory. One said that the missiles would be taken ashore on a remote beach and then picked up by tractor; another that they would be transferred to fishing boats – and another reported that the ship itself would dock at Port-Vendres and the Exocets, hidden under the fruit, would be offloaded into lorries. The last option, however, seemed unlikely for there were no Libyan-registered ships scheduled for docking in Port-Vendres in the next few days.

Catesby sat on the terrace of the holiday flat and stared at the commercial dock opposite and muttered, 'Oh shit.' What really worried him was that the whole thing was a charade, a feint to distract effort away from the actual routes that the Exocets were taking. If the intercepted messages were disinformation, it wasn't the fault of GCHQ. Their job was picking up the stuff, not evaluating or interpreting it. But if the reports were true,

Catesby thought the most likely option would be a sea transfer of the Exocets to fishing boats – and this seemed to tie in with what happened the next day.

It was early evening on the fourteenth when the colonel in command of the *11e choc* arrived at the holiday flat. They weren't going out that evening and Catesby was planning to grill fresh sardines he had bought off a fishing boat. The colonel was dressed in camouflage battle dress and somehow Catesby knew that he would have to leave the cooking to his wife – and that it would be a lonely meal for one.

'We have spotted the ship,' said the colonel, 'and have been ordered to intercept and search her. I assume you would like to come with us.'

There were two patrol boats involved, one of which had been commandeered from French Customs and Excise. The *11e choc* boat was armed with a 20mm canon and two .50 calibre machine guns and had a maximum speed of twenty-five knots; the Customs and Excise boat bristled with the infantry weapons of the *choc* commandos.

'If necessary,' said the colonel, 'helicopter support is available and on stand-by.'

Catesby felt that he was an extra in a film. The French military know how to put on a show – and the show aspect was important. Psychological intimidation is part of the game of force. They left the harbour an hour before sunset in a blaze of spray and evening colour.

'The other boat,' said the colonel, 'will deal with any smaller craft that attempt a rendezvous. We are going after the ship.'

'Are you authorised to stop them outside territorial waters?'

'We can stop them anywhere.'

For the next two hours the Libyan ship seemed to be playing a cat and mouse game of slowing down and changing course.

'She is,' said the colonel, 'waiting for dark – and we will wait for her in the dark.' He ordered all the patrol boat's lights to be doused.

At midnight the *11e choc* boat was within twenty nautical miles of the ship – which, according to the radar, was now heading full speed ahead for the French coast. The colonel smiled and rested his hand on his pistol. 'We could be boarding her within forty minutes.'

The patrol boat continued to plough into the night, illuminated only by the phosphorous of her bow wave. It was half past midnight when the radar operator shouted up the companionway to the bridge.

'What is it?' shouted the colonel back.

'The target, colonel, has changed course – completely changed course by 180 degrees. She is now heading back towards Africa.'

The colonel turned to Catesby. 'She could not possibly have spotted us visually from this distance – and, if she saw us on her radar, there is nothing to distinguish us from large fishing boats or commercial traffic. But we can still catch her.' The colonel ordered the patrol boat into full speed ahead.

It was nearly two o'clock in the morning when they finally made visual contact with the Libyan ship. There was nothing about her that was clandestine. Her running lights were ablaze and she was still heading towards the African coast.

'Can we sink the bastard?' said Catesby.

The colonel smiled. 'I am not authorised to do that – and, even if we were, I am not sure that our 20mm could manage it. But we could shoot her rudder off and make life difficult on the bridge.'

A voice called up the companionway. 'Colonel, there is an urgent message for you in the radio room.'

The colonel picked up the intercom phone on the bridge. 'If it's urgent I can take it here.'

'It is, sir, from the director of DGSE, so…'

'Fine.' The colonel turned to Catesby. 'I think it's best I take this call in the radio room.'

Catesby stared into the night. They were still closing fast on the Libyan ship. Three minutes later, the colonel returned to the bridge. His first words were to the helmsman. 'Turn around. We are going back to Port-Vendres.'

Catesby looked at the colonel with an expression of shock and betrayal. 'What's happened?'

'I have been ordered to let the ship continue unmolested and to return to base.'

Catesby stared at the colonel in stunned silence.

The colonel returned his stare with a knowing smile. 'The director would now like to have a word with you.'

The message from the director was short and sweet. THE ARGENTINES HAVE SURRENDERED. THE WAR IS OVER AND YOU WON.

Agency News: 15 June 1982
Argentine Forces Surrender

Prime Minister Thatcher's office formally announced early this morning that Argentine forces in the Falkland Islands have surrendered. After ten weeks of hostilities, the war in the South Atlantic is now over. Major General Jeremy Moore, the commander of British land forces in the islands, radioed from his command post near Port Stanley: 'Falkland Islands once more under government desired by their inhabitants. God Save the Queen.' A spokesman for the general said that enemy troops were being disarmed and rounded up for repatriation to Argentina on British ships.

The Prime Minister had already signalled that the end of the war was close at hand in a statement to Parliament on Monday night. Mrs Thatcher reported that Argentine forces in Port Stanley had begun throwing down their arms and waving white flags. A short time later, crowds had gathered outside Downing Street waving Union Jacks and singing 'Rule Britannia'. When the Prime Minister returned from the House of Commons, the crowds greeted her with rousing cheers. Mrs Thatcher replied, 'What matters is that it was everyone together – we all knew what we had to do and we went out there and did it.'

Agency News: 17 June 1982
Final Battles Proved Bloody and Fierce

The last three days of the Falklands War saw some of the conflict's bloodiest fighting which included bayonet charges in the dark. A total of forty-six British soldiers and marines were killed in the land fighting and another 158 wounded. The HMS *Glamorgan*, while providing close naval gunfire support, had thirteen crew killed and many more burned and wounded when she was struck by a land-based Exocet. Argentine losses are thought to number 125 killed and nearly 300 wounded. The fiercest fighting took place on the high ground overlooking Port Stanley where dug-in Argentine forces made their last stand. The most decisive battles were for Mount Longdon, Mount Tumbledown, Two Sisters and Wireless Ridge. The weather and lack of helicopter transport, owing to the sinking of *Atlantic Conveyor*, made conditions dire for troops on the ground. Many had to carry loads of over a hundred pounds and suffered from the wet, the cold, lack of sleep and diarrhoea.

New York: 15 June 1982

It had, thought Talbot, been going so well. The British and the French had been duped into believing that the Libyan Exocets were heading for Argentina via the south coast of France. Pretty stupid, but the deception had been superbly carried out by well-known arms dealers – who, aware that they were being monitored and tapped by the intelligence services, passed on false information under Talbot's guidance. The Libyan ship heading for France – laden with Tunisian fruit – was also an excellent ploy. Talbot smiled at the thought of heavy-booted French commandos squashing around through tons of haemorrhaging watermelons and cantaloupes in a fruitless – *hardly* ***fruitless*** *ha ha* – search for the missiles. But that, alas, was not to be. Meanwhile, the Exocets had been heading across Africa to Dakar from where they would have been flown across the Atlantic to Brazil, then on to Argentina via Peru. As soon as he found out that the Argentines had surrendered, Talbot ordered the delivery convoy to turn around and return the rogue Exocets to Libya. At least, that part had gone smoothly. A coded message delivered from Libya via a series of intermediaries had confirmed the return of the missiles.

The next problem for Talbot was siphoning back as much money as possible without leaving a trail. There would be losses, but most of it would come back to safe havens that he controlled. The Argentine polo ponies and breeding stock were now a forgotten vanity project. But Talbot would think of another one. Well, he thought, Argentina may have lost the Falklands, but they kept their polo ponies – which, in Talbot's view, should have been much more a matter of national pride.

The final problem was the banker. He knew too much. Everything else that Talbot had arranged had been carried out by go-betweens who didn't know who he was or where the money was coming from. But the banker, who was one of the best in the world at arranging dubious financial transactions involving hundreds of millions of dollars, knew where the trails eventually led.

Blackfriars Bridge, London: Midnight, 17 June 1982

'Hey, wakey, wakey!' The man in the back of the car slapped the nearly comatose passenger hard in the face. He then turned towards the driver. 'I told you we overdid the dosage. Just because he's overweight doesn't mean you have to overdose.'

The driver turned off the Embankment towards a derelict building site that was poorly secured. The man in the back got out and pushed open a loose metal entrance gate and then got back in the car. 'I hope,' he said, 'the cops don't see us here.'

'No problem, we'll just say we're trying to help our pal sober up.'

'You know, at first, I didn't recognise him. It's amazing how much difference shaving off a moustache makes. That was his trademark feature – and his nice suits.'

'And his Patek Philippe watch. Don't nick it. It might be worth a hundred thousand bucks, but they would track you down. This has got to look like a suicide, not a murder.'

The man in the back picked up the banker's left hand and

looked at the watch with its rose gold case and hand-stitched alligator strap. 'It is pretty classy.'

The comatose banker suddenly stirred. 'Hey, leave...'

The driver smiled. 'That got him going.'

The man in the back slapped him in the face again. 'Hey, wake up, Roberto. We're going for a walk by the river. It's a lovely evening.'

The banker opened his eyes. 'My name isn't Roberto.'

'It might not be the name on your Nicaraguan passport, but Roberto sure as hell is the name your mama and papa gave you.'

'Where are we?'

'We're in London, near the river, and we're going for a little walk to freshen you up before we take you back to Chelsea.'

The driver turned around. 'Make sure he hasn't got the Nicaraguan passport and make sure he does have his Italian one in his proper name.'

'I already have. Shit, he's gone back into la-la land.'

'And the money. Make sure he has all the money.'

The man in the back went through the banker's pocket and wallets. There was more than ten thousand pounds of cash in three different currencies, but mostly US dollars. 'Check it's all there.'

'Remember. This is a suicide – not a killing for money.'

'But it would be nice to take the watch.'

'Don't even think about it.'

The banker stirred.

'Are you ready for a walk?' said the man in the back.

'I just want to go to sleep.'

'Good. You'll be going to sleep soon.'

'We need,' said the driver, 'to find a couple of bricks to weigh him down. Stay there. I'll get them.' The driver came back with a pair of broken bricks and passed them through the rear window. 'Put one in each trouser pocket.'

'Okay. I'm not stupid.'

'And leave that watch alone.'

'Shall we drive him there?'

'I don't think so. The car would look suspicious.'

'You're wrong. There's a place you can park opposite the bridge – and no restrictions this time of night. And, in the state he's in, we'd have to carry him.'

'You're not stupid. Off we go.'

There was very little traffic when they parked. And, when they took the banker across the road, they looked like a couple of friends helping a drunk, perhaps helping him find a taxi after a boozy City banquet. They leaned the banker against a low parapet on the downstream side of the bridge.

'We have a real treat for you, Roberto...'

'My name no Roberto.'

'Sorry for my mistake – but we still have a treat for you. We are going to take you for a boat ride back to Chelsea.'

'Good. I like boat ride.'

'But you've got to get over this parapet – then it's easy.'

The banker didn't climb over the parapet. He was rolled over it and struggled to find his footing on the scaffolding planks under the bridge. The man from the back seat threw a rope over a bridge girder, then secured the rope and formed a noose while the driver steadied the banker.

'The rope's too long,' said the driver.

'It's not too long. We have to take him down the ladder.' He turned to the banker. 'We have to go down to the river to get in the boat. My friend will go in front of you and make sure of your feet on each rung.'

The banker suddenly seemed much more awake. 'What's going on? I don't like heights – I have vertigo.'

'Get on the ladder.'

The banker did as he was told. The driver made sure his feet were steady on each rung. 'Easy does it. You're doing fine.'

They were more than halfway down the ladder when the other man slipped the noose over the banker's neck. The banker was now fully awake and shouted, 'Stop.'

The driver pulled both the banker's feet from the ladder rungs and swung him into eternity.

Blythburgh, Suffolk: 18 August 1982

As the last remaining mourners dispersed, Catesby went to his car and picked up the sail bag where he kept his swimming things. The tide was perfect for a dip – and, at this time of year, the river far warmer than the North Sea – almost like a bath. He nodded farewells to two black-suited grey-haired men as he headed towards the shadowy path that led down to the Blyth. Catesby undressed on the rabbit-cropped green that met the riverbank. He was naked when he heard someone behind him. He grabbed a towel for decency.

Catesby recognised the person who surprised him as one of the mourners – a man with a beard who looked in his late twenties. He wasn't in uniform, but there was something military about him – and the pallor of the skin and the beard suggested the navy.

'Apologies,' said the bearded man, 'for disturbing you at such an embarrassing moment – but at least you won't be able to chase after me asking questions.'

'Most of my life,' said Catesby, 'is composed of embarrassing moments.' He noted that the man was carrying a bag which seemed to contain a flat object that looked like a ledger.

'My name is Bellman First Class. I've just come back from hunting a snark – and have decided to devote the rest of my life to the Snark Protection League.' He laid his bag on the grass. 'And this is my first action.'

Catesby watched as Bellman First Class turned and made his way back up the path disappearing into the leafy darkness. Catesby knotted the towel around his waist and picked up the bag. The contents were in fact a ledger. The stiff cover had gold embossed letters: *Log of HMS* Conqueror.

Catesby did what any conscientious intelligence officer would do. He returned the submarine's log to the office of the Chief of Naval Staff in Whitehall. The fact that the log was returned anonymously and without any reference as to how it came to be in his possession was not, perhaps, what every intelligence officer would do, but was not a procedure completely unknown in the trade. Catesby also did what any new member of the Snark Protection League would do; he photocopied all the parts of the submarine's log which related to snark hunting – and proved the Prime Minister had lied. He then passed the copies on to a Member of Parliament who passionately believed that governments must be held accountable and their decision-making should be transparent.

There were, however, lingering mysteries that had never been solved. The matter of the submarine's log was bizarre. Catesby knew for certain that the navy had the log, but the MoD still declared that it remained missing. The other mystery was what had happened to the reams of cables and transcripts of telephone calls that had bounced between Peru and Washington and London in the eighteen hours before the *General Belgrano* was torpedoed. A pity, Catesby thought, that it hadn't happened in January instead of May. The heat generated by Whitehall's incineration furnaces would have saved thousands of pounds in fuel bills.

Halesworth, Suffolk: 9 April 2013

A lot of Catesby's social life took place in the aisles of his local Co-op supermarket. Despite having turned ninety the previous February, Catesby was still nimble and could often be found perched around the wine racks. On this occasion, however, he was in the newspaper aisle choosing which papers to put in his trolley. The previous day had seen a historic passing and the headlines blazoned it. As he picked up his third and final newspaper, he sensed someone at his elbow.

'Hello, William.'

Her voice was still peremptory and clear. Catesby fought an urge to salute. He smiled at the colonel's widow instead – except now she was twice widowed. He nodded at the newspaper headlines.

'I wonder,' he said, 'if your wish has come true?'

'What a memory you have. I was thinking that too, but we'll never know on this side of the grave – and probably not on the other side either.'

'I've heard,' said Catesby, 'that red creatures with pitchforks and tails were seen going in the back entrance of the Ritz.'

The widow shrugged. 'But I'm not going to buy a bottle of champagne to celebrate. She doesn't deserve the recognition.' She looked at Catesby. 'Did I ever tell you that I met her once?'

'No.'

'It was a year or so before she became Prime Minister.' The colonel's widow paused. 'And what do you think was the most frightening thing about her?'

'What?'

'When you stared into those blue eyes, there was nothing there – nothing at all.'

Postscript

I want to make it clear that I have nothing but admiration and praise for the British soldiers, sailors, marines and airmen who fought in the South Atlantic. Their determination, professionalism and bravery was of the highest standard and should never be forgotten. They deserved far more than the tawdry triumphalism that greeted them on their return to the UK.

It is shocking that disabled Falklands veterans were only invited to the London Victory Parade after a media outcry. Another breach of propriety and custom was that Margaret Thatcher, rather than the Queen, took the salute of the armed forces as they marched past the portico of Mansion House. The tactless triumphalism of the day was epitomised when Mrs Thatcher asked a sailor, blinded when HMS *Antrim* was bombed, 'How are you enjoying the day?'

In the immediate aftermath of the war, very little, if any, mention was made of the three Falkland Islands women – Mrs Susan Whitley, Mrs Doreen Bonner and Mrs Mary Godwin – who were tragically killed by naval gunfire in the final days of the conflict. Such accidents are almost inevitable in warfare, but referring to their deaths would have been an embarrassing acknowledgement that some of those whom the Task Force was sent to protect were killed. Likewise, mentioning Argentine war dead was forbidden. There was a public row between Mrs Thatcher and the Archbishop of Canterbury, Robert Runcie, when she accused Runcie of a lack of patriotism in praying for Argentine as well as British dead during a memorial service.

The human cost of political ambition was 258 British killed and 775 wounded. Argentine losses were 649 killed and 1,657 wounded. There are no definitive statistics on how many British and Argentine veterans have committed suicide or are suffering from post-traumatic stress disorder. Argentine President

Leopoldo Galtieri was removed from power a few days after Port Stanley was taken by British forces. Galtieri was arrested in 1983 and charged with human rights violations and mismanaging the Falklands War. In the June 1983 general election, Margaret Thatcher's Conservative Party won an overall majority of 144. Firmly entrenched as Prime Minister, Mrs Thatcher was in position to carry out a radical agenda.

I would like to end with a personal message to any readers who lost family or friends in the South Atlantic. My thoughts were always with you as I wrote this book. May your loved ones rest in peace.

Acknowledgements

First of all, warmest thanks to Julia.

Maggie Hanbury, my agent, continues to provide guidance, support and good sense to an author who needs it. I am grateful to Piers Russell-Cobb who is a delightful and supportive publisher. A chat with Piers always brightens the day. And thanks also to Joe Harper at Arcadia Books for being ever helpful and efficient.

My editors, Martin Fletcher and Angeline Rothermundt, have once again waved their magic wands over a raw manuscript. Martin's editorial suggestions always show intuitive creativity as well as professional insight. Angeline has now edited six of my books and continues to breathe clarity into my prose.

Although this is a work of fiction, I try to get my facts right. I am very grateful to Guillermo Makin from the Centre of Latin American Studies University of Cambridge for his valuable advice. I would also like to cite the British Diplomatic Oral History Programme at Churchill College Cambridge as a wonderful source of frank and often amusing recollection. The Margaret Thatcher Foundation Archive also provides an interesting part of the jigsaw – even if pieces are still missing.

A number of real historic events are mentioned in this book and real places are mentioned, but I would like to emphasise that this book is a novel. A few real names are used, but no real people are portrayed. This is a work of fiction. When I have used official titles and positions, I do not suggest that the persons who held those positions in the past are the same persons portrayed in the novel or that they have spoken, thought or behaved in the way I have imagined.